Process
of
Illumination

A novel

Karl L. Caldwell

PublishAmerica
Baltimore

© 2004 by Karl Louis Caldwell.

All rights reserved. No part of this book may be reproduced, stored in a retrieval system or transmitted in any form or by any means without the prior written permission of the publishers, except by a reviewer who may quote brief passages in a review to be printed in a newspaper, magazine or journal.

First printing

ISBN: 1-4137-0870-6
PUBLISHED BY PUBLISHAMERICA BOOK PUBLISHERS
www.publishamerica.com
Baltimore

Printed in the United States of America

For my patron saints, Billie & Steve

for Family and Friends

for those who help me to be in a world that I cannot be in

for Daniela, Cris, Betta, and Marzia. SEI SEMPRE NEL MIO CUORE E NEI MIEI PENSIERI. RINGRAZIO.

And for those who've not yet been illuminated....

Enjoy....

KLG

– CHAPTER 1 –

SOMEONE WAS GOING TO DIE.

The boy was yanked around the warehouse doorway, his small feet leaving the ground. His angry father mittered a fearful curse. He turned his thick Slavic head, as vexed black brows creased. The boy clung to his father's thigh and accepted the pat on the head without a smile.

"Francesca! Franny?" he shouted, then stopped.

I heard the whistle of impending doom that closed too fast to react. I knew what it meant, but I wasn't sure it was happening. Then again, I wasn't sure of anything after losing so much blood. But I swore I saw their auras darken, and from an instinctual pool, filled with the experiences of a veteran dogooder/war correspondent, I knew their time was up. Some internal Pythagorean calculation, between the ominous sound, the increasing decibels, and where the father and son stood, told me it was over. "Move!" But my voice was a croak. I kicked a crate weakly, but the man only glanced, then looked up through the missing roof. No twinkling stars existed in this sky, only that sound. The horrible night song of late; high-pitched, yet sometimes only a whisper—

The explosion that always followed, a deep rumble, or a lightning crack, with titanium whiteness filtering up and out, like a huge flashbulb lighting up the sulfur-laced canvas above. Shadows were stripped away under the orange—yellow—white bursts. The details of every dirt clod, of every nick in the cobblestones, of cracks, and all those things usually unseen or ignored, were for a flash shoved into view by the blinding light of Class A explosives. American military grade; the best in the world. The dichotomy of the country that proclaims an antiviolent way of life, yet produces the best explosives and killing devices, is confounding, and hypocritical, at least.

But I am here and now, in an abandoned warehouse in war-torn Brno, on the southeastern border of the Czech Republic. I feel all the death that was and will be, with no one governing body learning these lessons in blood. And so distant, their puppets, those faraway button pushers, who send death on its way. Depleted uranium, heavy and sharp at once, rains without pause, and knows not the innocent from the guilty. Any living being within the kill zone will be voided from this inhumanity. I see father and son, and I know that seventy meters is too far for my legs, even if I wasn't carrying two AK-47 rounds in my right calf and thigh. It was too late anyways.

A flash illuminated the bones under my skin and flesh. My finger, unconsciously aiming the camera at the man and boy, depressed the steel button, guiltily. The heat blast was fierce, and my prayer for their survival vanished with my eyebrows. When I opened my eyes, I searched where they had been, where now a million million embers burned as the molten rock super cooled. I knew their fate. Flesh and bone, gone. Molecular structure of homo sapiens, gone. Scattered, exhaled in one explosive puff. And where once there was cement and gravel and dirt, there was a dirty glass-encased impact crater.

Pain, more of it, erupted behind my ears, and my nostrils flared under a familiar scent; the smell of my nightmares, and reality, when as a boy I had searched for Teza, my two-year-old Calico cat.

Food had been scarce as it was, without having to feed a full-grown cat, but Teza was a good scavenger hunter. One morning she didn't come for breakfast, a time when she knew I'd be tossing her snippets of egg or sausage. I ditched my 8th grade morning classes to find Teza, visiting all her haunts, which I'd spied and recorded in my journal. But I had recorded other rumors in my journal as well. You know, the neighborhood gossips; the old lady that eats kids, or the old man who kidnaps them. In my neighborhood there was an old woman who kidnapped and ate the neighborhood pets, which was why her house smelled like burnt hair. I would have to pass by her house on my search, I knew, and hoped I would not find Teza there. Like most gossip, the stories are usually only half truths, so I didn't expect what came upon me that morn. A noxious, almost caustic smell, just like the burning barber in the city who used a flaming ball of alcohol to cut hair. It seemed a thousand times worse, as I lifted myself on my tiptoes, trying to look into the kitchen window. I screamed at the sight of Teza. I swear it was her, unmoving in a steel sink, her beautiful coat of white, orange and black, ablaze in a bluish flame giving off too much smoke. She seemed to yawn at me, but it was the locked in scream of the dead. My mother told me I had been mistaken, and that when Dad got back from the war I'd be made to apologize to Misses Kricek. Cooking rabbit, my ass, I thought to myself now. I had stalked the good Misses Kricek, and took several pictures of her stealing two cats and one dog. Her catering service went out of business shortly thereafter.

"Shit—shit—shit!" I cursed, still blinded, but knowing that the smell of burning hair was my own damn head on fire. Fire, I tell you! Like an atomic blast isolated on my scalp, burning away my vanity. I felled the flames with dirty and scratched hands, my kevlar-encased camera falling harmlessly to the ground complete and total sacrilege, I admit. My palms patted, my fingers found bald patches, and I was sure I looked like a comic book fiend, with patches missing hither and thither, in a tragedy played out in real life. Her scream robbed me of my self-pitying indulgence, and also took me away from my pains. It cut through the cold air, much like whistling bombs, except this was much more unnerving, more damaging to my heart. It reminded me that for every man and boy there was a mother, a woman. Francesca? It had to be her.

There had been very few girls, or women, out and about in the cities. Not since the "revolution" began 6 months ago.

Male voices put me back in my hiding place amidst the stacks of old steel milk crates. My vision, returning slowly, was like a thermal resonance picture. I found my camera again and pressed 'Video'. I saw shapes around the edge of the crater; a figure on her knees crying, but more like screaming; soldiers in black surrounded her from behind. I felt the soft whir of my camera doing its job, and something in my thirtyish soul was comforted by it. An inner sigh, beneath the worry over this woman named Francesca. The Arabic sound of the male voices chilled me to the core. *UAN?*

A month ago I'd heard rumor of the United Arab Nations invasion forces, but it had just been gossip between fellow correspondents. I wished my uplink connection still worked, then I could find out for sure who was where, but the bullet that had hit my thigh had first passed through my forearm plate, which was where I had my PC mounted. As far as I knew the world was at war. Not just another Balkan battle. Well, it was already past that if UAN troops were here in the Czech Republic.

They dragged the woman away, despite her protests and screams. This was the UAN I knew well.

My leg throbbed, and the tourniquet bit into tender flesh, but I stood anyway. I had to get to a Red Cross center, but more than anything I wanted to see where she was being taken, and by whom. In the back of my mind I saw myself rescuing her and somehow vindicating cruel fate for taking away her husband and son. Maybe I could take her somewhere safe, give her a new life. If my leg didn't give out. The blood had stopped flowing under two tightly wound wraps—my version of a tourniquet—which only meant that I had been lucky no arteries or large vessels had been severed by the 7.62mm military rounds.

I was compelled by her; the sight and sound of a grieving woman being rent asunder by what cruel fates had today taken from her. "Francesca," I whispered, as my vision cleared enough for me to approach the doorway through which she'd been taken. Enough for me to see her blonde hair hang flacid between two soldiers with red berets.

I knew the wearers of red berets, the heretofore mentioned UAN soldiers, but the elite division. The soldiers that were loaned to governments to assist in the eradication of small pockets of resistance. Three years ago I'd snuck into their HQ and took six photos—award winning—of murder and cruelty and rape, before the alarms went off and I was forced to digress with haste. But they knew who I was and would no doubt have a contract out on my life, as did many other nations and entities of ill repute. They would without conscience put a bullet behind my ear, award winning photographer or not. (And get a secret medal for doing it, back at the UAN HQ. They loved their medals.) The egomaniacal rulers—I say monsters—that ruled the UAN gave no thought to human life, unless it somehow affected their political standing in the world. Life was cheap to them. I'd seen them kill two teenagers, and a middle-aged woman, as if they were nothing. I'd taken two pictures of the execution, behind the high walls of the elite forces headquarters in New Lebanon, and it showed a smiling red beret colonel, Fashiid Burak, a millisecond after squeezing the trigger. It was the cover of *Life*; a redheaded woman, maybe twenty-one, beautiful, but made ugly by the bullet that crashed so brutally through her forehead, matched only by the ugliness of Colonel Burak's smile, blurred by the red cloud behind her head, frozen like the fog over a Chinese lagoon.

I could envision Francesca's fate; Rape, execution, or slavery, unless I could follow and free her. Then again, maybe I was wrong. Maybe I lost too much blood and this was all a nightmare, and paranoia was overriding common sense, and the molten rock wasn't sticking to the bottoms of my boots. Could be those were Chinese soldiers, not UAN soldiers. But my instincts said if ever I was right, I was right now. The wife, woman, mother, or daughter was in trouble. If I didn't get moving soon, or get my computer satellite connection uplink online, I'd lose her. My only hope was that my camera hand had been faithful to my hunches and taken a good picture of her face.

I concentrated on slithering towards the door, staying in the shadows that had returned to the interior of this warehouse, which now had no roof. If I could get to the Red Cross, maybe find Dean—my reason for coming here in the first place—I could get her to use her doctorly ways on me and give me a new set of supplies. Then she could reveal to me the secret she'd wanted to tell me in person. But here was no more Brno, and most of its five hundred thousand citizens were gone, replaced by war. I only hoped that my friend had made it out of this hell, or that the warring parties were respecting the Red Cross insignia, and not using it as a bull's eye, as they did in many other countries. Those countries of ill repute. I hobbled, wobbled, but worked my way slowly around the crater, and out of the explosively decorated facadeless front. But all my concentration could not keep the little boy's face out of my thoughts as I left his unmarked grave. His pained expression, that universal look of shamed embarrassment and pouting yet fearful obstinateness, even as parents enforce their will. I looked back to the cauterized wound, its edges still soft like hot new asphalt. "Poor kid." I was thankful that the bomb had blinded me, that I was kept from seeing what it looked like to be concussed and incinerated out of existence.

But I'd seen it before, and all I had to do was cut and paste in my memory. My camera eye had shown it to me; Chechens, Chinese, and various other persons had been caught on film. Men, women, and children. That digital nanosecond exposed every detail of supercompression demolecularization, when the body actually comes apart at the molecular level, fragmenting into carbon atoms, depending on the position of the being to the explosion. I will not divulge incremental stages, but you may have seen them in documentaries or magazines, from which I profit not.

My mind fixed the little boy's face on the pictures I'd seen, or taken, and I relived it in detail, even as I stumbled out into the Brno night. Even the father joined my theatrical danse macabre. Memory's a bitch, sometimes. If I lived out this day, and ever slept again, these new acquaintances would revisit me. They'd all come back to my Cort Falcon Theatre for their encore performance that never failed to keep the dead alive in my heart, and remind me of my fate.

Past the Swiss cheese walls, cordite and ozone wafted past my singed nostrils. I felt the coldness upon my newly burned face and scalp, which was tender and malcontent, and let me know about it by giving me a headache. The breeze, running down the western face of the Carpathian Mountains, was cool upon that pink flesh. I searched for the red berets, and Francesca, but saw neither. I was glad to not have to exert any more energy to avoid them, but sad that I couldn't track her. I had a good idea of where they'd taken her.

The mountains and valleys and forests surrounding Brno were like mounds of pepper, salt, and oregano, each area separately distinguishable from the air. Hopefully JD was tracking me via satellite, and inadvertently catch which way the UAN had taken her. Pines and scrub were almost completely nonexistent, and where they were growing one could most always find a camp, or field HQ of sorts. The opposing air forces had only to aim at the trees to hit something that was foe.

I had no sides, only preferences, and the truth. A bomb is a bomb, no matter who drops it, and a life is a life, no matter who dies. And in my adjustment from "photographer/war correspondent" to "documentarian/dogooder" I have found no gray areas, only right and wrong. Good or Evil. The bullet-riddled conscience, of just watching, without acting, was sluffed off two years ago after the red-haired lady had been executed before my eyes. I was a hundred meters away and bore the marks of two days of torture. And so saying, I have neither friend nor foe, but view, instead, this corruptibly beautiful world with an eye to actions, not political propaganda, constitutions, policy, or speeches, unless they have an affectation upon actions, from which I, and you too, can say; "That's horrible," or "That's good."

I turned, as well with my thoughts, toward the inner parts of the city, hoping that the hospitals had not been shelled or evacuated, as they had four years ago in the tenth "revolution." The streets were paved, just like any small town in America, except that the debris was not in the form of candy wrappers and beer cans. Here the ways were littered with sharp fragments and a hardier permanence, scattered not by man's consumption, but by man's destruction. I imagine ghosts, recently dead, mumbling around just beyond the astral plane that is the reality I now walk in. At least, for a moment. On each side of me, as I step, drag, step, drag (envision the Hunchback of Notre Dame, scuffling along the cobblestone streets of France), were battered storefronts, which were like cheesegraters with millions of tiny holes. Should the sun have been shining, or the ambience bright enough for me to see, I may have been able to look through the brick walls and wooden roofs, to the horizon and the sky. I was glad for the darkness. I was glad not to be able to see the cockroaches and flies that always existed in these burned-out husks of humanity, which had once echoed with the sounds of neighborly love and laughter, or so I liked to think. *One foot forward, drag the right leg, do it again,* I kept telling myself.

My camera, attached now to my right hand, took several pictures, that I hoped my night vision software could clean up. My right finger depressed, but it was more an unconscious act. I stuck to traditional snapshots, instead of the video, which would drain battery as well as film. And my solar booster, which was half ruined, wouldn't restore a fully drained battery. The housing of my digital camcorder had been renovated, first to make it silent, second to make it water- and roughproof, and lastly to make it bulletproof. But silence was always the most important. I have scars to prove it, though the manufacturer claimed their "quietcam" was not the fault for my capture by North Korean soldiers near Panmunjom. I still believe it was the "click" from the shutter drive motor that made the soldier turn and look down between the barracks.

But that was then. Tomorrow can be no worse than yesterday in my book, for I've tasted the fire of the devil's breath. In plain speak; when the Chinese interrogator, Think Ink (I shit you not), pressed the glowing orange tip of a hot poker into my chest, I believe that's the worst it can ever get. What with having to smell his opium-laced breath, and forced to watch sweat beads roll across the lenses of his retinas—which I'd never have thought possible— there's not much else anyone can do to me. Man, his breath was like a year-old breathing sewer pipe, with a couple dead decomposing rat corpses thrown in for good measure.

I guess if I died today, it would be a shitty day, I thought cynically.

At an intersection, where wet wood burned and coughed in fifty-gallon barrels, a dozen or so raggedy-looking people huddled. I'd forgotten just how cold it was here. Two of the men wore potato sacks as coats, I saw as I neared, but I stayed in the shadows. I wasn't prepared to battle for my pants and long sleeve shirt, or the hardware I kept hidden in a backpack beneath the latter. I kept to the right. Down the road I saw hope. A field hospital.

My leg was throbbing, my camera getting heavy, and nothing was automatic. I hoped this place was up and running, for I saw no activity, and as I neared I smelled death, not life giving antiseptics. So one could understand my sagging facial muscles as I approached the door, with a Blue Cross insignia set into the olive drab material of the field hospital.

"Lordy!" a nanny like voice scolded. "You look awfully drab, sir. Sir?" the nanny-like voice continued, though I was beyond such reproof.

My legs gave out a moment before my mind did. However, I was told that I would not release my baby, also known as the camcorder, which I take to be true, seeing as how I woke with it still in my hand. In whose arms I fell, I know not, but those hands were strong and supple on my arms and under the crook of my shoulder, keeping my head from smashing into the scarred pavement. And I am no light load, being six foot two inches tall, weighing about two hundred pounds, which varied depending on which country I happened to be in.

In this blood loss induced sleep I revisited the beginning of my trek through the Balkan badlands, starting back at the Manse de la Rosa, in Seville's highlands, where Mrs. Maggy Mantera's devilish green eyes and sultry pouting had nearly resulted in my violating the trust of my dear and only brother. Harry, good and naïve man that he was, never suspected his Spanish wife's sexual proclivities. Or maybe he did, and didn't care, so long as he got something every night? My brother was smart enough to have just such a relationship, for he was, is, one of the world's best and successful users. I say that in kindness and admiration, even as his wife's dialogue resounds in my dreams.

"Cort, you've such brilliant blues," Maggy said over the rim of the crystal wineglass. Her toes, simultaneously, and quite dangerously close to my 'package,' squeezing my thigh from the opposite end of the couch.

I heard her say, "I want to fuck you." And the thought of it on a physical level was enticing. I'd seen her in a dental floss bathing suit on a hot day, and had even rubbed oil on parts of her body no one but her husband should rub oil on. But the emotional consequences would be too great, and I was, and will be, loyal to the elder Harry, as I knew he was to me.

So I left. No words. No good-byes. Harry was used to me doing that. In fact, everybody was. My reputation nearly demanded a disappearing act. As for Maggy – sure, she was good-looking, but good looks were a dime a dozen in this world, with hearts and personalities not so disloyal. I'd have to talk to Harry some day, but I'd plan on forgetting about it, for things that were harmless or obnoxious were best filed in the subconscious, where every so often I was disloyal to my brother, but only in my dreams.

On my way to Sardinia a nuclear mushroom cloud had been spotted in the Czech Republic. Dean, my European contact, also called and said something big was going down, in addition to having a secret to tell me, in a maddening conversation that replayed like this;

"Come on, Dee? I'm on my way to the sunny shores of our old stomping grounds. What gives?" I looked at my phone, for Dean had never been shy before.

"Look, Cort, it's important to me—I'm in Brno, but I'll be—"

And that was the end of our conversation. Kaput! Whether the cellular node got cancelled, the satellite fell from the sky, or whether she didn't pay her phone bill, I could not say. Two days later I'm in a foxhole, two bullets in my leg, limping towards the cityscape then being bombed.

Though I would have come to Dean's assistance, emotional or otherwise, the bonus was the chance to investigate the nuke blast, which Lars Van Holdt, an independent reporter from Sweden, had reported seeing. Nobody had seen him since. I wanted to see if I could get in where all the reporters had been banned, behind the Czech border.

Inside the deteriorating country, the civilians were expendable, except the rich in their dachas and highrise buildings, mostly located in affluent and major cities, otherwise known as the power hub of politicians and generals. Those safe dens of thieves were hardly ever hit with shells, at least not since

EU and NATO bombs had fallen indiscriminately upon Bratslava, Slovakia. The same thieves, probably, who were involved there were most likely influencing the events here now affecting the region. The tragedy of technology was readily apparent. The advances in modern warfare increased steadily, while the politicians still existed under Machiavellian rules. The reasoning of each individual country was usually the old axiom; "Let them deal with it." "Let Europe or Asia mend it."

However, with modern day weaponry one didn't have to exist in, or occupy the country in question, to cause damage to it. A terrorist general, or "revolutionary" general, could literally sit back in a computer headquarters and press buttons. With the advent of SMSs (satellite missile systems), running at about five hundred million dollars per twenty tactical space-launched missiles, any country with a budget or credit line to cover the Chinese-built system could have their national star wars launch system.

But then again, why should the powers that see interfere? Their own economies were burning suns, and besides, humanitarian aid was too expensive, since there was no repayment or interest affixed to the assistance. Additionally, cultures were agoraphobic when it came to meddling, especially when it meant giving national blood for another nation's struggles, unless affecting the aforementioned monetary or other interests; oil, minerals, or forestry products. It was usually poor countries who were trapped in states of crisis.

World harmony, Global peace, Universal unity, and whatever other term you wanted to apply to the dream of world peace, was a long way from being listed in a Webster's. More to the point, it had yet to be accepted by all peoples. Maybe that's why I still took pictures of war's aftermaths, of what the world without peace looked like. I also wrote slanted articles, though Barry Greenburg, my New York agent, warned me that the publishers and newspapers weren't buying it with a smile.

"Bring me pictures with more emotion," one editor, whose name I'll leave out, told me. No matter, I continue to push the truth of violence into those middle-class homes, those rich households, those working and white-collar abodes, those politicians' studies, pointing out with blood and bone and bereft that horror beyond the picket fences. There exists a real surreality outside your neighborhood or national borders, beyond the weekly paycheck and comfort zone that we, as human beings, find ourselves hypnotically immersed in. Only grudgingly do we raise our heads out of the mire of our daily trivialities, and gaze upon the cruelties of the world. It's like pulling teeth to get most to abandon their routine, to actually lend a hand toward stopping war. I give credit to the few countries whose soldiers have been sent to do the dirty work. But it is not enough. I freely admit to shaking the tree steadily, so those beneath it will look up, see the rotten bloodfruit about to fall on them. I've learned that even if the whole world were falling apart, there are people who're so caught up in their own little frivolities that they cannot be disturbed by the 5-year-old girl bashed against the tree because she's from the Shaka tribe.

I wanted to find whose nuke had been fired, where had it been dropped, and what was the human toll—i.e. how much would it cost you and me. My last story, "Betrayal of Innocence; The killing machines in America's prison system" (Based upon the novel, at www.xlibris.com), had been seven months ago, and my hiatus from the *Yorker*, and *Post*, was making me nervous. Though I didn't need the money, thanks to dear old Dad, God bless his lost soul, I needed name recognition to wield some measure of influence. All for good, I declare. Plus, as my fellow creativists know, one likes to answer the old demand; "Do I still have it?" Yes, even I, prize winning photographer and journalist, bow to the devil named insecurity.

And so, once again, I went willingly into the shit.

Winter was late, and I was truly thankful for the brown and green patches amidst the rubble of blasted mountain granite. It matched my clothes, and the cold was not so bone deep. I avoided any open areas and tried to stay within what scrub cover there was, but whenever I neared a town, a powerplant, or any other marker of civilization, I found nature obliterated, replaced by huge craters and scorched rubble. I ducked, hobbled, stopped to tighten my makeshift bandage, but continued towards my goal. To find Dean, and/or get medical assistance.

I reached Brno, pronounced "Bor no," at first light on a Saturday—according to my trusty watch—and felt light, both in mind and in body. I didn't see, hear, or intuit any threats from neighboring mountains, as I passed by the first intact buildings I'd seen since a small border village. It was hard to believe that five hundred thousand people lived in this pantile-covered suburbia. Yet I heard nothing. I saw an elderly couple sitting at a corner cafe that had long since stopped serving coffee. They smiled at me, and I raised my hand in greeting.

I heard the streak, not quite a whistle, but falling within the same connotation; *Bomb's coming!* They must have seen my bloody pants, my expression, or did they comprehend? Surely the latter, for living in this region bred knowledge of the instruments of war. They gripped each other's hands, and I saw them smile at each other; a sadly romantic foreshadowing of their life and death. The sound, which I knew to be incoming HE (High Explosives) rounds, was now clear. I believed I saw their acknowledgement, and they were standing, maybe make for cover.

BOOM! The flash blinded me, and the concussion compressed my flesh, my bones, throwing me, with my heavy gear, backward into the windowless facade. I expected to crash through the wall, or onto shelvings, but found that space cleared away by the blast wave. My fall was more like a dropping backwards behind the small brick base, which would normally hold the large windowpane. I shook my head, but knew instinctively what was happening. Brno was under attack. I had to get down, and get deep.

Bombs, mostly artillery and rocket-launched, began to rain down upon Brno' s suburban areas. I crawled into a pit used for cold storage, the stores gone of course. It was a small, family-owned restaurant, but large enough to have needed a large cold room below. I searched for another, smaller door, sometimes found in these old basements. I knew of a tunnel system, previously a sewer and overall disposal system beneath all of Brno, except the banking area. They had dug deep to plant foundations for the highrise buildings, during the 1980s boom.

A three-hundred-pound RLP (Rocket Launched Projectile) crashed into the old bricks, some five stories above, and shook the entire building. The cement and stone shuddered around me, and then began to fall like rain. But in the new cracks I saw the old steel door, near the rear of the room, and I crawled, my right leg screaming each time my kneecap was relied upon. Rockets blasted off, with as much rumble and inner brain concussion as a Cape Canaveral shuttle launch. Just above my head! I made the latch, pulled, and dove, as the ceiling above me caved in.

The tunnel was black, as I'd imagined it would be. I switched on my light, which was part of the mini personal computer, or MPC. Dust filtered through the stone ceiling, an arch that seemed to be compressing under the strain of the aforementioned collapsed building. Just above my head! Need I repeat it again? There was no return through the trap door, but if my layout of the city had been correct—a computer system I check before entering any city—I could head east, under the buildings, into the oldest part of town, where Saint Paul's church was located. Surely they wouldn't bomb the churches, for that was where most religious centers congregated, in all their competing variations, as if to say, 'Bomb the people, but not our Gods!' (Excuse the plurality.) On that side of the city the Carpathian Mountains looked down upon those pinkish tiles that were a fixture of the locale. A part of town where wolves still drifted near, and where work horses still pulled carts filled with goods, even under the horizon filled with 20-story highrises and mirrored bank skyscrapers.

But the Eurodollar brought more than just a united monetary unit, it also brought the barracudas, loaning and foreclosing, loaning and monopolizing. But unlike "civilized" countries, where governments and corporations take billion-dollar hustles with a smile, the Balkan bad men tended to go to war. Research had told me that this war had been created by billion-dollar borrowing, or, more correctly, the outright refusal to pay the loan. I still didn't know which entity, or who, but I was sure it was all connected to General Luk Rakelivic. He of previous war crimes infamy. Never captured. He'd bloomed, like a wicked alien flower.

I knew Rakelivic personally, and he me, for I had taken the photograph ten years ago; Rakelivic gripping a skinny 70-year-old woman, by her white string hair, bodies in a mass grave in the background, gun pointed at her head. Outside Timisoara, in the hills, the scene played out, with me a thousand meters away, my finger squeezing the trigger at the same moment as the then Colonel Rakelivic. My camera watched the entire scene in cold thoughtless digital reality. Every drop of blood, chunk of brain matter, and the expressionless scream that never came, all exiting her right lobal area. Her frail frame jerked, a squirt of blood pumped out in a three-foot arch, and disappeared into the open pit. Rakelivic put his boot heel onto her left shoulder and pushed. Diedre Kovak, grandmother to one American judge, and three priests, and faithful widow, was discarded like a masterless marionette into the horror.

I dream, some nights, that the crosshairs of my camera's zoom lens had actually been attached to a high-powered rifle, even as much as I have a repulsion towards killing.

It was that film which had gotten Rakelivic convicted by the 1994 session of the U.N. Counsel, and therefore imprisoned in the Czech Republic, caged in the Balkans like one imprisoned. I am sure he knows my name, and therefore I avoid announcing my presence when I'm on his turf. I enjoy being a field mouse in Maine, just one of many.

As I moved on all fours below, I imagined those above me, swimming through the caustic dust and smoke and fire and fragments. Faces tear streaked, wondering why, but at least not virgins to war. Even so, there would be wails and tears, just as there would be fire and destruction and death. We have, as a world organism, not yet reached the humanitarian capacity that would bind those idle hands from mass slaughter and genocide. There are corrective and financial solutions, but none willing, and sometimes not financially able, to support such sanctions, be they corporal or fiscal. So the bones of the present, and the future, will continue to unfairly join those of the past.

PROCESS OF ILLUMINATION

Those horrors; walking into a two-bedroom villa in Albania to find a hundred Muslims stacked head to toe, one atop the other, seven bodies high. I saw the petrol poured over the house and put to the torch, and I tasted the smell of human beings burning, heard the screams of some who weren't so dead. I photographed, with the inability to do anything but run and shoot, as NATO shells and bombs landed wetly in the thickets of human flesh, young and old, crippled or in good health. Nor did they stop when I sent word to the military HQ in Trieste, or high command in Germany, and I spoke personally to two generals on top secret lines—my talking upon which set them to setting aside resources to find the culprit, not adjusting their fire. Serbian citizens, not soldiers, writhed and screamed if they lived within the flare and flames.

Now, only bones can tell the story, but without the reality of the moment at which life was struck out. Very rarely will the rotting corpses reveal the horror. My photographs of mass graves only tell us that genocide took place there, but it doesn't show the evil leer upon the face of the murderer, or the tears of the young soldier who's been commanded to kill his neighbors, on the basis of race, religion, or creed. And those blights upon humanity, which have infected humankind since Cain slew Able, have still not taught us our lesson, have not compelled us to debark from our course. Even our peace keepers slink away under threat by the murderers.

The Hague is overrun with bones, and time.

I reached a T connection, and shined the flashlight from my left forearm to my right wrist. The compass on my gadget watch said I was heading in the proper direction. I turned right, and in twenty crawls I was able to stand up in a larger tunnel. My right leg was heavier, due to the blood-soaked pantleg. I figured two miles and I would be near the churches, where there should be a few field hospitals set up to tend the injured that were ever present during wars such as these. Every church basement, at least in the Balkans, was stocked with medical supplies. Hopefully it hadn't, or wasn't, being bombed. My tunnel trek lasted no more than fifteen minutes, even as the earth around me rumbled and shuddered under the tons of HE rounds denting mother earth's ear lobe, like a finger flick from a little brother, or sister. Pain, nonetheless.

The sky suddenly appeared, and I was in a crater. Snow was falling, or I thought it was, until I choked on a breathful of ash. I knew the city must be on fire. Indeed, a rumbling sound, much like that of thousands of zebras stampeding, was in the air. I heard thumps, heavy artillery being fired from ten miles away, being pumped into a mostly civilian population.

I dragged my sorry ass up out of the crater, into a swarm of panic. People were running in the black and acrid smoke, east, while I stood in what used to be a clothing store. Across the street was a McDonald's, incredibly open for business and not a window broken, as if their golden arches were a force field against the ravages of war. But it was no new thing for me to see, for I'd seen this same miracle of modern warfare, in many countries where big name brands were located. I'd seen warehouses and factories of certain American and English brands, standing amidst the piles of rubble, unharmed. A certain fee was paid at a later date, or some terrorist would blow up the factory that had previously been spared. The two-lane road was not packed with people, but dotted here and there with groups and pairs. Mostly women and children, struggling with their luggage.

But from what were they running? I saw faces frightened, and I heard the flow express fear of the troops coming down from the mountain pass. I'd spent many summers in this country and knew their language well, but it is hard to understand completely any language spoken on the run and in the smoke and thunder of bombs in the background.

I limped along the eddy, staying on the raised cobblestone sidewalk, as the bombs continued to fall. Thankfully, the UAN had more of an interest in bombing the old business district. I passed by the subway entrance, where smoke billowed up from the hole. I doubted trains were running in the thick gray pus. Besides, where I'd be going trains didn't run. Cordite was thick in the air, and sat like smog over the cityscape, even blotting out the sun and sky. Behind the light-colored smoke was an even blacker hue of air, which did not bode well for Brno, or the few forests nearby, should they catch fire. I ran, limped toward a warehouse, when I heard the UAN troops adjust fire, and whistling RLPs began to fly in. Small arms fire joined in, and I knew troops were incoming, or outgoing, whichever, it does someone unarmed no good to be in their way.

I was not alone. Flashes and glimpses of movement and colors passed along my periphery. But I doubted they took any pleasure out of running away from home. The thrill of the chase not so thrilling to these poor citizens. I would be lying if I didn't admit that I thrive in this climate. (Note to self; *Buy bulletproof pants!*)

I darted through a rusty doorway, into an aluminum-sided warehouse. It was the size of a good football (when in Rome....) stadium, filled with steel rafters and rats, crap and empty crates piled to the roof. I headed for the latter, to find a place to hide and rest for a moment, change the bandages, and maybe catch a glimpse of who was chasing who where. I had a pretty good view of an open delivery door.

Bombs, NATO type, began to fall; first on the outside of the city, where,

PROCESS OF ILLUMINATION

I guessed, the Czech Revolutionary forces were or where the UAN troops were. It was hard to decide on which side NATO had lent its support. I hit the ground when those class A explosives began to fall on my little part of the city. In the background I heard the screams of fighter jets. Antiaircraft cannons and surface to air missiles (SAMs) erupted from the ghetto.

Beneath the ruckus of war I felt the presence of troops. Hostiles. I lifted the Kevlar flap on my forearm and tried to dial home, maybe get Johnny Dempsey, my technical support team, to get me a lookdown satellite photo of the area I now found myself bleeding and trapped in. Nada. I checked my power, a combination of solar, kinetic, and battery, and found it well supplied. I checked my photo bank, where I stored all my digital film. It was holding.

"What the hell?" I muttered as the building shuddered, and the digital screen joined in simpatico. Nothing worked, except my send and input, which meant that I could send messages and download film into the computer bank, but I couldn't receive any mail or information. I wondered if I could still send photos, and at least keep my agent happy.

Boots. Hundreds of them stomping outside. I crouched behind the empty crates and pulled a stack so as to completely surround me. I could actually see through the steel and plastic boxes, but was far enough away so as not to be seen. They were all around, revolutionary forces, searching haphazardly, laughing and joking with each other, even as bombs were exploding half a mile away. Small arms fire erupted outside, and the men ran past my little warhouse haven. I pressed myself down, watching silhouettes shooting, being shot, and facing the subsequent consequence of death.

How, ask you, did I know they were hostile? Any soldier in the Balkans is hostile towards persons with cameras, and bearing the name Cort Falcon. Secretly, and maybe illegally, I have passports claiming me to be a Muslim, Christian, or Catholic, with correlating names and country of origin, just in case. Lately, after NATO bombed Serbian TV stations some years ago, it signaled the end to press untouchability. They'd kill me if they found my name database. I'm pretty certain my face was on a wanted poster in several countries of ill repute. But I didn't mind, as stated earlier, I loved these moments of anticipation and exhilaration, so close to being caught. I carried no offensive weapons, save a few knives. No guns. Possession of such would mean certain death, while having a camera with a direct satlink—i.e. the ability to broadcast a live picture from the field to a million viewers— sometimes scared the shit out of others, respective, of course, of the terminations as of late. Only once have I felt my number was up, back in North Korea, but I was slowly realizing in the here and now that death was trying to creep upon me once again.

How, ask you, do you know when death is "creeping up on you?" When you're in the freezing cold and you want to go to sleep; that's death. When you've been shot, or hit, and you feel tired. When your lids are trying to shut like lead garage doors. *Just for a moment*, I tell myself, but that's death's voice, and I know it well, having argued with him on several occasions. That's how you know, the internal warning signs that have no real connection to the machinations of mankind, save the infliction of the wound, if wounded you be when speaking with the devil in your head.

I knew this was death, asking me, lulling me to close the door behind me. Forevermore, no more.

The soldiers outside fled, I opened my small pack and ate two energy bars, and a packet of gofast, then sipped some water. This opened my eyes, but death was still there in the throbbing pain of my right leg. I tightened the bandages, while waiting for the distant sound of an army's approach, which usually followed the retreat of another. In my head I planned a route to the hospital, and was just about to get up, when I heard the footsteps of a little boy, followed by the heavier boots of his father.

Another horror to my collection, maybe even on film....

– CHAPTER 2 –

I SAW THE FACE FIRST; a distinctly feminine obstruction of my view, and not just some ordinary lineage. A goddess, with Grace Kelly likeness, wrapped within a tangle of Sophia Loren colored hair. The breath of cold light, in combination with my after coma blurriness, was softened by the gentle curve that went from brow to the tip of her nose. The ambient shadows caressed two concave pale cheeks with lips like a half moon, beside twin pink—nearly purple—wave crescents that melded together in a gentle slope. Her eyes were closed, but I could see her lashes and brows, so delicate I would not have noticed save on second glance.

I had to move to see if this wasn't a dream, but knew that if this was my dream she would have opened her eyes....

From my hospital cot, Royal Army issue, lying on my left side, I looked around. The girl, or woman, was just an arm's length away from my face. Behind her, and at my head, I noticed the green tarp of a field hospital. I saw an emanation of heated air leave her oval nostrils, and sighed relief. I flexed my right leg and brought instant awareness to my injuries; a subtle tightness in my right calve muscle, and the pull of a bandage on my upper thigh. The worst wound had been the calve, but it was the quadricep that greeted me with pain. It subsided as I relaxed my muscles. Good thing I did deep knee thrusts, because I didn't think I'd be using those muscles anytime soon. Or so I thought. Anyhow, the small tent hospital was empty, execpt for me and my lovely porcelain statue. There was no sound to be heard, but this quietude only lasted a second.

The bad feeling was coming; this wasn't right; missing patients and doctors.

Old Faithful, the nurse that had caught me, rushed into the tent, red faced and worried. As the tent flap opened I heard the sound of small arms fire, sirens, and soldiers on bullhorns.

"Where's everybody?" I tried to ask, but found my throat too dry for that. I noticed a IV in my left arm just then. I prayed it wasn't attached to a blood infusion bottle. I sighed visibly when I saw the synthetic blood.

"Here." Old Faithful picked up a water bottle and squirted cool liquid past my tongue.

I watched as she looked from me to the princess next to me, but her actions were furtive and quick, as if she wanted to leave here yesterday.

"Who is she?" I asked, seeings how I got no response to my previous question. Did she speak English?

"Ah, an American. I thought as much." Old Faithful had a distinctly Scottish accent, maybe Edinburgh, about fifty years, and of good, sturdy stock. "She's Janet Doe, found in the rubble of an old hospital that had been bombed to the boots."

She wavered for a moment, so I asked my initial question again. "Why are we here all alone? Where's everybody at?"

"Evacuated yesterday, with the rest." She looked at the girl. "She could be a citizen. International law forbids us from taking her out of her country without her permission—such a tragedy."

Ah, now I understood. If my knowledge of international law was up to date, foreign agencies, humanitarian or not, could not transport citizens of a country across borders, unless granted specific permission by that country's United Nations Ambassador. In this case, the Czech Republic didn't have an ambassador as of late, and therefore couldn't grant permission. Being an American citizen by birth, and a world citizen by choice, any humanitarian agency in the world had my explicit permission to save my butt.

"My camera?"

"Your pack's right beneath ya, sir. Can you walk?" She glanced at the door as a shot rang out nearby.

"I'm not sure. Can I?"

"Only flesh wounds, and a nick. Might challenge ya some." Her crystal clear blue eyes laughed at my hesitancy, even as the rest of her postured for escape.

"I'll manage, but what of her?"

Old Faithful shrugged, and I saw how it grieved her to leave Janet Doe behind.

"Might be they'll leave her be...." But she knew better, even as the words left her mouth. She plucked out the IV. "But not likely"

I nodded. "Then I'll see what I can do."

"A fond favor that would be for my soul." She stood up, looking once more at the sleeping beauty, then to me. "Good luck to you, Cameraman." With that said, she spun and ran out a flap in the canvas, leaving me and my charge alone.

Her quick steps frightened me more than anything else, for she did not seem the type of woman to hurry about for anyone. I rolled up out of the bunk too fast, and my head swam for a moment. I was glad that they'd taken off my pants instead of cutting off the right leg, due in no small part to the poverty of the region. A pant leg was something to get angry about missing when you'd only one pair to live by. I checked my pack and put on a new pair of gortex long johns, and a set of winter camos, which I put on as fast as possible, then stowed my dirty clothes.

"What am I gonna call you?" I asked her quietly. I stood, testing my leg. The calve throbbed, but if I kept the weight off of it I should make it through the next few days, depending on what a 'knick' was. I reached down, touched her pale pink cheek, as the lights flickered and the ground shook and the air seemed thicker for a moment. My ears popped. But I was transfixed by her beauty, a thumb caressing her fine brow line. A hundred pounds, soaking wet, I guessed her to be, and decided to roll her up in two of the thermal blankets.

"Come on … Francesca," I said in remembrance of the woman who'd been kidnapped, who I could hopefully save from a worser still fate, while at the same time paying some homage to the man's last words. It seemed fit, this ghost name, to the circumstance, but I'd be surprised if she were a Francesca. I would have liked to ponder this further, but the boots were brow beating the cobblestone streets of Brno. Machine guns were being fired. Screams and shouts, followed by more shots, and in the background one could almost imagine hearing the dead falling heavily upon each other, souls escaping, but there was no time to dwell within this morose morbidity.

With gray blankets around Fran, and strips of linen tying those tightly around her, she resembled a rolled-up rug, which might come in handy. "Ready, Fran?" Her eyelids didn't blink open. They would have in my dream. I covered her beautiful face. "Up ya go, sleeping beauty." Ninety pounds was more like it. I carried her, not much different than Richard Gere carried Debra Winger in *An Officer and a Gentleman*, towards the rear of the FH, the sound of soldiers pillaging too near.

Outside, the night air was frigid. The whispers of war were close, as magnesium flares burned orange, yellow, and white in the—I checked my watch—ten after midnight sky. Jets screamed in, the clouds alight with their orange fire, like prolonged lightning strikes missing the boom. Orange and green tracers lit a path up towards the clouds, that echoed with the light of jets too fast to be caught by mere man-guided bullets. I continued on the way I'd been going before, except now I just wanted to reach the mountains, and hide my precious cargo, whose life I held in my hands.

I kept waiting for the leg to give out, but it held, the only discomfort a numb burning sensation. But I could run, using the flares to my own advantage, even though I felt the stitches pulling now and then.

"Hey! Who goes there?" a unseen sentry shouted in Arabic.

I didn't wait for the bullets or more questions, and ducked into the first doorway of some small shop, just as bullets ricocheted off of the brick facade.

"Sucker!" I retorted in good Hebrew, just to throw him off.

The empty shop, a clone of hundreds like it, was twenty meters deep and fifteen wide. I headed, carefully now due to the blackness, towards the backdoor. A counter ran the length of the right wall, but that would be the first place they looked if we were to hide. Out of the question. I kept moving. Like many of the buildings, the doors had long since been taken for firewood, and this was no different matter. I found myself looking at a ravine, a black sheen in the middle, meaning that water was trickling down it. Instincts said upstream, and I followed. One foot in the water, one foot on the cracking cement that was loose beneath my feet. Fran issued no complaints to my awkward movements, caused singularly by my singular good leg. The gunfire and ricochets didn't follow us, but stayed out front. Before long I saw a tree, and knew I was close to the easternmost part of the city, where were the churches, I wondered, until I came out of the drainage ditch and saw three of the domes on fire.

I'd seen many fires, some tragic, some mere losses of property, and some both. I hoped that the latter was not the case here, though it was always a tragedy when places of worship and nonviolence were burned down. Understandably, though nonetheless unforgivable, the government sometimes sought out the churches, because they were usually the places where villages came together. And you can put two and two together. Churches were often used as meeting places, or at the very least, where grievances were aired in a semidemocratic manner. But this area, though many proclaimed it otherwise and maybe even had the world outside believing it, was filled with tyrants. Yes, even in this 21st century. Two Muslim mosques and an Orthodox church, each within five hundred meters of each other, consumed from the inside out. I watched, transfixed yet aware of my surroundings and my package, waiting for God to come down and extinguish the flames. *Maybe next time*, I thought.

I stepped over some grave markers, some fresh, some hundreds of years old, though of this latter kind there were few in comparison to the former. Many cities buried their dead just outside of town, in many different countries and cultures, and the mostly good citizens of Brno were no different. On the other side of the graveyard was the treeline of the Carpathian Mountain range, and safety. But before going deeper, I wanted to scout, without Francesca's weight in my arms, and so I laid her down in the soft green grass behind some bushes, though I doubted anyone had been following us.

I believe at that moment the chemical make-up in my brain was off, messed up, discombobulated, because I'd never felt so possessive of something, or in the case in point, of someone, in my life, like I did now. All I wanted—needed—to do was scout the first fifty meters, then move her deeper in, because I knew that many soldiers used the treelines as sniper foxholes. But I couldn't leave her. I peeled back the end of the blanket roll, to check on her condition, though tracing the outline of her face was only necessary to find her nostrils, from which emanated a soft warmth. I replaced the blanket, chiding my excuse for such an invasion. But it was necessary, I declare. I wondered if she'd eaten, and if not, or even so, how could I feed her in the future? I guessed I'd get to it when it got to me.

A blinding flash, not quite nuclear, but close, lit up the skyline. I counted the seconds, and figured the explosion to be about 5 kilometers away. Probably the oil fields or the powerplant, on the other side of the city, which meant that NATO was cutting off the city and its revolutionary government, with UAN troops being used as enforcers. Not a good sign.

Small pops filled the sky, and soon night was no more. Hundreds of flares floated down from the clouds, and anything they landed on would burn. Explosive blasts rocked the city, as specific targets were pummeled by the new stealth Tomahawk missiles. The flares blotted out satellite infrared recon. Why this was being done was a mystery, but if any mistakes were made, wrong buildings blown up, there wouldn't be any satellite film. I felt the armies moving, scrambling, in the maze of streets. It was time to go into deeper cover. I'd have to take my chances with revolutionaries, who'd fled like rats from a sinking ship to the higher ground.

Riddled with caves, mines, and ancient tombs, the Carpathians were like anthills. Some of the ancient tombs still reeked of sweat and toil of the slaves who'd pickaxed through them. In communist USSR, before it became Russia, slaves and criminals were synonymous. Antiruling party line supporters were deemed criminals. Any act or thought revealed, which bespoke of an ideology contrary to the then current governing body, was criminal. To Siberia. To the Carpathian copper and gold mines. To a variety of death inducing camps, factories, and mines. Dig, sweat, work harder, and die. These haunted caves were notorious hideouts, and so I approached with as much silence as I could muster, not daring to shine my mini flashlight, thereby giving my position away. At the same time I hoped there was a cave close by.

"Stop! Don't come any closer or I shoot!" someone barked in native Czechoslovakian.

I froze and waited, turning my back to the barker, just in case he shot anyways, fearing that the 7.62 round would pass through the bulletproof material of my camo shirt. If it was steel or copper jacketed, I'd be in trouble, and considering those were usual military issue, I was probably in trouble. Unless the guerrilla forces had been forced to revert to lead, which was common due to the expense of smeltering steel and copper, compared to lead, which liquified and hardened quicker than most metals.

"Where is he?" I heard a girl's voice say in the same native tongue.

"I don't know."

"I don't know—I heard something though, I swear," Jacques Pavlicek whispered to Terese Bocetz. "Move forward or I shoot!"

Too bad I heard their tiny young voices. I stood still and waited. Did they realize how close I was? I didn't believe they were part of any revolutionary group, and if I had my night-vision glasses I'd bet I'd see empty hands. However, in this area, 13-year-olds were common among the fighters.

"It's nothing, Jack. You're going crazy," Terese teased. "Put the knife down and come back inside before a bomb blows up on our heads."

The boy made a threat, inferring some sort of sexual activity. They weren't that young, I guessed. I listened to their retreat, gauging where their movement was exactly. I saw a lighter's flame, about five feet into the cave. Bombs exploded nearby, and I used it to mask the snapping of twigs and rustling of decomposing leaves, as I went towards the black hole that marked the entrance to the runaways' cave.

Many runaways formed quasi familiar bonds with other runaways. They spent their days huffing gasoline, paint, or other toxic agents. Anything to escape the pain of poverty, anything to provide the relief, short of death. Young girls and boys sold themselves, sometimes were sold by vagabond pimps, who were nothing but survivors who'd been there. These castaways were not loved by any but themselves, and sometimes not even that, while the governments of more countries than not were to give these "scamps" and "little thieves" and "disease carriers" a portion of their budget. Most children, too young to work legally, or too dirty to work in any place respectable, did indeed turn to thievery and beggery or prostitution. This latter degradation usually following a violent series of rapes by elder vagabonds. No one washed their clothes, their faces, or made sure they were healthy. Many froze in the winter, after being kicked out of the underground subway systems, or various other public transportation depots. Their tiny bodies like small innocent puppies, stiffened in death's repose, awaiting no coffin, for even that measure would be too expensive, and is the final unkind act they will face in this reality. Those living drift, avoiding local police and local toughs, who prey upon the younger girls and boys. They move in a vicious cycle with rare charities and rarer reprieves.

I hoped someone, or some world group, would have the decency to provide these wandering children with some love. Some kindness that their parents would not, or could not, afford, financially or emotionally. Either that, or teach the delinquent parents responsibility.

I'd once made rounds in Prague, with Dean, through subways, handing out food and drink to dirty-faced children, who upon receipt of a genuine hug from an adult would break down into tears that slashed through the crude of abuse built upon their bony gray cheeks. So used to distrusting adults, yet so in need of the adult supervision and approval, some didn't know how to react. Some checked the sandwiches for poison, others were bulldogged out of theirs. So hard to leave those teary-eyed and pink-streaked faces, and so I didn't. There's an orphanage, which I pay for, outside of Prague, run by the church nearby.

I stopped and set Fran down, just inside the tunnel, careful to keep her parallel with the incline, though it was only slight. Still, that's all I needed was my girl rolling down the hill. Ah yes, "my girl" already. Slowly, quietly, relying on the blessings of many American hunters and their camouflage to keep me invisible, I moved further into the cave, having to crouch as I went.

The invisible man entered the wider passage, praying he was not announced by the muffled bangs and flashes—though I was just as, if not more, worried about bringing Fran deeper into the mountain. I saw their tiny shapes, huddled together, a dim candle burning in a tin can. No gun, but a serious-looking machete near the girl's head. I heard bombs, this time too close, and decided on action.

"Jack?" I said in a noncombative tone. Both looked up instantly, the girl grabbing the machete, the boy a switchblade. "I have an injured woman who needs the safety of your cave," I said in decent Czech. I knew those street smart eyes, and waited for what I knew was coming.

"Do you have food? I want two meals—" The girl hit Jack. "—uh, I mean we want two meals, and you can stay for a while." The girl hit him again. "Cigarettes?"

"All right. Please put your weapons down, and help me."

"Wait, how do you know his name?"

"I know you too, Terese." She looked fifteen, but her eyes revealed those of a fifty-year-old woman. I knew the outline of her story, just like I knew his, by looking at the paint stains on their fingers and around their mouths.

They'd been sniffing away the pain with paint, which was comparable to a newborn baby sucking on toxic chemicals, each having only one outcome; braincell retardation and physical death or worse.

The boy, up close, was only fifteen or sixteen, a hundred pounds at most, with those Slavic features and dirty—everything about both of them was dirty—brown hair, and glassy eyes. This latter was a symptom, or the effects of the paint. He helped lift the feet, while I took Fran's head, and carried her back into the cave.

"Are you American?" he asked hesitantly.

I smiled. "Yes." *I am the bane of the Balkans. An American.* But to the poor vagrants I was considered a gold mine, but then again, I was a mark, or easy pickings to two thirds of the planet, which was both a blessing and a curse.

Over the years I learned to judge the intentions of my fellow impoverished human beings, child and adult alike, to see those furtive eyes, and tiny, but adept hands and fingers. The shaggers in the shadows, who controlled the stage, be it a busy street, a sidewalk cafe, or a train depot, were always easily spotted if one knew what to look for. And though I never carried weapons, as aforementioned, I did have some nasty defensive devices sure to put a tingle and spark into any would-be pickpocket or mugger. I love my gadgetry, though I must confess to finding many of my techno toys in Germany and Japan. The lethal items I use only in emergencies.

"What's wrong with her?" Terese asked, true human concern marking her young face as I laid Fran down in the furthest part of the alcove we were in.

"Don't know." And that was the truth.

"Looks like she's sleeping," the girl commented, when I adjusted the blankets so Fran's face was alighted by the flickering yellow candlelight.

"Move the blankets!" Jack ordered Terese.

"I am!"

They shouted back and forth, quasi parent to quasi parent. I knew this was their way, the abusive but caring shouts, which ended with the girl pouting. Had I not been there Jack may have struck her, to make her comply, but maybe not. He seemed a good enough sort. Not too jaded. I threw him a pack of Marlboros, which I packed just for bargaining purposes, choosing to see them huff on filtered cigarettes rather than unfiltered paint. I went to my pack, a thirty-kilo number, depending on how much water was in the tank.

"Jack—cooking fuel," I said, then adjusted my aim. "After you finish." He exhaled, I smiled, cringing inside. "You hungry, Terese?" I asked her in Czech, then tossed her an energy bar.

"What about me?" Jack said.

"Enjoy your cigarette, go get some firewood for dinner, and I'll give you one too. I'll let her hold it." I handed Terese another energy bar, which she looked at, then looked up at me in disbelief, then smiled viciously at Jack. She finally had something he wanted.

If I didn't speak Czech he would've warned her about the repercussions of filching his food, but instead he glared at her, then smiled at me, then started towards the entrance.

"Put your cig out before you leave the cave, and don't bring back company—"

"Ha! I've been doing this as long as I've lived," Jack said in confident, but broken English. He put out the cherry with spit, and tucked the butt away for later.

"He's from Kosovo," Terese said, after Jack was out of hearing range, as if she were betraying some secret given her. "Were you in Kosovo?"

I hesitated. "Yes." I was in Kosovo, and I knew all about it.

It was in the Secretary of State's office, in Washington, D.C., that the war in Kosovo began. The President and lesser included politicians joked about the Balkans. That area of the world was always full of troubles, and would always be, many American—and international—politicians said.

Albanians chaffed under Serbian oppression, and once Yugoslavia was broken up, and the reins of Mother Russia snapped, those in power abused their fellow countrymen.

A plague of ethnic "cleansing" and campaigns to eliminate nationalist rebels, and their supporters, turned out to be massacres. Photographs of the dead, many just children or skinny farmers, were shown to the world, and acted like stones on a scale, that, once tipped, acted as a lever that opened a door through which military might would burst. And once the politicians were safe in their cubbyholes, and the first missile and bomb salvos launched, there was no turning back. But violence begets violence, and death, Balkan style.

The Red, White, and Blue stepped in once NATO powers committed, after much pressure from U.S. politicians and ambassadors, who at the latter part of the lobbying seemed to be doing just that. However, it had taken some media bullying, through increased "war crimes" and genocide coverage, to get the U.S. onboard, and one could only speculate who was behind the media's role.

When the big media corporations have ties to defense companies and businesses that benefit when war is alive in the world, one must question the conflicts of humanitarian interest. ABC has ties with Caltex and Texaco; CBS has ties with Hill & Knowlton; NBC is owned by General Electric, who is a Department of Defense contractor with ties to British Petroleum and *The Washington Post*; Knight Ridder, Inc., has ties with Raytheon of Tomahawk missile fame, and much much more; *The New York Times* has ties with Caltex, General Dynamics, and Texaco; Gannet Newspaper Co., Inc., has ties with McDonnell Douglas and Phillips Petroleum; *The Washington Post* has ties with General Electric, NBC, and Ashland Oil; *Times Mirror* has ties with Rockwell International; Time Warner has ties with Mobil Oil and the Tribune Company. Et cetera et cetera. If a conspiracy theorist were to take a long and deep look at the connections, ties, and monetary links, he'd be abuzz with grassy knolls and shadow corporations. Let me disclaim right here and now; though these are actual ties, they are subject to rapid adjustments and changes, as acquisitions and mergers take place. Still, the template for uncertainty and speculation lay openly to any who would look, and ask, 'Is it a conflict of interest for the news anchor to be hyping tragedies, pushing the public against a certain act, for America, Europe or your country to go to war, when they will profit from the war?'

America claimed the KLA (Kosovo Liberation Army) were freedom fighters, and Serbians claimed they were terrorists. The media aired pictures that reflected the freedom fighters argument, while showing the genocide committed by Serbian forces. It did not show the Serbian citizens who'd been killed, or worse. Both parties were guilty of murder. However, due to the singular focus, Serbian soldiers (and probably rightly so), became the enemy of the international world.

Oiling the pinions of the machine were the huge defense contractors whose stocks had been falling since Saddam Hussein and Desert Storm. Greedy CEOs sent out schools of piranha—we call them lobbyists—with big sharp teeth and fatter wallets, which gave two choices. Get bit, or get paid. When the scale tipped there were no squeals or squeaks of protests. Defense contractors , energy companies , stocks went up and up and up. Five years after Desert Storm they fell and fell and fell.

Then it began again, this war process, but this time I was out of that Israeli pit, and lucky to be alive, after two years in one of their prisons. My sideburns—no razors allowed—gray enough to match the jail clothes. I'd still be there, waiting for a trial that would never come, if not for my brother, and our money. My own journalistic connections shrunk like snails do when sprinkled with salt. I watched the war, the Kosovo one, heavily slanted and censored, on a black and white television set, before I could fully understand the Hebrew language. Thankfully I've a gift for picking up languages, and did so.

I knew the situation, historically and politically speaking, in the Balkans.

I majored not in journalism, but in History and Political Science. What good is a journalist who doesn't know the entire history of a piece of land which he or she will write about, or the ghosts that roam therein. Could be the reason for my early success. I knew the ghosts by name, and sometimes they talked to me, between the exploding bombs and screaming jets, foretelling of a future. And believe me, it's nice to know the future, because what you know you can try to change, or if not, escape.

The Israelis don't take kindly to foreigners, world citizen or not, killing one of their "businessmen." Why didn't I write? Frankly, I was in a jail cell, not dissimilar to the current human warehouses in America, and other "civilized" countries, which was called "Haifu Hell" by the prisoners, and me, within. Many political prisoners, and aliens waiting forever to be tried. Why was I there, in a dirty and hellish world, with gladiator rules, and prejudices unchecked, where torture is legal, and where there were severe consequences if you didn't take a stand?

Since dinner is cooked, Francesca sleeps, and the kids are smoking, I can elucidate upon the reasons for my stay in "Haifu Hell."

Why was I there?

The charge; Homicide of an Israeli Citizen.

What say I? Guilty! Guilty! And Guilty! And I'd do it again to the kidnapper, rapist, molestor, and monster.

– CHAPTER 3 –

THE THEORY WAS THAT I killed a man who was about to kill a Russian prostitute. I killed him, all right, though I did not want to, and even now wondered if I could have fired my knife at not so lethal a point on the man's body.

The victim, Yassir Yeffat, a plump humpty-dumpty-built fifty-three-year-old businessman who ran two "men's only" clubs in Jafo and in Haifu. Men's only because there were 20 to 30 girls who lived and worked in each club. He was the usual thug made good by bad, with black hair, a thin mustache, and slits for eyes. He wore a Yarmulka on certain days, but by his own faith he should have been struck by lightning, plague, or paralysis long ago.

I'd been working a story, not about the ring of prostitutes—that story had been played out, according to Barry Greenburg—but about the allegations that women, wives and children alike, were being kidnapped and forced into slavery far from their homelands.

Some of the women were from Europe, but most were from Russia and Asia. They were judged only by their beauty, and the way in which they could be trained to use it. I'd played the game, hired a pretty 15-year-old girl —Vayna Yacovick—and a room, and then got her to open up by speaking my best Russian.

Vayna had been working in a dance club in Murmansk when she'd been approached by Petyr Peterov, a sleazy "Euromodel" representative. An investigation into Euromodel showed me that it was a phony name on a business card which made the person bearing it seem legitimate. (The only way I knew about Euromodels was because she'd saved the business card.) I bought it. She'd only been going to take photos with Petyr, when someone had given her a shot from behind. She felt a prick in her arm, and awoke on a train out in the middle of nowhere. Desert was all that surrounded the train. Two big, sinister-looking ex-KGB enforcers, faces scarred, lips tight, always watched them. Her, and two other pretty girls from her region. Vayna, Airiao, and young Tatia, the latter still dressed in a school uniform, were all trapped in a first class compartment. Airiao told her what was happening and she panicked, felt another prick, and woke up at the border. Strange languages, customs, and much whispered talk between officials and her guardians took place outside their cabin window. The man returned, and each girl was given another shot. She woke up alone, in the very bedroom we were talking in; a five-foot-wide stall, six feet deep, with a small bed, a dresser, and three hooks to hang dresses on. And there was a bill; ten thousand dollars, which she owed to the club owner.

"How shall I pay?" she'd asked Yassir Yeffat.

"How can you but pay? You are pretty, men will pay for you, no?" He grinned crookedly, like the devil.

(I'd seen his grin and believed her.)

"You have a problem?" Yeffat said, taking out a needle filled with heroin.

She showed me her arms, and I knew what had happened from that point to the then present day.

"Do you want me to?" Her innocent eyes belied the pain in her soul, and the lonely longing for home in her heart. "Please, or Yassir will fine me, and I like you. You are the only man who understands what I say, except some of the girls."

"Here." I handed her a U.S. fifty, and she was naked in the flick of a shoulder strap. "No—no—no," I said softly, careful not to bruise her self-esteem. "You are too beautiful for me. Only talk." I could think of nothing else to say, so I lifted her dress back up. She was still breath taking, not yet made gaunt by the abuse and drugs and ripping away of her soul, and the man in me had to remind myself that it would be rape. I hugged her, and she kissed me on the cheek. "I'll get you home." Why I made this crazy proposition I don't know, but I did, and I always keep my word. I began then and there making the plan to get her out.

Twelve in the afternoon is midnight to the girls working the clubs, and it was then that I crept into Vayna's "cell." Why they call them rooms, I don't know.

I found two little girls crammed together on the small bunk-like mattress. I wore dark gray Ninja style clothes, and was armed for defensive combat, but was hoping for a clean getaway. It was Tatia who opened her eyes and mouth first—"No, I'm here to take you home." I looked at Vayna. "Are you the man she spoke to earlier?"

"Last night, yes," I whispered. "Are you Airiao? Or Tatia?" She looked only 13 or 14 years old.

She smiled at the mention of her real name, then looked toward the door behind me, as if someone might hear her self-recognition of her individuality. "Yes." Tears flowed.

I touched her hand. "Wake her up, and we'll all three go back home," I said with some urgency. I'd left one of the protectors behind the bar counter, and I didn't know where Yeffat was. It was hard to keep track of people from the lookdown satlink, but he was in the vicinity. Reconnoitering the area had proved no sign of the pimp, or of his pimp mobile. Crowded cities like Haifu tended to disrupt technology; too many closely built buildings and small alleyways between. Big new cities weren't so bad, but the Romes and Parises were hell on spy gadgets and satrecon and electronic ears. Even the filters of the top secret Echelon Project's super computers couldn't differentiate a voice or call from within a confusion of frequencies and static.

(Echelon Project; a top secret-but exposed-American, NATO black project that encompasses messages, e-mail, and computer doings, since 1950.) More on this later.

Rumor had it that that was how they got Carlos the Jackal, Manuel Noriega, and a few other drug lords.

"What's wrong with her?" I asked Tatia, when Vayna didn't wake up. Then I noticed the needle and spoon on the dresser.

"Mr. Yeffat sold her.... She couldn't take the pain after—"

"Why?" I said, seeing the tears in Tatia's eyes sprout anew. I felt for Vayna's pulse. Youth has its strengths, and resilience was one of them. I hoped this would help her. "Does she have any jeans, and a long sleeve shirt?" I saw Tatia, who was familiar with everything in Vayna's room, go to the dresser and take out two items of clothes. Jeans and a shirt.

I saw the blood dripping from her anus, and the bruises on her back—
"What the fuck's going on in there?" Yeffat said in a mix of Russian, English, and Hebrew.

"This is my daughter! You've kidnapped her!" I said in the most guttural and indignant Russian voice I could muster.

Yeffat considered this, then squinted his eyes so he looked like a potbellied pig suspicious of a carrot. "Who are you?" He stepped in closer and looked at the two girls, adjusting his blue Nike warm-up suit as he did so.

"I am her father."

"What's your name?"

"Pavlo Bruschev. I demand my daughter."

"This is not your daughter, sir," he said smoothly. "Come, I show you. I have passport."

I didn't say anything, but made to follow him, but quickly turned to Tatia. "Pack your things." I told her, then went with Yeffat, glad that he hadn't made me from the other night.

He inserted a key into the lock, on a door marked "Manager." The dark blue door swung inward, lights flicked on, and the vulture hobbled with light steps to a small steel desk. He opened a drawer, and after a moment, pulled out a stack of passports and contracts.

"Ah, here we are. Vayna Yacovick." He produced the passport and the contract, one inside the other, and handed them to me. "You see?"

Sucker, I didn't say. "Thank you." I put the documents into my pocket. A background file and character assessment, provided by JD, did not give me any inclination of his next move.

He pulled a gun. "You're no father."

"I'm taking her home."

"You'll have to pay her bill. Twenty-two thousand. Cash." He was, after all, a business man first and foremost.

So much for her paying it off in the past few months. "Okay, I'll take her home and mail you the money." I spoke in English this time.

His belly jumped up and down. "You think me a fool?" Now he pointed the gun. "Give me the documents, or I shoot."

I'd have to talk to JD about our psychological profile people, because this WAS DEFINITELY NOT in his file. He'd never before gone to war with any rival gangs to own his business and he'd stayed free from racial and religious conflicts. There were indications that he assaulted the girls every so often, but nothing close to murder. He had two traffic tickets, and one health code violation about the same time ABC exposed his men's only club five years ago.

The U.S. President had called the Israeli Prime Minister, who sent the harassment hounds to Haifu, and then it all was forgotten, except by the parents whose children were kidnapped, or the children who were enslaved or killed. But the politicians had covered themselves, and could fain serve the morality of the opposition, if need be.

And me, I could care less about adults selling their bodies, but when someone—child or adult—was forced into it, or enslaved, a certain moral line was crossed.

"Are you sure you want to do it this way?" I slowly brought out the passport. "I will pay you, Yeffat."

"Pay me now!"

"Do I look like I have that much money on me?"

"How much?"

"Five—U.S."

"Where?"

"Right here—" I saw his eyes, and his pudgy little trigger finger. It was pulling, and I, instinctively, squeezed my own device's trigger.

The bullet, since he'd pulled instead of squeezed, hit me in my right upper chest.

A knife went into Yeffat's throat. The gun dropped, with much blood, to the short, cruddy-colored carpet. I remembered thinking about that short shag, which seems to find its way onto the floor of many a seedy establishment's manager's office.

Then Yeffat crumbled, hands grasping his neck, while I dropped, suddenly out of breath, and knowing that I'd just lost a lung.

Tatia rushed in at the moment I dropped, and I spoke to her in Russian. She was smart, and I sensed a toughness in her. "Take this, and find your passport, and leave now. Don't wait, Tatia. Hire a cab if you can't carry Vayna." I handed her the money, an envelope with fake passports and train tickets back to Murmansk. "Over there is your passports. Use the same picture."

"What about—" She pointed to the blood. "You're hurt bad?"

"I'll call the police when you're gone. Hurry, before the guards come back or other girls try to stop you," I said with the last of my breath. I turned onto the side I was shot, hoping to be able to breathe.

I dialed a number on my personal computer, I don't know who, but the next thing I knew was I had a problem.

Heavy footsteps getting closer. A siren nearby. Then pant legs and black shoes all around me, lights in my eyes. I woke in a prison hospital ward, my leg in irons, a nurse pulling something out of my dick. The latter, after much difficulty in interpretation, was a catheter. An odd sensation nevertheless, having a woman you don't know fondling the 'long johnson' so intimately, and—I swear the expression is worldwide—with a gleam in her forty-five-year-old eye. My right leg, seemingly always in trouble of some injurious sort, was linked by ankle cuff and chain to the steel bed rail. I thanked God I was already circumcized. (Purely for health reasonings, my parents told me, may they rest in peace.) The nurse left me, thankfully covering me up as she did, and a moment later a police officer looked in, and, without a word, left.

An hour later a pair of plainclothes Israeli detectives came in, carrying my defense gear, my MPC, and my passport, and began asking questions. I told them, with more detail than I told before, what exactly had happened, and following this I requested to speak with someone from the American embassy, or from World Citizenship, also located in the American Embassy. I spoke to someone at the embassy, so they said, and supposedly they would make sure my rights weren't violated. This, however, did not stop the Israeli system from keeping me in prison for nearly two years, from 2002 to 2003.

So there you have it.

Back in the here and shaky now, I was hoping that NATO wouldn't start blind bombing, which meant dropping uranium heavy bombs—the contents of which were not assured to be depleted either—from 15,000 feet and above, upon anything that looked as if it could be used for military purposes. Years ago, during that war in the '90s, NATO had accidently bombed tractors and trailers, some filled with Albanian or Serbian refugees. You don't want to know what 1,000-pound HE Uranium depleted bombs did to tightly packed human beings. Body parts melded, fused, integrated and disintegrated. The pain of the living broke the soul, and the gray shell shock hung about like a heavy fog on the brain that no voice or reality could penetrate. Except the inner pain in the eyes, of seeing the headless, armless, legless, children, or the mother and father evaporating in a gristly cloud of blood and bone. Blank, opaque eyes bulging grotesquely, looking nowhere in this world, but assured some corporeality.

I am about people over institutions, especially the institution of nation and pride.

But politicians sometimes thwarted the generals with the culpable responsibilities and collateral damage worries, so I doubted an all-out bombing schedule would be approved in the here and now. If the warriors were fully unchained to do what had to be done, it would be done quickly and ruthlessly. If you declare war on some nation or notion, then the air of civility can only be a detriment to the declarants' cause or goal. Yet man still sought to make omelets without breaking eggs, on account of possible repercussions in the next election campaign.

Meanwhile, the warriors were stuck with the impossible situation; Win, but don't hurt anybody, as the enemy laughed with innocent blood in their sinister smiles, massacring just over the border where it's "legal."

"Sir?"

Her voice brought me back to the cave, where it was cool, but winter was coming to the Balkans. I did not want to be stuck in it either, not by myself, and especially not with my sleeping beauty. I looked down at my hand, where I was dribbling dehydrated ice cream down Fran's chin, instead of in her mouth.

"Sorry, Fran," I said, and smiled a thank you at Terese. Looking down at my task, I hoped that the dehydrated ice cream had enough protein in it to sustain such a frail creature. I was able to get a good look—Hey, I'm just a man—at her body, her skin, her build, the shape of her bones to which that soft silk clung. I am a sucker for helplessly innocent beauty, and though this might one day lead to my downfall, it made me feel good. Not "bad" good, but that "good" you feel when you walk a blind old lady across a traffic-filled street. The kind of good you feel when you pinch a drowned baby's nose and breathe life into water-filled lungs. Seeing Fran's face, pure innocence wrapped in pale flesh, frightened me deeply. Would I be able to protect her, care for her, keep her away from the murderers of war, worse, from the monsters that war makes of men, who under the hypnosis of cause or liberty or justice, dole out such misery and malice?

"Sir? Here, let me, you re dribbling all over her." Terese took the packet from my hand, chiding me, and I took up the sponging and toilet.

My college buddies would boot me from the fraternity if they knew my deepest feelings. I felt like crying, something about the contact of my hand with her flesh, even her not so small feet, caused an instant chemical reaction. I knew the chemistry of love, and rarely, if ever, gave in to its hypnotic embrace. I could not help myself. She, Janet Doe, Franny, Sleeping Beauty, whoever she was, had my heart and soul. I would gladly attach myself to her till death do us part. Words do not rise to explain the imploration of my heart; my chest cavity swelling invisibly, my gut churning, my skin hot and my pores sweaty at the thought of losing her, whether by rejection or circumstance. It was a feeling, not a description of bodily functions.... No, it is everything. The bombs exploded, walking nearer God to me and the injured doe lying before me....

Let him cast the first stone....

– CHAPTER 4 –

MY NAME MAY BE KNOWN from Afghanistan to Zimbabwe, in the circle of journalists, and my fee is top scale, but for all the 15 years of walking within man's immorality I've yet to understand the hood of unethical and inhumane reasoning that drops over men's eyes in wartime. Not all, but most. Forgive me, I only wish to establish that war, as time turns the black and white of history gray, does things to human beings. Men and women alike. Horrible acts are committed in the name of cause or creed, race or religion, land or love, et cetera. War is also like a prison, in that there is an enemy —whichever side you're not on—that devises all sorts of devices to keep you in check. Wherein men live in cells, called "foxholes," and where war is waged on many psychological and physiological levels. Oh, not so glorious these warrior/criminals, but I met many an innocent person in prison.

In my most recent prison experience, in Haifu Hell, my battle against the Israeli warders was true. I fought—mostly mentally—for my survival, and for my respect. It seems prison guards around the world suffer from the same psychosis; power freak syndrome. Coupled with little education and intelligence, it equals, powerus controlus freakus, or PCF.

But I digress. Most catalytic a creed is religion; India v. Pakistan, Hindu v. Islam. Pakistani young are raised to be anti-Indiacentric. India's young are taught to be anti-Pakistanicentric. Who is to blame? In 2001 Taliban leaders in Afghanistan declared that anyone who was not Muslim was to be executed, and that anyone who tried to convert to another religion was subject to death, and anyone who tried to convert someone from Muslim teachings was also subject to the highest penalty. Who is to blame? Americans, who created the Jihaad, which now finds the enemy amongst its own silver-lined cities.

None see the fallacy of war, the inherent wrongness of battle, which, if allowed to grow exponentially, would lead to the perpetual death and genocide of mankind. Do the "Gods" of either religion call for the destruction of the species, for this is the penultimate goal of war in the 21st century? Do the "Gods" call for the ceaseless weeding out, the genocide of a race or creed? Do those "Gods" call for the cruelty and evil inherent in the deeds of war? The slap, kick, brutalization of humankind by humankind makes atheism psychologically and physically more appealing.

An example was once pointed out to me; A man holds on to a rope, which hangs over the edge of a bottomless chasm. Anything that falls is lost forever. The prize on the end of the rope is so heavy that it's dragging the man to the cliff edge. There's no tree or rock to tie off the rope. Just him, the rope, and the prize that will soon pull him to his death.

"Would you like some help, my friend?" Kosaam asks the man.

"Who—what—go away! You're trespassing on my land!" Jafaa replies, eager to get rid of this interloper; for the prize will make him and his people the richest in the world.

"But you are being pulled over, sir."

"My god will assist me before then."

"I don't see your god," Kosaam says, looking around at the open plateau. There is nothing but sand and rock.

"He is in the air you breathe, in the rain that falls, for he is all," Jafaa huffs, losing a foot of ground.

"As is my god. In fact, I will ask my god to help and he will save you." Kosaam promises.

"Your god is a manmouth!" Jafaa says angrily.

"Your god is a manmouth!"

"Baaa!"

"Baaa!" Kosaam spits and walks away.

Jafaa, in his stubbornness, slips to the edge. The prize that is so heavy a burden—peace and compromise—pulls him over the edge, for it takes two people to gain hold of this prize.

We have reached a technological point where victory is actually defeat, in terms of annihilating an enemy. Radiation poisoning is only the tip of the consequential iceberg. By warring amongst ourselves the human races inculpate themselves in the crimes of waste and excessiveness—a product of war. Sadly, the characteristics of a vainglorious and egomaniacal society. Even in our attempts to quell evil leaders, we sometimes forget about the trapped citizens. I hate to say it, but maybe if we could go back in time and imprison Stalin, Hitler, and the likes, the world might be a better place.

Look in the mirror, deeper, you might see what I mean in the house full of material excess. Call me homeless, or a loner, but my home is my pack, or the hotel I'm staying in, or with my brother, up until the time I need to raise a family, if the "gods" should allow me that comfort. This morning, my home was a cold cave, under a blanket, with Fran.

The bombs stopped dropping at about 3 in the morning. I see she still

PROCESS OF ILLUMINATION

breathes, and for that I am utterly happy. The two runaways, Jack and Ter, have left the safety of this cave in hopes of making Prague, where they will both be taken in at the orphanage, and given a bed, a hot meal, and a choice to stay and work.

"Well, it's you and me, kid," I whispered to my sleeping beauty in the best Humphrey Bogart impression I could muster, though I admit the cave was no amphitheater.

The cave, no bigger than an Israeli detention cell, smelled much better in the morning. A sense of adventure that was quite the opposite of the prisoners' outlook flowed through my veins, as I cleaned and dressed Fran in my only extra set of clothes.

Sometimes I cannot shake the unrest caused by Haifu Hell, or other places with even more sinister and painful demands. I remember having to sleep with a shirt covering my eyes and ears, with wadded newspaper rags in my nose, just to keep the bugs out at night. And it was a very fine line between sleep and wakefulness. After the first day in any place of imminent threat, a human survival mode instinctively heightens. The human senses are enhanced, allowing for more alertness, acuity, in sights, sounds, and sensibilities. Homophobia and paranoia were all a part of the crazy game of life in close quarters with sociopaths, antisocial personalities, and psychopaths, where the only thing respected was fear. If you could instill in them a fear of reprisal, then you'd have a chance of making it, but if you couldn't, then you'd better have hope, money, or bend over and kiss your manhood good-bye.

Funny thing about prison, and war, for each day brought the possibility of death. Even if you survived inside, there was so much secondhand smoke, or ETS, that you had a good chance of getting lung cancer.

Prison is a cruel and lonely existence, exacerbated when human rights and other civilities are not extended to those behind the prison walls. Even the concept of innocence until proven guilty is missing. I endured a year and some days before my people found out where I was, and why. Barry Greenberg, my agent, lifesaver, political lobbyist, and friend, truly earned his commission that year.

The SOS had been smuggled out of Haifu Hell in the bum of a very good friend, whose bum I saved. Literally. A common smuggling custom, called "keistering," which was sometimes the only way to get contraband in or out of the prison. I've yet to have the pleasure and hope it stays that way.

Barry sent in the troops, and at 62 he has some powerful friends in lots of places. As soon as my story leaked, was force-fed to Israeli, American, and

European press corps, my case was scheduled for an immediate trial. It never came. Hard to prosecute someone who threw a knife after being shot.

So, I went to hell for 469 days. (I counted each one.) And one day the devil, a guard named Bezrahi, who was an American hating tub of matzo balls, who happened to be one of Yeffat's best customers, for the aforementioned reasons, let me go. He told me himself, his malevolent matzo breath burning my eyes, after he'd threatened to have a Palestinian equivalent of "Bubba" teach me to get in touch with my sensitive feminine side. I'm a sensitive man, but I leave the wrangling to those who enjoy the wrangling. To each his own. C'est la vie. Bezrahi found out that my kindness and quietude were not a sign of weakness or frailty, but a residual effect of infection and fever. He also found out that not many men could be paid enough to try me, but that didn't mean he stopped taunting me from the other side of the bars, where cowards talk loud.

I am free, and so are you, Fran, I thought, shaking off the imaginary matzo breath, and breathing in the sweet scent of freedom. A sweeter scent could not be found, even in the Hanging Gardens of Babylon. It is a powerful thing, freedom found; heady and poignant. Makes me ponder, maybe pity, life in countries weighted down by dictators and fascist policies, virtual prisons, only with more privileges to take or lose, however one looks upon such punitive penalties. At times, in the complacency of this vast garden, one forgets to stop and smell the roses, or look and see the colors. What we call mundane, I call a continuing daily explosion of sights, scenes, and sensory input.

Two days passed in similar fashion, we hiding in the cave, the soldiers fighting outside. I repaired my equipment; Francesca repaired her mind. Or so I prayed. I fed her with a makeshift straw, blowing rehydrated powdered food down her throat. (It's the food you buy in normal sporting goods stores, the powdered kind that hikers pack.) Time was passed taking stock of each moment, before it passed, analyzing every fork that makes up the choices I would make in the near future. Like getting Fran to safety, finding ground zero.

Outside, on the second day in the cave, the rockets' red glare and the bombs bursting in air, but I saw no proof that anyone's flag was ever there. After they—NATO—finished, I stepped out. Movement. Ten soldiers creeping. Their many boots scrunching on the rain-soaked forest floor; a soft snap of a twig, which is antinatural to the vibrations of nature's cacophony. The water dripping from laden leaves, bugs scrambling on matted foliage, as each molecule adjusted to the end of fall and the coming of winter.

My own bones spoke to me, but only in whispers. I listened to the enemy,

PROCESS OF ILLUMINATION

the unknown. I had an idea it was the Arabs searching for revolutionaries, or for women of any race, had they not got their fill in the city? They weren't good at jungle warfare, quiet steps and silent hand signals to direct squad movement, because they were from a desert country. My eyes searched for colors and shapes that did not belong, while hoping that my own camouflage was still fresh. I only hoped our scent wasn't so strong, or that they didn't have their canine squads.

Even the dumbest dogs, or mixed breed mutts, had noses that could sniff us out in a heartbeat. I rue the day man builds an olfactory enhancing device, much like a pair of binoculars.

The search and kidnap—at best—teams passed on, but if I knew their tactical propensities, and I did, I knew they'd be back in about six hours. If another patrol passed by it would mean that their was a new HQ in these here hills. If the same troops didn't return, it meant that it was just a brief scouting party, either from Brno, or a nearby village. Most likely Brno's banking district, where NATO bombs wouldn't fall without specific target acquisitions; i.e. which door of what building. The usual TA information; Who, what, where, when, and why. The needed fodder before okaying the target for destruction, by laser-guided or scope-guided smart bombs. If important enough, they'd launch a volley of cruise missile; aka Tomahawks. Maybe some satellite launched missiles, or SATLMs.

It's truly a wonder that the generals got to even fight anymore, with all the bureaucrats and politicians mucking up the process. Too bad they couldn't put a stop to it altogether. But maybe the political and bureaucratic delays did do some good, by sparing some school bus on Monday, or Tuesday. Too bad for the bus on Friday, though. And when the latter did happen, when innocent victims were killed by stray bombs and bullets, the squirming politicians and bureaucrats called it "collateral damage." Like they were some sort of lost stock portfolio.

What the hell has "collateral damage" got to do with a dead family, a road filled with burnt out tractors and charred statues of children on roofless school buses? Above, F-111s and F-15s screaming past, their pilots yipping and yahooing in victory, below, babies burning, mothers crying, fathers, daughters and sons dying. Most die instantly, if that's any consolation to those suffering from "collateral damage."

On the third day, while out and about;
"Psst!"
I heard the whispered call, too close to just be curious.
"Psst?"
"Don't move." A K-bar rested against his jugular.

"Please, *monsieur*, Deana sent me to fetch you."

"Deana who?" I tested.

"Deana, your female doctor friend who—"

"Turn around and be quiet. Keep your hands down, not up." I ordered him towards the cave, after inspecting him with a quick glance. He had a weapon, but I was safe. "Come on."

Henri had on silver wire-rimmed glasses over dull brown eyes, which sat upon a long, straight nose. Short. Skinny. If he were a woman he'd be described as a mousy little French girl, with no upper lip and a fat, pouty lower one, which currently bore the sores of amore, or a punch in the lip. I felt sorry for him—he drew that kind of empathetic response—but not enough to let him off so easy. I'm hated, as stated, by several countries who wouldn't be stooping as low as they've gone to hire an assassin or set up a trap for me. Admittedly, I have found, pried, dug out and bribed many a state's illicit secret. I have exposed countless frauds (easily done with the carrot and the stick), many a hidden bank account with stolen IMF (International Monetary Fund) money, surely not doing the citizens of the country any good in the retirement fund of a dictator or general, or whoever had managed to lull some U.S. and IMF official into believing democracy was soon to be implemented in such and such a country. Leeches. Greedy ones, taxing the poorest citizens in the world at a higher rate to pay the interest rates on money they'd never seen. Interest rates so high they made the bankers seem like criminals, and which would never be paid off by the country.

"What's your name? Quick!" I hissed in his ear, the knife going back up to his throat.

"On-Ray Gee-oh-knapolis." Or, Henri Gionopolis. "Deana sent me, *monsieur*, I swear. How else would I know where you were?"

Hmmph. I could've given fifty different answers. Something wrong with his French accent as well. His whiny voice was believable enough though, so I pushed him past the bushes, and into the darker cave. Still, I never trusted Frenchmen, nor would I. Some stigmatic response that dated back to the Vietnam war era, and the nuclear testing violations of the 1990s. Something sneaky in their non-superior superiority.

"How'd you get past the patrols?" I asked, leading him deeper into the cave.

"What patrol? I have just now entered the woods."

"And checking the caves?"

"Deana said you might come to this area, and my map shows these caves—"

"All right, Henri, I believe you." If he knew my safe zones—places I would go to in times of duress, which were pre-planned, then he'd probably spoken to Dean. "I have many enemies."

"Yes, I can see why." He rubbed his neck, where the dull back edge of the knife had left a red line. "You wouldn't have, really...." But he saw my smile. "Well, never mind, *monsieur*."

"Call me Cort, or Falcon, and have a seat." I reached into my pack, and brought out the fixtures required for a cup of French Vanilla coffee. (Not all thing French were bad.) "Coffee?" I looked to him for a sign.

"*Oui, monsieur* Cort." He had a gun pointing at my face.

"Shit." I feigned shock and surprise, and passivity.

"*Oui*, Falcon, 'shit' is what you're in. Go ahead, make the coffee."

"So, who're you?" But I had an idea. I'd met his kind many times before. Hired assassins or bounty hunters. In the dim light I saw how his mousy looks had changed, as if he'd folded back a mask to reveal something not so vulnerable. Someone with an edge. His French accent remained though. He didn't answer my question.

"Who's there?" He spotted Franny's shape, just in the shadows. "Get up! Come here!."

"She's in a fucking coma, give her a break."

"Who is she?" he asked, strictly business, the small caliber gun still on her.

"Hell if I know. Found her in an abandoned hospice."

"Let me see her—"

"Leave her alone." But he didn't listen, and I hadn't expected him to. I hated to zap him before I found out who he was working for. "Did Fakul send you?" A French heroin dealer I'd robbed a few years ago, so he claimed, when I sunk his boat filled with drugs and guns in the Bay of Biscay.

"Very amusing situation there, but no. Minister Parovich requested your presence. Move the blanket so I can see her. Now."

Why idiots always think they've got the upper hand, just because they have a gun, never fails to amuse me. Don't bad guys, or good guys for that matter, know that there's been defensive weapons other than bulletproofed apparel invented, and on the undermarkets for years. Well, some of the stuff I have they don't know about, but still, there's lapel tasers and chemical delivery systems that cause instant paralysis, boomers, laser blinders, and numerous mechanical devices. The forearm knife gun, which I used, strapped under the sleeve and fired by flexing the correct muscles. I've even got a pair of sunglasses that fire an ELL (extreme laser light) 4-second pulse that causes near instantaneous seizures. But my favorite devices are electromagnetic, developed by JD and company, which cause most metallic mechanisms to seize up. I like goop guns as well, but they're a mess.

"Never heard of the Minister," I said.

"Well, he's heard of you, and would like you to pay him a visit."

"Then why the gun?"

"You have a reputation."

I laughed. "Not for killing people indiscriminately."

"I can't take the chance you'd say no, before hearing what the Minister has to say."

"Well, I ain't going anywhere for a while," I pressed.

His mouth twisted in angry frustration, but the gun kept a straight face, never wavering. He was a pro in that respect.

"Don't be a fool, Falcon." A sneer on those lines, but hesitation in his eyes.

"Put that gun down before you hurt yourself, or else." I let him figure it out.

"You know something I don't?" The gun waggled in his hand, as if emphasizing his possession of it. A big mistake.

I took it from him; a pinch to the nerves between the thumb and index finger. Men without strong hands are instantly compelled by this, causing disengagement of the metacarpal nerves and muscular functions, loosing the hand's grip. In other terms, it hurts so bad the victim forgot all else but the pain, which shoots from thumb to brain.

After Henri finished cursing and whining about and me going to kill him, "Shut up, and take it like a man," he began to raise his hands, seeing as how I had the gun. Geez. "Put them down, or I will shoot you." I leaned forward and checked his sleeves. "What's in the pack?" I felt the familiar straps around his waste.

"A satellite phone, on the chance you'd refuse." He was matter-of-fact about that happenstance. A bit too much, I thought.

"Well, let's have a little conference with your boss, so I know what to do with you."

"You're going to kill me?"

I'm glad gossip grows like weeds in my circle. I've only killed in defense of my, or another's, life, but it was nice that my enemies thought otherwise, and advertised my dangerous nature. Fiction or not.

"I might," I lied. "Now let's talk to your boss."

"There's a war out there, and the fan has to be placed high, *monsieur*?"

"There's war everywhere. Gimme your setup, and I'll attach a signal booster." It's about the only thing I had that was still working, after my attempts at repair.

A moment later, after connecting his antenna cord to my booster, I told him to dial up his boss. "Dial."

"Uh—it may not be appropriate to call the Minister at this very moment, *monsieur*."

"Dial him up!" I raised the useless gun. "No tricks." I could give a damn about interrupting Minister Parovich's schedule.

I watched him closely; a nervous little mouse twittering about with a five-thousand-dollar satellite communication system. It was the best one available in the world.

"Who the hell's this?" a Russian voice barked in harsh Russian, and a bit nervously.

"You called?" I said in my best Moscowitz Russian.

"Where's Henri?" Parovich asked, but not too concerned.

"I'm here, Martinov," Henri blurted, sounding as if he were under the gun, with my finger on the trigger.

"Don't kill him, or my sister will kill me," Minister Parovich said calmly.

"I'll think about that. Whadaya want?"

– CHAPTER 5 –

THE HANGING QUESTION BROACHED, I wondered why the Minister of the Interior—third most powerful man in the New Republic Of Belakrainia, formerly known as Belarus and Ukraine—was dirtying his hands with me, the third most hated man in his country's shortlived history. (There were a couple of generals who'd sold Russian secrets to several countries; while I had provided reconnaissance photos and scientific evidence that President Putin had been transferring nuclear weapons into the Balkans. Yes, the Balkans! Circa 2001.)

"I want you to alert the world that we've lost four nuclear vehicles; two twenty-megaton bombs, and two ten-kiloton warheads of the new variety—"

"What new variety?" I said, mouth dry, palms sweaty, and out of breath.

"A new concentrated plutonium metal, with an enhancement additive that allows for higher yields with less materials—"

"Miniature nukes?" Those were first-strike weapons of the foulest magnitude.

"Yes, but only two."

"Only two! And several warheads in the twenties, I bet!"

"Ten each."

"Impossible. UN and NATO pay for their security, and track all your nukes."

"We don't tell the West everything, Mister Falcon."

"True." I knew the Russians to be sneaky, but no more than those seeking and sneaking. It seems man always has to have a hole card. Machiavellian rules.

"But this secret can't get out," Parovich pleaded.

"You can't have it both ways, Marty."

"It must be, or they'll know I am—"

"Who'll know?" I demanded in Russian, so there'd be no mistaking my question.

The line was quiet for a while, then there was a muttered curse. "Okay, but you mustn't mention my name."

"I'll consider it—"

PROCESS OF ILLUMINATION

"No! I demand it if I'm to tell you more!"

Self-preservation was one of Russian politicians' best character traits. I weighed the monetary gain against the possible "collateral damage." Millions of innocents.

"Tell me, was that detonation eleven days ago one of yours?"

"Yes."

"Okay, I'll keep your name out of it."

"Good. We must act now. Henri has a vehicle—"

"Yes, sir, it's nearby—I was going to take him to the airport."

"Idiot! They'd never permit him—bah, never mind. Mister Falcon, do you have a recorder?"

It was already running—a sound-activated personal recording system (PRS)—but I feigned ignorance. "It's broken. I have a good memory. I wish I had a voice stress analyzer."

"The Minister of Defense sold the weapons to Prince Fahoud of Sudan."

"Didn't he just get a huge U.S. defense contract for software and processors?"

"He gave half the money to the Minister of Defense, and plans to build a cheaper processing plant, or default on the loans to make due. At either rate, Fahoud thought it more important his country become a nuclear power."

I listened to the story, but had no sympathy for the man, or his traitorous guilt. It didn't surprise me, the depths to which these men had sunk. Terrorism for hire. The detonation a demonstration of the quality of merchandise prior to sale. Bullshit. More than a few people knew. Why was Belakrainian airspace a no-fly zone, and why were they jamming satellite and standard communications?

It all stank of the putrid stench of man's need for power, or for money. The oil rich countries had the money, the independent countries of the former USSR had the technology and the power. Nuclear. I'd had nightmares about this type of thing happening, even though it was supposed to have been made impossible by NATO, and Western dollars and technological input, which was to pay for, and insure, the "safety" of nuclear devices in poorer nations, or nations still suffering from growing pains. All the conventions and treaties had been eradicated by secrets, and now, greed.

"How much?"

"Two point five billion U.S."

That was definitely more money than I had. It was a staggering amount, but realistic when one thought of the totality of all the possibilities. Blow up Wall Street, some major refineries, or corporations, and the collateral profits, i.e. the competitor profits, would skyrocket. A domino effect would race through the financial markets, burning through portfolios like fire through a wheat field in Spain. All the connecting fields would burn with it. If one knew which market to protect, dump, or invest in, two and a half billion was a drop in the world's bucket of cash.

Hell, nuke Seattle and half the world's software and airplane manufacturing would go up in a mushroom cloud. As would about a million people. Which would we mourn for?

"What's the catch?" I asked, once his calm soliloquy of events, rumors, and paper trails had wrapped. I only wished I had my computer online so I could verify what he was saying, as well as Henri's identification.

"Peace of mind, Mister Falcon, and resources to match the story that you alone will break in the European, then Western newspapers. You're already a rich man, so I doubt money can entice you."

Hmmm. I smelled a double deal. None of these old former Politburo guys did anything without a catch, as in they were getting something out of it.

"Here, Henri, you might need this then." I tossed him the Sig Sauer 9mm. "Advice; if you ever pull a gun use it right away. You ever see the movies, where bad guys always talk with a gun, and usually the gun gets taken away...." I saw him nod his head, and was satisfied that he got the point.

"I apologize, *monsieur*, but you realize the imperative nature of the objective."

"How the hell did a Russian end up related to a Frenchman?" I asked the speaker phone.

"I married his sister, bella Isabella." He added a sigh to affect his true remorse for having done so.

"And tell me again how you found me?"

"I assure you, it was as Henri explained."

"Then tell me where Dean is right now?"

"On the way to Kracow, with two very badly injured patients."

"Good, that's going my way." I had to get my gear, which Dean, as my European contact, always kept handy. In Russia I had an ex-KGB agent, Igor. In China I had Fong. And in India there was Rajiid. Each were paid handsomely to hold supplies for me, but it wasn't the money, it was the philosophy of the causes. One never knew where he would end up in my line of work, or in what condition. Here, on the outskirts of Brno, deep in a cave, I was talking to a Minister and trying to save love in the form of a comatose sleeping beauty.

"What about her? What's wrong with her?" Henri asked, once I'd broken the connection.

"I spoke the truth before. She's in a coma, and I'll be taking her to the nearest hospital." I saw his look of question, wondering if it was smart to pack dead weight through a dangerous battlefield. But he didn't need to know that this flesh and blood had changed my life, that her pale face had made me hope she was my soulmate, hope that she would open those aquatic eyes—I checked—and say, "I love you too." I know, foolish and dangerous ruminations, that are no more possible than two strangers meeting on a corner and falling in love. I'd spoken to her quietly in the darkness, after the two runaways had gone, praying that she would wake and speak, so I could adjust her voice to suit the woman of my dreams.

What was it about this woman? I asked myself, was it the shape of her head, the soft concave hollows of her eyes, her frail neck, or did she give off some pheromone that kept me chemically hypnotized by her silent form? Was it anticipation that drew me to hope she'd soil herself, just so I could wash her, though my conscience screamed; "VIOLATION! VIOLATION! NO! DON'T LOOK! DON'T MEANDER!" If there was a mirror I'd see a red face before I turned away in excited shame. But shame nonetheless. Like a schoolboy caught peeking up the teacher's dress from the first row. Though I'd cleaned her twice, I was afraid she'd wake at just that moment, screaming, and think I was doing something to her. That thought kept me honest, though I'd like to think myself a moral and ethical man untainted by temptation. Okay, that's a lie, but I would never, you know, do that! NEVER! And if you saw her, you would not either, for the innocence of her would scream to your conscience; "Not without her permission!"

Ackacks, or antiaircraft guns, broke me from my reverie. Too close. If the revolutionaries had setup ackack cannons, then they'd probably taken Brno back. Better them than the UAN forces, but if that was true then it didn't bode well for Francesca, the woman who'd been taken.

The UAN was mostly infantry, and rarely packed cannons or heavy artillery. Their presence alone was usually threat enough to keep NATO from bombing or using air power. They mostly protected Muslim and Islamic cities in the Balkans, but they were also used to occupy neutral areas already fought for by other NATO forces, as a sort of conciliatory recognition of the Arab Nations. But, for some reason, the "white" world bristled at Arabs policing their countries. And the incidents and rumors didn't help either.

On several occasions UAN soldiers had been caught raping women, and what made it worse was the rapists would admit to assaulting the women, but claim that it was the woman's fault for not wearing the *hijad*, or veil. Under their own law the soldiers would be found not guilty, and sent back home. Nor were the UAN known for their equitable treatment of prisoners or even civilians within their areas of control. Cultures clashed and the temptations arose along with the consequential problems.

I'd experienced the temptations, as in taking advantage of the cultural vulnerabilities inherent in the differing peoples of the world. Sometimes that vulnerability was simple kindness, or trust. An evil man given that wreaks havoc upon the trusting.

"We gotta leave now. Pack this stuff, and I'll get her ready."

Henri nodded his head, visibly frightened by the shaking of the ground and the bits of dust falling from the ceiling, which served to quicken his actions.

"Where's your weapon, *monsieur*?"

"I don't carry one." Only a small lie. Just in case we were captured. I didn't think Henri could hold out under threat. Blunt, cold, hot, sharp—the four main ingredients to torture in the field. Fists, water (or snow), fire (or cigars), and knives. I bear the scars, both internal and external, and the permanent rasp in my voice—sexy or not—is the result of three sessions with Colonel Fun Traak, pronounced Foon Trayack. A Cambodian bastard. Henri would crack the moment they put a gun to his head and dry-fired. Probably pee his pants. In the interim, I'd be the first one Henri squealed on, with any info he knew about me. I didn't see him as the kind of man to even have a cyanide tooth, let alone use it.

I wrapped Fran in the gray blankets, folding her arms over her small breasts, much like a corpse, and while doing so I was envisioning a route to the train station on the northwestern side of Brno, if it hadn't been bombed out of existence. I imagined it would've been. We could use Henri's car, and take the highway, which was a dangerous course, as I explained before. Sometimes civilian vehicles looked like tanks to the fliers above, with their itchy trigger fingers.

"Shit!" I realized that she didn't have a passport, and my scanner/printer, and sometimes document replicator, was in a bullet-riddled house on the other side of the country.

Henri jerked his head around, waving the gun. "What. What is it?"

"Nothing," I said. "Just have to hide her when we cross the borders."

"Oh."

"Where's the car?"

"Near the bridge, a few hundred meters north by the wash."

I knew the spot. It might be hot, but if I had to I could play a Serbian, Russian, or a Westerner, depending upon which enemy stole upon me first. "Okay, let's get to it."

Outside the air flowed east to west, through the oaks and cypress trees, stirring what still remained of the fall foliage. The latter canopy, though thin, provided some manner of protection from hypersensitive eyes above. Wet leaves muffled our footsteps, and anyone else's, I reminded myself. We went north, towards the barrio that is Southern Brno, where the rebel forces of Brno were still hiding, if they were still alive and not in the mountains. Probably empty of UAN forces, because there was not much loot, which interpreted to account for a lack of looters.

Sadly, many Balkan forces, and UAN forces, took "to the victor go the spoils" seriously. Certain countries, whose soldiers were paid well enough, didn't dirty themselves with theft and looting. However, many countries were paying their bureaucrats and politicians more than their soldiers, which forced the latter to scrounge for a living. We kept our footsteps light, and I was thankful that Henri's feet could be as quiet as the mouse he portrayed. He also exhibited some common sense as a point man, but how his pistol, which still wouldn't work, would do against an AK-47 would prove to be interesting. I'd be standing over by the AK bearer, with my precious cargo.

At a ravine, Henri paused.

I stopped five meters behind him, testing my leg, and not liking the twinge in my calve muscle; a tear, I figured. I was glad for the cleanliness of the wound, thanks to the kindly nurse at the field hospital. I'd also been gulping Amoxicillin, so if anything bad were to happen it would be physical, not biological.

Across the brook were the back lots of the ghetto, but we didn't need to cross. I saw the bridge a hundred meters east, right along my mental route to Kracow. I tend to think in distances.

"Henri? That car on this side, or that side?"

"On this side, just off the road."

"There could be traffic. Come over here." I led Henri to a thicket of bushes, where I set Fran down and shirked off my pack.

Henri, wide-eyed, looked at me. "Where're you going?"

"Can you carry the pack and her?" I asked him, and he nodded, like a man will to another man when manly things are needed done. "Go to the front of the houses, and I'll meet you there. I'll honk once."

Henri opened his mouth to speak, then shut it. "Good idea." He fished out a single key and handed it over.

"Fifteen minutes. Stay out of sight, and come running when I honk."

"*Oui, monsieur.*"

"Guard her with your life." And saying that, I felt trepidation leaving her in his momentary custody. Something about him wasn't right. From his quick attitude change to his military bearing when we were stepping through the forest.

I walked down into the ravine, and followed it to the bridge. I felt my money belt, and made sure I had my separate identifications in grabbing distance. My left hand would get a Russian ID card, and my right an American. Depending on who stopped me. Out in the field it was easy to make such quick changes. Grunts, or soldiers, rarely knew what official passports or identifications looked like, except when near HQs and border checkpoints. Choosing the wrong identification could cost me my life, so I had to be prepared. Without my computer I didn't know who was where, and was therefore blind.

I saw the car—a silver Benz—the kind driven by rich Euro yuppies. It was parked off to the side of the two-lane road, surprisingly intact and undamaged. A bomb crater was no less than fifty meters away. I stayed within the treeline, which followed the road for about half a mile. A perfect ambush position. Ten feet away I checked my watch, making sure it was still activated and armed.

Technically speaking, an electromagnetic pulse was emitted in micro bursts, and welded parts together by magnetizing the intricate trigger mechanisms (so long as they were made of metal) and making the gun worthless. My fillings all had to be changed to porcelain. One reason why I didn't carry exotic or complex weapons with metallic workings. I wasn't the only one with this technology.

It was supposed to render locks useless, but every so often it didn't work right. I took out Henri's key and approached the driver's side door.

"Stop! You!" A deep bark in Russian.

Shit, I thought, and turned slowly, then spoke in Russian to a bush that blinked at me. "Don't shoot, comrade. I am a photo journalist from Moscow." I slipped into character like a fish being released into water. I flicked my tail, tested my gills, and darted to freedom. I smiled, like all comrades do upon greeting one another from Mother Russia. "I spoke to General Bogeskiya last week. He said some good troops would be here."

"Papers! Quiet!" he cut in.

I saw his Spetsnaz insignia, on his right sleeve, near the shoulder. A shiver vibrated down my spine, almost disrupting my smile. These were the robots of the Russian Army. The special forces. *What are they doing here?* I wondered, trying to look past the green, black, gray and brown face paint.

Oftentimes I'd found many small Balkan armies trying to pass themselves off as Spetsnaz forces, with similar patches and insignias, but one could tell the real from the phony. This one was real, from the Gregorov boots to his beret. I looked for Cyrillic tattoos on his inner left forearm, which would denote their affiliation with the Russian mob, who paid the wages of certain battalions. It was rumored that if the Russians went to war the mob bosses in Moscow would be the ones to make the decisions.

Oddly, the Russian mob, having usurped such power through corruption, had now developed national discretion and objectives and pride. A quasi government that controlled the marionette faces that danced for the international audiences. But that's another story.

I saw no such markings, but that meant something even more disturbing; Russia was in the game, and they'd not been invited to play.

"Papers, identification!" he barked again, snapping me from my indulgence with quiet aggression. Several years of training had given him the instant presence of a man to be listened to, obeyed, and respected. Like an alligator respects the hippo, the leopard the lion, the mouse the cat, me a trained killer.

Slowly, under his submachine gun, I pulled out my Russian papers; used passport, state identification, Moscow press card, military forces donation receipts (that showed I'd helped to pay the wages of the Russian military when the government wouldn't or couldn't). The later was sort of like being pulled over for a traffic ticket in Los Angeles, and having a 'Policeman's Charity Ball' receipt next to your driver's license. I saw Igor had done his job well, when the soldier handed back the papers with a snap.

"Komrade, is this your car?"

"I must confess, I stole it from a Frenchman in Prague," I lied, and looked down, ashamed.

He laughed. "Good. I hate the French too, snobby Euros!"

"Aren't they all!" I cursed everything but Russia, as was common. I tucked away the papers, careful not to reveal the key in my right hand. Pretty odd to steal a car and have the keys, I told myself, and did some magic. *You're slipping, Cort*, I warned myself. "May I take your picture—"

"No!" His smile was gone, the killer returned. "We are not here, Komrade, understand?"

Something was up. "I've never seen you then. Nor had my camera. If it is good for Mother Russia."

"It might be, Komrade. Go."

I reached out and shook his hand, slipping him enough money for his entire squad. "For your troubles, Komrades. I know the bureaucrats don't pay you properly!" I spat out the last in disgust and indignation.

The money disappeared, and he nodded his head. "I hope you didn't kill the Frenchman," he said, letting me know he'd seen the key. "Go."

"I have rations in my car—"

"No, thank you, Komrade."

That was when I knew he was a true commando. Spetsnaz platoons were always well supplied, and deservedly so, even though they're paid less than privates in the U.S. military. But, again, what were they doing here? Russia had backed away from the Balkan conflict ever since they'd been caught violating the nonproliferation treaty by smuggling short-range nuclear missiles back into the Balkans. The only reason I could think of was that it was somehow connected to the nukes.

– CHAPTER 6 –

I HONKED THE HORN, and waited. Surprisingly, there were still ragged and weary-looking people walking up and down the debris-filled cobblestone streets. Vagabonds, in their own city. Some wore tear-streaked faces and long stares, which fell upon the rubble of their own neighborhood.

I wondered, if whoever came upon this planet of humans, homo sapiens, warring, killing, destroying, would they shake their heads in dismay at the negative acts we employ against one another? Would they laugh at our stupidity in not fighting our common enemies, like natural disasters and space-born threats, instead opting to bicker over words, religion, and land?

And I, pushed along this quest by man's impetus to self-destruction, am I therefore responsible for my antithetical acts committed in my forward progress to seek out the destroyers, the reapers of the inherently weak, those evildoers? Am I responsible for the man who dies in his attempt to murder, or enslave, or entrap, or rape, or impoverish, or war? Am I a sinner under someone's religious bylaws? A God waiting for fates to cut my string, so He may further punish me in a 'lake of fire', for committing consequential sins in my endeavor to do the jobs that the gods were slacking in. Although I am not without personal blame in some instances when human weakness pulled me assunder. Should I stop, live off of assets and interest rates (a sin in itself, so says the Bible), or should I continue on in the name of justice, peace, and the environment? Do we do what we do because we can? I often wonder, as I ponder the vicious cycle called humanity. So far.

Perhaps my vexations and questions can only be answered by death, like those of the world.

A figure darted out from behind the half wall of a burned-out home.

"'Bout damn time!" I grumbled, and pushed open the door.

"I heard soldiers," Henri worried aloud.

"Let me have her." I reached over and grabbed the end of the rolled-up blanket. A thin strand of blonde silk fell out of the blanket, and rested upon my forearm. Once safely in the back seat I shifted the bundle so she was lying down, upright. I reached inside, followed her skull, down her neck, and felt for a pulse—"Ow! Son-of-a—" Something clamped down on the underside of my forearm, like a crab pincer trying desperately to take a chunk of my flesh.

"Snake!" Henri said, shutting the door.

"No, she's biting me!" Then the vice grips released me, and I saw two rows of teeth imprints. "Why'd you bite me?"

"We've got to leave, *monsieur*, regardless."

I followed his stare. Down the block two dozen red-capped UAN soldiers were coming our way. *Shit. I can't play an Arab without make-up.* A common problem for Caucasians.

"Yes. If you can hear me, be quiet in there." I tapped the roll near her face. "Or we'll all be killed." I stepped on the gas, gently, and prayed for the invisibility of gray. In the back of my mind I was desperate to hear Fran's voice, the timber of her femininity, but heard nothing. The car moved, scrunching on those little bits of gravel, a common hazard in the Balkans.

A man in the mirror raised a model 900 Remington, one of the best sniper rifles in the world, and my foot stomped down on that rectangular piece of rubber, which pulled a cable that ran to a carburetor, which opened butterfly valves that allowed a mixture of gas and air to flood into the six combustion chambers, where sparks from electronically fired spark plugs detonated the combustible mixture, exploding beneath the piston, consecutively, driving a crankshaft that spins the driveshaft, providing the rear wheels with power to move a 3600-pound vehicle and its occupants forward.

"GET DOWN!"

A bullet poked a hole in the safety glass. Spider webs appeared. Henri screamed, but got down. I turned the big car around a corner and mashed the accelerator down, and headed out of this quarrel. Away from this place where one day Christians ruled, and the next Muslims. Maybe these Balkan bickerers would do better with Odin, for at least then you knew what you had coming, and the simplicity of following the religion should not allow for too much deviation from peaceful practices. Then again, whatever man touches seems to be tainted.

"You can get up, Henri."

Behind us the madness continued; another Chechnya in the making, over half a million lives at stake, which I could do nothing about. I ignored the gunshots and screams, and kept my eyes on the surroundings, then jerked the wheel left and skidded onto the main road to the Poland.

"I would like to go back to civilization."

"What would the Minister think?"

"My life was not part of the bargain!" Henri's indignantly red face was serious. "My car! My wife will kill me."

I smiled, and kept my eyes ahead. On each side of the road were burned-out vehicular husks; tractors, cars, buses, cargo carriers. Victims of NATO pilot boredom—an unfair assumption—or mistaken military vehicles. As with all highly trained forces, be they police or military, the "gung ho factor" was maxed out. When fingers and minds were always poised to pull the trigger, accidents happened more often than not. If one's finger is always on the trigger, pretty soon the brain begins to imagine, or create, targets. A prime example was the fact that more U.S. soldiers were killed by "friendly fire" than from Iraqi fire in Desert Storm. I caught sight of a teddy bear, which had bounced from the window of a small compact car, now resembling a blackened frame, with skeletons inside, and one of them a small child. A mission gone bad. "Collateral fucking damage."

Henri stayed quiet, shocked at these massacres, which were not so readily ignored as they were back in Paris. Like a man who's now faced with his own mortality. There's nothing like seeing another human being dead to bring that home. Was his wife's happiness, and his own, worth the risk he was taking? He was a small-town politician, by trade, in the city of Dijon. He knew how to assign jobs, delegate authority, and smile while kissing babies to be reelected, but this spy business was supposed to have been left behind. He'd been out of the business for years, and his cover had been established, covered, painted, sealed and resealed for decades. *Money*, Henri thought. He and his family needed it. Ten million Euro dollars would go a long way. If only he could keep playing the game.

"Tell me about the Minister?" I asked Henri, who looked deep in thought, a suspiciously familiar expression returning to his face, like when he had the gun. I'd seen the look on other men as well, right before they made a move. But Henri wasn't the physical type; he was, or seemed, nervous, scared, and too much like a politician. He was a man who needed hot baths and expensive soaps and razors and thick towels and real beds in real rooms with doors that could be locked. Or was this a mouse who changed into a fearless rat?

I glanced at my watch, after every question; "Is your name Henri Gionopolis?"

"Yes."

The built-in lie detector in my watch said that he was telling a halflie. I nodded my head, as if believing him. The truth machine measured heat and body stress through an infrared analyzer, with micro processing chips that made it 80% accurate.

After Henri told me more about the mission, I said; "Bull! Don't lie to me!"

"What, you have a lie detector or something?" He smiled cockily.

"Yes, I do, and it says you're lying out your ass. Now tell me what's going on or I boot you out of the car right here."

"My brother-in-law found a telex in his office, which was mistakenly sent, his number is one different than the Defense Minister's. It was a top secret memo about six packages in the north; the symbols used were only used when transporting nukes. He thought nothing of it, until a few weeks later, when the explosion happened." Henri took a cautionary look at my watch, then at the bundle in the back.

"Who's selling and buying nukes?"

"I swear I don't know. Only the Minister can tell you."

My watch said he could be lying or telling the truth. "So, we're back to terrorists?"

"*Oui.*"

"Why don't you check her, Henri."

He rolled the end of the blankets down, to reveal her sleeping and peaceful face. "I don't know how she could've bit you?"

"Seizures."

"Ahhh...." He took care to wrap her up again after checking her pulse and breathing. When he had turned back around, he continued his story. "My brother-in-law went to the deputy of military affairs, Igor Primatov—"

"The villain himself," I said aloud.

"Ah, you know him?" Henri asked curiously.

"Of him, and his deeds in Serbia and Bosnia."

Henri clicked his tongue. "Yes, a bad man. But as I was saying, Primatov denied the existence of the memo, and asked to see it. Parovich personally delivered the memo, and has never seen it since. Later, they told him to mind his own affairs, if you know what I mean?"

"Yes. The Minister's under the thumb, so now he needs an outside contractor to save the country, the world, without anyone knowing he's involved, or bad things happen. About right?"

His mouth was ajar. "The Minister was right about you, *monsieur* Falcon."

"Redundancy makes experts of us all, Henri." Especially when it comes to human nature. "If you only knew."

"I read enough to understand."

"Yes, but nothing is better than the classroom we call humanity."

"My father once said something of that ilk before pushing me through the recruiting door of the Foreign legion."

I saw five men with green rebel arm bands walking along the side of the road. "Wave at them." I honked the horn and waved myself in mock support. They waved tiredly back, and smiled, as we passed by.

"Why'd you do that?"

"So they'd wave back, instead of shooting us." I was wondering what the Czech freedom rebs were doing walking along the side of the road, out in the open.

"How far is ground zero?"

"Do you have a map?"

"In the pack, upper left-hand corner." I usually didn't carry much paper, because it ate up the earth's resources, but I had to have the map.

Henri dug around in the side pocket and found the right one, then circled a small area on the plastic-coated map. "Here." His bony finger touched a valley in the Carpathians, south of Ostrava.

"Not an easy place to get to?"

"No," Henri agreed, though he didn't really know.

"And why are they not testing in their own countries?" I could only assume it was to throw off NATO and UN and UAN entities. "Do any environmental groups even exist in the Czech Republic? Or Poland?" I said aloud to myself, still not believing the audacity of the act. They'd had to know that the satellites would see, and that the entire world would object, as they did when France violated the above ground test prohibition.

"The Poles might, but there's too much selfism and greed in the Balkans to realize smoke stacks are killing them all, or that a nuclear bomb has just eradicated that entire area."

"Takes time for people to realize the poison that is killing them is coming from the air they breathe, the water they drink, or the food they eat."

"Some never do, *monsieur*."

The chap wasn't so bad after all, but he was still hiding something, I believed. "My father used to say that wise men can see death beyond the horizon, but only warriors could stop it."

"An odd thing for a twentieth-century man to say."

"Yes." And things had progressed even further from whence they'd once been, because technology allowed us to sew the polluted death of the many, while reaping the rewards from afar without toil, without tasting the bitterness of the fruit harvested. Those rich corporations, harvesting so, were at once a pariah on humankind and a Godsend—where would civilization be without their greed at all costs? For greed drove many an advance toward the betterment of human life, toward saving life.

"How 'bout we take a field trip?"

"Where?"

"Ground zero."

"I don't have any pills."

"I brought some, just in case." Ever since the scientific community, and U.S. Army specialists, had proven that even small amounts of radiation and microwave radiation caused cancer and genetic disorders, I had begun bringing pills to countries with poor regulatory commissions and laws governing nuclear power plants, and relay stations. They were bought under the counter from a man in Mexico, where the U.S. government contracted out the production. I'd even bought stocks in the company once tests proved that the antiradiation pills worked. Good thing, too, because I needed to keep track of Henri.

"It's that road, huh?" I said, pointing to my right, where a road went up into the rocky mountains. The green carpet turned rocky, almost serene in its openness. Sulfur and gunpowder still hung about.

"Wow, that's bad," Henri exclaimed, holding a brown silk handkerchief over his nose.

I had no such luxury. The smell burned the tongue, like strong vinegar, and coated the sinuses. Foul play had taken place up ahead, or somewhere close upwind. Lots of rifles had been fired, or lots of explosives detonated, or both.

"What's that smell?" Henri's muffled voice requested.

"War. Could you get my camera, left, upper-hand pocket, and check on Fran?"

"May I ask how you know her name?"

"I made it up." *To remind myself of a job that needed doing.* I said this latter bit to myself. I only hoped that ID had received my outgoing signal to track the woman, if possible. He had the photos and, I hoped, the idea to track this woman so he could rescue her if need be. I figured they'd take her to the UAN main headquarters in Slovakia, if she lived through the past few days unmolested. When I got my backup MPC I'd be able to update my info, despite the satellite blackout that was in effect over Belakrainia, Czech Republic, Slovakia, and Romania.

There were two or three ways to track her. First, I could use the top secret HKS—200 series satellites, which cut right through any attempt at interference, and were in stealth mode virtually undetectable in space. Second, I could use the horizon view satellites which looked across the land, instead of down at it, thereby avoiding most jamming techniques. And lastly, I could use the Echelon Project.

In the late 1960s, a little-known project called "Echelon" was started by the U.S. National Security Agency, or NSA, later joined by the United

Kingdom, and a very few select countries around the world. Geodesic domes, silver or white in color, began popping up like mushrooms all over the world. The technology stayed under the "blackops" of the NSA and M16. Polyglot computer programs translated the billions of conversations picked up over any telephone in the world, with special filter programs that weeded out unconsequential, or mundane communications.

The American—and the world—public's right to privacy from their own government's prying eyes and hypersensitive ears was subverted, by having Canadian Special Service Branch listen to American citizens, and NSA officers to Canadian citizens. And so it was around the world, a sort of you-watch-our-backs-we'll-watch-yours. All in the interest of "national security," but subject to abuses in the name of money and power. Information is power, as well as safety. Knowing the hearts and minds of your enemies, and your friends, strips away certain crucial elements of success, like surprise, influence, or knowledge of your opponents, to name but a few in this global politic.

The worst enemies, sometimes, turned out to be your closest friends or neighbors, for it is they who know you, covet your successes, and want a share—whether by theft, force, or intimidation.

With the development of bigger and badder satellites, with super ears and eyes, the richer countries could listen in on the world. Those less ethical countries could use the information to steer their stock market investments, money growth, and the thoughts of their own citizens. To combat this new, but old, technology came superencoders. Cryptographs based on algorithmic and fractal mathematics, as well as binary code more complex than the human genome. And as with all technology, it came grudgingly to the mass market, much to the angst of those prying governments. However, all encoders sold to the public were also given to the government, under NSA laws, so that the encoder couldn't thwart the government's "national security interests" in hearing your conversations. My own devices, or superduper frequency modulators, were programmed by Johnny Dempsey, heretofore known as JD. He made what military and covert ops used, which were unbreakable digital algorithms. I hoped. Even highly encrypted transmissions were still transmissions, and could still be traced, and sometimes that was worse than having an electronic discourse listened to. Even these poorer countries could afford to log on to a Russian SKY satellite receiver and see who was sending messages in and out of a country. If they knew I was in their country, all they'd have to do was triangulate on the only encrypted transmission not related to their own military. I doubted there were any countries in the area who could do an instant reverse transmit, or afford to rent one, if the NSA felt like divulging what was still top top secret.

The reverse transit system meant simply that if an electronic device were turned on anywhere in the world, four satellites could locate the exact position instantly. Even if the device (e.g. phone, baby monitor, computer, radio, etc.) was only used for a split second. Then, depending on who you were, a missile could be launched, or a team sent to "retrieve" you.

You're thinking "big brother" and "thought police," but you're on the late train. These systems have been in place for decades, without red flags being sent up to warn the public. As technology increases there are no laws to stop this silent invasion, and conscience was no longer a question. Indeed, it's been like this for years. The real difference between a China and a USA is that the Chinese know their government's watching them, and the Americans don't. Trapped in the glamour of democracy, only slapped back into conformity when straying from the herd, Americans rarely suspected such deception of their own elected officials.

The Branch Davidian Syndrome, for example. The Weaver Mother and Son, who were also killed for religious separation beliefs, by Department of Justice snipers. The mother was shot while holding her infant child. A blood red dawn marked, appropriately, the family's surrender, but also the survival of two young daughters, a father, and a friend. The official charges; Mister Weaver had, or had not, sawed the barrel of a shotgun off for a associate. For this "crime" he lost his wife and son. Will this happen again? Yes. Can we get rid of the problems that are growing like cancer in the marrow? No. It would be like outlawing gas-fueled engines. But who knows, even that might be possible.

But those in America are not alone, nor are they so selfish of their own jackbooted thugs, for America lobs spears of hate at any country defying their entreaty. Be it a country, or a single human being, they are none immune without a viable threat of retaliation. (Sadly, that hypothesis supports nuclear arms, but I do not.) Many who live in security, the butcher, baker, salesman, automechanic, and even the politicians, are afraid to speak out, don't want to cause ruin to their shuttered thoughts and consciences.

The soul of man's innate evil unchecked cannot turn back in certain circumstances. The heart of darkness, man's untethered will to suppress those he deems necessary for the heightened exultation, for greed, for survival, and for pleasure. I've looked at, and felt, the cold black force of men who've gone unchecked out in the field, left to rule over a kingdom of thirty soldiers, their only orders, "seek and destroy." The ears, and fingers of their victims hanging on strands of not so dried gut around their necks; fleshy reminders of the screaming deaths. The night powwows in Cambodia and the

PROCESS OF ILLUMINATION

Congo, severed heads and cannibalism, torture and rape, and much worse. One leader, with too many willing puppets, whose wives and children live in the cities, far away from the killing groves, until the killer comes home. Another day in the life of institutionalized evil.

A 'Lord of the Flies,' but for adults, for we are all sinners at one time or another, for life or love.

– CHAPTER 7 –

"HERE, TAKE THESE." I handed Henri two anti-rad pills, one with a secret transmitter, and watched him swallow. As soon as the gel capsule dissolved the titanium on lever would open, the battery would be engaged, and a transmitter activated. Another device from Q, or JD.

"My wife's going to kill me for missing tomorrow's palace luncheon," Henri mused aloud.

"Palace?"

"*Oui*. It's our second invitation." There was a bit of pride in his voice.

"Thought France got rid of its kings and queens?"

"Yes, but billionaires took their place."

"Ah." Now I understood. "Play things of the rich, with the minions kissing ass?" I jibed playfully.

"I'd take exception to that, *monsieur*, but you're mostly correct."

"The wife's idea?"

"*Oui*."

"Bet you'd rather be watching football?" I started the car and continued up the two-lane mountain road.

"I'd rather be with Michella...." A sigh.

I didn't ask, because he wasn't done, but I figured it to be a daughter, or a mistress. The tires buzzed over the cracked pavement for about fifty seconds.

"My little gem. She's six years old." The pain was loud in his voice and tone, and tears welled, until he coughed to camouflage his emotions. "Cerebral palsy, which my wife pretends she doesn't have. Sometimes she tries to pretend that little Michella doesn't even exist. A sad situation. Doctors say she may live a while longer, but mostly in pain." He choked on those last words.

"Sorry to hear that, Henri. Lots of shitty things in the world." But something about his story sounded theatrical, and with the underlying Russian accent it sounded fake. Even still, I sometimes wondered in the face of shitty things, if all we were meant to do is to be born, eat, and die, if we were lucky. No big picture. No gods. No "He above" watching over us. No afterlife. No reincarnation. Just us, left to our own fate. Are we, or some of us, born with a screw loose, evil, or with a debilitation that brought a life of pain? Or is it the treatment that is the driver, the causal touch that creates the subsequent pain, the initiator of insanity. Products of society? Products of nature? Or pawns in a cruel game played by Whomever above?

Those were men's voices, 24-year-old Sylvia DeNoel thought from within the rolled blanket. She could hardly breathe due to the tightness of the cloth wrapped around her. She relaxed, and listened to the distinctly different voices; one a deep and easy voice, the other a weak French imitation combined with something else. She could feel the movement of the car, and wondered where she was, who she was with, and where they were taking her. Why?

She tried to remember her name, but couldn't. She tried to remember where she came from, but no memories came to her. In fact, she couldn't remember anything, except an inherent sense that all was not right, that she should have a name, and that she had to have come from somewhere.

Tilting her head back, she looked up and out of the gray tunnel, to the gray upholstery of the car. She smelled her own scent, which was clean. That meant someone had tended to her, or she had, just recently. Hands and fingers explored the texture of her garment, and found a durable shirt.

What happened to the hospital gown? She remembered the hospital suddenly.

There were popping sounds—machine guns, she remembered—close by. She was thrown to the side of the vehicle as it zigzagged. Something exploded near her head, and she heard the weakest of the voices screaming unintelligibly. All these sounds were muffled by the blanket wrapped around her head. She opened her mouth, and realized it was wet. Somebody had indeed been caring for her. She willed her toes to wiggle, and they obeyed. The vehicle swerved, the motor gunned, and she fell into the footwell, behind the front seats. She heard them cursing and muttering, as the gunfire grew louder and more intense. During all this she was testing her muscles, which began to burn and grow tight. She felt tired.

The car swerved violently, as if spinning around. Popping sounds were too close, and a big explosion rocked the earth, as tires screamed on cold pavement.

This was wrong, she thought to herself. Everything was unfamiliar, as if she'd just been born. The sounds, whose source she could not name, were strange, yet deep down she could sense the danger they meant. The voices were now louder. This scared her more than the other sounds of violence, for if those who had her were in conflict, then she might somehow be vulnerable to their embittered whims. Or was she already slated to be abused in some manner?

But how could she be abused, she wondered. There was not much she could do with her skinny body. Surely not slavery, she thought, but then received flashes of women behind windows near the border stations of some unknown country. She shivered. There were no muscles needed for that kind of abuse. Had she already been used like that? She ran through a mental checklist, after realizing the physical sensations of her unused muscles.

She checked her creeping desire to scream out, to rid herself of the claustrophobic wrap. At least until she found out if her captors were good men, or bad men. To do otherwise might be dangerous, some intuitive sense guided her.

But who am I? was her last thought, before an irresistible tiredness descended upon her without mercy.

"Check her for bullet wounds." I saw the bullet hole in the top of the backseat. Hopefully it had gone through after she'd fell into the foot well.

"Are we safe?" Henri said, looking up from the well, where he'd been hiding.

"Unless that tank can go ninety." I looked down at Henri, who was still pale from fright. "I doubt there'll be any more rebs ahead," I lied. The soldiers had looked like Belakrainian forces, and their equipment had as well. So much for visiting ground zero.

"She's breathing. I don't see any holes," Henri said, after putting the bundled woman up onto the backseat. He sat back heavily. "War is hell."

"You ain't seen nothing."

"I heard you know about war...."

"I seen some."

"True what they said about Serbia?" Henri asked with reverence.

I hated being admired, but I loathed hero status. "Yes, I went in, saw them dumping radioactive waste, and put a stop to it." I swerved around a body in the middle of the highway. *Poor bastard,* I thought.

"I heard it was more than that. Barbarous." But he did not press any further.

"We are all not so lucky to live in a country where we may pursue our happiness."

"Yes, the 'pursuit of happiness.' That old American axiom that has infected so many."

"And for the better, no?"

"Quite so—quite so," Henri agreed.

"You know in Asia they still abort little girl babies, or smother them after birth, for economic reasons?"

"A barbaric practice," Henri said with a nearly British bite.

There were still countries where during the day fascism robs you of dignity and money, and during the night the robbed robs what's left, because they have to live too. No rule of law. No real courts or judges, just a suppression of happiness, usually disguised as religious dogma, or political demigods, whose failure to wake up and change the oppression is based solely upon greed and power. He who has the gold makes the rules, or vice versa. It was no different in Serbia, or Siberia, where Vladimir Volstok controlled the mines and owned all the big companies, which he thought entitled him to dump waste products from the Murmansk meltdown into the Barents Sea. And he was selfishly pragmatic, as well, filling the empty mines with radioactive waste. The only problem was that the waste seeped into the water table.

"I remember the children who were ... damaged." Henri shook his head. "I've always wondered how the waste positively connected itself to the deformities."

"The company in Serbia tried to deny that fact, until they were shown the chemical analysis of the poisons found in the children and the drinking water, which matched up with the water linked directly to the dump sites."

"I saw the televised findings. Were any of the company records real?"

"You mean the Russian Regulatory Commission findings, that the levels of radioactivity were harmless? Not one. Each was forged, or falsified."

"Did Vladimir give you copies?"

I shot him a look, and he was smiling back at me with an 'I know what you did' look on his face. "They fell into my possession, you might say." I smiled right back. Never give up your confidential sources.

"I must say, *monsieur* Falcon, you have a way of getting over these powerful forces."

"Every dog has his day," I told him. I firmly believe in that saying; "What comes around goes around." But sometimes Karma needed a push, and I don't mind putting my back into it.

To plow under the killing fields of the Cambodias, the Chinas, the El Salvadors, the Nicaraguas, and the Panamas takes more than just fate, or luck. How does one stop countrywide killing and inhumanity, where politicians undertake to glorify the murderers, or to assign them government official statuses? Take Zimbabwe, where the dictatorial President has institutionalized murdering whites, by ex-military men and youths, having the effect of further debilitating "his" own country. So, for the sake of power and greed, violence is used to enforce the status quo, even when the majority has voted otherwise.

Cambodia was a prime example of mass slaughter, used as a political tool to rid the country of its intellectual—and therefore a threat to power—individuals, but which did nothing, save cause pain and suffering and millions of deaths. I have observed the players upon these killing fields, and know that evil does exist.

Evil; a person who kills for self-gratification. *Not* the felony murderer. Not the soldier. The one who kills whole villages, whole peoples, and dashes the skulls of babies on rocks to save bullets, or kills the unarmed populace with axes and machetes, or gases towns to test chemical and biological weapons, and who would do it tomorrow if given the opportunity. *That* evil, which, like Lucifer himself, must be put down. Vanquished to a sad reality of homosapien history.

Too many memories; Bone fields and rats, dogs and maggots, innocent blood and mothers asking, "Why? Why? WHY?" Maybe I would not give a damn had I not been exposed so early. If my aunt Violet had not married Jim, things may have been different. I may not have been able to sneak out "Gray's Private Investigation" and stuff. When I turned 18, John Gray made available my first paying job; he sent me to an Army recruiter he knew. John said he'd done it out of love, but I bet it was to get rid of the kid who was always tampering with his gadgets.

"Make the Special Forces and I'll give you a job when you get out," he promised me with a handshake. Then he secretly made a phone call to his contacts at the Pentagon, who controlled the lives and destinies of the men who joined. And with that push, my fate was sealed for the next 10 years.

"Get down, you MAGGOTS!" were the words of introduction from the U.S. Army Drill Sergeants, once I stepped off the cattle cars, which were used to transport new recruits. "Hop-tu-hee-or! Hop-tu-hee-or!" went on being screamed as Hell week began, and my freedom ended. I cursed John Gray for every pushup I burned through, for six of the first thirteen weeks of advanced infantry training, during which I woke at 04:30 hours and went to bed exhausted at varying past sundown times. I put on 20 lbs of muscle, grew 4 more inches, and began to like the education in soldiering. Surprises were thrown at us until surprises were no longer surprises, and we were ready for anything. And after many weeks, even the DS banging a trashcan lid two inches from my head didn't surprise me, though it did jolt one from a dead standstill sleep to instant wakefulness, like a bolt of electricity tapped directly into your brain. Bzzzz!

PROCESS OF ILLUMINATION

Following graduation from basic training and AIT as an eleven bravo (infantryman), which I topped, I requested special training and a chance to take the Special Forces entry exam. And for another year of military training I cursed John Gray, for the exam was both physical and mental torture. First was the physical; does the man have the capacity to push his body to the limit, to the point of death (some have gone that way), to achieve his goal.

At 28, I stepped out from under the umbrella of the armed forces of the United States of America for ethical reasons. I was not, after all, the trained robot they'd taught me to be. I could not squeeze the trigger upon defenseless villagers. I was looking for God to save them from me, until I realized that I could step out. I was offered a sixty-thousand-dollar retirement bonus, but money was not the issue.

But then again, maybe I exaggerate, as I believe man tends to do about past experiences, be they good or bad.

I confess, that while in the 2nd ID (Infantry Division) I came to realize how the world worked. If someone dies, they're gone forever. On a grander scale, if a hole is poked in the ozone layer the sun heats the earth, causing it to heat up, in turn causing more greenhouse gases to plug up the hole. During the process we humans would undergo the wrath of the changing climates and nature's fury. A simple philosophy; try not to kill, or cause harm, and don't pollute.

I love my life, to be sure, for each day brings the opportunity to make a difference, but sometimes I long for the adventure of the military mission. Maybe that's why I was a war correspondent slash adventurer slash dogooder slash bull's-eye. And if all I could do was think and write, to that end I would lean. Make a difference for the good of humanity.

What slosh!

Then again, maybe I digress to the point of fallacy, adding those self-aggrandizing details that make screwing in a lightbulb seem like diffusing a bomb with ten seconds on the counter. Or maybe the newspapers and media have placed such story lines so deep, and gave such little priority to them, so as to keep them from the consciousness, and therefore your conscience. But, as I vow to you herenow that there is a Zimbabwean calling himself "Hitler" and killing white farmers, I vow that everything herein related is a product of experience, truth, and actual events.

Hup-tu-hee-or! I heard, and thought maybe I was losing blood from some unseen and undetected bullet hole. Sounds from the past memory were invading my herenow. Henri saved me.

"Hear that?"

I sure did, but I kept my mind occupied on the horizons around us, which were dashed here and there with trees, rocks, and bushes, with mountains in the background.

"Sounds like a basic training camp?" I murmured aloud.

"Hmmm?" This thought piqued Henri, for he grew quiet for some time in thought, no little worry marking his face.

After a few minutes, and no sign of any trainees, I saw the border village of Ostrava, formerly known as good old Moravska Ostrava, until someone decided to delete the river Morava precursor. The latter was a frequent occurrence in the changing Balkans, whose inhabitants felt so much horror from past connotations to persons and places. They thought by transposing the name it would bring independence, or erasure of the past acts. I felt for these people, who for generations had known little peace or prosperity, and whose sense of closure was to simply change a name.

"Shit! Don't say a word, Henri," I ordered Henri when I saw the checkpoint ahead was occupied. "Let's see what side they're on." Always a safe bet in this neck of the woods.

"I must tell you, I am a practicing Christian," Henri spoke adamantly, pride replacing his previous worry.

"Well, when Allah points an AK-47 in your face we'll see how your affirmations hold up."

"Hmmm? You have a point."

I left him to think over the dogma that has dealt death, in one form or another, since the beginning of time. Man's will was best represented through religious dogmas, which require those who would follow (or not), to live and give, or perish in a hell of one form or another. Most religions have been so polluted by man's will that it is now a common translation that man kill man in certain situations, for certain sins. Certainly, a "God" who created man would not want, or have, man usurping His authority by killing His creation. Would He? If so, we are all trapped in some game, for Who would have His own creation destroyed by said creation, unless it was some sort of test. A game in which we are all expendable, liable to be picked off one by one, naturally, or unnaturally. I doubt God would want some of the things man says He wants, but then again I'm only a man.

Buddha's philosophy save us all, I said to myself, though I've no preference for any religious dictum. Rather, I believe in lasting peace, good conversation and compromises, working to extend life and make that life as full as possible, feeding the children, housing the homeless, rehabilitating the wretched and not just throwing human beings away in prisons to be released ten times worse, and a bunch of other sappy shit I won't repeat, but am sure you've heard before. Simply, I believe in that innate common sense. But I love the meditation regimen practiced by clear thinking Buddhists, and find that it is actually good for you, as are many teachings and practices in many of the religions. To each his own.

– CHAPTER 8 –

AS WE APPROACHED THE GATE I took a few deep meditative breaths in through the nose, hold for eight seconds, and exhale in four. I searched for explanations of this situation I now found myself in; a Frenchman, who I sensed wasn't really French, carrying a gun in the seat next to me, a comatose woman who I was obsessed with wrapped in a blanket in the backseat. I smiled as I saw the uniforms of the border guards.

I braked gently, and smiled into the two new M16s. I knew they were Americans, for everything about them suggested cockiness and expense. But then again, in today's world it was hard to tell who was from which country, except for the Asians, who rarely allowed Caucasian refugees or citizens.

"Where you coming from?" the blond-haired soldier asked, looking warily into the backseat, while the other soldier backed away to provide cover. "Please pop your trunk and step out."

I nodded my head, and kept my hands visible, toed the trunk lever. Henri followed my subservient lead after a questioning look. We both knew that citizens who were fated to die were usually asked to get out of their vehicle, especially a nice one like this. Be a shame to waste such a piece of German American engineering. For any would-be murderers, ordering victims out of the car solved two problems; the bodies of the victims would not alert the next unsuspecting victims; and the vehicle would remain usable. But I didn't see these two lone gate guards as the likes who would do such a thing, and their accents were straight of the Texas panhandle.

The outside air was brisk. Each soldier wore a U.S. military issue jacket, as did I, while Henri looked like a blue-coated ski bum.

"How long you guys been stationed here?" I asked in American-English. Yes, there's a difference.

I could see clearly now that both were young. The blond one was a Corporal, the junior one, a redheaded farm boy dressed up to be a soldier, was a Private First Class (PFC). The patch on their shoulders informed me that they were from the 101st, where my own military training had begun.

"You do basic advanced infantry training Benning?" I asked.

"Yeah?" The PFC looked at me with more interest, as his squad leader checked the trunk. "Whadayouknow bout Benning?"

"SF out of Benning," I answered. "Lieutenant Colonel Falcon." I put out my hand and the kid shook it. A major no no in combat situations, but I didn't take his rifle or knock him out. "How long you boys been here?"

"Clear back here." The Corporal slammed the trunk shut.

"Hey, John, dude's a Special Forces Colonel outta Benning," the PFC said excitedly, as if I was some celebrity, or as if I brought a sense of security with only my presence. The latter happened quite often, if I gave away my element of surprise.

"Wow, sir, I was gonna try out...." The PFC looked down for a second, embarrassed about giving up.

"There's no forces without you grunts." I smiled easily at them both. "What's your mission parameters?"

They looked at each other, as if deciding whether or not I should be privy to that information.

The Corporal said, "We're to monitor and check any small non-military vehicles, tell any refugees which way to go to reach the UN camp—"

"—and bug out if we see anything military!" the PFC cut in excitedly.

"How many troops we movin in?"

"Don't know, but at least four bats."

That was at least two thousand personnel, I figured.

"What was the pep talk about?" I asked, because one could glean the real intent of the mission by listening to the officers' briefing, known to all as the "pep talk."

They both laughed, and knew I was indeed ex-Army. The Corporal spoke again; "Some two-star said we were going to the Polish border to bring some peace and justice to this part of the world.

"And to make sure civvies weren't being executed," the PFC added.

"I see they're still feeding you boys the same old same SOS." Same old shit

"You got that right, sir," the Corporal agreed.

"What's it look like in Kracow?" I asked.

Sylvia DeNoel! That's my name, she thought happily the moment she awoke in the tight confines of the blanket, which was down in the foot well again. Memories began to fill her mind, vivid pictures of unknown faces and places.

She was in a room, on the fifth story, visiting an antique dealer. A bomb exploded somewhere below, shaking the foundation of a building. A concussion of supercharged air rushed through her body, throwing her across the room, into an old vault. It all went blank after that. Why was she at an antique shop in Brno? But she couldn't remember.

She began putting together basic memories. She was 24, from—from? *Oh, come on, Syl,* she chided her failing memory. Well, she was thinking in English, so that meant she was English, American, Australian, or a dozen other countries that taught their children English as a second language. She felt Italian, sort of.... Pidgin was what she was thinking now, but at least she knew what pidgin was, right? *Right,* she answered.

The vehicle stopped, and she remembered she was in a car. She strained her ears to hear, but God, she was tired. She yawned and her jaw muscles barked in pain from disuse. Something like maple syrup was dragging her thoughts into that black mire that was, to her, unwanted but inevitable. *Come on, Syl, you just woke up,* she tried telling herself, and for a moment heard laughing voices in the background. They didn't seem menacing.

Her lips turned to a soft smile, she drifted with those voices until the black mire of memory accepted her once again.

"Rule number one; keep'em smiling, Henri. Always keep'em smiling." I gave the two guards a wave, and drove slowly past the Hummer that was parked just behind a boulder near the tree line, on the Polish side of the border. There was no sign of the usual border and customs stations? "Check Fran, wouldya."

"I think you're in love, *monsieur*," Henri huffed, but did as I bade him. He lifted her back onto the backseat, unrolling the blanket a little bit, so he could see her face. "Ah, I see. But will she love you when she wakes? Does she even know you?"

"Just lookin' out for my fellow human being, Henri. That's it." But was I? I felt the sexual attraction, but I mean, the woman was beautiful, vulnerable, and if I were a dastardly fellow she was easy. I've been called dastardly by some of my own gender, but never by any women, for I still believed, and went out of my way, to be chivalrous. Love? No, no, no. Henri had it all wrong. I had just been musing in my earlier reportings. Hadn't I? "Use the chapstick and squirt her some water. Not too much."

Henri laughed, sure that his assumptions were correct.

"She can't lick her own lips, so...." But I found my explanation both redundant and embarrassingly inadequate. Maybe he was right?

"Thirty minutes or so, and we'll be in Kracow." And I could find a hospital for Franny, and get new equipment.

The car moved along at ninety KPH, the trees along this straight highway were all sturdy pine. Lucky they were growing here and not in America, where trees were being cut down at an alarming rate, even with the environmental groups watching and fighting the good fight. Too much money, too much comfort in having wood furniture. Ahead was another U.S. Army vehicle, and I knew they'd been radioed of our coming. All a part of the "mission."

The air around Sylvia DeNoel was filled with the dust of a building that had been unceremoniously deconstructed by two one-thousand-pound bombs, dropped from an aging NATO bomber. She heard the screams, felt the floor beneath her vault cocoon turn to liquid. Her medium heels toppled, and she felt her loose skirt fly upwards as she went downwards. She had to get out of the building, she knew, because there were five stories above her. Those thoughts ended when the ground met the walk in vault turned elevator.

She awoke, rolled up in a blanket.

They were moving again, she knew, because of the familiar drone of rubber on the crappy Balkan highways. Well, that's another thing she remembered, though she'd rather have recalled something more tangible, something with strings and webs that branched off into other memories and past experiences. What she wouldn't give for a memory, she cursed, then began working her muscles, trying to ignore the claustrophobia that tried to creep into her thoughts.

HEY! Someone touched her face, roughly applied pressure on her lips—

It began as a cry, then turned into something that sounded like this, in French; "Yeeooooooooooooowwwwwwwwww!"

Henri screamed in pain as something in the roll attached itself to his fingers.

"It's just a reflex," I quipped at his suddenly pale face, remembering his own words to me. *Serves him right,* I was laughing inside, until a thought slapped me across the face. *She's awake.* My heart began to race, again, at the thought of hearing her voice, of looking into her cognizant eyes. A sentient being to analyze this poor ragged soul that I be.

"She's AWAKE!" Henri cried. "She's no more asleep, that's true!" And he jumped back into the front seat, as if he were escaping shark-infested waters. "She's a devil! Why's she biting us? We're helping her!"

"Maybe Franny doesn't like you?"

"And remind yourself that she got you as well!" I showed him the Hummer, by pointing my finger to the side of the road. Four soldiers stood near the Hummer, well camouflaged.

I rolled down the window, and gave them a wave, and they returned a wave. I recognized one. I kept to myself the fact about the Spetsnaz's appearance, and now, the fact that American Special Forces units were in the area. Why in Poland? If I knew that the nukes had been detonated in the Carpathians, then I knew NATO knew. But did they know that Belakrainia was the source?

"You're a popular man, *monsieur*," Henri fished.

"Better wrap that up. There's some ointment and bandages in the first aid kit, where you got maps from the pack." I pointed to the pocket, in case he forgot. "But we should be in the city in a few minutes." I could see it, and so too did Henri. "Dean can fix you up."

Henri brightened at the sight of civilization. "Yes, I shall have a shower and a shave, maybe a drink or two. Ah, and the Polish women are beauties, *monsieur*. Beauties...." He faded into some fantasy.

As he dreamed, I listened for the sound of movement in the backseat. Was she awake, I wondered, then worked up the courage to ask. "Hey! Are you awake back there?" I said, loud enough to break Henri from his trance, and to get through the blankets.

"Yes, I think so," she whispered hoarsely.

"Did you hear something?" I asked Henri, keeping my eyes on the road and the fast approaching cityscape, that now began to bloom.

"I believe so?" Henri wound the bandage around his two injured right hand fingers.

"Check her!"

– CHAPTER 9 –

"BUT DON'T GET TOO CLOSE," I warned him, with a smirk that wasn't appreciated.

"Why'd you bite me, *madame*?" I heard Henri whisper down into the cloth pipe. "Okay, hold on." To me he said, "She'd like to be unwrapped?"

"She's her own person, and she's dressed.... What language does she speak?"

"Barely audible English, *monsieur*."

Hmmm? That was just as curious as her speaking any other language. I suddenly wished I would have had time to search that field hospital for signs of identity, Maybe she would remember everything. I wanted to hear her story, though I knew from experience that the mind tends to be in a foggy state following a long sleep. There were usually mementoes and persons who knew you that were able to poke and prod memories in the right direction. Here there was nothing.

"Water, please."

I heard her soft voice, and it sent a warm chill down my spine, and I wanted to turn and see her sentience, but didn't, for the city was coming upon me, and my eyes were needed to drive safely. The women may be beautiful in Poland, but the Poles still had some improvement to do on their driving skills. Feeling like a lovestruck teenager, I began to imagine her eyes on the back of my head, surveying every molecule, wondering about my looks, in turn causing me to worry about my own mug and grill.

"There's some water in my pack. Beneath the kit." My voice box let me down momentarily as I caught sight of her in the rearview mirror.

"*Oui*," Henri replied, giving me a look, because he knew I knew he knew where the water was.

"Ah, thank you," Sylvia said upon drinking the cool water. "Am I a prisoner, or something?" Sylvia DeNoel asked, while fiddling around with the blanket so as to be warm. "And do I have any women's clothes?"

"You'll have to ask *monsieur* Falcon. He's the one who's been packing you around, *Madame*." Henri looked from her to the back of my head.

"You were in a coma, I'd been shot. They didn't know who you were, and they couldn't take you out of country without violating the treaty. The UAN soldiers were taking over, and I know what they do to beautiful women, so I am taking you to a hospital."

"And what did you do with me?" she asked, but it came out like an accusation.

"*Madame*," Henri began. "I found you being cared for in a way that bespoke of a true gentleman's intentions, to care for you until he could drop you safely at a hospital, even as he himself was shot through." Henri pointed at my thigh, where there was a blood stain. Nothing serious, but proof enough.

I felt her eyes burning a hole through my skull, or was she caressing me with gratefulness? At any rate, I was glad Henri had vouched for my credibility, without voicing his suspicions about my intentions. "He's grown quite fond of you, *madame,* calling you Franny."

Big-mouthed bastard, I thought to myself, smiling all the way.

"I think you have him smitten—"

"All right, Henri! You can call me Cort—uh—what should we call you?"

"I am Sylvia DeNoel, but ... my mother's name was Francesca? Anyways, thank you, Cort."

"You don't sound so sure."

"I'm not—not sure of anything."

"I am Henri Gionopolis, and I'm pleased to meet you, *madame*." Henri looked her up and down. "When we arrive at Cort's friends' house, there should be some proper female attire—"

"Anything that fits, is all. Since somebody forgot to find me proper clothes." Sylvia threw the barb out.

"Ouch." Something in her tone gave me the impression that not only was she ungrateful, but that she also didn't like me. But she hadn't even seen my face yet, I said to myself. Maybe she was just one of those persons who bristled at the thought of owing someone their life, or that I had cared for her most intimate needs, and therefore knew more about her physically than she felt comfortable with. I knew that some people reacted differently to people that knew too much about them, or even just one important item. Vulnerability made one defensive, sometimes appropriately.

"Where we at?"

"Kracow," I informed her.

"I was hoping New York city, but oh well. Good thing there's no checkpoints at the border, eh?" Sylvia said, while fixing up her clothes by rolling up sleeves and pant legs. "Do I have any papers, or anything?"

"Nada. Like I said, I didn't find you, I only rescued you in—"

"Brno. I remember, oh, sorry, go ahead."

She was an independent little snod, I thought, but immediately forgave her. "Oh, it's nothing. The nurse told me that they found you in the rubble of a building, or something. And when she left us, I knew the UAN solders would use you just the same as if you were alive—"

"How'd you know what they'd do?"

"I've dealt with them before, but that's another story. Let's just say I know."

"I have friends with the UAN, I think, so I doubt they would have used me." She took a sip of water.

Henri kept quiet, knowing that the introduction was not going well for Cort.

"What's the name of your friends?" I was suspicious, but kept it out of my voice.

After a moment, she said, "Tell you the truth, I can't remember."

"Then I doubt you could have called your friend, IF you'd been awake to do so." Game, set, and match.

"Yes, you got a point there. I owe you a big thanks."

"You're welcome."

"But who's Franny to you?"

"A woman that was dragged away, after her husband and son had been killed. The UAN took her."

"At least it's not an ex-girlfriend or ex-wife or someone like that."

Henri couldn't keep his laughter to himself. "My apologies, but I can't contain myself. She's a tough one, eh? Just like you, *monsieur* Falcon."

I looked up and found her staring at me in the rearview mirror. She smiled, those soft pink lips my fingers had made sure were kept that way arched slightly. Or was it a smirk? "Why'd you bite me?"

"Why'd you touch my face?"

I smiled. She was a fighter. "Chapstick. When you're in a coma they tend to get chapped, just like your throat and mouth go dry, tongue swells, you know, all that stuff."

"Sounds like you know what you're talking about," Sylvia said with not little sarcasm.

"I do." She didn't need to hear my resume, and I doubted she'd let me finish, with all her inquiries, interruptions, and smartass remarks. "A long time ago."

"You don't look that old."

Ouch. Henri kept his face away from me, so I couldn't see him laughing.

We drove past an outlying warehouse and factory, with parking lot and all. Civilization suddenly crashed upon us, as we hit the first crowded intersection, and cars began to bunch even more. Big lorries, small compacts, motorbikes, and all the other old vehicles one finds in an unrestricted Polish city, horse-drawn wagons included.

The sky was the normal Polish gray, which befitted the chill that was in the air. The Polish pedestrians beneath this canvas were dressed in light weather coats and sweaters. Poles were used to the cold weather, and their lack of outer wear showed this fact. As we went deeper into Kracow the streets grew more crowded with traffic, but also better maintained. All the traffic lights worked, and chaos was kept to a minimum. Buildings went higher. The clothing of the natives grew more affluent; suits and long coats, business skirts and briefcases.

"What time you got, Henri?"

"Three thirty, Balkan time."

"I'll drop you off with a friend at the hospital, and if you check out, I'll arrange for you to go home, if that's what you want."

"The least you can do after kidnapping me and transporting me across state borders." There was a tender bite to her words.

I looked up and saw the twinkle in those aquamarine seas. She was playing with me, this devilishly odd creature who'd just came out of a coma, I thought, while trying to regain some footing, some control of my place in her world.

"Look out!" Henri cried in French.

I swerved the car just in time, missing the corner of the truck by scant centimeters, and when I looked up she was smiling as calmly as a cat who'd just ate the family bird and wasn't copping to it.

"Yes, do be careful, Cort," she teased, enjoying the fact that she had the world around her off balance. He was a handsome man, very rugged and in control of himself, and no doubt, those around him, except her, Sylvia assured herself. She enjoyed this game of cat and mouse, especially with these friendlies.

Her stomach rumbled. "Is there any food on this trip? By the way, how have you been feeding me? I hope you haven't been chewing it for me and spitting it down—"

"I'm sure there'll be food where we're going," Henri cut in quickly, as if the thought of her suggestion was about to make him sick.

"Dean'll have some food for you when we get there, or I'll take you to Kracow Joe's."

"I've never heard of that restaurant?" Henri questioned.

Sylvia laughed, light and airy, filled with the confidence of youth and safety, and with a cute snort. Music to my ears.

I figured Henri for a fancy hotel, or somewhere where there was five-star food and a bath. He was a strong man, despite his frail facade, and shortcomings in the field. Deep down I knew something wasn't right, that Minister Parovich, if indeed it had been him, had some illicit gains to be made, for who brings in an American citizen—and an enemy to many of his comrades—into something as big as theft of nuclear weapons?

My enemies sometimes guessed that I worked for the CIA, or NSA, and therefore assumed that by harming me, or bringing me into their game, they were also connected to these U.S. entities. My military training also assisted this assumption, and I did little to dissuade that line of thought, because it's always good to have your enemy believe you're under the skirts of a larger agency. Especially big skirts like the CIA or NSA. More than once I've been guilty of impersonation and name throwing, but only in life threatening situations.

"I'm tired again—"

"No!" I blurted out, then added in a softer tone, "That's the worst thing you can do right now. Try to stay awake."

"I've read that somewhere?" Henri remarked seriously.

"All this talk's made me tired—"

"We're there," I said, turning into the parking lot of the hospital, where I hoped Dean was on duty. "Think you can walk?"

"I don't think so."

I'd worked her leg muscles twice, but I was no therapist, and I didn't know how long she'd been under. I knew that her muscles weren't atrophied, or flacid, but I didn't know if she was paralyzed or not, or what.

"Can you carry her?" I asked Henri, for as much as I wanted to carry her, to feel her arms depending upon me, I had business to tend to first.

"*Oui.*"

"Good. I'll go inside and find the doctor, and then I'll bring a wheelchair out to the lobby, okay?"

"A sound plan, *monsieur*."

I stopped the car next to a set of doors which, if I recalled correctly, led right into the main lounge.

I saw myself in the glass reflection on the door, and pulled off a couple of twigs that had somehow affixed themselves to my hair and clothing. I ran my hands through my hair. A good thing it was kept short, or I'd have a wild thicket up there. But all this was unnecessary. The difference between American and Balkan hospitals is that they would think I looked normal, whereas in other hospitals, in more affluent countries, I'd be rushed by doctors and nurses. My bloody pant leg would be scrutinized, and I would be deemed a homeless person without insurance. Ah, civilization....

I was right; the main counter was here, with a staff nurse writing on some forms. Yes, there's still bureaucracy in the Balkans. Behind her was a room with rows of filing cabinets. A room that I'd broke into one cold wintry night some eight years ago.

"May I help you, sir?" the older nurse asked in Polish, which I obliged to respond in.

"Doctor Van Clus?" Pronounced Van—Cloose.

The kindly nurse smiled, and her face wrinkled up, then she pressed a button and lifted the phone to her mouth; "Doctor Van Clus—Doctor Van Clus—you have a visitor at the front desk." She looked me up and down, then smiled once more. "I'm sure she'll be here in only a few moments."

"Thank you."

I waited at the end of the hall until I saw a tall, stringy-looking person walking down the hallway. God, those legs. The hem of her white coat blew back in her wake, a few strands of streaked brown hair escaped the green beret she'd stolen from me a long time ago, when we were "closer."

I'd known Dean since she was just out of medical school in Austria, some thirteen years ago, before she'd joined Doctors Without Borders, donating her life to travelling and doctoring. Her family was the second wealthiest in all of Austria, and she was like so many wealthy children who felt the need to give more of themself to those less fortunate. She was the type of heiress who didn't like associating herself with elitist values or views, which was why she was always helping the poor.

I had surmised this a long time ago, which suddenly seemed like yesterday. I suddenly had an aching for our "closeness."

She wrapped her arms around me and held me tightly for a long three seconds, then kissed me, tears sparkling in those naughty blue eyes I remembered so well.

"Wow. I haven't got that since Morocco."

She ignored my attempt at humor. "I thought you were dead. Someone said you'd been shot, then blown up, in and out of Brno."

"No, yes, and nearly. You look great, Dean." I stepped back, and looked up and down her 34-year-old body, which came straight out of *Swimmer's Weekly*. Long and thin. I knew every crevice, every smooth mound, every taste, every erogenous zone on her body. "Oh, I have someone you should look at—"

"You're bleeding," she said, and knelt right there in the hallway and examined my leg. "Does that hurt?"

"It's fine—look, Dean, I need to pick up and drop off—"

"Oh—no—ya don't. First I look at your leg. YOU ARE BLEEDING, Cort. I'll look after your friend. Have you noticed the squishing sound when you walk? That's your sock and boot soak through with blood." She rushed into a room, and came back out with a wheelchair. She was always rushing.

"Listen, Dean baby," I tried to say, as she pushed me down into the seat of the wheelchair. "I need you to look at a girl who's been in a coma." I turned around in my chair, trying to see Henri and Franny, no, Sylvia. I felt sluggish, as if I'd been driving on adrenalin for the past hour. "Right there!"

"That's no problem. I'll have a specialist look at her. Where's your gadgets? It's not like you to leave home without them."

I caught the sarcasm in her Austrian accent. "That's why I'm here. I need the package." Damn if I wasn't really tired. The walls seemed to be flashing past, and when I looked down I saw a long trail of blood, which went all the way down the stretchingly long hallway. "I'm tired, Dean."

I listened to Dean bark orders at orderlies I couldn't see, directing nurses to do this or that. *It's nice to have friends,* I thought, looking up to see Dean's beautiful eyes. Her face was covered by a green surgical mask. Something poked my leg. But I was thinking about how her nostrils seemed pinched, and how her lower lip was probably being bitten, like she always did when she was nervous. Ah, those catty blue eyes blurred, replaced by gun barrel blue. Oh-oh, something was wrong, I knew, because that's what happened when she was pissed or angry or scared straight. I grinned at her, and then drifted into a whiteness that was my unconsciousness.

– CHAPTER 10 –

HENRI LOOKED AROUND to make sure nobody was watching, before he dialed a private number; Minister Parovich's mansion on the Dneiper River, just North of Kiev.

"Where've you been for the past twelve hours? Have you got him?" the Minister of the Interior asked urgently. "Wait, is the scrambler on?"

"Yes." Henri checked it again. He spoke into a microphone that encoded the voice into an electrical signal, which was indeed virtually unbreakable. The problem was with the backwash. If he spoke too close to the mouthpiece of the phone an unscrambled shadow voice would be detectable. "We're in a hospital in Kracow, miles from where you're moving the—uh—equipment." Henri smiled at his own impromtu. "I doubt he'll even suspect where they're going."

"You just stay with him as planned."

"What about our agreement?"

"Your wife's in possession of half the money right now, as we agreed." There was a pause. "Can you kill him?" Minister Parovich wondered quietly, but loud enough for Henri to hear.

"No. He's too good. He has these these gadgets that protect him."

"Well, you're good too, Mikeli Stiebski, or you once were...."

Henri sighed at the sound of his real name, which evoked memories of long ago. The family he'd once loved, and abandoned. "I'm just an actor," Henri said in his native tongue, Russian.

"Well, maybe we should hire someone.... Hmmm. I'll see to that. Check back in twenty-four hours, or when you have a location."

"Yes, sir." But he was speaking to a dead line. Henri sighed. He'd been afraid of the Minister ordering him to try and kill *monsieur* Falcon again, which was something he did not want to try to do, at least, not without help. Maybe that's what the Minister meant, Henri wondered.

"Whatcha doin', Henri?" Sylvia asked from behind. "Whadaya think?" She twirled in the new clothes that Dean had scrounged up for her.

"Madam DeNoel, you're a sight for sore eyes, and walking just fine, I see."

"How's Cort?" Concern marked her voice, and worry her eyes.

"*Monsieur* Falcon was hurt the entire time he was saving us, it seems, and bad too." Henri felt a bit of thankfulness for the man's efforts.

"Maybe I was a bit harsh? But I didn't know either of you." She didn't ponder it. "I'm starving, Henri!"

"Does *Madame* remember what type of food she likes best?"

"No, but I could eat a horse."

"We're in Poland, so that is entirely possible, madam."

"Not a real horse, Henri. Something smaller, like a sheep or a goat!" She laughed, and placed her arm through Henri's, and they walked towards the hospital exits. "Will he be okay, Henri?" She looked back towards the hallway, down which Cort was being operated. She felt a pang of guilt. *Why,* she wondered.

"Yes. He's a tough cookie, as you Americans say."

"I don't think I'm American, Henri. I don't feel it."

"Hey?" Dean asked, smiling down at Cort. "You feeling better now, with a couple of pints back in you?"

"Damn." I was in a hospital room. The horror.

"I'll take that as a yes. By the way, that bundle of energy and that fellow left the hospital."

"Why?" I sat up, and realized I was in a hospital gown with a hard-on to boot.

"Calm down, and I mean that doubly." She reached down and patted her patient's thigh. "Has it been that long?"

"I don't go running into women's beds just because I wake up with a boner each morning. How insulting you'd think that!" I mocked righteous indignation.

"Well, I'm going to go make my rounds, and then we'll take you to my house and discuss it some more over dinner and desert. Prosciutto, crackers, salad and wine?"

"*Molto bene!*"

"Where's my clothes?" I asked.

"In your bag. That shifty fellow brought your bags in.... Who is he?"

"Don't know. Says his name's Henri, French, but he's got a barely perceptible Slavic lilt, if you know languages."

"Yeah, that's it. His accent's off. No matter, I'll be back, I'll be dressed."

I watched her rub her chin, mimicking my suspicions, as she always did, before she turned and walked out of the room. She was a beautiful woman, and doubly smart, but knew that our lives were on different paths. She was a healer, I was a helper, and those two trails, though similar, were quite different. I answered the cries for help over here, and she over there, and vice versa. We'd tried, but it was either one of us give up our livelihood, or one of us would have to adapt to the environment of the other. And my environment, though it usually did contain individuals who needed doctoring, was usually a dangerous one. Sometimes her work areas were hairy.

When Putin began bombing Chechenya, and genocide had once again reared its ugly head upon this world, Dean was off and running. With her money she chartered a flight with as much medical supplies as the plane could hold. I went behind the lines and took pictures of war criminals doing what made them so, on both sides. Neither Russians, nor Chechens, were innocent of murder, torture, and genocide. But we, me and Dean, were able to each do our own thing.

Only later did I find out that she'd been as sick with worry as I had been, diminishing our joy we each found in our jobs. And so we dissolved our singularity, and she disappeared for a year or more, during which I found myself arrested twice in small hick towns in America, where I'd decided to drink away the pain of not having Dean's love, which included her mind, body, and soul. She was loyal to the bone. Always would be, I imagined.

But I ached for her, as much as I ached for the sleeping Sylvia during the hours that I cared for her body. Dean would've been my perfect match, one who could hang out on my travels, and who I could count on not to get me killed, or be killed, on a mission. Plus she was a doctor. I doubted there was another person more perfectly suited to being my partner than Dean. Yet, on the few occasions when we had gone out together, into situations that turned dangerous, I cannot deny that I wasn't worried for her safety. Distracted.

I flipped the covers and saw the soft cast on my lower right calve and foot. It was made of two pieces of hard fiberglass, which were molded to form. At least it had snaps and could be taken off quickly. I didn't like impediments, especially when I was on a mission. I liked to move fast, if I had to. For a couple hours, and during the night, I'd wear it, then I'd toss it.

I worried about Sylvia in Henri's possession. If Dean thought his accent was funny for a Frenchman, then Henri was a fraud. I'd find out soon enough. Tonight, when I had my backup computer and satcom system I'd verify everything he said, beyond the fact that he had indeed talked to Dean about where I might be found.

I also wanted to download as many satellite photos as possible. With them, it would be easy to see who did what, and where they were headed. And these would be nothing compared to the scientific clues; radiation, airparticulate contamination, infrared heat signatures, radiation ion trails. All these would give away the direction of the nukes. All this would be available once I picked up my new supplies.

"Where is Henri?" I wondered aloud, slipping my pants over the cast. That small balloon of mistrust had blown up slightly, once I thought about the certain lies Henri had tried to lead me to believe—well, I didn't know they were lies yet, but I smelled the collusion between Henri and the Minister. I didn't feel a direct threat, but that wasn't to say he wouldn't do something stupid, like have Sylvia kidnapped to harm me, or bind me from assisting in the search for the nukes. A stupid stunt that never works, but which many still try for some reason or another. Well, there's a reason, just like there's a reason fish continuously suck in baited hooks. A brain the size of a pea, they say....

My jeans just fit over the soft cast, though I'd have to use a crutch or cane, which I hated, because it demarked me as prey in this sea of sharks. My mobility would be down, but there was an advantage; the cane itself. I put on a flannel shirt that Dean had picked out for me. Wait a second, it was the one that she wore to bed, when she wore anything. They must have been keeping her at the hospital late, for her to have sleepwear here. I saw one boot, and knew she'd planned this all along. Damn! I saw the cane next to the IV stand.

"Ah, I see you're ready." She had a bag over her shoulder, and then my bag in her hands. "You ready? I checked with your fancy suppliers, and they still haven't made a smart bullet that can track you. So you can stay in one place for a while."

Oh, Dean, how much you don't know, I thought. How much I wouldn't tell her either, so she wouldn't have to worry about it. Besides, she hated it when I spoke of new weapons and gadgets and death. There was a smart bullet, only the bullet was a .50-caliber shell, which meant you needed a large gun to fire it. This fact alone made it impossible for a covert operative, or an assassin, to carry one, except under certain circumstances, and then only from a distance.

"I'm anxious to see you in your non-doctor duds. I see you've been keeping it all together?"

"Hey, two hours a day in the gym—"

"Didn't know they had gyms in Poland?"

"There's more here than just pretty girls, Cort." She took my left arm and guided me down the hall. "Stop being facetious."

"Always, Dean baby."

"Aren't you gonna ask about your leg?"

"Why? You always fix me up proper. That's all I need to know, except when's this cast coming off?"

"A week or two."

"Oh, hell no." I exploded softly, not unlike a dog shaking his head at a muzzle. Dean tended to have this effect, but I also knew she was bidding high, trying to get me to commit to as long a period of wearing the cast as she could. "Try overnight, and then it's off."

She grinned and pushed through the door, stepping out into the rear parking area of the hospital. I knew she'd won.

"That vein needs time to heal, no matter how many stitches I put in it, or how many pieces of melt-away support I sewed around the wound."

That was good to know, and if I knew her well enough, I probably couldn't break open the stitching without a pair of wire cutters.

As I hobbled toward her car I watched her, considering our decision, weighing it against the possible feelings for Sylvia. Dean was solid. I wouldn't have to worry about her ever turning me in. She was all those things I mentioned. She spoke her mind, before retaliating in any manner, which was an infrequent event that I'd never experienced personally, only witnessed. She could also give it, as well as take it, mentally, physically, or emotionally. At the height of our affair I believe we could have sealed the deal, binding one to another in a Austrian chapel. But we chose to wait, to travel unbound upon that path of love that soon becomes worn and assumed and comfortable. These attributes are not bad, mind you, and we never strayed or had need to satisfy needs elsewhere, but we became so attuned to the other that we each felt the need to adventure, to go to our destinies, feeling that our departure from the other could not harm our relationship. We should have taken heed of the Hollywood marriages, which rarely lasted, because they were always separated by work. And so we went our own way, and at these separate locales and venues I received a call. Instead of vacillating and acknowledging her emotional need, and she mine, we both plead *nolo contendere*, and walked away with the fondest of feelings and whispers of a still unbroken love. With Sylvia, it was new, unexplored country that draws a man to those green seas, those blue mountains, those grassy plains, to the rivers and lakes, to feel that warmth of being able to lay one's head upon the very heartbeat of something possibly unattainable twice in one life.

"You know, you could have called me back," Dean said, as if reading my thoughts. She had a habit of doing that in the past.

"I was in the middle of a Khmer Rouge body pit, with death squads twenty feet away when I received your call. Dean, why do you think I said yes and no and I'd call you back? I said I love you. I got caught three days later—"

"That was why you didn't call back!" she snapped to the illogical logic of my hopeless situation, some three years ago. She thought about this for a long while, and her arm tightened around my bicep protectively. "Is that where you got that new scar on your chest and right eye?"

I tried not to remember the hot poker that sizzled against my sternum, or the straight razor that cut my right eyebrow in half, but it was useless. Had not Fong intervened, I'd still be in the stinking cargo hold of a Chinese junk, on the Mekong delta, in the hands of the Colonel.

"You still got this junker?" I changed the subject. I laughed at the sight of the battered BMW coupe, which I'd fixed more times than I could remember.

"I like the gadgets you and JD put in it, and besides, I only use it when I'm close to home," she said, pressing the alarm deactivator. Both doors opened automatically. "You see, doors still work." She laughed, guiding me to the passenger side like some invalid.

As I leaned down, my face came near hers, and her eyes locked directly, intimately, into mine. I was left with her scent, a familiar memory, then she slammed the door.

I saw a flash of pale white skin, just above her right stocking. Flesh that I'd caressed, kissed, and used as lovers do. I knew it was soft, with a firmness underlying that feminine pastel that men, and I, find so easily lovable. But I did not want to use Dean—though I doubted I could— and find out tomorrow that it was Sylvia who'd stoked my fires. Nor did I want Dean to feel that way, though she sometimes in the past partook of me at her leisure, and I knew she did.

To 'get the itch out of my system,' she said without a hint of shame.

In the close confines of the car I smelled her scents and they too stoked memories. Maybe that was why she kept the car. For the memories.

One hundred and eighty KPH on an iced highway, being chased by two East German secret police, or Stazis. That was not a memory easily forgotten. Especially when the car that crashed two road blocks, and flew over a river, was humming right there beneath me. And how many times had we slept in this car, and made love with the front seats fully back. How many times had we used the gadgets to escape or evade. Many?

I realized we hadn't said a word to each other for five minutes, and were already nearing the Kracow flat she shared, or rented, while the owners were gone during the winter.

At a stoplight she looked over at me. "Memories are powerful."

I chuckled nostalgically. "I was thinking of the time we were being chased by those Stazis, in reunified East Germany. Remember?"

"Well, that was your fault, but we had bulletproof glass, so I forgave you."

"That's right, huh? JD had just installed that new lightweight impenetrable glass. Is this it?" I wondered aloud, and knocked on the glass.

"That's not my favorite memory, but it was a good one, wasn't it, Cort?"

We both knew the memories she was talking about, and maybe we both missed it.

Dean laughed. "Remember when you pulled a hammy?"

"That hurt like hell—"

"The last time we tried that position...."

How long ago was that, I wondered. "Dean, why did you drop off the face of the world for a year? Where'd you go?"

"Please, let's not talk about it right now. Maybe later, when you're done trying to kill yourself, I'll tell you."

I saw the building,, unconsciously searching the architecture, the layout, for escape routes. Always good to know more than one way if possible. I'd never been here before, and since I couldn't do a walk-through, I did as good a visual as possible. It was one of the new buildings, made of steel and glass, about four stories, which kept it from sticking out too much from the rest of the high-rise buildings.

"Nice place." I was impressed even further when she turned into a driveway that went down into an underground parking lot, though I didn't think much of the trip hose activator. Anyone could jump on it and trip the gate, which did open and close quickly.

"Still on duty, eh?" Dean commented dryly.

There were only six parking spots, and two were filled with brand-new Mercedeses. Dean parked the beast as far away from the newer cars as possible.

"They hate it when I put the beast next to their beauties."

"Can you blame them? Self-destruct, electric shocking mechanisms, pepper spray, flame throwing ports, and on the list goes."

"Don't slander our baby," she said, patting the console gently, before getting out of the beast.

"Where's Henri and Sylvia?"

"I gave them instructions on how to get here. I figured me and you can have dinner here? If that's okay with you?"

"Sounds good to me." But I was worried. Why? For the reasons aforementioned. And for the reason that Dean was my friend, and I don't think my questionable feelings for the sleeping Sylvia—who was so much different from the wakeful vixen—would be enough motivation for fidelity.

Women have the upper hand in that category.

I was pleasantly surprised by the security system, which had a fingerprint ID pad with keypad override, and a lock, which would require burglars to have experience with high-tech and lock picking, though the latter required only a pick gun. A device that literally touched all the right tumblers, and made the lock useless, with just a few squeezes of the trigger. Inside was a sea of black and white and gray, and no other colors were obvious, save for the streaks in faux marble walls. The mirrored walls, two out of the six in the main room, made the space look expansive. The deep shag rug was almost hard to walk on, as it kept sucking at my crutch. I watched her athletic figure swish away down a short hallway, and into one of the backrooms.

"There's wine and glasses behind the bar, if you want to pour us a couple of glasses?" Dean said loudly from the back, muffled here and there by the motions of taking her clothes off.

"First I have to find the bar," I said to myself, looking around.

"It's through the archway and nothing hard!" She read my mind.

I limped through the mirrored archway and saw the chrome bar, with glass and mirrored shelves behind it, and a walk space for the bar tender.

She came out as I was pouring, and I caught my breath at the sight of her spaghetti strap black silk pullover, or was it a teddy? She was barefoot, and her hair was down, thick and curly, falling around her small oval face. She was beautiful. Her naughty blue eyes were afire, pupils dilated. Her hips were fuller than I recalled. Sexier.

"I've missed you...."

She saw my look of appreciation, and that made her temptation all the more easier. Apple, indeed!

– CHAPTER 11 –

I AWOKE TO THE SOUND of laughter; Dean's and Henri's. For a moment I suffered disorientation, until I rolled, and felt the silk sheets slide across my thigh, and remembered. I'd been had!

"Another glass of wine, my ass!" I whispered angrily at the nonexistent Dean. I knew it. That wine had tasted funny, but with a funny taste in my mouth already, I couldn't tell. The details of my getting I will not presume to tell, save that she was astride.

I did feel better, though, so maybe Dr. Dean knew best, but still, I did not appreciate being drugged, especially with Henri and Sylvia within my sphere, therefore dangerous.

I relaxed into the deep cushions of the luxury kingsize bed, and thought about what last night's pre-drugging activities meant for me and Dean, or for me and Sylvia. Well, there was no me and Sylvia, I reminded myself.

The dark gray duffel bag, on the floor next to the bed, caught my attention, and my excitement. I got up, *au naturel*, and punched the combination into the electronic lock. I trusted Dean, but not burglars. I opened the supply bag and began gently taking out the bubble-wrapped devices, from watch-sized items to the larger miniature personal computer (MPC) for my forearm. I always got excited over gadgets, especially mine. I searched out the battery units, and found them tucked safely away in their boxes. I use two kinds of batteries; a pacemaker type battery, and a lithium core. As a backup, I carry a kinetic power source, which can be wound and produce enough electricity to run the MPC, satcom systems, or even provide enough energy to start a car. But it is a backup only, and very large, which, as you may have noticed, doesn't fit too well with me. JD was trying to miniaturize the device, but prototypes have not been released to me as of yet. I found the voltage adapters, and plucked out the one for Poland, and got my MPC and satcom system online. I checked the satcom reception and the small 40x10-character digital screen.

After the ready character, a small green light at the upper right corner of the screen blinked, I typed a message to Barry, and sent him the pictures I hoped had been saved from my old MPC and DVC (digital video/camera).

Before he could reply I sent a flash important message to Johnny Dempsey.

"FALCON! THOUGHT YOU WERE DEAD? WHO'S GONNA GET TO SIGN MY PAYCHECKS WHEN YOU LEAVE UNCEREMONIOUSLY?" JD replied in an instant.

"THANKS! I HAVE A BACKUP BOSS THAT SIGNS CHECKS IN MY ABSENCE! SURPRISED YOU HAVEN'T HACKED INTO MY LAWYER'S COMPUTER TO FIGURE OUT EXACTLY WHO, AND WHAT! HA! :-). HERE'S SOME PICS! I NEED IDENTITIES FOR HENRI GIONOPOLIS (SUSPECTED RUSSIAN???) AND SYLVIA DENOEL (UNKNOWN). ALSO, DID YOU GET FLASH IMPORT MESSAGE TWO DAYS AGO TO FOLLOW SINGLE WOMAN, FROM BRNO, WITH UAN TROOPS?" I finished typing to give him a chance to reply.

"ONE MORE: MINISTER MARTINOV PAROVICH, BELAKRAINIA."

"WILL DO. WANT RECON PHOTOS?" JD teased over the electronic highway.

"THIRTY SECONDS!" I replied, while hooking up my fax/scanner/color copier machine. It was the most expensive device I had, due to the upgrades. It was required to print out maps, pictures, documents, and do it all in silence. The latter requirement took one year to meet. Prior to that I had to retrieve any printed matter on a screen that wasn't very clear, or make sure nobody was listening. The printer went to work, and I set it off to the side, knowing it would take a few minutes to shit out my reconnaissance photos.

"Oh, excuse me! I—uh—I—" Sylvia exclaimed, turning bright red when she noticed all of him was uncovered. Something hot inside her caused her to sweat, and she turned away, but not before taking another look. "Uh—sorry—Dean said you should be awake about now."

"I'm up." I covered that fact with a pillow.

"Yes, I can see—I mean—we're going to have lunch, if you want some?" She took down her hands and turned back to face him boldly. "You know, you've seen me naked, so it's only fair I see you naked, right?"

She gave a huff, as if she'd worked up the nerve to say what she'd said, and now didn't know what to do with the excess audacity. "Well, you've seen everything. So we're even. I hope you got a good look, then." I smiled back at her.

"Not hardly, but it'll do for now." The latter was said with no little hint of suggestion. "So? You hungry or what?"

"Thanks. Ask Dean to bring me a plate." I went back to my equipment. There was a small fish and tackle box filled with devices, one of which I wanted right then.

"What're you doing? Show's over, kid," I said, readjusting the pillow, and finally locating my clean pants. I looked at Sylvia. "Would you mind?" I swear I saw her thinking about making me walk to the chair right next to her to get my clean pants.

"Doc cleaned them for you...." Sylvia picked them up and threw them to me. "Are you and her ... you know?"

I caught the pants. "Thanks. A long time ago."

"She's really a nice lady."

"The best I know, so far."

"You ever been married?"

"No. You?"

She laughed happily. "How should I know? I can barely remember my name and country." Then, as if she'd gotten all she wanted from me, including the peep show, she bounded out of the room. And I could not imagine any man binding her down with marriage, at least, not this Sylvia DeNoel. It would be interesting to see what my resources came up with.

Speaking of which, I took a look at the first satellite photo that came out of the printer. It was just as I suspected; the Belakrainian military were knee-deep in this, at least a branch of it was. I didn't jump to conclusions, because in a few moments those conclusions would be drawn for me. I was more interested in the info I requested about Henri and Sylvia. "On-ray, my ass," I said to myself. Dean had as much as confirmed my suspicions, and a good night's sleep had reaffirmed my own intuitions.

But why would a Russian want me for help, and why would he try to shoot me, or threaten to, no matter how ineffective it turned out to be? And that ineffectiveness could in itself have been an act, a sort of wolf meeting the sheep to get more information about the flock.

I typed an encrypted message to Igor in Moscow, and gave him a brief description of Henri, and some of the details of the man's contacts and habits, and even a picture I'd covertly taken of the man. I also described the relationship between Henri and Minister Martinov Parovich.

"NICE TO SEE YOU ARE WITH THE LIVING MY FRIEND. STOP. WILL CHECK. STOP. THINGS ARE HOT. STOP. ETA TEN TO TWENTY. STOP. OUT," came the answer from Igor, my Russian resource man.

Igor Stanislov was an old KGB man, but also part of the new intelligence service, who for some reason—and believe me, I could name many that were not good—had become a reliable contact and a good friend. He was forty-five, married to Svetlana Butraskya, a famous Olympic gold medalist in gymnastics, and had two daughters, Silkya and Skyia, who attended the prestigious Moscow University. The last time I saw him, a year ago, he was a balding man with graying red sideburns. Short, but quietly powerful, and not too overweight, like many of his generation begot. He didn't know I knew he was a CIA asset, but there wasn't much he didn't know in his half of the world. Yet, the only way I knew, was because of an SF mission that took place along the Russian Chinese border, in which I was picked up by a Colonel Stanislov. Igor. I believe that was his first, and last, CIA mission in which his cover was risked. Otherwise, his duties were strictly intel gathering. Code-named FRANKENSTEIN.

I had an idea that he knew I knew, but he didn't let on, nor would he. It was part of the game.

He would have files on any assassins, spies, or suspects, from the 1930s on. Sometimes, spying ran in the family, well, it was actually the norm upon historical review. Oftentimes sons and daughters would die on paper, only to be reborn on paper in another name and a different city. Sometimes a wholly different country. But the Russians had files on all their 'resurrections,' and if they had them, then Igor would find Henri. It was still a matter of would he. I'd known him to deny me intel on certain subjects, which would jeopardize him or his family, though I hadn't known the danger at the time. But he was otherwise worth the risk. Risk was a part of the game.

"FLASH. STOP. NO SUCH DUDE NAMED HENRI GIONOPOLIS FROM FRANCE. HERE IS A LIST OF PAROVICH ASSETS. PICTURES INCLUDED. CHECK OUT NUMBER FIVE." I read JD's more informal encryption.

"THANKS. WILL REVIEW AFTER PRINT. WILL RESPOND. OUT."

"Come on, put your toys away, and get some real food in you," Dean chided from the door, a bright smile on her face. She caught the gist of my look. "Hey, it's been a long time, and you're still the best I've had, or probably will have."

"Thanks, Dean." There was more than just the bed, the comfort, the medical assistance, and food that needed thanking for.

"And the world's still here." She smiled.

"Don't think you've gotten away with drugging good wine," I warned her.

"It was cheap stuff, and you were tired after the second bout." She laughed with her naughty blues.

I put on my watch. "Where's On-ray?"

"I don't know. He left when I told Sylvia you were in the backroom sleeping. I guess he thought you were still at the hospital. I didn't tell him otherwise."

"Good goyle!"

"But Sylvia went with him."

– CHAPTER 12 –

I HATED NOT KNOWING what the enemy was planning, One of my many pet peeves.

"There's nothing you can do about it, Cort. And if he did what you're so worried about, you'll never find her."

Dean was right, of course. Not that I was totally wrong to want to chase after Sylvia. It just took me a little longer to get to the right, or wrong, course of action. My stomach settled it for me. The printouts were still rolling in at a painfully slow pace. "Breakfast ready?"

"Now that's the Cort I know and love!" Dean said with a playful lilt, then leaned over and gave me a kiss on the lips.

I gripped her hand and held her at eye level. "Did we, last night?"

"Don't worry. I did, but you were asleep, so it doesn't count if you're ever asked. Why? Are you ashamed of doing it with an old lady?" She cackled and pulled away as I tried to tackle her and give her a red belly rub (RBR). She deserved better, but I could not stay mad at her.

Dean was the damnest and smartest woman I'd ever known, yet there was a certain unexplainable lure to the fragile blond-haired beauty, which had nothing to do with the latter coloring. I've never been partial to any hair color, for what is color compared to what really counts? Besides, anyone could change the color of their hair in an instant. Sylvia had me bewitched. Maybe it was her innocence, turned precocious, or her vexatious teasing. Though at that particular time I didn't recognize my own internal capitulations towards her. Then again, it could have been that she gave off pheromones, which I was susceptible to. Her, Dean, and a few other women as well.

All these things I thought about as I did another survey, while the printer was working. With a slower and less anxious view of the penthouse, which is what it was, I saw that it was sparsely furnished, yet what decor and furniture was here made it seem fashionable. A few blown-up pictures, maybe fifty dollars each, hung on the walls in chrome frames that were more expensive than their passengers, but they took up space. That was the key to their continuing existense, I guessed. The only really extravagant item was the long-haired white rug that covered the entire floor, with the exception of the bathrooms, dining room, and kitchen. There were big black wine jugs, circa 70 AD, sitting in the corners, or used as lamp stands. A few white jugs were also in existence, I saw, upon entering the living room. I went down the short hallway, the same one I'd previously gone down to retrieve wine and glasses for me and Dean. From the bar, which was at the rear of the dining room, I could see the modern kitchen, with its white multitask appliances and stations. Someone had definitely gone overboard for black and white, I saw, looking at the black fork handles and white spoon handles.

"Go sit down!" Dean said, slapping me on the ass, making me jump. "I've got something in the oven."

"Thought it was too soon to tell?" I joked with her. "Go—go sit down?"

"Get!"

A moment later she placed a hot tray piled too high with eggs, potatoes, and fresh tomatoes. "Ta-daa!" she said, raising her oven mittens out to her side. "I learned to cook while you've been gone.

"I see." I picked up a fork, then hesitated. "Anything I should know about? I can't afford to be hazy with Henri's ass around."

"No, so eat up. You'll need your strength in this weather."

She watched me eat, and we exchanged smiles. I didn't mind her kindly eyes, though sometimes when they turned to adoration I got a little embarrassed. But they never did. She simply watched, and I simply let her. We were comfortable with each other.

"I figured you hadn't eaten a full meal in a while. And those protein bars aren't real food either."

"Thanks, Dee, I needed that. But keep away from my protein bars, baby." I patted my belly as she took away the tray.

"Go get your gadgets ready. I know that's what you wanna do anyways."

I stood up, and grudgingly used the cane, though my leg actually felt like it was nearly brand-new.

"Really, thanks, Dee," I said from close behind her, and kissed her on her neck, where she liked it most.

"Unless you want soap and something else on you, I wouldn't kiss me like that." But she smiled, and flicked some soap back at me as she did the dishes.

Back to the gadgets I went, and found many satops printed out, along with other interesting items. Whoever had taken the horizon photos had done so expertly. There was a zoom angle through two northern peaks in the Carpathian Mountain range, to ground zero. But most interesting was an area circled in red, where there were limos and Belakrainian military vehicles along with a red delivery van, marked "Canrari Vineyards" on its sides. A very common thing in all of Europe. There were faces available, and I went through the pile of prints until I found the digitally enhanced close-up of a face I knew all too well.

Henri Gionopolis. He was shaking hands with a man with graying hair and a black Vandyke beard. I put the man at about fiftyish. I bet he was the Minister. The men around them were military and paramilitary. I suspected the paramilitary men, who wore winter camouflage, to be the buyers' soldiers. A few looked dark enough to be Arabic, but skin color was hardly a key to judging someone's homeland by in this day and age.

I still didn't understand why Henri, or the Minister, would be at ground zero. I looked at the other photos, and found the one that showed the entire site, complete with detonation pit some twenty meters down, but not deep enough to act like a proper shape charge. "Idiots," I whispered to myself.

"Hey you?" Sylvia snuck in through the doorway, and sat down next to me on the bed.

"Where's Henri?" I asked her.

She shrugged her shoulders before answering. "Said he had to contact the Minister, be back in a few hours, and dropped me off."

"Listen, Syl...." How did I tell her to watch out for Henri? What if she was taken with him, or so set against me that she'd believe anything he said. I took my eyes off of the photos and looked into hers. She saw my worry.

"What?" Sylvia asked. "I would have told you I was going with him but I figured you was still mad at me seeing little Cort and all—"

"It's not that," I cut her off. "Look. I know you don't know me, or Henri, but it was me that saved you. Not him. He came to me with a gun pointed at me."

"Henri? Oh come on, Henri wouldn't, and couldn't, hurt a fly. Would he?" She was thinking about it now.

I watched her charming lower lip tuck behind her upper teeth, as if she were pouting, but was instead in deep thought. I watched her round face, now animated with question, as she tried to decide where her loyalties lay. It was a beautiful face. Just plain beautiful. Even her crooked nose was equally appropriate. Her eyes were fat almond-shaped, though not related to any recent Asian lineage. Her lips were very pink, without lipstick. Her hair was pulled back into a ponytail, as if to thrust her facial beauty out to the world. Was this how she was, in her pre-coma society? I doubted it. Once she realized, or found out about the perks of being a woman, I could see her rushing to the salon, the boutique, the make-up counters, and shoe stores. To those places men shun, and women flood. In Dean's white blouse and khakis, she was a perfect goddess. I hoped that I could persuade her into believing this, so she wouldn't tarnish her natural allure.

I found her watching me when I came out of my own shallow and self-serving trance. She was smiling at me, in a fond way that at least gave me a hint of her appreciation.

"Dean's told me all about you, so I'll keep my eye on Henri and not go off alone with him again, since you say he's dangerous. Okay?"

"Not dangerous, just a liar. I don't know what his intentions are. And he's no Frenchman—"

"Well, you're certainly right about that, Cort Falcon," Henri said from the doorway, with a gun pointed at Dean's head. I checked her wrist for the watch I'd given her; it wasn't there. "I don't know how you got your information, but I assure you it's going nowhere."

He was ten feet away, and I saw his gun was a new carbon fiber, U.S. military issue, 10mm. It was immune to magnetic infusion. I thumbed my watch on anyways.

"That won't do you any good, so don't waste our time."

"So what's going on? You and the Minister got a deal going with terrorists? I thought better of you, Henri—"

"Oh, it's much much better. The UAN is buying as well, to add a more mobile military threat, seeing as how NATO won't give them the responsibility to hold nuclear weapons. And the terrorists, well, you Americans wanted to war in two thousand one, so now you have to pay the price of escalation." Henri snorted. "You Americans think that only you can control the world's opinions, but it is only because you control the minds through threat. Not for long."

He sounded just like a terrorist, justifying the deaths of innocents, for which there exists no qualification. A good thing he didn't start talking about a god or a prophet, or I might have rushed him right then and there. But he kept to the party line of hatred of one group or country, which gave defense to the deaths of anything, and anyone, associated with the the enemy, innocently or corroboratively. A spiel only the bored, dense, disenfranchised, or young bought into.

I'd heard similar theories, juxtaposed, in nearly every country, from Afghanistan to Zimbabwe, and each of them in between. What it came down to was this; everybody hates a winner when they themselves are losing. The haters see their crumbled society as they sit around doing nothing to improve it, and while oppressing and killing their own, as they empower themselves through multiplicious bureaucracies that stifle the system, trying to control the masses, when it is the governors that need controlling. The masses are shepherded by propaganda created specifically to propagate nationalistic fears, and beliefs, that one or another country, or peoples, are oppressing them in some form or manner, when it's also always the contrary. Colonialism was dead. The only place where there was still true oppression was in certain parts of Africa, and in the oligarchic republics within the United Arab Nations, and in a few Asian countries where the last outposts of communism struggled to survive. Each country, save for those mentioned, had the opportunity to better their own economy, to get billions in loans to do so, to evolve into the super economies that were beginning to sprout upon our small globe.

I've my own vision of the Earth, but no Plato am I. Nor was this the time to divulge my scheme of things, with Dean's life in jeopardy, and my play at hand.

"Henri, or whatever your name is, put that gun down, will you, before you hurt yourself." This had the desired effect of angering him. The gun began to move from her head to me, as I raised my hand in mock fear. I saw Dean close her eyes, and wondered how she knew about this new device. The pressure pad underneath the watch activated the blinder at the clench of my wrist and forearm muscles. A green light, so bright he'd be blind for twenty-four hours, colored his face, disorientating his brain for approximately three seconds. I had his gun in one, and so his snarl of realization was quite appropriate. I added some plasticuffs to his discomfort.

"Rookies," I said to myself. "You girls okay?"

Dean nodded, but looked at Sylvia. "I'd better check her though?"

"Shit!" I saw Sylvia on the ground. At least the rug had cushioned her fall. "I'll go get some water."

I also wanted to check the perimeter, just in case, because it was obvious that Henri had been ordered to make an offensive move. And such steps were rarely taken without reinforcements. I hoped the glass was custom insulated, since there was so much of it, otherwise we were sitting ducks to a high-powered sniper rifle with a thermascope. I hoped that this was a case of 'some people never learn,' but I doubted it, or Henri would've gotten me while I was asleep, which meant he had gotten orders from the Minister, or someone. I had to proceed as if backup was already here, or on the way.

The penthouse was clean, and I could discern no new suspect vehicles parked along the side, or front streets. But that didn't mean anything. I checked Henri's gun to be sure it was ready to fire, while I thought about the implications of a UAN deal. But if they were doing a deal with the UAN they could just blow this place up, if they didn't care about bad publicity. It also meant that the Minister had lots of guns on his side. If the connection was true then it was a good thing I avoided them in Brno, and quite an act put up

PROCESS OF ILLUMINATION

by Henri.

I carried the glass of water into the room, where Henri was spitting and cursing me to death, thankfully in Russian, which Dean hardly understood. She was an Asian language specialist, while I was good for most Slavic and Romance dialects. But one didn't need to know the language to understand the intent of Henri's words, so I clouted him once on the nose.

"Sorry," I told Dean, then to Henri. "Next time I break it and put you out. You gonna be quiet?"

I watched Dean pat cool water on Sylvia's pale face, and prayed that she would snap out of it, and hadn't looked at the light.

"Margaret?" Sylvia named Dean, a questioning tone in her brow. "No, it's you ... Dean?"

"Of course it is."

"What happened?" She saw Henri on the floor, and that he was now face down and tied up. "What's going on?"

"Henri wasn't who he thought he was," I told her point blank.

"Oh?"

"Don't you remember our talk?"

"Who's Margaret?" Dean overrode my question.

"I've no idea." She thought about it for a moment. "Maybe it's a friend's name, or something."

"Think on it while you re getting ready to leave, you too, Dean."

"I'm not sure she should be moved now?"

"Doesn't matter. Move or die."

"You sure?"

"I can feel'em, and so can you. Sorry, but you're in danger, so you gotta take a ride."

"Cruddy diapers! This always happens when you come around." But she felt that old thrill returning, reviving that old moxie in her bones. Maybe she should have chosen to venture out into the unknown dangers and adventures when Cort had offered, before they decided to separate, she pondered for the umpteenth time. Was Cort enamored of this girl, Dean asked, seeing the look of worry for Sylvia in his eye. A look that, at one time, had been solely for her. Damn his ruggedly handsome head.

"That's why you love me so much," I joked, not knowing how close to her thoughts I'd come.

Dean huffed, but began packing her get up and go bag, which I had also supplied her with six years ago.

"How ya feeling?" There was tenderness in my voice, which I should have hidden from Dean. "I mean really? Are you in working order, Sylvia?"

"I think so. My body feels fine. It's my head that's fuzzed over. I saw the gun, and...."

"That's to be expected of a virgin, I guess," I said offhandedly, and saw her blush pink.

"That's none of your business!"

"I meant it another way," I explained poorly. At least she knew what a virgin is, though, and I told her so.

Yes, she did, Sylvia thought to herself, and blushed red again, then sat upright without feeling lightheaded. The mirrored room looked bigger than it actually was, she noticed, when she tried to see how bad she looked after fainting.

"You have any winter clothes for me?" Sylvia asked.

"Yeah. Pick some out." Dean opened the closet door, revealing racks of clothes. You should wear the best stuff, and pack for emergencies. You're so thin you'll fit into anything I wear."

"I've already seen you both naked, but I leave you girls to it. Remember—"

"Hurry up," Dean finished for me.

"And take him out of here too." Sylvia shuddered at the sight of Henri.

"Yes, boss." I received a pillow in the head for that. I got the research materials, all the printouts, and carried them into the living room. I kept the gun ready for use. Then I went back and dragged Henri out of the room, while he bitched and moaned about rug burns. Not like he didn't deserve it, and worse.

"Oo-la-la," I jested Dean, who was taking off her blouse. "I'm gonna shut this door, but don't come out no matter what you might hear." And Sylvia shut the door.

"How long till backup arrives? Is it here already?" I asked politely, as I began to put on my travelling clothes. I slipped on my gray longjohns, then a gray undershirt, and lastly, my over clothes. Everything was neutral gray, sort of like an overcast sky, but neither too white, or too dark. My shirt was bulletproof, and had a plastic suction flap on the left sleeve where I strapped the personal computer brace, then fitted the slender MPC.

I pointed the gun at a spot next to Henri's ear and pulled the trigger. He couldn't see, but he felt the bullet go by his ear. His blinded eyes opened wide in shock.

"Give me the information, now!" I pressed the hot gun barrel to his head, and said, "I know you and Parovich were at the test site, and I know you and the UAN aren't involved. Now, I want to know what you know."

Henri spilled his guts, after a momentary realization that my reputation might be real, not just some advertisement. I wouldn't kill him in cold blood, but I might put a bullet in his tennis elbow, or make him think I had. His information could mean life or death for me, for my two girls, and for over a million people. I had my lie detector on as he sang, and only once did he lie. I bonked him on the head with the butt of the gun.

"No, I swear, a squad is waiting down the road at the gas station!" Henri cried. "They're Columbians! I swear."

"What time were you supposed to call, and what are Columbians doing here?" But even as I said it the pieces were beginning to click into place.

"One o'clock."

"Why'd you contact me, Henri? I mean, I've seen you at the meeting site, and know you must've got a healthy cut of the sales. What gives?"

"They insisted something be done about you. A diversion or something?" He paused. "That sniper was supposed to kill you, but he lost you." The lie detector told me he was lying.

"So that was your man?" I chuckled. "And all this time I thought it was some kid who didn't know shit from shinola! So you figured on distracting me while you snuck the weapons out of the country?" I kept my suspicions to myself.

"No. We were going to lead you to some of the weapons."

That was the last clue I needed. They were going to run the old shell game; show the nukes going here, while sending the bulk over there. I would discover the nukes, and the world would think it was safe.

"I thought all Soviet nukes had been displaced under START?" Strategic Arms Reduction Treaty. A treaty that in theory is supposed to clear the world of major atomic weapons strongholds, and thereby lessen the risk of destroying the planet. But, as with all man's plans, it wasn't perfect. Russia was selling nuclear secrets, no matter how much money was given them. Greed.

"I was telling you the truth when I said that Belakrainia had secret nukes," Henri said in mock indignation.

"All right, Henri. Now tell me, how many nukes are going where?" I pressed the muzzle against his crotch.

"Twenty-six.

The lie detector said he was telling the truth.

Twenty-six nuclear bombs, I said to myself. There was good reason to keep certain irresponsible, still warlike nations of the world from having nuclear weapons, which was why the major powers had agreed to keep their secrets under their vests. It didn't prohibit the invention of, or the development of small nations' military nuclear weapons, but there were perks to those nations who were non-nuclear, and a part of NATO.

"Let's go, ladies!" I shouted.

"Coming, Pa!" the smartass shouted back.

I was glad to hear her wit return, but the remark about my age wasn't very nice.

I gave one last comment to Henri. "If your boys show up before we can clear the building, it'll be you that dies. You deserve a bullet in the brain, you piece of shit, and if the Russians find you first, that's what you'll get." And I believed he actually felt sorry for what he did, and for risking so many lives. NOT!

I checked my watch, and my portable office material in the pack, to make sure it was just right. I tested the weight of the pack, and decided I could lose the cast. I'd have to chuck it and settle for a tightly wrapped ace bandage, which I did immediately. Back in my boots, I could feel the wound tighten and pull, but it felt like it would hold. I hoped.

"Let's go—wow?" I exclaimed, and caught myself at the sight of Sylvia's tight khaki pants, which did her figure justice. A matching blouse, and something different about her hair; a bun. "Very nice."

Sylvia spun around. "Watcha see is watchya get, and two pairs of thermals underneath." She smiled.

Dean smiled in the background, carrying a pack that was similar to mine. There was a look on her face that revealed a jealous streak.

"Did you have to?" Dean said, bending down to check the gag I'd put in Henri's mouth. Ever the humanitarian. She put a finger in the bullet hole. "As usual destroying property."

"Yep. Sorry. I knew you'd hate it. Can't have him screaming out." I checked my watch. "Come on, we gotta go, girls. We're cutting it close."

I took her pack and handed her the gun, which she checked, sighted, then stuck in her jacket's inner pocket. Dean was a damn good shot, and I'd rather her carry the gun than me. Her only problem was that she'd never shoot to kill. She always shot to injure or disarm, but never to kill. It was a good sentiment, because it saved human lives, but I always believed it would cost us one day. So far it hadn't, so I let it be. Besides, we both hated guns, and rarely had possession of them, unless, like in the instant matter, they fell into our laps.

"What's going on, Dean?" Sylvia said, somewhat warily, upon seeing Dean handle the gun so expertly.

"We're getting out of something, if we can, Cort'll tell us all about it once we get out of here, okay?" Dean answered for me.

Sylvia stepped way around Henri, as if he were a pile of shit, which he was, and stepped towards me.

"Stand back." I pointed a thermal scanner at the door, and found nobody waiting on the other side. "Okay, it's clear." The bad thing about these new buildings was that there were no stairs. Only elevators down to the lobby, or to the carport.

"Did Henri see the beast?" I asked Dean, fearing a car bomb. "Come on, everybody into the elevator."

Everyone's eyes were on the elevator indicator as we went down, hoping against hope that Henri had felt confident enough to take us on his own.

Dean handed Sylvia the pack. "Here, stand to the side." She took out the gun, cocked it, and took a shooter's stance. She exchanged a glance with Cort, then back to the door as the electronic bell dinged.

"Get behind me!" I pulled Sylvia over behind me as the doors began to open.

Sylvia took the rough handling in stride, as if she were in a state of shock, trapped in a game she didn't know was real. Ever since she'd woken up, life had given her nothing but obstacles. She'd seen a man who'd been kind to her pull a gun on the man who'd saved her. Now she was playing commando with people she hardly even knew. And this man, Cort Falcon, who the hell did he think he was? Dean had said he was a reporter, a spy, a pariah to bad governments still in existence. She knew he was handsome, and resourceful, for she'd witnessed and heard as much. He was a man who could ask a doctor to pull up her roots, and move, on the basis of what she could only so far see as a hunch. Her heart beat faster when she thought about him as a man, and herself as a woman, but she disliked him for his assertiveness and confidence, which now had her trembling behind him. Was it dislike, or was it just that she didn't like this entire situation into which she'd awakened. Awakened because he'd cared enough to rescue her from a bombed-out city. At the restaurant, where Henri had taken her, she'd gleaned enough information from a newspaper to realize that she would have been dead had it not been for him. Or worse.

And her friend from the UAN, Arul Bashik, was only a pen pal from Egypt, and then, they'd only written to each other for two years. He was married with five children, and only twenty-nine years old, commanding a battalion in the UAN forces. She had explored the memory of their friendship, and had remembered that they had met at the customs office that was being raided by the UAN along the Egyptian and Jordan border. He had saved her from embarrassment and possible arrest. The customs officials were stealing original artifacts and supplanting them with fakes, then selling the originals on the black market. They'd been caught due to one of the fakes being of poor quality, and the buyer being affiliated with the UAN customs office.

A new revelation: She was an antiques dealer slash finder, which meant she'd gone to college somewhere in America or an English speaking country.

The door began sliding open. To her it seemed like everything was underwater, slow motion. "Open," she willed. A moment later she ducked out, gun at the ready, just like in the movies. A scream echoed in the underground parking garage, and she heard the gentle doctor bark orders. The scream cut off instantly.

"Clear!" Dean barked.

"Come on, Sylvia."

They passed a frightened young couple, who were still standing with their arms raised, not knowing if they were to be robbed or murdered.

Dean started the car and backed it out of its parking space before me or Sylvia could reach it. The door opened.

"Come on, Sylvia," I told her, lifting the seat for her to get in the back, where it was safest if there was any gun play. There was a look of fright in her eyes, not much different than a scared doe trapped in the headlight beams, a flash away from bolting. But she got slowly in.

"What's the matter?" I asked, worried her mood change was indicative of something more serious. Sylvia looked at me with fear in her eyes. Fear of something only she knew.

Meanwhile, Dean approached the ramp with caution. If we were followed there were defense systems that could assist us, but if we were front-punched, a tactic used by many professionals, we'd be screwed.

"Put your seat belt on, there, that's it. I'll explain all this in one minute." *If we're still alive,* I didn't say. I turned around once she was secured, and put my own five-point harness on. "Gun?" And Dean handed it to me.

"Ready?" Dean asked no one in particular, stepping on the gas, rolling over the trip hose. "Come on!" she hissed at the slow rising door. "Oh, which way we going?"

I smiled at her attempt at humor. "We're heading to Belgrade. But you two can get off at the nearest airport. If they're still operating after the pulse." As much as I hated to lose Dean and Sylvia, I knew that I'd be risking their lives if they came along. And Sylvia's presence would distract me.

"Think they've got the airport watched?"

"They run the airports here."

"The Poles wouldn't like to hear that," Dean commented.

"When someone's told indigo is lapis lazuli they start to believe it."

"I'll take the old highway, right? They'll think we're heading towards the airport." Dean turned to me for guidance, and we exchanged a look that brought a smile to her lips. Then she looked down and saw the tiny hand in mine.

I hadn't realized its presence, for it was so natural a thing for me to comfort Sylvia. Even when I cared for her, during that short period, I had held her hand during the night, and it seemed she'd held mine. "I need both hands, Sylvia."

But I was looking dead into Dean's hurt eyes. I shrugged.

"Hold on!" The wheel spun, and the beast shot up the ramp, and out into the street, with surety. She neither slid, nor screeched.

"Turn right, quick!" I saw two black Euro SUVs, the vehicle of choice for punch attacks, because they were sturdy. "That little bastard," I cursed. I'd believed Henri was telling the truth about the backup, but I hadn't believed they were waiting just down the road. Or I'd misjudged the proximity of the gas station down the road. I doubted any one of their SUVs could stop the beast, for she was just as heavy, and probably better put together. But the smart man avoids the expenditure of resources, e.g. conflict. I was thankful for the tinted windows, but still unconsciously sat back in my seat, as if to hide behind the door post. "Don't think they saw us."

"It's clear," Dean said once we'd travelled a hundred meters down the road, then she stepped on the gas. The business district turned into homes, and finally she cut right, heading towards the highway.

I took a look in the rearview mirror. "Still got the touch, Dean." Then I saw Sylvia in the mirror.

Sylvia smiled back. "So tell me, what's going on?" No fear in her eyes whatsoever.

– CHAPTER 13 –

"SEE MY BAG?" I asked Sylvia. "Open the big pocket and take out the pictures." And then, with photographic proof, I set upon the tale which has previously been related. The pictures making it easier for both women to understand and believe.

"Those bastards!" Sylvia impressed me with her vehemence. "Oh, excuse me."

"No need. You're right on target." I live my life for days such as this; to open the eyes of those who have theretofore been blind. But such moments as these were too far and few between. Too singular. I held that moment, wishing she'd curse them more. I had made a convert, and it had taken just a few moments.

I think that even if I wasn't a war correspondent slash dogooder, I would still endeavor to make a change. If I could put an end to the violence and classism that kept the world in a constant state of stress, war, and oppressionism, with words and pictures, I would.

There are other evils. Newer. Industries that have sprung up, in the same manner as the old vices. Prison and law enforcement industrial complexes who push for war, but a different kind of war. One that is aimed at its own less affluent citizens. Those whose death and ruin go unheard.

Sadly, it is America that has been the catalyst for a bloated and corrupt prison industry. But they knew better. In the 1970s, after the slaughter at Attica, a rehabilitation and reformatory position was taken up by the nation. It was because the world was forced to look inside those hells we'd created, and the world didn't like the cruelty that went on behind those iron curtains within American borders. But in the '80s and '90s, despite the decrease in recidivist rates, a new prison industry, the offspring of the law enforcement branch, sprouted up like a black rose. It began lobbying for more money, for more prisons, for more power. And it got it. Soon there were no educational or rehabilitative goals in the prison. Sentences became longer, and "habitual offender" laws went into effect, which would take away a man's life for stealing a piece of pizza, or a pack of cigarettes.

The sentencing schemes are almost vile; on one side the legislature is saying that they're not going to allow the poor (the majority of all inmates being poor) to rehabilitate themselves in prison, so they become more criminalized, but hauntingly, while on the other hand, the legislature enacts laws that basically terminate the freedom of this "class" of people with harsh sentences, when they go out and commit more crimes. It's as if the industry is feeding the prisoners wheat, and expecting them to shit soy beans.

The current state of warehousing human beings for twenty-four hours a day in 8x10-foot boxes, alone, only exacerbates the cruel intentions. And with the judicial and executive and legislative branches, in the global politics, benefiting from these misfortunes. Call them crimes. Call them what you will. It is misfortune that usually leads one to criminality. Or youth. Or mental decompositions. And yes, even immorality. At any rate, the industry will not soon stop growing unless the citizens wake.

Do not think there are no others, for the media too shares some guilt. It is they who push their propaganda upon the masses, exciting them against certain classes, pushing victims upon stages, where instead of mourning they are used as a bully pulpit to push even more laws, more prisons, more police. Example; In 1991 the big three American networks showed 571 crime reports, compared to 1993 and 1,636 crime stories, even though the crime rate had dropped from 1991 to 1993.

Common sense, in many instances, has been replaced by greed, power, and a subtle fascism hidden beneath the facade of a growing criminal element. This latter created by those corrupted by the need for "more action" in their news hour, more heroes, and more zeros. However, unlike big corporations and normal citizens, criminals, or suspects, get no apologies from networks that inadvertently slander them in the reaching for higher ratings.

Thus, it's a vicious and clearly visible cycle that has been on earth since man has invented government to govern. It's covertly beneath the surface in some countries, and overt in many others. There are indeed still countries who sponsor murder, even though there is proof that not all persons who are found guilty are truly guilty. Anything man makes is imperfect, so too is a system that finds one guilty or innocent. But common sense is not in strong demand, for it thrusts those who purchase their rotting pork belly husks into the light of day.

Is there a perfect way to decide the guilt of a human being? I have some ideas....

I smiled at Sylvia. "Hand me the photos, please." I didn't want to take them from her, but needed to review some of them. I took a magnifying glass out of the glove compartment; never underestimate the power of a magnifying glass. I looked at the faces, imprinting them on my memory. They were the enemy. It was always nice to put a face on your foe, in any adversarial endeavor.

A face stood out amongst the terrorists, but it was only a profile. He was only in one frame, which meant that he'd only stayed a short time, or had stayed in the backseat of one of the limos. Or the man was very smart, and knew about the capabilities of long-range horizon scanning satellites, which no satellite missile or laser could disrupt. His lips were thick, ruddy, and familiar.

I scanned it back to JD for a computer-generated frontal shot, which would take an hour. It was possible he was already doing it. I made it a point to debrief after each mission, and found it a wonder how small the world truly is, for many of the same faces begin to pop up. Descriptions of clothes, watches, shoes, and various other items of apparel could foreshadow a person's attachment, affiliation, and intent. If I saw Basnk shoes, it meant the person was with the KGB, while if I saw a person wearing a dark trench coat I knew that person was with the new Russian Intelligence Department, or the new KGB. Various agencies dressed in varying ways, with the poorer countries being limited to, frankly, generic clothing that spotlighted their presence. But the most important part of the debriefing was the facial recognition descriptions that JD pulled from me. Surprising how many of the same individuals are always involved in illegalities.

"JD. IDENT CHECK/COMPUTER FACIAL. CHECK DEBRIEF/NSA/SF FILES. THANKS."

"ALREADY THERE. NO IDENT YET. LATER."

JD was on the job and that was good to know. Probably spurred on by my disappearance.

Ah, the satscan radiation trails. I hadn't had time to review all the maps, wanting to get the players memorized first. Now I saw a lookdown topical map, with very dim lines that went out from a red circular area, the latter being ground zero. The radiation blanket created by the blast would cover any radioactive signals. They must have known it too "Shit!" I cursed under my breath, and brought out the photographs of the area, this time covering a hundred-mile circular area. Lines began to appear, like a spiderweb from the center, with tiny red lines going out from the cloud, which indicated radioactive materials being transported. It made no sense, the lines went out in all directions, and no line was more clear than the other. I doubted there were that many nukes being moved, or a few would have already been snatched up by surrounding governments and at border checks, none of which had the radiation detection devices. I knew that Austria had the radiation detection monitoring system at its border checkpoints, yet there were five trails going into the country. What would give off a similar radiation decoy signal, and more importantly, which trails were the real bombs? I guessed there could only be as many as 20 separate trails, and that was if they broke apart the warheads, which contained as many as 8 apiece. The bombs were singular, but powerful. City destroyers.

"Bad news?" Dean asked.

"Yes." And when I didn't provide more details, she knew not to bother me. I drew lines next to lines which I thought had to be decoys, either because of their destination, or because the nukes could not be gotten through that border crossing. I was giving the border guards the benefit of the doubt, and the antismuggling devices their due. I turned 28 red lines to green, indicating my 90% no nuke probability. That left 35 red lines, and we were following two, by taking this highway now, though some eight hours behind, I surmised.

I felt the car accelerate. "Problems?"

"Possibly." She kept smiling, kept her foot down on the gas pedal, and her conversation with Sylvia about amnesia.

"I see a black car behind us," Sylvia said a moment later, looking through the small back window. "It's gaining." Her voice trembled.

"Shoot!" Dean's memory was definitely intact, I thought.

When travelling in not quite so democratic countries, like the Balkans, who still had secret police, one should always beware black Mercedeses, otherwise known as "bad guy cars", or BGCs.

Four years ago me and Dean, on our one last excursion together, had had a run in with the black Mercedes men, and one woman, and we hadn't even done anything illegal. Yet. We were innocently eating ice cream in a shop overlooking the Black Sea, in Bulgaria. We'd no reason to believe they were after us, but just in case, Dean had advised that we get back to the boat and watch. And watch she did, with a pair of high-powered binoculars, as five men, and a mysterious female leader, scoured the ice cream shop for us, and not believing the counterman, they had beat him up pretty badly. Their black Mercedes parked just outside the pink and white awning, soiling the gentility of such a kindly establishment.

That was one of about thirty run-ins we had with the bad guys, and one girl, whose evil intentions were somehow betrayed by the car itself, which does not mean that the car itself was evil embodied, but that for one reason or another people of a darker nature really like that car. You'd think they'd change after seventy years of black Mercedeses. Just to throw off the competition.

"Beegees?" Dean said, meaning 'bad guys.'

"And a woman," I added, to ease the slanderous tone of the gender reference, implying that women could be just as evil. And they could, I guarantee. In fact, I remember— "Yes, and a woman!" Dean stopped short, changing her glance, looking not at the BGCs, but at Sylvia. "You?" I glanced over at Dean, aware of the hitch in her voice, the accusatory tone, which Sylvia hadn't recognized. "What?"

"They're coming!" Sylvia worried aloud, as she turned completely around to eyeball the enemy. "What do they want?"

"They'll wait for us to get to the winding road, and then they'll try to run us off, to make it look like an accident." Might as well give it to her straight.

"But they're not Henri's men." Dean was trying to tell me something.

I looked at her, and mouthed a "What?" to her. She did a head jerk towards Sylvia, but I didn't catch what she was saying, again. "Love makes you blind."

"Sit down, just in case they start shooting," I told Sylvia, and she did.

"I thought this was bulletproof glass?"

"Nothing's for sure." No matter how bulletproof the glass was, and no matter how much armor plating we had in the body of the car, there was always something that could penetrate.

Dean tried jerking her head, as if to point something out, then gave up, after I looked at Sylvia, then back at Dean.

An odd silence ensued.

"So what'd you remember, so far?" I asked her, keeping my eye on the bad guys' car about a half mile back. I was like a chef with salt, but with distances.

"I am an American-schooled female, twenty-six years old. I've been to France, and I speak it. I have a friend named Margaret, and the UAN friend is actually only a pen pal named Arul Bashik, from Egypt. I am an antiques dealer. And—"

"You remembered the black Mercedes?" Dean asked.

Aha! Now I was in sync with Dean.

"It's familiar for some reason.... I don't know why."

"Remember the woman from the ice cream shop in Bulgaria? The woman?" Dean said forcefully. "Remember, you said she was too young."

I looked at Syvlia, and looked into my memory bank, trying to bring up the face of the woman. No, the hair was darker, the face tanned. The shapes were similar, but Dean had been the one with the binoculars, while I was controlling the boat. I'd looked once, but only to acknowledge the odd presence of a woman, and by that time I only got to see the side of her face and her back.

"What's going on? It's like you two are talking in code or something?" Sylvia said with genuine concern.

"I think we've met before," Dean said, now suspicious of Sylvia and her stories. "And I think they're are after you, not us?"

"Me! Why me? I haven't done anything?" Sylvia's eyes pleaded with mine, looking for some sort of support.

"Stop it, Dean. You don't know for sure, and look at her, she's just a kid and that was three years ago.

"I'm not a kid." Quit calling me a child!" Sylvia rebuked my implication.

"See, there it is there." Dean grinned triumphantly.

I looked from Dean's serious profile to Sylvia's innocent expression that begged my assistance. But what could I say amongst the memories of this car, where I had faithfully relied upon Dean, and she upon me? The facts said I should rely upon Dean, yet my heart would not abandon Sylvia and leave her to the wolves.

"Let me have the first aid kit, in the side pocket." I pointed to the pocket, so Sylvia could locate it easily. Once in hand I opened the plastic case and took out a small syringe. "Let me have your leg—just put it between the seats."

"What're you gonna do?" Sylvia hesitated.

"Trust me.

She put her leg through the seats, and I located the perfect spot near her calve muscle.

"Ow!" She jerked her leg back. "What was that for?"

"Stop rubbing it, or they'll see." I swatted her hands away from the injection site, where a micro transmitter was alive inside of her body. My heart hurt, I swear, at the thought of losing her to some other warders' care. It seemed to take more effort for each beat, as if my internals had suddenly been placed under 5 G's.

"Who?"

"Them," Dean said, looking up into the rearview mirror.

There was two of them, I saw. "Get ready, Dean." They were a hundred meters behind us.

"Cort? What's going on?" Sylvia pleaded, looking from the bad guy cars to me.

"Dean's sure she seen you before," I told her outright.

"Impossible or I'd—" She knew better than to complete her sentence, because she wouldn't remember.

"There's American troops to the west, at forty-five long, fifty latitude?"

115

"Too far! We'll never make it!" Dean drove, looked, and barked. "Shoot! They're making their move." She stamped on the accelerator.

"There's gotta be another way?" *Think, Cort, think!* I cursed. But I knew a way.

Dean laughed sourly. "Then why'd you give her the tracer?"

"Stop it! Stop it right now!" Sylvia shouted in panic. "I have a say, don't I? You can't just hand me over. I've never seen them. I don t remember them." I turned away when her eyes widened, because Dean had taken her foot off the accelerator. "Dean? What're you doing? Dean? Cort? Stop this right now!" Her last words were a plea for help, with tears streaming.

Her touch scalded my soul. I felt like shrinking myself into the molecules of the foot well rugs, which is where I put myself at that moment. I couldn't meet her eyes, and I felt despicable, though I knew it would save all of our lives.

"No, Dean! I've an idea—"

"Too late for that!"

A bad guy car was blocking the road ahead. They'd no intentions of allowing us to even reach the mountain roads. Whoever they really were, they wanted what they wanted alive and kicking.

"What's happening, Cort?" Sylvia squeezed my hand.

"Listen to me." I took her face gently, but firmly in my hands. "I didn't save you for nothing. I will find you. I will. That device in your leg is a tracking device that will last a full year. I will find you and get you back, Sylvia DeNoel. On my life, I will not forget."I don't know why, but I brought her innocent face towards my guilty one, and kissed her softly upon the lips. There was no other way to kiss such lips, without bruising them. I felt her heartbeat quicken, under my fingers, which rested lightly upon her neck. I tasted her tears, which ran down her cheeks and collected upon her upper lip. I pulled away, and found her eyes closed, a smile on her face. "I'm sorry, but it's the only way. I think they think you're one of them. Be one of them, but don't forget. Okay?" She nodded back at me, and sniffled.

Dean brought the car to a stop, and knowing I had no heart to say it, said it for me; "Get out, Sylvia."

Was there a bit of harshness in her voice? I wondered, as I armed the bigger magnetronic device, which acted as a sort of bullet shield. A side effect was that it wreaked havoc with electronic devices that were outside of the beast's frame.

– CHAPTER 14 –

I STEPPED OUT OF THE CAR, then stood off to one side, checking the horizon for snipers, though in the back of my mind I knew better. If they were any good, I'd never see them. I kept silent, trying to ignore the sniffles, trying not to look at her, to see the betrayal I knew was in her eyes. The anguish I felt could not be snuffed out, however, and I grabbed her hand to help her out of the car. But it was more than that. I wanted to touch her one last time before she was gone, without giving away my feelings. If they saw it they might use it against me, or her.

"I will find you," I whispered into her ear, as she stood up. "Say it."

"You'll get me out," Sylvia said, raising her intense blue eyes to mine. She believed him with all her heart. "You'll get me out."

I heard the faith in her words, my own pain lifted some, and my hand let her go. Nobody got out of either of the three cars, until she began walking. I kept the gun and watch within the frame, unsure of whether of not the gun would work at the same time.

"Get in! Get in, Cort!"

I heard Dean's voice calling me from somewhere outside the fog of my brain, and then a hand tugged me back into the car.

"Put JD on it," Dean ordered naturally.

"Right."

"JD! URGENT! THREE BCG'S AT 20L0—50LA. TRACE DEVICE IN FEMALE SUBJECT SD. NEED FACES, PLACES. PRIORITY TRACK!"

I was thrown back into my seat as Dean punched the gas, and we headed straight for the black Mercedes that was blocking our path. I turned my head and watched Sylvia's shrinking figure. A man in a black longcoat stepped out, and I swore I could see him smile in a more friendly manner than befit the occasion. Or was it my imagination? I tried to look harder, searching blindly for my binoculars, and finding them too late.

"Is it moving?" I asked Dean.

"Oh, it'll move, or get plowed. You might want to turn around and buckle up."

As I turned I saw the whites of a man's eyes, as we rushed at the rear quarter panel (the best place to hit when looking to clear). The rear wheels smoked, and the car shot forward, into the shoulder ditch, the man jumping in with it.

"I forgot what a devil you are."

"Just doing my job," she said with a little bite.

I knew what for. "Sorry, Dean, but I had to give her something to believe in—"

"What a load of crap!" she barked derisively. "What? Are you fuckin' Casanova!" She snorted. "A kiss and the women swoon?"

She was pissed. I'd never known her to say the F-word in all my years, save once, when she was arguing with Taiwanese black marketeers who'd had me stowed in the hull of their ship.

"I was talking about getting you into this mess—"

"Oh, I love a little adventure now and then," she said in her most sarcastic tone.

I heard a bitterness within the sarcasm. I'd hurt her, I knew, with my affections for Sylvia. "Sorry." I said it again just because I knew I'd trounced on her at some point, be it with the kiss, or simply by showing up with another woman, comatose or not.

She didn't respond to the second apology.

The first incline and curve approached. "Easy. Remember the angle of the road on this first incline—"

"I know what I'm doing." Anger still apparent in her tone. After a moment she sighed. "Sorry," she said, realizing her jealous feelings were overriding her common sense. She lifted off the accelerator, and looked into the rearview. The BGCs were gone.

"I know."

"You don't know shit," Dean said with a friendlier laugh.

"I know," I said again, just to pester her.

She glanced at me with that quirky smile of hers, which consisted of the left corner of her mouth rising. A look I was very familiar with, for she used it whenever she didn't believe what I was saying. I gave her the tongue.

She laughed.

I breathed a sigh of relief, for I didn't want to lose this woman's friendship, or her love.

I went to my work, and she to her driving, without speaking for an hour. That was how it was.

"They're heading towards Moscow, by Russian MAC," I told Dean, once JD responded.

She only nodded, but made no comment, not really feeling like talking about the competition. And competition Sylvia was, for though she'd let go of Cort, there was always the unsaid hope that once he got all the P and V out of him he'd come back to her, and they'd settle down. But it had to be his choice, not something she forced upon him. Her secret had been kept for just that purpose, because if he knew, he might give up his dreams, and maybe the world would be far worse off without him. She wanted to say something, but didn't quite know which way, or from whom. A friend, a lover ... or a mother?

"Is Budapest far enough?"

"Plenty."

"She's very young, Cort?" she said.

"And she's somehow connected to the Russians, except she spoke perfect English. A perfect American accent? Oh, I've been thinking about the ramifications for a while, Dee. But I gave her my word—"

"And sealed it with a kiss?" Dean looked at me sideways, then readjusted her gaze to the road. "You know she has deep feelings for you, but?" She said no more.

But. The big question. I'd gone through every 'but' in the world; but she's young...; but she's just come out of a coma...; but she could be married...; but she may be suffering from the survivor rescuer attachment syndrome...; but she could be royalty...; but she could be a covert agent for the big red machine. This latter 'but' was becoming more solidified as time passed, what with BCGs and charter airplanes to Moscow.

We entered Budapest, with its smells and small alleyways, its brown and white faces (and every color in between), its pedestrian crowds gawking at the dusty black BMW, unable to see beyond the black-tinted windows. These were the friendliest or at least most hospitable people in the region, where hunger and thirst could be easily quenched with little or no money, if you were weary travellers needing such sustenance. Dusty-faced children searched pockets, in their frenzied greeting of strangers, but never took much, unless you allowed them to. Beyond these mundane beings were the rocket-shaped minarets and domes of mosques dotting the skyline. I imagined the hundreds of thousands preparing for *Maghrid*, literally, to prostate oneself in worship. Sewage scents crept in through the A/C, and carried with it the potent reminder that Hungary was an old country that still hadn't caught up with the rest of the world. But they were trying, and two French and Spanish companies had been contracted to build waste management facilities, though they'd need four to meet the bulging populace. Much like other Balkan capitals, where the hunted had fled during the wars. As we drove down the darkened lane food vendors of all sorts were involved in heated haggling, usually over a stick of lamb fry, lamb stew, or a glass of tea. But as I looked around and the city and its sights enveloped me, I realized Sylvia was gone. They could have killed her.

Dean was again silent, concentrating on making the drive without killing any of the pedestrians, and keeping her speed down until she found a three-wheeled cabby to race behind.

"Has it been that long?" I wondered aloud, looking above to the facade of our favorite hotel, El Barak. It was just outside the business district, and always clean. It had room services that were the best in all of Hungary, maybe the world, me and Dean had agreed once, a very long time ago. The five star hotels would be hard-pressed to meet what this 1200-year-old hotel delivered; taste and history; a sense of resting your head where many great people had so done; and the continuing evolution of a family-owned business.

"I wonder if Ali will remember us," Dean hoped aloud. Her mind was on them, their past, her decision to stop risking her life. How she loved being with him, sharing his excitement, pressing and passing the boundaries, all for the good. Who said doing good was boring? If only he knew why she'd really left, she thought with a sad smile. Her hospital monotony was certainly filled with risks, and even excitement, but it was always with someone else's life or limb, it certainly wasn't comparable to their challenges within the war zones, which Cort frequented as naturally as a summer traveller a beach or lake. Maybe she'd become desensitized to the medical tests she encountered daily, or needed a break from the hospital, with all its security. Maybe she was having a midlife crisis, or early menopause, Dean wondered with a sarcastic smirk.

"What's on your mind?"

He always knew when I was in inner turmoil, Dean thought before answering. "Memories and stuff...."

"Good ones, I hope?"

"And some bad ones...."

"Not the mother?"

She sighed, having long tried to purge that memory from her brain. The mother; a woman who'd walked a thousand miles with her baby, escaping and hiding from the murderous Musabbi tribe, who were killing anyone not directly linked to their peoples. The sun's anvil had pressed down upon her purple skin, as she hid her child under her wrap. She'd crossed the Kalahari Desert with no water, no shoes, wearing nothing but a wrap, with her child tucked beneath it. They came across her body with fresh pink scars. Slices and tears, and a variety of other injuries she must have endured before entering the desert, for they were baked shut. Vultures had congregated above, which had attracted our attention from Gaborone (South Africa). Beneath her body, resting upon knees and shoulders, her form in death still protected the little baby girl. Still alive, still smiling, the last meal still fresh upon her little lips. It was Dean who'd cried, both happy and sad tears, for to lose such a woman as this was a great loss to humanity. A mother who would give so much, even to the end.

"How is Kala?" I asked. We'd given her the name that best suited her mother's trek across the Kalahari.

"She's doing great. Smart. Won't give up no matter how hard it is."

"There's a spot." I pointed to a lucky hole behind the hotel, and Dean angled the beast around and backed into it. "That's good to hear." I was glad to hear Kala had survived, and would have a chance to succeed. Unlike many Africans who were born into poverty and war. The opportunities were slim. Life expectancy was the lowest in the world. And quarrels over tradition, religion, power, and the greed of a few often blossomed into genocide.

"Right below our room?" she said, looking up at the third-floor window.

"Nice shot."

"Thank you," she said in her best Hungarian.

"Okay, I'll carry the bags and you do the talking?"

"I'm a bit rusty, and you've always been better—"

"Go for it. You know how Ali loves to hear your voice."

I laughed, and felt somewhat lighter than before, as if being surrounded by humanity had taken the edge off of losing Sylvia. Had I attached too much hope in that skinny little blonde, whose biting wit and sarcasm irked me to no end? Maybe it was the loss of my own blood that had affected my thinking, and she was indeed a Russian spymaster, or the pawn of one? I'd pissed off plenty of their splinter allies in my brief history on this planet so that they could have put a contract out on me. But only the Minister and Henri would have had the foreknowledge to have set up such a fraud. And Sylvia had gone off with Henri. And come back safely. However, why had the Russians taken her, like some expensive state jewel? One chance I hadn't thought of, and that was the possibility that she herself could be an enemy of theirs, or possessed some valuable information. But worth the trouble of military aircraft and a team of covert agents? After thinking too much I didn't feel as light.

Our old room was available, and it still had the fire escape, which went right down to the rear parking lot. Inside, nothing had changed, save for new curtains and bed covers. The same frankincense smells lingered, and two jasmine-scented candles burned in the wall alcoves that were a necessity to mask the sewage odors. It was a square room, with a tiny bathroom set off to the side, furthest from the bed.

"Some things never change, eh?" Dean said wistfully. "Even the incense is the same."

I set our bags down. "Wonder where Ali's at?"

"Don't know, but I'll call down and see if we can't get some dinner up here, and you can set up your little command center, as usual."

She knew me well. "Yeah, great," I answered reflexively, and continued unpacking my equipment, and affixing the satcom systems. What I wanted most was the satellite photos of Sylvia's journey, and her current residence, and, if possible, her. Dean disappeared, but I didn't realize this, for all the attention I was giving to the tracking program, and the photos. JD had activated the same digital signal tracking satellite function that tracks a personal beacon like the one inside my body. When visual or thermal tracking was lost, signal tracking could continue. At that moment Sylvia was inside Moscow, and although it could pinpoint her to the exact room, or place, it was dangerous to do so, and JD knew better. It would alert the Russians that someone was looking for someone, possibly her—if she was the only action in town. The passive sonar was virtually undetectable, but also not that site specific, however, like a submarine, the satellite could "ping" the beacon—only in emergencies—that would in turn give off five strong bursts of radio pulse waves that would enable the satellite to pinpoint the person. The downfall was that once the beacon was used, it shortly thereafter lost power. This was why it was important to follow her visually by satellite, or ground resources, as far as possible. I guessed Sylvia was in the Intelligence Services building, being debriefed. The new Lubyanka.

Conflicting feelings wanted her to be a Russian agent, because the debriefing would be much easier on her, even though this meant that somehow she was involved with the Russians, dealing in the secrets and double dealings and unspeakable matters involved in being a spy. But for her safety and health, I swayed to the hope that she was somehow friendly to their side. It didn't mean that Russia was bad, but they'd still found themselves unable to pull out of the corruption of the old communist government, and the aftereffects of the change.

When democracy was shoved down the USSR's throat, it brought into the new Russia one-time opportunities for thieves and entrepreneurs. Banks who held government monies used those same funds to buy State properties and businesses, while other upper-class citizens, and even non-Russians, bought up State lands and properties for fractions of their actual value. The change had been done without changing the Russian judicial system, at least to the extent that it would stop monopolization and the consequential price gouging, which in turn forced the citizens to pay outrageous taxes, and exorbitant prices for food, warmth, and hygiene. Without the uncorrupted judicial system, and with no regulatory laws or enforcement bodies, there could be no working democracy within which all could prosper. Instead, classism took root, with criminality. Unions were trying to have a positive effect, but many corporations were either owned, or involved with the Russian mob, and sent out hitmen to take care of any union leaders. But because the poverty was so great, versus the individual wealth of the few, these strikes by the many were the only way to bring the bosses to the table. Without workers there is no product, and without product there's no business. I had to give them their due; many were trying, but it was still a long way from being a democratic society.

A few horns bleeped outside; they bleep in Hungary. The night took over the sky, and shadows deepened. Budapest came alive at night, with outside cafes that could seat a whole neighborhood, and oftentimes did. People laughed and talked freely, and I remembered me and Dean used to take tea and sweet breads just a few hundred meters away from the hotel. There was no classism to be found here, in those familial night spots, where anyone with a working knowledge of Hungarian, or just a smile, was welcome. Indeed, all manners of speakers were welcome, and most Hungarians understood English well enough, though it was actually rare that outsiders found these cozy cafes where locals gathered before settling for the night.

Dean brought two brown bags, filled with bowls of rice, stew, meat, and a roll of freshly baked black bread.

"Room Service!" Her smile faded when she saw Cort packing his travel pack, a smaller lightweight alloy framed backpackers pack, which could be used as a tent as well, she remembered. He didn't look up or acknowledge the food, or her, for that matter, and she thought, *I must be jealous, because I'm a little upset at how much time you're spending on that little girl.* I had narrowed the radiation trails to two definite targets, and twelve other possibilities, where the bombs and warheads could've been taken. JD was putting all resources into the lookdown satellite surveillance, using proximation course headings to catch up with the terrorists, or whoever they were. I wasn't going to bite the bait Henri or the Minister had given me.

"Chow time!" Dean shouted.

"What was that about, Dee?" I wondered, looking at her strangely.

"You're not listening, and I'm hungry and won't eat alone on our first night out in years."

I noticed something in her eyes, which were greener, or seemed so because of the white blouse she wore. Was it sadness I saw? Had I caused it?

"What's going on?" I washed my hands at the small alcove sink. The running water still came from the huge tank atop the roof, as it had a thousand years ago. Only now it was covered to keep the polluted air from contaminating it.

Dean thought about it while she set out the contents of the bags on the table. "I guess I just think you're devoting too many of your resources to a girl you hardly even know, and who might even be a Soviet spy." She fidgeted with the customary ceramic dunking bowls, then set the steaming miniature pots of hot food on the wooden table.

I knew what she was saying, and it was far from what she actually said. My heart was heavy with the realization, and the conflict it created in me. "We agreed to be friends, Dean, because you wanted to settle down and not get killed." I dried my hands. "Remember, I'm a walking war zone? And you were right, too."

"What did you expect of her?" The last was a slight, though officially only a pronoun. "To sweep her off her feet and take her with you into your battles?" She snapped off the caps on two beers. "She's a fragile little creature. Pretty, but glass. She'll break."

I came up behind her, and put my arms around her, feeling her muscles resist, then relax. I kissed her cheek, then the corner of her angry mouth. "I love you too, but I can take care of myself."

She was frustrated, but wooed by his heat, his hug, into silence, even though he hadn't grasped what she'd been trying to say. She sighed. "Come on, let's eat then, before you go off on one of your adventures."

"Ah, my favorite. By the way, my leg feels great. Thanks, Doc." But I hadn't grasped what she was saying. I am a man, after all.

"You're welcome, though I'd still like to see you in that cast for a few days."

"I bet you would!" I was referring to last night, though I still wasn't quite sure if we did, or didn't, though it really didn't matter. "Should I check this for sleeping powders or aphrodisiacs?"

"No, you were quite good enough last night, though I wouldn't mind a more willing subject...." Her catty green eyes gleamed.

The lamb was tender, and the oily stew was mouth watering, full of paprika and spices, which would affix and soak the black bread, softening its natural tendency to be coarse and grainy. The Hungarian beer was lacking, but it was deliciously cold, and perfectly matched their meal. Alexander the Great, and many other notables, had eaten this same meal centuries ago. Thanks to Ali's family, and to the lack of change in the culture of Hungary, it remained simple, easy, and scrumptious.

My mouth enjoyed the food, and the memories Dean orated through the meal fed my mind. We'd had a great eight years together, and I still loved her. After all, our friendship was more of an umbilically connected partnership. But I'd cut off hopes of having Dean, of possessing her, as a man does a woman in marriage. Not physically or emotionally, but that willing and unbreakable chain that two people attach to each other, physically and emotionally. I am yours, you are mine; that willing possession. And the realization that I could not have Dean was a long time getting over, a heartbreaking experience that nearly destroyed my friendliness towards her. The only thing that saved us was the fact that she knew my thoughts, and had always kept contact, except for that year, about three years ago. Could I risk that type of pain again? I wasn't sure. After a while those feelings of loss left me. She took a year hiatus from me, during which I adjusted to her missing presence. But there in the hotel her jealousy was attractive; a cool-headed and beautiful doctor who got mad at the passing of a pretty girl. I could not see her wanting me back, not now, after 3 years of separation, after getting over the year of silence and absolute rejection. Yet, with each description, of each small memory, I perceived sadness in her tone. And her descriptions of our lovemaking—places, times, positions, and hemispheres, were said with a wistful voice that touched me, and made me realize something. I could love her again like that.

She couldn't look up at him, couldn't stand to see the feelings shut down, and knowing she'd been the cause of it when she'd backed out of his proposal years ago. *And for what,* Dean asked herself, *to go have his child in secret.* Still, she hadn't told him, hadn't even hinted at it. Why? She'd known what she'd be giving up in letting him sew his oats, but had somehow thought to possess him, as he had sought to possess her. Now she saw her mistake; distance. He was a man, and needed a woman's touch, as much as her presence. Unlike women, men were visual creatures, and tactile, needing to see, hold, or play with their possessions, be they material goods or women. Her absence from his sphere had forced him to seek out the attentions of others, and had closed down his feelings of love for her. Maybe after this mission she could lay her heart on the line, put her head on the chopping block, and reveal her needs to him. Her need to share with him the joy of parenthood. Her ache to be, to go with him, wherever it might lead.

"Remember the cabby?"

"The one who stole the suitcase that was actually a bomb planted by his own boss to get us—"

"—and ended up getting the boss and the thief!" I laughed at the memory, made seven years ago. "That was great."

"That was God watching over you," she said seriously, knowing my feelings towards man's dogmas.

"And you too. The timing was perfect." I smiled, and drank the rest of my beer.

She sipped her beer, smiling at the memory of the huge fireball that lit up the skyline of Hue, Vietnam. "That was great."

We sat in silence for a while, until she got up and went over to the window, a tear in her eye, which didn't go unnoticed. I stepped in behind her, placing my chin upon her head like I used to. We looked out through the opaque silk curtains that whispered with the breeze.

"I've always loved you, Dee, but you chose, no, we both chose our careers." She gripped my hands to her breasts.

"I know. I'm having second thoughts, Cort. I need you, and—" She coughed.

Something pushed her backwards, into me, as if a ghost had placed his arms on her shoulders and shoved.

"What's the matter, Dee?" Blood! Too much crimson ran down the front of her blouse, and I knew what had happened, and why. I pulled her out of the line of sight, away from the open window.

Sniper! Sniper! "Dee! Hang on, baby. Cort's gonna get you some help."

But she was smiling sadly, as if she knew this day would come, and had accepted it already. She shook her head. Her legs were already gone, numb, and she could feel the cold tide creeping up her torso. As a doctor, she knew the wound, knew its course. Had she been on an operating table when she was shot there would've been only a 50/50 chance of her surviving, even with a dozen staff, and one of the best surgeons. And there was no place in all of Hungary, that she knew of, where the best of the best could give it a go. She knew without knowing that she'd been shot, into one of her main veins, maybe even the heart itself. It came up to her stomach, and she knew firsthand what patients meant when they said they felt cold.

"I'm dead, Cor—" she told him, savoring the warmth of the blood on her tongue. Coppery. She couldn't hear her own voice, but she saw his look of fright, and it caused her to smile, for it told her his true feelings. "I love you.... Take care of Karl, and ... forgive me for not telling you."

"Forgive? There's nothin to forgive, Dee, just hang on and we'll get you to a hospital." I'd sent the emergency signal to JD, by pressing the help button on the side of the MPG. It gave my location. I typed the seriousness of the injury, and, in this case, who'd been injured.

I hoped there were friends in the area, doctors preferably, who could get here in time. There was too much blood.

What was this? Absolution? Who was this Karl character that she wanted me to take care of? Come on, Dee, talk to me, love. Keep talking, baby—"

Her face, pale, went gray, and her usually sparkling eyes went flat. I saw life leaving. She was right. She was always right. Damn her! Her hand, already in mine, squeezed an SOS. What was she smiling about, I wondered, as hot tears ran down my cheeks. My gut was afire, filled with the rage and anger of vengeance, yet cooled by the guilt. That bullet had been meant for me, I knew. I also had an idea who did this, and they would pay. They would pay.

I typed in a photo recon request for JD, and informed him that Dean was dead. Then I held my friend for a while, pondering what may have been, and what she'd meant. What life could be like without her.

– CHAPTER 15 –

THE QUEEN IS DEAD! THE QUEEN IS DEAD! My friend, gone. People came and went, while I slumped in my darkened corner of the hotel room. Then they were gone. Nobody had spoken to me, as if I was contaminated, or frightful. Where was the remnants of Dean, the blood, the beautiful face that even death's repose could not dispel? Had they taken away everything? Were they so accustomed to be so fastidiously adept in cleaning up murder? I had to get to work, to push myself up and out of this wooden comfort chair, and put my nose above the waters. Breathe. Breathe. Then find those cold-blooded bastards. I found myself dominated by thoughts that would not redeem a peacemaker, or dogooder.

A knock at the door disturbed my packing. Oh yes, I'd been thinking about how a sniper knew which room we were in, and had come to one of two conclusions; a rat. I'd also thought about Henri's opportunity to plant a device, but my watch would've have instantly detected it on my person, or on Dean's.

"Who is it?"

"Ali, sirrah Falcon, with much grief...." A muffled sniffle crept past the thick wood door.

"Go away, Ali, it's not safe." I didn't want to see him or anybody else for that matter.

The door opened, and Ali's eyes were red and watery. In his right hand was the master key, in his other a bottle of honey-flavored grappa. His eyes widened.

"You shouldn't have come, Ali." I pointed Henri's gun at his face, my finger on the trigger. It would be nothing to squeeze the trigger, but was Ali the rat. Would this fifty-five-year-old brown-skinned and battle-hardened man give up two of his friends? Were we his friends? I wondered. Was there some sort of situational ethos that I wasn't aware of? I refused to believe, but my mind cried for vengeance.

"You would be justified to pull the trigger, my friend. I apologize." He turned his head to the side. "Bring him in!" he barked in unintelligible Hungarian, laced with vitriolic curses, and spitting.

PROCESS OF ILLUMINATION

"What gives, Ali?"

"I come to conclusion that one of my household has spoken to strangers about you for money, and I believe—" A man was dragged in through the door, his hands crudely tied behind his back, a gag tightly fixed in his mouth. He wore a dirty sheet, tied at his waist and pulled down so that his skinny upper torso was bared. He was thirty-five, maybe five feet two, and scared to death "—my son, what blasphemy, has killed our friend, Madam Van Clus." The two men—also Ali's sons—held the betrayer by his arms, while Ali slapped the man's face around, then yanked off the gag.

I noticed the tracks first; marks of a heroin addict. This man couldn't have pulled the trigger, my barely in control thinking side told my vengeful side. But maybe he knew the person who did.

"You may shoot him, if you think it just." He couldn't hide the shame in his voice, for ever having fathered a creature such as this.

"I would like to know who he talked to, and how much heroin he got, and from whom!"

Ali bowed his head, deferring to my request, almost sighing in relief that I hadn't squeezed the trigger. Ali slapped the face of his son and spoke harshly, giving the traitor no room for bartering or holding back.

My arm hung at my side, the gun ready, as I watched and listened, suspicious of everything. I didn't think it was a ruse, for all the slapping the man took, and genuine tears he cried. I watched the two brothers, and wondered how they could be so cold to their own brother. Then again, I'd seen worse when it came to betrayal, or disgrace to the family name.

"He says a man with a scar?" Ali gestured with a finger, running it across the right eye socket. "On cheek and eyebrow, very thin. This goat say also that he receive one ounce of heroin?" He slapped and cursed his son again, then turned back to me. "How did you know?"

"Have you been missing money? Complaints of money missing? Thefts?"

Ali rubbed his bearded chin, then barked at the shamed son, whose eyes went wide with fear.

"Is he your accountant, Ali?" I asked.

"Yes. I shall have my wife do it as she has done before, and if he has stolen from the family, or further disgraced our family name, we shall deal with him."

"His arms, Ali. Those are the track marks of a junkie." I saw realization come over his face.

"He said one other odd. The man wear a glove on right hand?"

An icy stalactite shot down my spine. Boris! It couldn't be. Nobody with that kind of money wanted to kill me that bad. Boris charged two million dollars a target, and never failed. I'd only heard of the assassin but it could be no doubt, not with the glove and the scar.

Boris Valin was a hired hitman, who'd defected from the Russian Spetsnaz, and went on a reign of terror in Chechenya. His last known target had been the President of Uruguay, just a year ago. Me and JD kept a file on the man, as best we could. The Uruguan President, Francisco Padilla, had been murdered over his stance against drugs. For someone to pay two million dollars, it had to be treated like an investment. A business decision. I knew Boris had worked for the KGB, and other State-sponsored secret entities. He had no country or credo, just a two-million-dollar price tag and a 100% guarantee.

Was he out there now? Or did he see my silhouette fall? "Oh, Dean?" I whispered to myself, while putting on bulletproof clothes. "Maybe I should've killed Henri?" *And be a cold blooded killer,* my silent voice mocked me.

I unflapped my sleeve, and typed the following message to JD; "FLASH! BORIS IS AFTER ME. NEED INSTANT RECON PHOTO. NEED BORIS FILE. CHECK PERSONAL FILES, AUTHORIZATION ZEBRA FIFTY DELTA ECHO ALPHA." I pressed the send button, and the message was sent up into the sky a hundred and thirty miles, bounced off a satellite and routed along an electronic highway to JD's home in Virginia.

I felt the vibration on my arm, which signaled the incoming message. "SORRY, BOSS. SHE WAS THE QUEEN. TAKE CARE OF YOU. I'LL TAKE CARE OF BIZ. PHOTO RECON DATA COMING UP. DO NOTHING STUPID."

He knew me too well. I smiled. "THANKS. ALSO. CHECK FOR KARL IN RELATION TO THE QUEEN. NOT URGENT, BUT IMPORTANT. I'LL TRY TO BE SMART."

I watched as lookdown photos were printed out, near the time of the shooting, and knew it was no good. The buildings were too close, too hot. I saw the hotel's lighted sign, but everything else was dark. I used the magnifying glass to look at shadowed faces, but all I got were the tops of people's heads.

But I knew that; lookdown photos were only good for the tops of heads, unless they had a good angle.

"Damn!" I cursed to myself. This was a waste of time. But I looked at all of the photos, and even a distorted side view.

The last photo to be printed was one of a brown stone building in Moscow, which I knew very well, having rescued an American from that very same building. It was the converted KGB headquarters. A prison, torture, and execution area, respective of the offices on the top floors. The prison was in the basement, and if one looked closely, small six-inch slots could be seen, where once were the tops of tiny windows. But they'd long since been welded over to protect the dark secrets. In the center of the large building were the interrogation areas. There were two kinds of interrogations; ones that ended in death, and the other that left you scared but friendly. There were also two areas for interrogations, which also depended on who you were. If you were cooperative, you were interrogated by an intelligence officer. If he caught you in a lie, then you could be subjected to the other venue, which included physical and psychological torture. This ranged from long-term solitary confinement to pulling fingernails out to electrocution to other much worse happenings. Must I go on? Let me just say that the Russians have nothing on the Chinese when it comes to torture and interrogation techniques.

Sylvia was there. And I only hoped, for her sake, that she was a friendly in their eyes. I would keep my promise. First, I had to get the nukes. Or at least find them, and point them out to certain authorities that could do something about them, or retrieve them. By force, if necessary, before any bombs were put into irretrievable positions of imminent threat, for once planted, the bomb, or bombs, could be detonated by remote. Most likely a simple cellular connection, which the government couldn't shut down, or jam. Dial a number, blow up a city.

I needed bodies! More resources. If only I could rally the greens (environmentalists) and peaches (humanitarians) to come and assist me, but that would be impossible. There were secrecy elements. Even if I wouldn't dare print a story that nukes were now in terrorist hands somewhere on the European/Asian continents, there was always some idiot that would. A panic would ensue, and more people would die. JD had certainly alerted the CIA, and the NSA, and possibly his British contact, and maybe they were ahead of me, or just behind me. Either way, I just wanted to get this mission over with, and get Sylvia out of that pit. I'd lost too much already in losing Dean.

"Let's go then," I pumped myself up, picked up my bags, and Dean's single bag, and left our room. I looked at it one last time from the doorway, then left. Forever.

Outside the room, in the hallway, it was quiet. Hungarian time had it at one in the morning. Even though it was suspicious to be driving at this time of the evening, I'd rather risk questioning by the police, over a hit squad rushing my hotel room while I slept. I didn't know if Boris knew he missed, or not. I felt the hairs on the back of my neck tingle as I stepped onto the new elevator. Anyone expecting me to sneak out would be looking at the side door, not the front. I only hoped they didn't know the car.

I saw a woman at the hotel check in counter, but her face was behind the newspaper.

"My husband say it all clear. Go." The woman didn't move.

"Thank you."

She humphed a you're welcome, and kept on doing what she was doing. Nothing.

The small tinkle of the doorbells faded as I stepped into the Hungarian night. Government-bought incense burned at the corners, and filled the night with sweet airs. There were a few cars passing to and fro, and one old couple walking home after a night on the plaza with friends. I moved towards the side of the hotel, and spotted one of Ali's sons. He nodded.

I found the BMW unmolested, and pressed the alarm release button when I was twenty feet away. The car's horn beeped in response, instead of blowing up. Though the "special" alarm system would have blown the car up right when a contaminant had been placed, thereby blowing up whoever tried to attach it to the beast. Had someone tried to place a passive bomb, a bomb that used the vehicle's electrical system to detonate the explosive charges, then the car would blow up upon depressing the infrared alarm deactivation device I held in my hand. Before deactivating, the electrical system purged itself by running electricity through all systems. Had someone tried to place an active bomb, the horn would have beeped five times, which meant that someone with gloves or nonconductive material had touched the car.

Q would have been impressed.

Another touch of the deactivation device and the driver's side door unlocked for me. I put Dean's bag in the backseat, my pack with it, then got in. My head hit the steering wheel. I saw one of Dean's mittens on the floor, picked it up, and turned it inside out. I pressed it to my nose, smelling the scent of my friend, remembering her touch, her hands which had once filled that purple mitten. I felt the desolation of grief trying to wash over me like a thirty-foot wave.

"Stop it, Cort!"

I started the car, and for a momentary pause waited for it to blow up, always remembering that for every defense and detection device there was a gadget to get past it.

Me and Dean had had several of those moments, apprehensive in that split second, as we awaited the explosion. They flashed through my memory, lingering like a fog on a warm morning, as I put the beast into "drive" and cut out of the parking lot.

The stars were gone from this Hungarian sky, unlike so many years ago, when one could see even the dimmest twinkles, without the smog of industry trapping humanity's dreams on this fair planet of apes.

"Yeah, Dean, remember the nights atop the hotel, making love through the night, waking up to the sound of kids playing soccer in the streets below," I remembered fondly, wondering if Dean's ghost was haunting me, trying to ignore the vibration from my MPC. "Remember we promised each other that whoever died first would come back and give the other a message about the thereafter? So you still owe me, Doc." The sleepy city, stone and adobe buildings in this section, passed slowly by on each side of the beast, which was too big a car for a city like this. The buildings were so old that it was blasphemous for me to be driving through it without chariot, or at least a horse-drawn cart. Here and there water rained down into small alleys from upper floors, or from open drains that poked out of the exterior walls. In the newer buildings, all such waste and plumbing was concealed, behind the facades of newer architecture and materials. "Things are changing, baby," I whispered, not wanting to keep her from any place brighter than this world, if she was being called upon at that very moment, though she'd decline such a calling if she thought she could help me in any way, which added more weight to the scales that might judge her purity of heart. And I, the fool to let her go in the face of a pretty young blonde, who may or may not be a Russian spy. "I'm an idiot, Doc." My admission wasn't as sincere as I'd like it to be. But I didn't want to stop to examine my false voice, or its implications. "Sorry, Doc. Maybe we just moved on. I by accident, you—I guess you didn't, because you were too busy saving lives to have a social life.... Remember we used to say we were lucky to have each other cuz we were too busy saving the world to meet anyone else? I don't know if we ever saved the world, though, but maybe we did? Ah, Dean, I'm gonna let you go. I'll try to save the world." My laugh was choked with tears and snot. "Damn! Like a fuckin' baby, eh! Tough Cort Falcon! Bullshit!" I slid the window down and spat, then heard a buzzing noise.

A scooter had been following me from the moment I left the hotel, and I let it, keeping my speed slow enough for the little motorbike to keep up. That was my link, I guessed.

"Oh, one last note. I think Boris Valinkov got you, Doc, so it was a two-million-dollar bullet, and now I know he's out there." I smiled at that thought. "I'll get his ass, Dean, you can bet yours, if they have asses up there? Don't forget to give me a sign. Now go on."

I let her go, wiped my nose with her mitten, and brought most of my faculties back on line. I depressed the small A/C button (which normally slides left to right, if one wants A/C), and the speedometer slid to the left, and a small 5x5-inch screen appeared, with the scooter directly in view. On the rear bumper, in the right and left taillights, sat two cameras behind colored glass. I hoped the lenses were clean. The picture on the TV screen looked good, and I plugged my printer into the cigarette lighter, which doubled as a computer hookup to the beast's systems. I zoomed in, took a couple of stills, and noticed a discolored area near the man's throat. Like a tattoo? Or better yet, a microphone.

With my left hand at the ten o'clock position, I undid the forearm flap and punched in a quick message. "AM BEING FOLLOWED BY SCOOTER. SEEN A MIKE AT MAN'S THROAT. POSSIBLE TRACE TO LOCATION. MOVING EAST, SUBJECT APPROXIMATELY 50 METERS BACK." Because the beast had two transmitters emitting a crypted frequency, the car could be tracked by JD. It was also how I kept track of Dean, not in the spying or stalking sense, but in a friend watching over another friend manner.

The forearm pad buzzed again, undetectable to the ear, but felt on my arm. I checked the message.

"COLUMBIAN FREIGHTER SPOTTED ON BLACK SEA. POSSIBLE DESTINATION FOR NUKES. WILL RELAY INTEL AS FOLLOWS. I'M IN THE GAME. IGOR OUT."

"Right on, Igor!" I relayed the message to JD an instant latter. I ran the implications through my head. Columbians?

It was common knowledge, when it came to who was behind the "war on drugs." The United States of America. A forty-year failure, without seeing this future, thinking themselves superior—as many American politicians did—not realizing that like the Cold War there would be a downside. A threat unlike any terrorist organization, group, or even rogue country. It was predicted, quietly, by myself, that any war escalates, and so would this useless one. They should have seen this as the only way out for the drug lords, and those involved. The traffickers had their own army of guerrilla soldiers, who were the ones fighting against superior technology in the jungles of Central and South America. These guerrillas fought not for drugs, but to eat and support their families. It was such an exercise in jungle warfare that many countries sent their soldiers to train there. As if this were some sort of academy, which used live targets and preached a creed that rang hollow in the throats of those with the slightest trace of intelligence. War on drugs, indeed, had killed more men, women and children, than drugs ever did, or would.

As the drug lords were backed into a corner, running out of banks and places to launder their billions, they'd finally purchased the penultimate weapons. Nukes.

And they'd use it more readily than any other group in the world, even quicker than a terrorist organization. In fact, I would bet money on it that a U.S. city would be nuked just to show the bold U.S. politicians what they had. And it was the U.S. politicians that had snuck America into a mini Vietnam under the heading of "war on drugs." It was the politicians who kept speaking for Americans, and much of the world, to this supporting of the warmongers that needed war to keep their power base secure, to exort their might upon some tangible enemy, in a world that was scarce of easily identifiable foes. If these drug-trafficking bosses would bomb planes filled with innocents, shoot judges and prosecutors, families of police officers, they would indeed have no qualms about setting off a nuclear bomb in Boston, or even Manhattan. If this happened, America would be forced to make a Hobson's choice; risk millions of people's lives by escalating the war; or doing what it should have done some thirty-eight years ago and rehabilitate buyers/users. In the 1980s, after seeing that the "war on drugs" wasn't working, the politicians had a choice to rehabilitate; however, since police agencies around the United States had a lobbying voice and drug addicts and criminals didn't, it was an easy bribe.

The "war on drugs" was an industry, that involved a fat prison complex, weapon making industry, military industry, law enforcement industry, and several other industries needed for the continuous running of the war. And if you think the deaths of ten million people in one flash of a 20-megaton nuclear explosion in the middle of New York City at 12 noon is enough to wake the U.S. politicians up, you'd better think again. Remember the lies of Vietnam, and several other wars, where in the losing of wars American generals and politicians lobbied with warmonger rhetoric to allow them to throw more flesh upon the fire, only later realizing what a defeat truly was, and how stupid the war had been in the first place.

And that latter stupidity would be balked at by the wrinkled soldiers from an era gone by, when war had been necessary, but had now faded to a possibility only in the extreme, as with "Desert Storm" against Iraq, or the several small skirmishes, which the U.S. had lent its powerful right hand of military might to squash what its left hand had deemed foe.

What would they do in the face of millions dead? Would the folly of "wars" on drugs, crime, or whatever's the flavor of the month, finally be revealed for the propaganda that it is? Would "War on Aids" or "War on Hunger" or "War on Hate" or "War on Diseases" or "War on all that's Bad" finally take its rightful place as foe against humanity? What would the world do in the face of losing Paris, Rome, London, Moscow, or Hong Kong? Did we not unite to save Venice from the floods? Makes me want to give my forty percent worth of taxes to rehabilitation centers, to take away the buyers of these drugs, and therefore the market for sales. But I campaign for naught, only voice my opinion as I see things, as I've experienced the basest of experiments, or the consequences thereof, which many of you do not see, enshrouded in your backyard, biweekly salary, and what the local news tells you to believe. "Never happen to me," I picture the ignorant saying, while a drug dealer lives next-door with four million cash and a tunnel going under your house to the gas station down the street, where the drugs are loaded and unloaded. That same place where your children buy the candy and sodas on the way back from school.

Maybe it's a good thing that traumatic incidents don't occur often enough to keep the possibilities fresh in our minds. For we carry on, "MIB" style, not knowing and not wanting to know. Life is peaceful there in America, if you've the money to buy it, save for the shattering moments of cruel reality when a plane flies into a building, or a police chase ends with a child dead, before fingers can depress the channel change button. But ignorance cannot erase the half a century of tragedies since the U.S. of A. began its "war on drugs," and took the strike offensive, no matter the crumbling results that have only shown true that this war is a war upon the poor and middle classes, and upon minorities and foreigners. It was a war upon the farmers who grew the plants in the Americas and in Asia, whose only fault was being born into a weakened economy and oligarchic political system, which forced them—by necessity or threat— to grow crops that would provide food for their families and some semblance of civilized life. It was a war upon innocents as much as it was a war upon the drug lords, and for all the technology America possessed, it was odd that more innocents were injured or killed than drug lords caught or killed. Maybe it's a good thing the tragedies are downplayed, if they're even shown, which is rare, because people felt comforted by peace within their own backyard. Out of sight, out of mind.

My eyes tracked the motorbike as it suddenly stopped at a darkened tea and tobacco shop. There was nobody there, but the rider dismounted, went through a doorway, and pushed it open, and was gone from my sight. Something was up.

A horn brought my eyes back to the fore, and I saw my trouble bearing down upon me. A large garbage truck.

– CHAPTER 16 –

THE BEAST WAS NO MATCH for the truck, and there was no room to outmaneuver it. I pulled on the wheel and shot down a littered alleyway that during the day would have been clogged with people and vendors. How did I know the truck was part of some setup, one may ask, but it is only a matter of intelligence and coincidence; this latter a circumstance I always view as suspect upon finding myself in the face of; the former intel is a matter of knowing how a city breathes, how its heart pumps, which is free knowledge gotten by asking the city comptrollers or a local.

Upon entering any main city I tap into the kilobites of information, which JD keeps updated, and find out when trash is picked up, among other things. Needless to say, a garbage truck that size was not used in this part of the city, and was in fact, according to the city code, banned by its weight alone from travelling in this area of Budapest. Besides, garbage trucks without garbage men were suspicious.

The alley was very slender, and I felt like a fat mouse in a skinny snake, wondering when I would begin to bulge out into the brick and rock walls. An opening to the left appeared, and I took it, accelerated, spinning the wheels to make the turn radius, which otherwise could not have been made. I was parallel to the garbage truck. I shot past an opening, and had time to press the satdirect button, which showed me the streets, alleys, and unmarked pathways on the little screen above the radio. It was more than a radio, since it contained a telecommunication device, as well as secret frequency links. One could, if necessary, talk to someone on the other side of the world. The downfall was that any old satellite could pick up the signal and track it to the beast. I looked briefly at the screen, which showed thick, zigzag, and thin lines, each representing the byways aforementioned.

"Voice recognition?"

"Alpha code twenty two softly." I remembered her name.

"Yes, Cort?" the computer asked, remembering me as well.

"Ha! You still work!" I said, bemused.

"Yes, my lord. How may I serve you?"

I couldn't help bursting out laughing at that, followed by a hollow feeling of grief as I looked to the seat where Dean had once sat. It had been her idea to program it to say 'lord' and 'lady' every other time it responded.

"Destination Ruse Varna, Bulgaria. Avoid Yugoslavia".

Less than two seconds later two thicker lines appeared on the screen, and showed separate routes to the port city on the Black Sea. I wondered if the NSA or CIA already had men there, as they did in most countries. One good spy is worth more than an entire army, an old Chinese man said. How right he was.

"Thank you."

"You are welcome, my lord."

I smiled, and tried to figure if the Minister had the technology to track me via satellite, or whether Boris the assassin was using it to track me.

"Voice recognition?"

"Yes, Cort?"

"Are we being tracked?"

"Yes, my lord."

Shit! Why wasn't the detection device blinking? "Where is the signal coming from?"

If it was coming from the ground I could evade it, but if it was a sattrack, I couldn't.

"A signal is being bounced off of the rear bumper, and up to a tracking satellite, Cort."

I slammed on the brakes. Satellites tracked hoods and flat surfaces, not cear bumpers, unless there was a device! I ran to the bumper, leaving the car running. I didn't like how the walls closed in on me and the big BMW, but at least there was no immediate threat that I could see. I found the patch with the flashlight; a half inch sliver of tape with a solar-powered transmitter embedded in it. If they'd known the color of the car it would've been more difficult to find. How it went undetected by the beast's sensors I did not know, but it had, and that worried me. If the motion, heat, and emanation detectors weren't working properly it placed me in danger, for car bombs were famously popular amongst my cruder enemies. It could have been placed while the car was moving, when the sensors were dampened. In fact, that was the only way, unless someone were wearing an invisible man suit that didn't emenate heat or electrical pulses of any kind. It had to be attached while I was moving, because JD's little miracles were never topped. At least, not until now.

Back in the vehicle I took numerous pictures of the patch with the digital camera, and saw an early morning taxi driver getting ready to go to work. Perfect. Yet I was too aware that even then I was being tracked. It was a tight squeeze, which suited my purpose, as I rolled down the window and aimed for a clean spot of paint on the cab. I slowed to a near stop, with the cabby on the other side of the car, and stretched my arm out and pressed the sticky-tape onto the back trunk lid of the cab. I waved at the cabby and smiled, then rolled up the window and turned left on the first side street wide enough to handle the beast.

"Voice recognition?"

"Yes, my lord?"

"Is there another tracking device emanating from you?"

"None leaving the vehicle except my own, Cort."

"Please inform me if one should pop up."

"Yes, my lord."

"Thanks."

"You're very welcome, my lord."

Something sarcastic in that voice tugged upon the synaptic tendrils of my memory, like a whisper in the dark, an intuitive assertion that the VR voice had changed. I knew Dean was not a techno junky, but she was very capable of programming a computer, or rigging a comlink, for I had taught her those things myself.

But first I had to make choices, and I did. The route would take me to Timisoara, Romania, over the baby Carpathians, then on to Bucharest, then across the Danube, and down to the Black Sea port city of Ruse Varna. In the meantime I would let my support services track down the targets of interest, including Sylvia, among others you have heretofore been informed of.

I thought about Igor, now that the Russian assassin was imposing upon my life, much like a dung beetle rolls its ball of nutrients, pushing, pushing, taking paths of least resistance until the monumental task, of which I hoped to prove myself thus, was accomplished; Igor had helped compile the file on Boris. He was one of three who knew about it. I recalled the Boris file, in which there were dates, targets, weapons used, manners of approach, methods of egress, and resources needed to accomplish all of the above. Assassin number 1; the two-million-dollar man. He was very wealthy, I'd heard.

Two hours later I sighed over the unguarded border of Romania, making good time, figuring on four more hours of mountain roads ahead.

"Cort?" Dean's voice echoed in the silence of the car, scaring the shit outta me, until I realized it was coming from the VR speaker.

"Yes, it's me?"

"Please say the password we agreed on in nineteen ninety-seven, if ever we were separated."

What the hell was she talking about? I wondered, then remembered as the year unfolded. "Dino—do."

"Good enough. I guess I've been killed or injured?"

"Yeah, you guessed it right, Doc." I whispered. I knew it.

"Then we gotta talk, because if I haven't told you about Karl, then I have to make my confession and hope you can forgive me. Will you forgive me? I hope so. I don't know why I did it, but I felt you were just too bright burning to put a stop to you, or placing an extra burden on you with my—our problem."

"Well, come out with it," I muttered to myself, as the green pastures turned into jagged rocks with jutting pines rising from the earthy tones. For a moment I thought the program had been seized by an electronic hiccup, until I found that it was Dean's breathing I heard, not my own. How I wished for a time machine to take me back to the moment when she'd made this tape. To a point where I could rearrange the series of events in time to save her life, even if it meant giving my own, fully aware of the master plan He who is had for all of us; though sometimes I question His presence, for what creator would snuff Dean's life, greedily taking such a gift from this world into the skies above? Such cruelty to leave us below without her delicate surgeon's hands and fixated goal of saving those whom He who is may have deemed prudent to be in suffering, and therefore in need of Dean's hands and heart. Now what would they do, I pondered, and committed mental ablutions to He who is for any slight I may have made to His end designs upon our little world. Not the first time for that.

She spoke finally, her words curved with the roads, winding back through valleys of reason, disappearing in short tunnels laced with the darkness of guilt, but always with a pure quality, which did not upset or mire me in questions as to her love. Up we went as she explained and explained, and her tears flowed like snow melt streams, coming down, sometimes like glass, sometimes a torrent of white bubbles, fast and thin, slow and powerful. She moved, as did I, until finally reaching the peak of her explanation, and as if we'd hiked the peak together, we both, one dead, and one alive yet dying, were exhausted from the climb.

"—Karl is your son, born October 11, the year after I left you to return to work in Austria. He is named after my father, and bears your last name. When I made this he was three years old, and soon will need his father, though my mother and father have done great. Please do not take him from them, though I know you wouldn't do that. I have set aside some personal videos, I hope they've been kept up to date. They are in a case, in the secret backseat compartment. I hope you will enjoy them as much as I do. I'm sorry,

Cort. I love you with all my heart, loved you, and am even now thinking of telling you, for I know you'd make the best father in the whole world. I could not have Karl be the reason you stopped taking risks. I know your love of the game, which is not really a game. Who knows, maybe in a couple decades Karl will take after you, and you'll know what I'm feeling now, even as you are in China and haven't contacted anybody." She paused for a moment. "I think in a few years I might join your dangerous entourage, if you'd accept me back. The boredom of my safety is killing me. I think you corrupted my alpha waves, which now require serious adrenalin rushes, and the danger to produce them. But if you're listening to this you've either stolen my car, or I have rejoined you and I am dead or seriously injured. I leave you and Karl Falcon my properties, and the beast, or my BMW. A copy of this tape has been left with the family lawyer, so you'll get a copy of this and more tapes of Karl's youth, no matter what. So, my love, only you and my parents, and the doctor who signed the birth certificate, know that Karl is your son. If for reasons unknown to me you'd rather keep it that way, then I accede to your judgment, as always. If I have died in your arms, in some foreign country, on some adventure, all would be right with me. I mean it, Cort. Don't beat yourself up over it—"

"—Shit happens," we said in unison. The words hearkened memories of telling Dean the same thing, after she'd lost a patient on a table in the middle of the Congo, in sweltering heat, with mosquito netting as our trauma room. Shit happens, I'd told her, just like she was telling me.

"So this is good-bye, Cort. My life is most enjoyed when I spend it in your dangerous sphere. I just want you to know that. I love you. Maybe we'll listen to this together in thirty years or so, but it was a relief to put this on tape. Good-bye lover, and don't do anything stupid...."

The car pulled over as if of its own accord, and I got out. I don't know for how long, and told myself I didn't care if these few moments might be risking millions of lives. For a while my voice echoed in these craggy valleys, and sometime later I got back in the car, thankful that her voice was no longer heard, alive and playful, but to me a rusty and barbed knife upon an open wound.

A father? A FATHER! The joy of it assuaged my grieving, yet also acted to enhance it to an unbearable point, for there was no Dean to share it with. Why hadn't I picked up the signs? Or had they been there, but I, being so tunnel-visioned, could not pick up the hints? I recalled that she had begun to glow, like a woman with child, though hindsight is a prophet's paradise. I had noticed a change in Cairo, but had thought that she was just fed up with me, though she surprised me with her proposal, not just for marriage, but to give up the life.

I reached back and touched the secret latch. Ah, the HK 97 was still there, fully loaded, disguised as apart of the frame and cushions. There were the discs, small videodiscs that recorded images clearly and digitally, which would also play on the beast's video system.

With a lump in my throat I pushed the first disc into the CD player, and pressed the red video "on" button. I put the car in gear, and drove slowly, looking at the tiny screen, listening to my boy and his grandparents' exchange in Austrian, pondering, smiling, mourning, and finally accepting what was Dean's gift to me, and to the world.

As if hypnotized, I drove through the dangerous mountain curves, with my son's—MY SON'S!—voice in my ears, no matter he hadn't learned to speak until the tenth videodisc.

I heard Dean's parents speaking intimately, in the background, and later on I would find Dean playing with Karl, laughing, speaking, and being a mother. She was beautiful.

Romania was half gone when the fax machine behind me chattered, like it shouldn't have, until I noticed that it was the thermal paper brushing against the upholstery. I reached back, my mind still enmeshed in the emotions of fatherhood, and its joyous lassitude, and ripped off a wad of soundless paper. Yes, soundless. No matter which way you wrinkled or crinkled it, it was not supposed to make any noise. I pulled myself from the joyful mire, and went back to work.

The ship had been found; IL MARICELA. I looked at the picture out of the corner of my eye, and saw it was still offloading cargo from whence it came, and no doubt had a rendezvous which would take place before I got there, or which may have already taken place.

Leaving the mountains, I next entered a green hilly area, filled with farms of all sorts, but not one gas station. However, I knew that gas stations in Romania differed from those in the rest of Europe. The beast was sucking on fumes from the second of two tanks. I was glad to see a "Bucharest Ahead" road sign pass by, along with various other signs that I could not understand, because they were so worn. Baling wire was present on some of the battered signs, whose need for repair had been on a day twenty years ago. I pulled into the first gas station I found, which was only a two-pump setup, with no store or station. Just two pumps sticking up out of the ground, with a rusted Shell Oil sign hanging dangerously from a wood post. The latter being the demarcation of the farm as a gas station. There was another sign, leaning against the boot of one pump, that said; "Petrol." I honked the horn and saw a boy spring from a shack some fifty meters away, buttoning his pants, and carrying a five-gallon bucket. I saw his eyes sizing up my affluence. I'd been through this song and dance a thousand times during my travels, but knowing the poverty line began at the edge of the big cities, I usually gave in after a bit of haggling, just so my intentions wouldn't show and they'd think they got the better of me, but also to stop too much exploitation of my charitable nature. Charity's one thing; disrespect's another.

"Fifty gallons? Do you have it?" I asked in rusty, but decent Romanian.

The boy nodded, his eyes wide at my use of his native tongue. His bare chest was rippled with rib bones, and he was dirtier than a child after a wild pig chase through the mud.

"Three dollars a gallon, no more, plus twenty U.S. for your troubles. Or you can try for more, and I go down to the next one, or into the city, for much less." A dollar, the screen on the dash read. So I knew he was getting a good deal.

"American?"

"Gas?" I ignored him, and started the engine.

"No—no—it's good—it's good!" He panicked, but smiled with four black and five yellowing teeth, which ruined his perfectly rustic farmboy face.

I watched him work, then fell back into the small screen on the dash, where Karl was evolving before my eyes, from birth to one month ago, captured on twenty-four discs that captured approximately 3 years. 3 years I missed. I could not let myself become angry at Dean, for I had forgiven her. How could I not? It was sometimes painful to watch, as if forced to see a party your friends threw, but had not invited you to, and when you stumble upon it, there's all those feelings of humiliation, of anger, of self-esteem issues; why wasn't I invited? I thought we were friends? Don't you trust me? Don't you like me? You prefer them over me? Why did you even bother...?

I kept the sound up, and was glad, for they had mentioned my name when he'd grown old enough to notice something was wrong; where's MY daddy? *That-a-boy, Karl,* I thought, and was happy when they told him I was on a mission, and even showed him a picture, which caused me to look. I rarely allowed myself to be captured on film, let alone had custom ones made for friends.

"Dean, you sneak," I said to myself with a smile, and laughed when Dean turned to the camera and stuck her tongue out, not letting her parents or Karl see. She'd read my mind, two years ago.

I turned back to watch the Romanian farmboy, as he went back and forth to the rusting tank, filled the five-gallon bucket, and brought it back, then poured it through a funnel with screens inside of it to catch the rust flakes. His short arms worked fast, as did his legs, as he went to and fro. I scanned the horizon, but it was empty save for the shack, and a farmhouse some hundred meters behind that. And beyond that cattle grazed, and even a tractor was seen on the side of the barn.

It took a half hour from the time he started, which allowed me some time to go over the most recent intelligence.

Il Maricela was still offloading, and no suspicious activity had yet to be captured. No radiation detection in the entire country, so the radiation scanning satellite's reported. But I knew there were ways to conceal rad signals, even from weapons grade plutonium and uranium. A flash report came in from Igor, and I wondered what for, until I saw her name.

Sylvia.

– CHAPTER 17 –

SYLVIA HAD BEEN TAKEN to the protectorate building, following a short debriefing. (Shortest in the known history of the USSR or Russia, Igor claimed in amazement.) She had then been taken to the Balderov Hospital. This latter was a hospital where only government officials—and only high ones at that—went for medical treatment. The average age of its patients was fifty. She was currently resting there, with two teams of guards, who were posted at cover positions around the property. No one came or visited without permission from high up, and no permission had been given yet, except for two doctors and one military nurse. No other agency knew of her existence; in fact, she didn't exist on paper.

This latter part was disturbing, because it could mean that she was probably one man's handler. She was a pawn, a covert operative. A sleeper? (Someone born and raised in another country yet conditioned to allegiance to the Soviet Union, it being too soon to condition them to the Russian Federation.) I hoped she was not one man's pawn, for man had more pride than a government entity, and was therefore more likely to make sacrifices that government entities would not. Deaths were usually the result.

I tried not to think of Sylvia, as the beast coughed past the Ruse Varna city limits.

The Port of Varna was not a large port, but being one of the first ports after the main one in Istanbul, it was reputable, and supplied much of the region with goods coming in from the Mediterranean and the rest of the world.

If the satellite recon photos were correct, I should be able to see the Columbian freighter any moment.

"There you are." A big white elephant, and I, the great not so white hunter. Bingo! I typed to JD and Igor; "WHITE ELEPHANT IN SIGHT. STOP. ANY TRAFFIC OR SUSPICIONS? STOP. GIVE LAYOUT OF PORT AND SECURITY. THANKS. GOING IN. OUT."

Now, if only the nukes would jump up and sing the Star Spangled Banner, or otherwise give themselves away. I didn't care much to run into the Columbians who were transporting the bombs, ruthless bastards that they were, but I'd sure like to see where they were. If you know where the snake is you can avoid being bitten by it.

My past experience with Columbians, or any "drug lords", were far and few between. I don't think drugs, per se, are going to lead to the end of the world, unless an epidemic of cocaine sniffing Presidents breaks out. However, the industry that has been built upon the manufacture and sales, obviously run by less than moral characters, can be quite dangerous. Indeed, most of these drug dictators wanted to survive this "war on drugs," and the only way was to escalate. With enough money to purchase nuclear weapons, they'd have to be recognized as a small country. They already had small armies working for them. Armies that could, and did, take over the governments of the South American countries that they operated within. It was survival instincts. In all reality they should've stopped, or moved, but they were bound naturally, economically, and politically to that area of operation. The world television news reports always showed the "kidnappings" of any drug lord who ventured past the borders of his little kingdom, whether he was on vacation with his family, or on a legitimate business trip. And they do run legal businesses, only they've been gotten by dollars of illegitimacy.

"GET ME INFO ON SUSPECT DRUG LORD," I typed to JD.

I checked most recent reconnaissance photos, comparing them to three hours ago, and found that I did indeed have a tail. A black Mercedes, otherwise known as the bad guy car. You'd think they'd drive something original. But why? They'd gotten Sylvia, and Henri's amateurs had been left alone in Kracow. The Russians had had their chance to kill him. Whoever it was had stayed back five miles, which either meant I was being sattracked, or that car had a ground radar system that JD was only just procuring for me.

The problem with ground radar was interference, and until computer software had been invented to figure out the millions of signals, while tracking the subject, it had been worthless except on flat deserts with not too many trees or high scrubs.

"JD! FLASH! POSSIBLE GROUND RADAR TRACK SYSTEM FROM BGC FIVE CLICKS BACK. CHECK OUT EMANATIONS."

"I'VE BEEN WATCHING IT FOR A WHILE NOW. NO SIGNS. NO RADIATION EMANATIONS. NADA? WILL CONTINUE TO COMPLETION."

I knew he would too. He would dog it down from the question; how was Cort being tracked from five miles out? And there were only a few answers; covert satellite tracking, radar, or site on. The latter was nearly impossible at night.

PROCESS OF ILLUMINATION

I shut off the second to last videodisc, and pulled into a half-full parking lot, just as the sun peeked up over the Black Sea. The dark blue tint above was replaced with a softer hue. I took a minute and put away all the photos, and put them in the secret compartment with the videodiscs, then, with my bulletproof gray longcoat, I stepped out of the car. The defensive knife gun was comfortable, and I dry-fired it twice, in the car, before loading it. I armed the beast, with a press of the button, then walked over to a cafe.

Food! my stomach cried, as I took a seat near the window front, where I could see cars coming and going. The small two-lane road went from the main highway out of Ruse Varna down to the docks. If the black car passed by, I would rule out coincidence.

I ordered a plateful of morning scallops, covered in a local sauce, which was discinctly fishy, but good, and two slices of peach cobbler with a coffee chaser. Ten of the twenty tables were filled with longshoremen or sailors, each still wearing their thick coats, as if unable to shake the chill, even in this hot cafe. It was going to be a nice day, I saw, as the sun painted the sky with golden rays unfettered by clouds with malintent. But my brain kept an eye on the road, waiting expectantly for the black car, while the seamen came in, quickly ate, and left. Maybe their ships were calling them back, or better yet, their wives whom they'd thus far avoided since returning. The tables around me filled and emptied and refilled, like the tide. Fish, potatoes, eggs, and black coffee was the usual request, and was anticipated by the cook wearing a dirty apron, whose gender was difficult to discern. Rich voices full of character were heard bantering back and forth, rumoring locales of fat fishes in fat classrooms. Not a truth to any one story. Each man, or crew, kept those secrets for themselves, yet it was all done in the friendly banter of competing fishermen, who lived and worked together. And while there were some shouts to the cook, and the reply just as boisterous, there was not a hint of a budding barroom brawl or anger. I found a few faces staring at me, but that was to be expected, and I was accustomed to it. Travelling makes strangers of many persons. The coffee was excellent, thanks to a dash of cinnamon and fresh beans, while the scallops and peach cobbler that went before it were even better. The peaches weren't soggy, but were crisp and sweet, with a perfectly caramelized crust that was gummy on the inside. By far the best meal in a month, I apologized to Dean, and then contemplated ordering something else.

Thirty minutes later I stepped out, better replenished, better informed, ready to face what troubles may come, though still wary of the black car, which had not yet passed by. If it was Boris, then I was quite sure he wouldn't drive past a glass facade to identify the BMW in the parking lot. He would park spot that change in terrain, and walk into the city. Then again, if it were Boris, he wouldn't be stupid enough to be driving a black bad guy car, unless he was working for them, or had specific intentions. I too had to get rid of the BMW soon, have it shipped back home to Austria. I wondered if Boris was using human resources to track me, like the motorbike driver. That was his weakness, using less than reliable persons, and that made him not so esteemed in my eyes. I didn't think it was he who now stalked me, yet another voice said it was.

A tinkle of doorbells and I was out in the morning air. A cold breeze coming in off the Black Sea, which carried with it the smell of industry, and of what nature man hadn't yet managed to extinguish. Behind and in front of me, on the 30% grade sidewalks, men were coming or going from cafes.

"Hi there!" a man greeted loudly, catching me by surprise. I nodded and smiled, looking closely at his live blue eyes, and the kind wrinkles of his weathered face. Then he was gone to replace my seat in the tavern.

The colors of the buildings were mainly dull, almost color-coordinated with the dark waters of the Black Sea, as if this deep partnership with nature had permeated more than just commerce, but had affected a change upon human nature. The structures were mainly box-like, from the homes to the giant warehouses. Gray, brown, off-white, dark blue and green hues. Even the clothes, I now noticed, matched these colors. I saw no children, but nor did I see any homeless people, as I continued to walk towards the docks, keeping my eyes leeward. The streets were clean, and newly paved, which was a stark contrast to many inland countries I'd passed through. I arrived at the docks a few moments later, and saw another gathering spot called The Seaman's Bar. Oddly, the sign was in Bulgarian, Turkish, Greek, and English. Nobody had followed me, that I could tell, and the beast was self-monitoring. Anyone who even looked askance at her would be under video surveillance. My own camera was tucked neatly inside my coat pocket, hardly bigger than a small pistol. I'd also left a micro camera just under the table of the cafe, angled to capture the entire parking lot across the street.

I looked out at the *Il Maricela*, safely anchored a mile off, but clearly visible. Boats were ferrying cargo to and from chartered ports—privately rented docks for companies that can't afford the big cranes, or whose cargo is private.

A helicopter roamed somewhere above the city, but was too far away to be connected to me. A pontoon boat landed at a small manmade harbor airport, its engine growling, then quieting, as it touched down and skied into its offloading area. I lifted my camera, and used its internal zoom mechanism to survey the airport and its property. Always good to have an escape route.

I saw three other small planes, sitting on the shore, tethered by a single rope. A perfect getaway route if necessary.

I began my short trek back up the road and caught sight of a red yugo. I used my eyes, not my head, to scope it out, while staying behind a group of sailors walking up the hill to eat. I saw a fortyish man inside, but couldn't take a photo without breaking cover behind the men. I saw the gray mustache, dark sunglasses, and the black leather longcoat. The latter I guessed to be KGB issue. All of these were merely surmisings from my intuition, for I could not see the length of the coat, nor its true color.

"Gotcha," I said to myself, and greeted a passerby in Bulgarian, catching him off balance, and receiving a serious nod.

My phone buzzed, and I tapped the earpiece, which turned it on, I didn't like doing it, especially since Echelon heard all.

"Speak," I muttered into a specially modified collar microphone.

"Sorry, Cort. Know you're busy, but *Life* wants your article, and Dean—"

"Dean's dead, Barry," I knew this hit him like a ton of bricks swinging on a ten-story rope and socking him in the gut.

"Sorry, Cort," Barry Greenburg started.

"Send the check to the bank. Can't talk now, Barry, sorry." And as much as I hated to leave my friend in the crater of death's subsequent doing to loved ones and friends, I hung up on him. With a tail I didn't have time for distractions or grief, and that simple conversation could easily be tracked to the nearest communications node. Easily, since not many Ruse-Varnans had cell phones. No matter the communication was encoded and encrypted, the signal was like a huge global pointer stick; there he is! There he is! In fact, Barry knew better....

If the man was KGB I guessed it was Sylvia's handlers who were sent to eliminate me, like they had Dean, or they were merely checking me out. The more I acted naturally, the better. But I didn't have much confidence in that, for I'd lost most of my anonymity in these parts when the story broke on the leaking Smolensk nuclear power plant.

I'd done one short interview with a BBC/PBS station, out of a sense of duty, because nobody but me knew exactly who, how, what, why, and where. Afterwards, I went back to work, on that prostitution and kidnapping ring, previously mentioned. So my face and name were déjà vu to many; "Haven't I seen you before?" I get sometimes, although I'd altered my appearance for the show. That was the last time I did a piece, for newspaper or television networks. And any pieces sent in had a privacy clause, so that they wouldn't print my face.

So my name and face were out there, and I was assuredly certain as I walked towards my car that they, whoever they were, were not there to investigate who Cort Falcon was. And my subtle disguise was not that good.

I didn't like walking up the hill, but the incline wasn't too bad. Not that I shied away from exercise, for I tried to do my daily ration of pushups, situps, and squats each day. I was thankful for the crowds of seamen, coming and going, crowding the pristine white sidewalks. Most were stocky men, or had weathered faces only the sea could create. No women were within these groups, and they were smart to stay home, for it was hard work these men did, best suited to the male human species, or an uncommonly robust female.

I reached the diner where I'd eaten, and saw my seat was taken. The entrance was nearly filled with men waiting to get inside. Out of the corner of my eye I saw the beast, seemingly undisturbed. I pressed the alarm button to make sure. Two seconds passed—WHOOMPF!

Windows shattered, in front and behind me. I felt myself airborne, turning my face while clenching my jaws to lessen the effects of concussion, even though I was thirty meters from the BMW. The cars next to the beast exploded, and the shack crumbled like match sticks suddenly unglued. The concussion of air was visible, moving like an ocean wave at over 1000 feet per second, and knocking down anything not sturdy enough to withstand the pressure. The fireball, orange with angry black snakes twisting and curling at the edge, mushroomed up into the air.

"You okay?" a man asked me, and I looked up at him from the ground where I lay.

I checked for KGB indicia, and not seeing any, took the man's hand and stood up. My head felt like it was 3 fathoms under water, as if, well, as if it had indeed been concussed. I felt the pressure of the man's hand on my forearm, which was as good as touching me on my genitals, but I resisted the urge to snatch that part of me away. I regained my senses, and some clarity, and thanked the man.

"JD," I spoke into the microphone, and waited for him to answer. "The beast is dead, and I'm on my own. I believe these are Syl's friends, but I'm not sure."

"Holy smackers, Bird. They used enough bang bang to make the lens reprogram itself! Want me to send god?"

"No, but say a prayer.

"Will do.... You okay, man?"

I heard the concern in JD's voice, and smiled. "Nah. I've seen worse. I'll run a diagnostic on my MPC and be back that route. If it still works I'll give you a bonus."

"Take care."

"I'll be outta touch, unless I need help from god, for twenty-four."

"Anything important will be routed through the quiet line once you confirm its status." Meaning encoded digital signal to my MPC. "Don't do anything stupid."

"Thanks. Oh, and I know who Karl is."

"I figured she'd tell you," JD said, then clicked off.

"That sneaky little bastard knew all along!" I huffed to myself, but knew better. Nothing went on in the world that JD didn't know something about.

"Damn!" The videos! But Dean said something about I would have received them anyway, so that meant she'd made copies.

Maybe I should just let the spooks at the CIA or the Britons take care of this, and were it not for my mistrust of the self-serving natures of those in power, I think I may have been tempted to pass the buck.

The sirens were coming.

– CHAPTER 18 –

NOBODY HAD DIED AS A RESULT, I saw, before walking back down towards the docks, which would be the best place to keep an eye on *Il Maricela*. Maybe even get a job for a couple days, rent a motel room and lick my wounds. Ha! What bullshit! This whole fucking thing stank to high heaven. Dean WAS DEAD! Goddammit!

I felt a trickle run down my cheek, and thought I was crying until I swiped away blood. I pushed through the first tavern door I came upon. Bar tenders were renowned for their surgical prowess!

"You're bleeding, friend?"

The bar was completely empty, but appropriately so at this time of the morning, and with the new show up the road.

"Front row seats to a fight," I answered him in English, for that was the language he'd addressed me in.

"Aye, I see?" And he reached under the bar and brought out a plastic fish and tackle box. One of those plastic ones; when you open the lid a hundred little caches fold out. I saw a pair of wicked-looking needle nose pliers at the bottom of the box, with the bandages and other stuff.

"I hope those aren't necessary?" I said with concern.

"Not less you have a fishhook somewhere in ya?" He dug around, took another look at my brow, and took out some ointments and tape. "Good thing we're not busy, you'd be doing this on your own." He winked.

I took out a U.S. $50 bill and put it on the counter. "Is it too early for a double shot of your sturdiest whisky?"

He picked up the bill, snapped it, ran it under a hidden black light to reveal the secret authenticators, then smiled. "And you'll need it too! Aye!" he said, all in a friendly manner that belied the fact that he was a bartender in a dockside barroom, where toughness was a mark of good character, and friendliness a sign of weakness.

He went to a locked cabinet and brought out a bottle of twenty-year-old classic black label Jack Daniels, and snapped the seal off it. Two glasses appeared on the counter, and they were soon filled.

"Look out, here it comes." I tipped the shot back, and felt the fire burn down my throat.

"Here's another, on the house. And you'll need it too." He watched me down it, then moved in for surgery. "Now be still and I'll leave your face the way you brought it in."

And with one eye on the mirror, which gave me a clear view of the front door, I stayed quite still.

"Twitch like that again and it'll be a flap of flesh," the bartender warned. I felt a moist huff cross my cheek.

I had jerked because Henri, that's right, 'On-ray,' had walked in through the door.

"You've a problem with the boyo?" Alex the barkeep asked in a whispered voice, then moved to block my face from Henri, as well as hide my profile. "Be with ya in a moment! Come on in the back, Dirk, where I can see! That fin damn near took your head off!" He said it loud enough for Henri to hear, then guided me back, his large hand never leaving my face open to exhibition.

I walked with a purposful slump that would make me look inches shorter, and altered my gait somewhat, at least differing it from Cort Falcon's.

In a small storeroom, with boxes of bottles stacked floor to ceiling, I escaped recognition.

"That should do ya," Alex said, pressing down on the flesh-colored butterfly tape.

"Thank you," I said sincerely, but didn't offer him money. He was the kind that wouldn't take it. "If you ever need help...."

"Aye. And that's the back way out."

"Do you happen to know where the crew of the Columbian boat, *Il Maricela*, stays?"

"Never heard of 'em."

We shook hands, and fighting the urge to walk back into the bar and grab Henri up by the throat, I left through the backdoor. I'd like to know if he, or the Minister, had hired Boris. But personal matters had to be put aside for the greater good. I had to find the nukes. They were somewhere here. I could feel the heat emanating from their radioactive hulls. Henri would lead me to them, somewhere between here and the *Il Maricela*, this I knew, unless Igor's intel was faulty, which had never before been a factor.

Henri's appearance in a bar on the Black Sea coast, in the same one I was in, was eerie, like someone playing favorites from above. I don't mind a little divine intervention, though it's disturbing in its disproportionality, and ambivalent delivery. *Why now? Why here?* I asked Nobody in particular,

Stepping out into the alley behind tavern row, I took a small pathway between the buildings. My left eyebrow pulsed as I crossed the avenue towards one of three bars, and I pushed into the first one. A Greek tavern. I took a seat near the small glass porthole that gave me a view of the bar I'd just evacuated.

"Thanks," I said in Greek, as the bartender set down the beer fifteen minutes later. I dropped him a $20 tip.

He grunted, and I took that as a friendly gesture. He also snapped the bill and checked it under a black light. Counterfeit problems, I guessed.

"Where's the crew for the Maricela? The off dock loader?" I asked him in conversational Greek.

"That big rust bucket? They've come and gone to town. All work now."

"Thanks."

I sat for five more minutes, nursing my beer, figuring Henri had left while I was in the backroom of Alex's bar. I stepped outside at exactly the same time as Henri did across the street, and froze on the doorframe. If he turned his head we would lock eyes, and I doubted my sunglasses were disguise enough. He wore a dark brown coat, gray pants, and the same half boots he'd worn when with me. The gold-rimmed glasses still rested upon his birdlike nose. He turned, I breathed, and waited until he'd gotten halfway to the first loading dock. It wasn't difficult to follow him, as everyone was still mesmerized by the black plumes of smoke.

It was like this for ten minutes, me following Henri from dock to dock. 1 through 25; each had a cement peer, like parking slots for big boats. Some double, and even triple. There were two ferryboat docks, whose pier ended in a T-shape, and had offices and postable gangways. One had to be aware of the goats, which carried huge steel boxes from the yard, across the street, to the cranes, if the ship was big enough. There seemed to be only a few of those massive ships, and the *Il Maricela* fit into the massive category. Why was it off dock loading, then? It was expensive, and dangerous, and the owner still had to pay for the use of dock 25. Henri, as I figured, turned down Dock 25, which was basically a long cement road going out into the sea about three hundred meters. Then I saw the men, dressed not like Black Sea shoremen, but in newer clothing that mimicked the colors of the city. Someone had tried to do their homework. Henri didn't approach the men, but went, as if planned, to a black-haired man with distinctly Columbian features.

There were the trailer-sized containers; big enough to hide detection containment devices and insulation that would distort or hide the radiation signature left by plutonium. Even a micro scan, in which the satellite would pinpoint its sensors on a specific subject and search the very molecules for taint. Ah, and now I understood the new clothes. The men had all been scrubbed clean of radioactive particles, which would indeed be traceable, and given the new clothes. Even the boots. It went without saying that someone had gone to a lot of trouble.

I kept between two containers, which gave me an angle on Henri and the workers from about a hundred yards. I saw the seagoats, or boats that carried up to four containers out to an off dock seagoat coming and going from the *Il Maricela*. I could feel the illegality in the air. If there was any official monitors, this place would be raided. It was too distinct, too clean, and foreign. Where were the customs officials?

A black, tint-windowed Mercedes rolled past me, up to Henri, and stopped. Nobody got out, or in. The Columbian and Henri walked over to one of the containers, which had three more atop it, that were next in line to be loaded onto a seagoat.

If I were the druglord buying these nukes, I wouldn't put all my eggs in one basket. I'd have a simple backup plan. Some sort of insurance, if not for the safe passage, then for extorting. I could even sum up the druglord's argument in support; if you guarantee the safe passage we will leave Rome as is, for we only want the threat of nuclear power, like other countries, so that we may guarantee our rights in the future. Bla bla bla, or we'll detonate a 20-megaton nuclear bomb in Rome....

Henri came out of the cargo container carrying a larger than should be silver suitcase, which physically weighed down his right side. He had to set it down, and call his driver. They got the suitcase loaded into the backseat of the car, and both men got in. I saw the Columbian shaking his head in disgust at Henri's weakness, until he turned his attention back to the loading of the empty seagoat.

I watched the Mercedes make a large U-turn, come back my way. It would pass no more than ten feet from me. I hit the ground, pulled out a blowdart gun from my boot, and waited from my little alley.

The front grill came past quickly, and I aimed for a quarter panel, then gave up and blew. I didn't want to hit a window. That would instantly draw attention to the dark microemitter patch. I hoped I hit the backdoor.

"JD TRACK BGC. MICRO EMITTER HAS BEEN INSTALLED. POSSIBLE MALFUNCT. CHECK. REPEAT. BGC HAS SUITCASE NUKE! CONFIRM AND TRACK. OUT."

"CONFIRM TRACK BRIGHT AND CLEAR. SUSPECT TRAVELLING THROUGH RV. GOOD SIGNAL. SUPPLIES ARE IN ODESSA WITH IGOR. MEET HIM AT TEN HUNDRED HOURS TOMORROW. TRAIN DEPOT. STOP."

"HAVE YOU ALERTED SPOOKS ABOUT MARICELA?"

"AWAITING YOUR COMMAND, SIRE."

"CONTACT A FRIEND AND HAVE RESOURCES PREPARED. I BELIEVE NUKES ARE ABOARD SHIP, WHICH IS GUARDED BY COLUMBIANS."

"I KNOW. WILL DO. GET TO ODESSA."

I folded the flap over the MPC, and stepped out into the street. Henri's car had indeed disappeared. It was up to JD now. I don't think I'd asked for as many satsurveillances since India. In fact, once again, I was humbled by the power of the satellites.

Dockside workers and sailors on shore leave were beginning to trickle down from the explosion. I searched for the long-coated man, sure that he wasn't part of Henri's consignment. This time I would corral him, press him, and get answers from him. Even though I'd been dazed after the explosion, I had still panned and scanned for the man, and had not seen him. Maybe he had also been dazed by the blast, which meant that he may not have planted it. Maybe he'd been in one of the several nearby cafe's? Who was he, and was he the driver of the black Mercedes that had followed me into Varna?

I walked towards the train station, hoping they took the Euro debit card. I needed my supplies, but also to speak face to face with Igor, who didn't like to speak of super secret subjects over the airwaves. And rightly so.

What was happening to Sylvia? Who was she? Still, those questions barked from the distant corner of the doghouse I called my brain.

The train station was well manicured, though an indignant and angry crowd was upset about the lateness of the train flowed from the ticket windows to the food vendors, or stood listening to the musical venues. Small violinists, or quartets, but no rock'n'roll allowed, nor screaming guitars. Scattered here and there, under the great steel circus tent, were signs of westernization; a Burger King sign said you could "Have it your way." A Dunkin' Donuts promised pie, cake, and coffee (or tea). It was like an amusement park, with many treats wafting on the air; candies, popcorn, hot dogs, baked bread, and even fish on a stick. The scents filled the station, compelling one to buy, to eat. There was even a steel dining car, where cooks accepted orders, cooked, then shouted; "Order up!" in Russian. However, even with the quantity of food served and eaten, there was no trash or wrappings laying around. Near the tracks, where the trains pulled to a stop, the ground was a scuffed red stone. Sweepers, an army of teen sweepers in dull brown coveralls, would dash back and forth after each departure and arrival. Once past the red stone, under the awning, the ground was a shiny, polished cement that was so aged and waxed it looked like marble. And this too was swept clean on the hour, and the cleanliness of the entire depot made diligent and respectful individuals of everyone who used it, for who would dare throw down a piece of paper or ketchup packet in the face of the army of teenage sweepers. This station's attitude brought about a quietude, save for the soft live music, not a clear-cut oppression of all speech, but a decibel reduction, a normal tone not usually found in train stations. Even the trains sliding in seemed to be just a little quieter than trains in other nations, their horns softer, their brakes less squeaky.

I joined the crowd, train ticket in hand, and boarded the northbound train for Odessa, which would cross one soft border, or one that wasn't as heavily guarded, as they had been when it was part of the USSR. Either for economic reasons, or because there simply wasn't a need, it was basically a look by, with one or two officials watching tourists or travellers go into their country.

Inside the 20-year-old passenger car I found the rearmost seat available, and sat. No luggage, just me, my emergency fake passport (well, not fake, but not actually honest). The cars were also kept clean, which not only spoke of the character of the people within the region, but of the necessity of trains as transportation.

There were no city airports, like in many American and European cities, because fuel was simply too expensive, and maintenance costs were way too high, which made air travel nonfeasible for all but the wealthiest. This also kept the pace of life slower than those countries filled with jet air traffic from city to city or country to country. "Things" were not as urgent, the skies not as crowded, and the air was much cleaner. There weren't brown clouds to be found along this northeastern coast of the Black Sea.

As the train went inland, to avoid the uneven terrain along the coast, I tried not to recall the last time I'd been to the Ukraine (before it melded with Belarus), during the revolutionary *coup d'état* attempt. A faction of the military still clinging to the corruption of the previous communist regime. General Volkstad had sent tank divisions to the capital in Kiev in hopes of finding battle, but instead found something similar to the slaughter between Kuwait and Baghdad during Desert Storm. The train wouldn't enter Kiev, and those who dared would have to walk three miles at their own risk. I didn't see the first tank or supply truck for fifteen minutes.

Inside the charred husk of a ten-ton supply truck were the scabby remains of a burnt human being. He was charcoal black, yet his features were visible, his nose and facial lines clear, even his eyeless eyes were open and staring back and up, towards something that had been and gone. A huge hole adorned his head, like someone had taken a hammer and smashed in a clay pot with one good whack. Yet there was no blood, or bone, or brain, for it had all been consumed by the instantaneously intense white phosphorous explosives that had torn through the hundred plus tanks, supply trucks, jeeps, and civilian vehicles that had attempted to enter Kiev in hopes of sanctuary. The man's arms were through the backwindowless frame of the cab. The left arm went only from shoulder to elbow, while the right had everything but a thumb and a pinky. An indication of a ring seemed visible, or was a trick of the blackness. Part of the man's right shoulder was gone, much like a stone statue that has had a jagged fist-sized chunk chipped crudely and magnanimously away. A wind blew stiffly from the south and I turned to face it, to see if it brought ill tidings, and when I returned my greedy camera's gaze to the statue it disintegrated into black crystals that caught the waning sunlight and sparkled upon the breeze. Further down, similar statues bearing their own uniqueness slowly lifted into the sky. *Ashes to ashes, dust to dust,* I said to myself.

Although the massacre was a stand for democracy, and in defense of the capital, it was poignant that so many had died in vain, blinded by a minority that had once again tried to assert itself over the majority. The latter mostly occurred during times of trouble or economic lows. It didn't matter, I guarantee, for the dead were the dead, and a massacre is a massacre, be the dead victims or pawns or aggressors. Death is death.

Back in the present, my subconscious warning bells began to chime, arousing me from memories of mayhem and massacre, and I looked past my tinted glasses at the man who entered the car. And he knew I knew, even as he hesitated at the door, hoping I hadn't seen him. I gestured for him to come on back and take a seat next to me, then waited to see if he would play ball or play cat and mouse. I didn't much care for feline games, but I would, as my job required me, play along however he chose. The Russian agent stood confused and exposed for a moment, every passenger in the car, being from this region and fresh of memory, knew him for what he was. The silence went on for ten palpable seconds, and then the man made his choice.

"Are we still that visible?" he asked in fluent but heavily accented English.

"The longcoats and dark looks give you away every time," I said, matching his tone and demeanor, then smiled as I activated my watch. Much like a shark circling.

– CHAPTER 19 –

THE SPY WAS UNCOMFORTABLE, unaccustomed to direct confrontation, yet his willingness to throw down his game and directly attend to matters also meant that he possessed some intelligence and rank. This authority showed in the man's shoes, Italian loafers, with the black horseshoe buckle on the instep. Expensive. His skin had that slightly ruddy look, camouflaged by a tanning bed tan. His wrinkles showed him to be between forty and fifty. He was not tall, but he was slim, probably five foot eight inches with the loafers.

I waited for the man to light his cigarette, a habit quickly disappearing. "Did you plant the bomb?"

The man blew out a cloud of smoke too forcefully, shaking his head. "We don't plant bombs or detonate them in public areas. The collateral damage and political recriminations are just too great in this age. But to answer your question; no, I didn't and nobody I know did." He puffed, blew, and sighed, as if tired of his job.

"Then why have you been following me since Slovakia?"

"Yes, that." He puffed, looked at me to gauge how much I already knew, then looked me dead in the eye. "We wanted to know what you were doing."

"My question exactly. Why follow someone you already know, unless you're planning to terminate?" Now I looked him dead in the eye.

"We're interested in WHAT you're looking for," the spy fished, expertly covering any emotional tells. "What are you doing in our corner of the world again, Mister Falcon? It makes my superiors nervous when you're around. Like there's a viper in our nest that we don't know about." He smiled at that, as if he were pleased about something that made his superiors nervous.

The thought of divulging my mission to a Russian spy would have been blasphemous in the past, but now the gray areas encompassing tactical decisions were much broader. Technically, this man was my ally. The man had obvious intelligence, and authority, for they too were just as forbidden from revealing mission objectives. However, the thought of loosing Russia's vast security forces, though tempting, could be dangerous if Minister Parovich found out, which he definitely would. Yet it might be a risk worth taking, if they could be made to understand the details.

"What's your authority here?" I asked him point blank.

This made him adjust in his seat, as if he noticed a pebble underneath just then. "I am Nicoli Telza, Colonel in our intelligence service."

I lifted my sleeve and the flap, then typed his name and sent it e-mail to JD. "Precautions must be kept for what I'm going to reveal and ask of you. You understand?" He nodded his head and we waited for JD to send me a description of Colonel Nicoli Telza.

A moment later Nicoli's face appeared on my small screen, and it matched the face looking down at it. It also matched the lie detector's results.

"Many times I would have killed for a gadget such as that. Do you know where I can get one?"

"Maybe we can make that part of the trade?" I typed a quick thank you to JD, along with some pertinent information and updates. "What would you say if I told you that one of your ex-states had sold nuclear weapons to a drug lord?"

"Bahh is what I say. The START treatises have virtually locked down most of our nukes. It would be impossible, besides, we have taken back most of our nuclear weapons from independent states." He was lying.

"Do you have drug dealers in your country?"

"You know well that answer. Every country has drug problems, except the countries that have made them legal." He puffed. "But that is not what you get at? Please, get to the point, as you Americans say."

"Not until I have you and your superior's promise."

"I cannot speak for him."

"Then we shall wait until we arrive in Odessa. You will contact your superior, and I will conduct some personal business, and then we'll meet wherever you like. Be assured, I know your superior's face, and will have him voice-matched."

"What is the compromise we will be asked to make?"

"Boris." He started to speak, but I put up my hand. "I know he has been placed under contract by your country in the past, and I know you know where to reach him. I neither require you to admit or deny, only give me his whereabouts and access information. Also, I will want to be there at the end."

"I must know the subject matter, or I will be demoted to a Corporal."

"I've told you. Nuclear weapons and drugs, and I'll give you this. I believe one or two major cities in Europe, and Russia—" I added this last tidbit for shock value. "—may be annihilated by a nuke."

"Are the Americans involved yet?"

"They will be, you can bet on that, but I haven't spoken to them." But

Nicoli knew, as well as I did. American intelligence intervention was unavoidable. They could only be kept out of the loop if it was a tribal war underneath the remaining canopy of a South American rain forest, with spears and arrows the only weapons in use. So much money had been spent from 1988 to 2008 on intelligence gathering, both on technology and personnel, that virtually every country in the world was wired for sound. Those countries that were patently aggressive towards America were observed intensely, and covertly. It was hard to diagnose whether or not this Orwellian approach was harmful, or just an ambiguous part of future society. Irrespective of man's inherent nature, does constant vigil impinge upon the privacy of those guaranteed their right to privacy, when only criminal acts are reported? Does the absolute nature of the Echelon scan, and the HKS space surveillance system, which has the ability to monitor every electronic or vocal act, transmission, et cetera, violate and thereby oppress our creative nature?

For example; nonviolent protestors over the past twenty years have run up against authorities who were amassed prior to the actual demonstration, because of the government's ability to preempt the planned demonstration. Therefore, in a country where there is a guaranteed right to demonstrate and associate peacefully, such an estoppel is clearly violative. Yes, authors and speakers are still allowed to print or speak whatever antigovernment slogans (be they lies or truths) without fear of death or imprisonment (in most modern day countries). However, the moment peaceful protest is mentioned, especially against one of the many giant organizations (WTO, Democrats, Republicans, etc.), you would find the streets to the summit blocked, the public transportation systems shut down in the area where the giant organizers were meeting.

Since the World Trade Organization protest in Seattle, Washington, no protest has gone unmonitored by U.S. Federal and State authorities. Precaution, or fascism? Do we all secretly long for fascism, as Mailer opined more than once, or do we not truly know what fascism is, like many before us, who until they felt the bit in their mouths didn't grasp the totalitarian evolution of a fascist rule? Human nature; absolute power will corrupt absolutely. A rare man it is who shuns the corrosive effects of power, for even the godliest of pastors have "sinned" due to its course. The virus power flows in every human's bloodstream, awaiting only the catalyst, the external input, the situation that releases the sometimes deadly strain that affects one, or all. From stepping on the gas pedal of a powerful V8 to spanking a child too often, the underlying altruism is the corruption of power.

The train rumbled over a switch and slowed for the Belakrainian border, which I saw now had a serious contention of border guards. Trees and green pastures lined horizons, and little white dots represented the sheep herds that roamed the region. The small border station had a small town in the background, with an equally small Orthodox church in good repair, and one hotel that did need some attention. A few people waited for family and friends, others to board the train for the next stop, which was the bigger city of Odessa.

"Shall we get something to eat?" Nicoli offered, and stood up.

"Sounds good to me."

"We'll have a few minutes."

"More like thirty." I checked the layover times before boarding.

"Exactly." Nicoli was impressed. "I know a good place."

I sensed his affinity for this small town, which had been created solely for the border watch needs, and rail maintenance. It had evolved with Russia's railway system to become a nearly self-supporting township, with a mayor and all. There were plots of green square hectares stretching out and melding with the horizon. The town was made up of two-story villas that almost looked Victorian. The colors, as if the Black Sea had infected all those who lived near it, were similar to those in Ruse Varna. The streets were clean, and only a few cars that were held together with baling wire and ducttape.

I followed Nicoli, discreetly and behind my sunglasses scouting the area for traps, but Nicoli walked normally and led me into no alleys or small roads. In fact, the shop had a perfect view of the train. It was a small glass-fronted cafe, which was filled with the crackle of frying food, and the scents of heaven, at least to some of us connoisseurs of the palate. To this list I later added Nicoli.

"Try the chicks and peas with a brandy sauce," Nicoli suggested, leading us to a table and sitting—again on purpose—with his back to the window, affording me the seat to watch incoming diners. A sign of trust.

There were a few people from the train, those in the know, that trickled into the small cafe, but none that I deemed suspect. A chunky, redfaced woman swooped around the tables, hollering out in Russian to the chef each and every order, and soon came to us. She smiled at me and paid Nicoli no mind, despite his draped longcoat.

"You can tell me no more?" Nicoli pressed lightly, sipping on an after-meal glass of an unnamed local wine that should have had a name.

I sipped the wine. "Nice flavor. Fruity. Almost Tuscan."

I looked at my watch. I heard his question, but ignored it respectfully. "Shall we?"

The train's airhorn blew, giving all a fair five-minute warning.

As we boarded the border guards left me and Nicoli alone, and we found our seats at the back once again, with only a few changes; the previous passengers in the nearby seats had moved forward. I hoped this was not by arrangement. We both sat, much more at ease with the other, and more prone to the offhand remark. We needed, or I needed, to be sure of his unambitious sincerity. I knew spies, for I live like one, and am forced to be one now and then, so I know about taking the opportunity when it presents itself. Sometimes, however, when things are not in your control, the best thing to do is go with the flow, wait for that fortunate opening. That's what I was doing with Nicoli, and I could only rely on my reputation, upon the rumors that had me tied to the NSA and CIA to keep me afloat.

"Colonel."

"Nicoli, please."

"You know my resource capabilities?"

"I've heard of them, and—" He pointed to my left sleeve, indicating my MPC, with a slight nod. "—I see you have an intelligence service at your beck and call."

"I will keep my end of the bargain, but I cannot have you or your men following me while taking care of personal business. Are we clear on that? If my recon satellite sources find any ground, satellite, or air surveillance, I'll ghost on you, and you'll look foolish in front of your superiors, and they will look foolish when it leaks out what is truly going on. Even now your intelligence services are rummaging records looking for missing nukes. I doubt you'll find them until the covers are pulled off the entire scheme."

"I will make arrangements for your unmonitored passage to wherever you must go in Odessa, but I must have reassurance that you will meet me at the meeting place."

"Let me have your phone." I held out my hand, knowing it was probably his most precious object, with the exception of his Makarov pistol that I knew was under his right armpit. Reluctantly, at first, he handed it over. It was a standard Nokia, sold at almost any electronics store in the world. It had a memory service, into which I put my non-secret beeper code, then handed it back. "Press memory six and you can contact me for any changes, or fax me a four-page message. I already have your number, so if there's a problem I will call you.

He looked down at the phone, wheels turning; could he trace forward the number to a spot location, without me knowing?

"Impossible, Nicoli."

He smiled guiltily.

"You'd have to beep me more than once for a prolonged period, which would set off warning bells, et cetera et cetera." The latter meaning that I would trace back the trace, possibly sending back a nasty geometrical virus that would overload the systems of even the biggest-capacity computers.

"Ah, but the American GPS signal instaspot could locate you, no?"

"The Russian version could do that too."

"Yes." He chuckled. The test passed.

"But the tracking leaves a mile-wide radiation signal, easily detectable, giving the subject time to ditch the device and move away from the area." I didn't tell him that America, and therefore I had an undetectable system, which was connected to the Echelon program.

"But still, your location would be spotted, no?"

I knew he was fishing, but I played along. "Sure, but you already know I'm in Odessa. What good would it do, unless you had agents right there when the position was located, but then, no system has that much manpower, save China."

"Hmm?" He thought on that for a while, nodding his head in agreement to my theory. "Very astute. Thank you."

"Nothing two friends with a common enemy might not share." As if I'd enlightened him! What an actor.

He laughed aloud, startling the closest passengers, patting me on the knee. I joined his jocularity, sensing the irony in my statement and heretofore suspicions and fears.

"Indeed! Common enemies create the strangest of bedfellows and collaborators." He took out a handkerchief and wiped his watery blue eyes. "Indeed," he mumbled.

Although not as prone to outbursts of hilarity, I was thankful for the lighthearted nature he'd adopted, and hoped that this friendliness was a precursor to some sort of working relationship.

Odessa loomed, a test fire range, full of perils and live mines yet to be stepped upon. Truly, a thriving Russian, technically a Belakrainian metropolis with over two million people. It was the largest city along the northern coast of the Black Sea. Its buildings were in the process of evolution, old bricks falling, new steel and composite materials rising. Half the city was new, the other half an interesting vintage soon to undergo a metamorphosis. It was among the first of the Belakrainian cities to undergo such a face-lift, it being one of the gateways to the entire area, and therefore in view of democratic and working foreign economics not corrupted by the plutocratic infestation that infects communisms ruling parties. Because it was one of the main thoroughfares into the country, it was chosen to be among the first to undergo the change. After all, almost every country in the world is image conscious, and prone to peacock fluttering, although this was a sincere renovation and upgrading of life in Odessa. Convicts cleaned the road, picked up the trash, worked in the new waste management plants, and at other basic menial jobs. Even the homeless had no reason to be in such a state, due to a new Western European system that enabled every citizen in need of a job, who could work, to have a task. And those who could not work were fairly treated until they could work, and fraud was prosecuted for the middle-class citizens who felt like living off the system for over a certain period of time were dealt with severly. The rest of the jobless were imprisoned, and therefore working.

The train creaked and groaned, unlike before, as it pulled into the crowded and not so quiet Odessa train station.

I let Nicoli step off first, and watched his signal; a hand scratching his right temple. "Very discreet, Nicoli," I said from behind. "I hope that was a hands off signal?"

"Yes, it was." He shook his head and put out his hand. "In two hours I shall fax you with the location."

We shook. "I'll be waiting, Nicoli." I held his hand a moment longer to gauge his sincerity.

"You will be alone. You have my word."

"Then I'll see you again."

– CHAPTER 20 –

IGOR TAPPED HIS FOOT impatiently on the sawdust-covered floor, not looking unhappy, but neither looking chipper. The typical brooding Russian. A certain tension hovered around him, maybe due to the set of the shoulders, or the way he twirled the glass of tea on the wood bar. His eyes darted back and forth behind his blue tint sunglasses, from the door, to the mirror behind the bar, to his watch. But his head barely moved, though it seemed at any moment he would jump out of his "normal" attire. A gray tailored suit with an off-white tie over a light blue oxford. His matching Vandyke mustache added to the tenuous appearance of importance; the man was somebody.

The "Moscowvite's Restaurant" was a very upper-class establishment, the interior being dark and romantic, or shadowy and sinister, whichever you prefer. The fact that it was in the basement of a twenty-two-story building, which was part of a complex made it an ideal place for clandestine meetings. One could come and go to the restaurant without being observed by surveillance, the biggest problem for the little guy in today's spy game.

I grinned inwardly, watching Igor sit at the bar nursing his tea. The latter a common fixture with Igor, and I constantly jibed him about being a closet Englishman, to which Igor matter-of-factly claimed that the Russians found tea first. I knew he saw me, but he gave no recognizing tells, which was impressive, due to the fact that I was thirty minutes late. He was a short man, who kept his size and shape hidden well with tailored suits that most Russians could not afford. He had about him an air of importance, a "hands off" aura, as if he were a KGB agent in disguise (which he was). Every so often he turned a certain way, reminding me of Stalin, with a tan, but as I approached he looked like good old Igor.

"Quiet in here?" I said, sitting down next to him.

"Yes, my friend. How are you?" Igor looked me in the eye. "Problems?"

"Nothing I can't shake. But I'm good considering."

"She was a great woman." He raised his glass of tea, as if in toast, and drank it down. "I believe I might have the information you want."

"Let's get a table. Are you hungry?" I offered. "My treat this time."

He patted me on the shoulder. "No, it is my treat this time, remember?"

PROCESS OF ILLUMINATION

We took a table in a four-person booth near the back, with a good view of the back and front doors. He ordered a small meal, and I a small snack. I didn't want to be fat and slow when I met with Nicoli's people.

"So, are the supplies still intact?" I asked.

"Yes, with new identification, permits, and passports. JD said you might need it after you get out of the shark tank, if you get out." He slid a key across the table. "You know the station?"

"Must be picked up before six. Thieves go through them about that time, but I've an assistant watching the locker until you arrive. He doesn't get paid unless you get the bag."

"You may want to stay in Odessa for the rest of the day." I looked across the table at those gray eyes that he tried to hide by wearing tinted glasses, though his sight was perfect.

"Do you have a scrambler?"

He took out a wavelength scrambler which would distort the reception wavelengths at 0:25-second intervals, creating a static to any listening device or monitoring system. It was to be used sparingly, lest it be compromised. Not many knew about it, since JD had created it himself. He flicked it on.

"I received it yesterday, inside the statue of Mother Mary." He shook his head at the blasphemy. "Please tell JD never to use such a ploy. I could not bring myself to break it for three hours."

I smiled. That was just like JD.

I related my plan, specifically, my meeting with the Russian intelligence directorate, right here in Belakrainia, and how I intended to control them. It depended on how much the Russians knew already, and that was why I needed Igor.

"So, you intend to use their resources by making them think that your resources are much more sophisticated than ours, or theirs, excuse that *faux pas*, but you will be the one that gets credit. And Boris? The girl, Sylvia?" He grimaced at the mention of her name. "You should leave her to her own." He grimaced some more, as he did when mulling over my risky operational plans, which sometimes conflicted with his training and experience as a KGB operative for over twenty years.

"Come on, it's not like I'm trying to catch a comet. From their point of view, with the pride of the Komitet gosudarstvennoi bezopdsnosti at stake—"

Igor smiled. "Yes, they will agree, or try to trick you. You know that you are in the Lion's mouth?" Igor eyed me to be sure I knew what he meant. "I assure you, if you see fat Minski, who is head of operations in this area, he is already planning your arrest."

I took a bite, savoring the excellent cheese, waiting for him to speak of her, to bring up her name.

"Well?" I said, finally giving in to him. "What about her?"

"Stay away from her, my friend." He wiped his mouth and looked around. "I do not warn you of many things, because I know your capabilities, but I'm telling you, I believe she's a deep cover plant. Do you know Vladimir Peroskvi, General of Moscow forces and KGB commandant?"

Any good reporter worth his salt knew who he was, and Igor knew I knew. Commandant Peroskvi, as he was called by those within his sphere, didn't allow himself to be photographed, but he'd been captured several times on film, for it was hard for any public official not to be caught on tape, no matter how camera shy he was.

"I could find no information about her, only where she was staying, which I've relayed to you, and possible family members. I have that information here." Igor slid the envelope across the table to me.

I ripped open an end and shook out the typed report, which was a commodity with Igor, who was either a good typist, or had good assistants. I knew the latter to be true, but he never revealed much about his network to me, and I didn't expect it of him. There was nothing significant about the one page summary; Sylvia DeNoel was 24, she lived in France, but was born in Kansas City, Missouri. Her parents were Griffin and Margaret Chofsky, also American citizens who'd migrated from Poland in the 1950s. Everything else I knew. I dipped the edge of the paper inside the small red glass that trapped the candles flame and set the summary on fire, tossing the ashes to the ground when the flame reached my thumb and forefinger.

"She is a closed book, my friend, and I would leave her thus, for nobody is a closed book, if you know what I mean."

"I gave my word, Igor."

"Ahhh." He shook his head sadly, considering the ramifications, and having been my Russian contact for ten years, knew that I didn't give my word lightly, nor had I ever broken it. "I will try to look into some pages, but this is not an easy task...."

I knew what he was saying. This may be one I couldn't solve. "We'll see. So, do you have any advice about the meeting, or Nicoli's superior?"

"Ahh." Igor grinned. "I trained Minski myself, twenty years ago. A politician, not a genius...."

I listened to his didactic speech, filled with information on how to tailor my request, so as to highlight the political gains, and gloss over the consequences, if one could ignore a nuclear blast that destroys a major Russian city.

"Thank you, Igor." I shook his hand.

"Always a pleasure, my friend. I must congratulate you on your new fatherhood. It will give you a new outlook, I assure you."

"Yes, I am experiencing that." It was not a lie. The past days had brought something to me in the form of a new consideration about life, and how easily and accidentally it could be taken. There was no special consideration by Death, or God, given to those human beings, like Dean, who'd given much of their time to the betterment of humankind. There was no 'get out of death free' card, no reprieve, or even a few minutes notice, which might allow a "good" person to set things in order, or do one last "good" deed for the cause of humanity.

Cruel. Yes. The good die young sometimes, and though I knew all this, and had even come close to Death's scythe more than once, none of this deterred me in the face of the storm. Nothing stopped me from making more than a courteous check of the barometer when going about my business where death was most popular. Dean's blood stained my hands. My memory was haunted. I saw her in the laughter and smiles around me. Outside the windows of the cabby I could see her long hair and slim figure in the crowds. And in my indulgences, food, wine, conversation, observations, and various other tactile stimulations, I found myself choking back tears of loss. Selfish tears, mixed with an anger towards a "God" I didn't understand, not in His message, but in His delivery, His gamesmanship, His cruelty and illogic. Yet I try to see His way, ignoring the manmade dogmas, without prejudice, and each time I make a willing observance of some rite or prayer I am crushed by the death of innocents. Why? Why must we, as a global populace, be prodded by death, in its many forms, as a Godly disciplinary measure or threat, until we come around, until we self-rehabilitate, until we learn not just to live together, but work with one another while respecting the uniqueness inherent in each of our varying cultures. Is death the cattle prod, by which we are forced to go out into the pastures of peace and goodness, our free will a catalyst for our failures to date? Yet, if there are greener pastures, why must humankind suffer the agonies of death, of goodness stripped, of innocence murdered or killed, of the atrocities we visit upon each other in pains of growth? Why can't we be enlightened, given the necessary knowledge and intuition, to do the "right thing," to graze upon the peaceful pastures? Why can't we be given some other example, some other nonintrusive remedial course, by which to shape our path, if not an innate goodness? Or would this corrupt the lesson of death, which elucidates life, by allowing us the opportunity to experience gut wrenching pain, or would this easier grazing ruin the experiment we are all a part of?

A new outlook. A consideration of the perils that follow me as they affect to endanger those I care about, and those who are "good".

The cabby spoke some gibberish about nonexistent traffic, and I agreed with a nod, earning more of the same. I was transfixed by the melancholy created by Dean's death, and the loss of the videotapes. Even the smiling faces of the citizens of Odessa didn't cheer me as they normally did, for in their life was the poignant reminder of my friend's death.

At the station I picked up the suitcase, which was not the norm, but preferable when in the Russian states. A duffel was too conspicuous, except near the port.

It was 15:00 hours, or 3pm, when I walked unharassed through the doors of the government building. I had gadgets armed properly, and concealed, but was surprised to be allowed free entry into the large white building. It seemed all government buildings, especially capitols, were made of white, as if color alone could symbolize the inherent trustworthiness of those within. A man in a gray pinstriped suit, met me at the bottom of a great marble staircase.

"Mister Falcon, sir?" The officious man smiled down at me. He was a tall one. "Please follow me."

"Why the easy access?" I asked.

"We know you're not carrying anything. Computer olfactory, and X ray entry sensors have already checked you out. Nothing to disrupt your gadgets, I hope." He smiled back and down at me, as if to say, 'We know your hole card.'

Honestly, I hadn't thought Odessa, or all of the Balkans for that matter, wealthy enough for those types of detection devices, but I was glad that JD had built my gadgets with auto masking capabilities. It was good to have an edge, even among potential friends. Keep your friends close, and your enemies closer.

The wide staircase wound its way back and forth at the rear of the atrium, the buildings facade being the front, and we peeled off on the third floor into a wider hallway filled with oak doors along the oak-paneled walls. The hallway ran the length of the building, but we didn't make it that far, turning off into a small recess that led to a pair of double doors, which opened as we neared them.

Camera surveillance, I thought, as Nicoli exited.

"Ah, Mister Falcon, thank you for coming." He outstretched his arm and we shook hands like long lost comrades. He looked at my small briefcase. "May I have that taken care of?"

I smiled, and so did he, silently withdrawing his offer to have it "taken care of." We both knew what that entailed. A full shakedown of the contents.

"Mister Falcon," Commandant Minski Valitsk boomed in greeting, a huge smile drooping beneath his pink nose. He was a great bear of a man, a thick brown bush of hair barely manageable, but somehow pulling off the look. He had thick, ruddy lips, whose pinkness matched that of his nose and jowls. A thin pencil mustache adorned his upper lip, while a small thatch grew beneath his lower. His hand was huge, and strong. His suit, unlike Nicoli's, hung loosely, and was in dire need of a tailor and a good ironing. His appearance was deceptive, for though he looked jovial and kind, he was a cool and calculating man not prone to emotional reasonings or merciful dealings. His records showed that he'd made at least five "kills" in Afghanistan. His wife had been bought and paid for in the slave trade that was rampant in this area. His children were tucked away in boarding schools around the world, for which he had need to supplement his meager income.

I knew the man instantly. Not bad, not good, just the normal type of Balkan commandant, looking out for he and his, with a Russian twist. His file said that he'd been born in Stalingrad, before it was renamed Volgograd. He'd been a junior member in the communist party, when communism was cool. I read the man had also consigned two U.S. spies to death during the Hanson fiasco, when the FBI, CIA, and NSA had finally been tipped off about the deep cover Russian spy who was in the FBI's counterintelligence operation. A perfect place for a Russian spy, or heck, any spy for that matter.

The *entente cordiale* began, he representing his, and I the world. The doors closed behind me, and I heard the click.

– CHAPTER 21 –

THE ROOM WAS ELEGANTLY AUSTERE, with the same local oak wood paneling the walls, whose entablature was completely hand carved. The cornice, frieze, and architraves were carved to make the wood flow together, like a wave, with flowers set adrift upon the strip of sea that met a light blue ceiling. One great rectangular table, maybe ten meters long in a twenty-meter-long room, was surrounded by wooden, straight-backed chairs with deep red velour seats that had seen their share of use. There was one picture, that of the current Belakrainian President. The floor was not marble, but a sound trapping dark blue short shag. No windows existed.

Around the table we four men sat, Nicoli, Minski, the escort turned stenographer, who was most likely armed and dangerous as hell, and myself.

"So you want our assistance in exchange for Boris?" Minski came right out and said it.

"No. I want Boris, you get your nukes back, and save a European city from being turned to ashes."

He laughed, his entire body jiggling. "What do I care about a European city? That's the West's problem."

"Oh, weren't you informed that there's a trail leading to Moscow? A radiation trail?" I'd done my homework, and JD had filtered out three false trails. "One radiation signature had in fact gone to Moscow, and one to Varna."

"And the other?" Minski asked. "You said three?"

"Paris."

"I never much liked the French...."

"We should call Moscow right away," Nicoli insisted in dialectic Russian from the Estonian area.

"And give our position away to Vladimir," Minski snarled the name like it was a curse. "We'll be assigned watch dog duty while he takes the credit and gets the promotion. No. This is big, Nicoli, and I shall promote you accordingly."

The fool, Nicoli thought to himself. He didn't want a promotion. He wanted to stop the mass destruction of Moscow, which would have a catastrophic effect upon the entire Russian federation, destabilizing the government, the economy, while creating another series of civil wars, which would throw Russia back another twenty years. They couldn't afford that again. The wounds were just barely healing. They were just barely recovering from the communism to democracy change in the '90s, just regaining their former status as a super power, and their respect. This would once again cut their legs off, making them no better than nonentities or Third World representatives.

"Of course," Nicoli placated his superior, then looked at Cort. Did Falcon know, he wondered, the future implications of what would happen to Russia should what he say come true?

Minski turned back to me. "It will take some favors to get the information on Boris, as you requested, but I think it is possible." He rubbed his chin, in a perfectly choreographed expression of doubt.

"You'll have to do better than that," I said, knowing the most common of Russian tactics when I saw them; promise nothing, and therefore be obliged to give nothing, while dangling the possibilities before the subject. "You understand that at this very moment two twenty-megaton super bombs are en route, or are already planted in a major city, Russian, European, this I know to be true. There are also two warheads, each with ten one-megaton, or kiloton bombs. At this moment they are being loaded onto a cargo ship—"

"We've no record of any nuclear weapons missing, and if anyone would know, the intelligentsia would!" Minski looked around for confirmation, and the stenographer bodyguard nodded.

"—These same nukes will be used by drug traffickers to hold each of our countries hostage to the drug lords and criminal elements, who serve no ideological master save for money. They will be used to bind laws and governments by threat, and therefore place the population under an oppressive weight. There will be no remorse, and they will make an example first, so the world knows they have no compunction in killing a few million people. They are to be feared more than terrorists, for at least with those groups there is some sort of mental imbalance that can be predicted, or at least understood, whereas the drug lord carries no such burden, and no such enemy, for his target is the world under our protection." I had no time to argue or school him about his missing nuclear weapons.

"But where did the weapons come from? How can I expend my resources if you do not tell me from which coat pocket I have been robbed?"

"You have been robbed. Trust me. I will write your name in my story, as the hero, the helper, but we must act now. If you don't get involved now, the Americans will—"

"Are they involved?" Minski asked, perplexed and suddenly anxious. He still lived in the world where it was Russia versus United States. Many did, and shame on them.

"Do you doubt that they're aware of something going on? Belakrainia suddenly using offensive jamming techniques to shut down all satellite and radar surveillance? A no-fly zone? Troops on alert? Creating enough false radiation signals to light up half the country? You bet your ass America's on its toes looking over your backyard wall, and you'd better show your face before it's too late." I watched him mull it over, then played my trump card. "I'm sure Vladimir Peroskvi wouldn't hesitate to throw Boris to the wolves for a chance to get involved. Should I call him instead?" I saw Nicoli grin.

"No!" Minski blurted, then settled himself back down and spoke with forced tranquility. "We have a deal. I will reveal to you Boris, and you will assist me in locating the weapons.

"Do you have the resources?"

"Hmmph! I have a thousand men at my disposal. Nicoli will be my liaison."

"Then the weapons are right now aboard a white Columbian freighter, *Il Maricela*, probably just leaving the port of Varna."

"Good." Minski nodded to the stenographer, who took a gun and pointed it at me. "Now, you will leave this building and leave this country, and thank your god for your life."

"Too bad, now I'll just have to call Vladimir, and tell him how you wanted to take all the credit at the risk of the entire country." I took out the phone and began to dial.

"Shoot him!" Minski ordered with not too little mockery and superiority in his command.

The stenogapher turned assassin squeezed the trigger. The gun, a heavy Makarov, didn't even flinch. They all looked at it, even Nicoli. The dart hit the stenographer in the throat a moment later and he fell over instantly.

Minski, bug-eyed and flushed, looked on in horror as his powerplay went up in flames like a match stick house. Slowly, he turned to me, and waited for me to spit a mouth dart at him too. When he realized I was waiting for him to change his mind, he smiled, and put out his palms in supplication.

"I was only testing the odds." He couldn't hide the tremble in his voice.

"Boris! Now! Or you end up like him and I get Vladimir's assistance anyways," I said politely, holding the phone to my ear and mouth. "Yes, Commandant Peroskvi. Urgent code thirty-two communication," I said in the exact same dialect they'd tried to hide their language in. I enjoyed the effect my knowledge of their codes had on them. Jaw dropping effect.

"Wait! Wait! Okay—okay. Put the phone down please."

"Hello? Vladimir? Please hold." I pressed a button and looked up at Minski. "What did you say? He'll be tracing this call, so you'd better hurry. What is it?" I watched Nicoli, who looked both nervous and amused, at the same time. Minski brought out a sealed brown envelope, the contents of which I assumed to be the Boris files. Small.

"Here. Please cut the call," Minski nearly pleaded, dabbing the sweat from his forehead with a white handkerchief.

I waited approximately three seconds, then pressed the button that would cancel the call.

"Open it, or I reconnect." This I said to Nicoli, who was closest to me, as he was seated between me and Minski. Nicoli, I thought, was now looking quite amused by his boss' fiasco. The envelope didn't explode upon opening, nor did it emit a knockout gas or cyanide spray, so I accepted the contents of the envelope. It was a two-page report. I opened my suitcase, took out the mini scanner, and uploaded both documents with four up and down sweeps. I saw the address, and made sure to get it clearly. I handed them back the two-page report. "Thank you."

"It must not get out that I gave that to you—"

"Shut up! You've lost your rights," I barked at him. "I will go with Nicoli from here on out. He will be promoted next week, or I will call Peroskvi, and inform him about your clandestine operations, et cetera, et cetera. Am I understood?" I asked this latter part in Moscow Russian.

He nodded his head in defeat, but to keep him with some hope of improving his situation, I added, "And you may reap the benefits, political or economic. If we're successful."

Minski nodded his head, taking what he could get.

I sighed relief, my constipated breath expelling loudly as I passed the doorway of the building, and was nearly blinded by sunlight. But I knew Minski wasn't that dense. After all, I had made arrangements right there before his bulging eyes that in the chance of my death JD was to notify Vladimir and inform him about Minski's attempts, and to turn over my MPC, which had picked up every word of our little meeting. The latter had shocked and surprised Minski, and even Nicoli.

Right now commando teams—Spetsnaz forces—were en route to intercept the *Il Maricela*, and Minister Parovich. I had Henri tracked, so long as he didn't leave the car. I wanted to deal personally with Henri, and the location of the bombs. If all went well, the Belakrainian and Russian intel forces would be in position within twelve hours, and I would be having a chat with an old friend, over a switch blade and a pair of tweezers, if that's what it took to get him talking.

– CHAPTER 22 –

NICOLI CAUGHT UP WITH ME at the military airport, on the north side of Odessa, where we'd agreed to meet. We were to be flown directly to Skopie, Macedonia, where satellites had tracked and pinpointed a black bad guy car. Thee BGCs, with one Henri Gionopolis inside, and possibly a one-megaton suitcase bomb. Either that or an old satellite phone system. My guess was on the bang-bang. If I guessed right about Henri's weaselish character, he had been paid to use the suitcase as a backup to a backup. In the event that things went wrong he could easily sell it on the black market for a few million dollars. Some cult or terrorist group would love to have it.

"Nicoli," I greeted the man who was still somewhat of an enigma. He seemed quietly pleased that Minski was under my thumb, yet he had stayed reserved ever since. However, that reservedness, I'd come to notice, was part of the man's nature. I wasn't so much worried as I was cautious; many a smart man kept his deepest thoughts to himself, and his feelings in check, so as to keep the most important advantage in human adversarial dealings. The element of surprise. So says Tsun Tzu. The element of surprise by inferior forces can cripple superior foes, if done decisively and wholly without reserve. When your opponent is down, wound him permanently. A good thing terrorists weren't reading the classics, but then again, there were a few who'd evolved. But most weren't educated enough to even read.

To be a terrorist is analogous to being a private in an army, signing up for a hitch to escape poverty (though not all), except that when you signed up for state or national duty you kept the hope of a better life alive. With terrorists, the hope of creating a better life from terrorist acts was infinitely void, and most were either killed in action or assassinated by their own paranoid leaders. The vicious cycle, kept in place by manmade religious dogmas and self-comportment, had boys and girls learning religious texts, instead of free ideology and philosophy or other worldly items of import. Without getting into the gray area of fundamentalists versus conservatives, within certain Arab cointries, it's a hard way of life, and harder still to change. For to change to another route of living, would be to cause pains. Therefore, with religious leaders preaching secular hate against this or that, they or them, or whoever was the devil for that day, children grew up in a poor society, offered only war, terrorism, as an alternative escape from poverty. It is not a problem relegated to Arab countries, but one that has infected nearly every culture in every land. Give the downtrodden a heaven and a hell, then tell them how to get there.

My mind drifted, as did the plane into cold pockets of air, to the north, to Moscow, where she was being held. My red-haired, green-eyed waif, so in need of protection, yet able to survive on her own. Where was she? What was she? I'd thought to ask Fatman Minski, but to do so would be to jeopardize my position. It would possibly give Minski something to hold over me. Only now, alone, did I realize how much I missed Dean's advice. Her tendency to slap me back on track. Dean?

Outside the smudged windows, clouds rubbed up against the plane's metal skin, a cold corpse dragging its flesh over colder skin, leaving its dewy wetness, which was sluffed across the plane like a snake's skin peeling. I felt like one of the hundreds of tiny beads, the wind dragging me backwards, momentum opposite of normality. Instead of my intuitive forward progression toward some goal, I was sapped by the need for revenge, the need to find Boris, which deterred my progress from the initial need to save the world from nuclear destruction. Never leave stragglers behind; that was my motto. Until Sylvia. "Let her go," Dean had told me. But the act still pained me, for Sylvia had indeed been left behind. Only for a moment, I vowed, for I had indeed given my word, and that was gold. Damn right, I reassured myself, feeling better after the self-imposed pep talk. Besides, what else did a investigative slash dogooder have, but his word?

"That was professional. The way you handled Minski," Nicoli said, speaking for the first time since the plane took off. He'd been leery of Minski's spies, but there were only the two soldiers at the front of the noisy plane, and the two pilots, so he felt it was safe to speak,

I looked at the man, not the overcoat, which stood for the inherent deceptions and ploys of the KGB. He was a curiosity, in that he was either a sneaky SOB, or a reasonable man. The latter indicated his intelligence, and belied his current underranking position to Minski, though I knew Minski had a cousin related to a nephew in the old Politburo.

"Know your enemy...." I said casually, as if it were a given. For me it was.

"Ah, Mister Tzu. Yes, we've had Russian editions, but it is not as widely read as it should be. Too much pride in our own philosophers, too much ignorance. My people have sometimes lived and, sadly, died by their own unwillingness to adapt to better ways, and superior technologies."

PROCESS OF ILLUMINATION

"Unless you could steal it," I added with a chuckle, and saw Nicoli accept it with a knowing grin. KGB was one of the best espionage intelligence agencies in the world, no matter the state of their national economy. Although post Stalin premiers had lasted only short terms, it was the creation of the KGB by Krushchev that had left the mark, with exception of the Yeltsin changeover to democracy. The creation of the KGB was to guard over USSR interests, to gather intelligence from other countries through espionage and spying tactics, among others.

Stealing, yes, but it was official, and therefore not considered "theft" per se, but a victory against the West, or East, or whomever had been penetrated. All's fair in love and war. Even now, with the Cold War over, the CIA, Moscow Centre, British MT5, as well as the countries of the world's intelligence agencies, were as active as they'd ever been, Each continued spying through less than honorable means, and paid the highest price for failure. The old axiom that spies caught were traded back and forth was a lie. Most spies were simply executed, especially native spies, or spies that spied on their own country. And when an individual was caught openly, mostly in America or United Kingdom, at first an air of indignance and approbation was feigned, by the party who'd caught the other, but it was soon checked, once the political juice was bled dry, for each knew the other was just as guilty. But it was a risk worth taking, for to not know what the other was doing bred suspicion, insecurity, and paranoia. A bad trait for nuclear countries to have. Even with all the satellite surveillance systems, electronic listening posts, and super computer lookouts that predicted the "moves" —political and tactical—of every country in the world, there was still a need to have a "man on the ground." An ear to the keyhole, a human opinion of the entire situation.

"Each does what must be done," Nicoli acknowledged what we both knew to be true. "You did not ask Minski about your other concern?"

"What concern would that be?"

"The woman?"

I turned to look at him.

"Vladimir is my superior. I've received word that you were in the car from which the woman was rescued."

"Rescued?" I laughed shortly.

"That's how the official report is going to be filed, though we know you probably saved her life."

"Anything to do with the Spetsnaz team I ran into?" I asked, wondering how important she was. Had I uncovered a legend? A deep cover operative.

"I have no knowledge of their presence in that area?"

But he did. My watch said so, and so did his eyes. I was satisfied with that bit of knowledge, but the Russian military presence was worrying, if they weren't there for Sylvia.

If they'd not been in the Czech Republic for Sylvia, then it meant the escalation of military might in the area, which could lead to war between substantial powers. Unlike the current one-sided battle, against Islamic guerrillas, who nobody cared about. A sad inhumanity that permeated the world's conflicts. Like when the Kiwan tribes massacred one hundred and fifty-eight thousand men, women, and children of the Zuba tribes. None of the countries that could have stepped in did, because nobody gave a damn about the Africans killing Africans. Small human rights organizations, the Red Cross, Blue Cross, and "Doctors Without Borders," and even the powerless United Nations tried to help, but without the military and political support of member nations, their attempts were fruitless on a grand scale. Sure, a few lives were saved, but the unseen butchering of one hundred and fifty-eight thousand, three hundred and seventy-six human beings was barely reported on. Was it because the world public, all of us worker bees, didn't give a damn about Africans being hacked and bludgeoned to death (to save bullets), and therefore our politicians followed suit? Or was it racial, some inherent indifference to persons of another skin being murdered, or was it the current state of indifference to human suffering, so long as the suffering did not affect you directly? Maybe it was both. But whatever the reason, the uncaring attitude by the majority still existed when the immoral acts did not encompass their sphere of life.

Where did Nicoli fit in? He didn't seem the uncaring sort of person.

"So, who is the woman to you?"

"She's one of ours." Nicoli smiled.

"And?" I didn't ask why he was telling me, but he knew. It didn't have to be asked.

"What's your stake in this woman you barely know?"

Ah, so they'd gotten something from her during debriefing that led them to believe I had more than a vested interest in Sylvia. Moscow Centre had their special ways, their drugs that made your head swirl and your tongue loosen. They had their toggles and electrodes, their pliers and pincers, their isolation and hyperbaric chambers, which twisted your thoughts and broke down the loyalties of the stoutest citizens. They had their two faces, the good guy-bad guy routines. They had their softer approaches. But which had they used on her? Or did they have to?

"Just curiosity. See a young woman picked up at gun point, you tend to wonder what's going on. Why?" Was he proposing a champerty, or just fishing for information?

Nicoli eyed me longer than was polite, then smiled to break the tension. I knew he was looking for those telltale signs; change in voice, twitching, clenching, crossing or uncrossing feet/legs, inability to maintain eye contact, dry mouth, hesitancy in answering, inability to remain seated, need for cigarette or water, playing with hands, reddening of face, tapping of fingers, and other such signs that revealed liars. A great interrogator fed the interrogatee half truths, but never revealed everything that he knew, thereby keeping the advantage. But in the instant matter I was not under threat of charges, and had nothing to be held over my head, save the potential romantic feelings I had for Sylvia, and my promise to retrieve her. The former was my secret, the latter I had to assume they knew.

"So, you're not going to try and rescue her?"

"Not unless your agency is abusing her, and even then, what could I do?" I shrugged. "You're not torturing her or anything, are you?" Now I watched for the tells.

Nicoli searched his inner pocket for a cigarette, tapped it out, and lit up. Now, was that a sign? Or was it a reverse sign given between two men who knew them?

"I doubt we need do that with Sylvia," Nicoli admitted.

"I had named her Franny," I remarked, feigning disinterest in the subject by looking out towards the fading clouds.

"So what's the plan?" Nicoli asked after a moment.

Good, he fell for my disinterest. The element of surprise might still be there. Maybe it would stay that way, give me a shot at giving her a shot.

"Get Henri, make him talk, and save the world." That's about how I saw it.

Nicoli shrugged, as Russians do when faced with the simplicity that is inarguably correct.

If only it were that easy....

– CHAPTER 23 –

WE LANDED ON A MILITARY TARMAC of a decommissioned Russian airport just outside Skopie. Tires chirped, and out of the window I saw a black limo shoot out of a hangar and race down the tarmac after us.

"Welcoming committee?" I commented.

"Yes, and no secret signals this time." Nicoli smiled at his own dry humor.

"Good to know." But I'd be watching anyway. KGB were known for tricks, though it was not very seldom that they went back on their word, or on agreements, which was why they tried to word their contractual obligations so as to provide an out. In other words, if you were dumb enough to sign a dummy contract without hammering the details out, then shame on you.

The old Russian Tupolev TU-106, which had been converted from commercial to military transport, squeaked to a halt. The plane was bumped and jostled by the poorly maintained runway, but that was to be expected. The Russian military were the first victims of the economic adjustment under a democratic government, since their generals, most of whom had been on the take in one form or manner, had been cut off from the perks. In that median, between communism and democracy, the grunts had been abused and maltreated, because what scraps came down the line were first sucked up by the generals, then the commissioned officers, and then the higher-ranking noncoms. Unlike most countries, who paid and fed their soldiers first, Russia had turned its back on their once proud military. Soldiers begged in the streets, in uniforms, or deserted, if they were smart enough. If they held their mud, they'd wind up in Chechenya on a suicide mission, or at least in a war that was akin to Russian roulette. The equipment was poorly maintained, or falling apart. Only recently had the bear begun to rid itself of the fleas and ticks that were bringing its military down.

I speak of those fleas and ticks that can cripple any institution, whose hide is riddled with the sores of corruption and abuse. Any type of government, be it absolute monarchism or socialism or democracy, succeeds or fails on the backs of the rulers' integrity, and those with delegated authority. For thousands of years man has revolted in the name of one form of government or another, but it is not, in all actuality, the government type they were protesting, but the corruption of their leaders, who have been corrupted by that absolute power that had in turn infected the system of governing. Even tyranny can allow its people to thrive, until the tyrant becomes enamored with self instead of country, at which point the people suffer, and ultimately revolt. Plato, Nietzsche, or even Machiavelli's discourses on government, succeed or fail on the merits of leadership probity. It doesn't matter what style of governing is empowered, for it is the governors themselves that determine whether the governed will except their executive function.

In Russia, the judiciary and legislative bodies were still unaccustomed to their powers, of legislating, and then enforcing those legislative laws, because throughout their communistic history their power was all too often usurped by one Politburo member or some other "official" that had the power to command. Laws and courts were necessary in the running of a smooth democratic society. Without the judicial function, there could be no equality between the classes, no protection of the poor and previously disenfranchised, and without these basics there could be no democracy. And because the judiciary still shook on newly acquired legs, the corruption and convoluted bureaucracies posed a substantial threat that could possibly topple the democratic system that was just beginning to right itself in Russia after years of floundering. And to attempt a reversion back to communism would be too costly, too bloody.

The air was brisk, carrying on it the scent of cattle, which was common to this region. Though controlled by its own democratic government, its past ties to Yugoslavia and Russia were still intact. It relied upon their parent countries, like a daughter relies upon her father for money, her mother for emotional stability. Therefore, Macedonia sat heavily in Russian hands, and Russian military bases were common in certain areas of the country, though they were kept low profile to the citizens of Macedonia, lest it become common knowledge. I stepped onto the tarmac, and saw why the plane had bucked and jostled down the runway; pits, cracks, and one-foot-deep potholes! I cursed the latter. My briefcase in hand, I watched Nicoli conversing with the limo driver. They argued about something, which was very uncommon, and then the backdoor of the limo began to open on its own.

My body went rigid as I waited for a shooter, wondering if these clothes were made of the bulletproof material I usually had all my clothes made from. The electromagnetic pulse might deflect the bullet, but the timing was next to impossible. I would have to press it the instant the trigger was squeezed if it was a silenced pistol. If it wasn't, then the watch had its own sound activation system.

I saw red hair, and black glasses on too white skin, and a chill ran up my spine. I was glad my sunglasses were on, or I'd be telling on myself with bug eyes. I looked from Nicoli to Sylvia, then back again.

I walked as naturally as I could towards her, and gave her a smile.

"Surprised to see me?" Sylvia said, red lipstick contaminating those pink lips I'd wiped after feeding.

I swallowed and went forward, aware of Nicoli's look. "No. I was just telling Nicoli here that I was worried about your safety." I went forward and gave her a hug.

Her lips tingled against my ear, but her words burned my soul. "You bastard, why'd you let them get me?" she whispered into my brain.

Our hug must have surprised Nicoli, for he thought about moving closer, then thought better of it. I hoped that our tactic of genuine concern, instead of pretending to be distant, threw them off their base. Nicoli, and several cameras located around the area, were recording the entire scene.

"You're welcome," I told her aloud, and with a smile, as if to answer her whisper of thanks in my ear. I could only hope she wasn't bugged. "How're they treating you?" I asked, as Nicoli closed in like an unnecessary third wheel.

"I'm afraid Missus—" an emphasis on the last word— "DeNoel is booked on a flight back home," Nicoli said, more to her than to me, as if chastising a child in front of company that you don't want to know. The problem is, they always know.

"What? No getting to know you? No reminiscing over trails travailed, pains passed? Am I not the rescuer?" I asked Nicoli with some indignancy. I looked then at Sylvia, who was still embarrassed about the revelation that she was supposedly married. A revelation that had not passed by me without sending a subtle shockwave through my heart. That thing I sometimes refuse to acknowledge, where hope of new love had existed when Dean had said, "No, my love, I cannot marry you now."

"I'm afraid Mrs. DeNoel is far more important than you or I suspected, and must return to run her husband's company."

Nicoli gently guided Sylvia by the elbow to the transport we'd just landed in, and I didn't envy her at all. In fact, I worried about her and that plane. Some phantom of intuition creased my thoughts, yet was there anything I could do?

Not so important that she'd rate a better plane than that junker. If she'd been that important they wouldn't have driven her all the way out here to accidentally run into me in an out of the way changeover. I would wait for an explanation, but they'd given away their suspicions, and therefore their edge. They suspected some romantic link, when in all reality there wasn't. Sexual tension, maybe. Mutual attraction, probably. Yet they'd wanted to rid me of all romantic aspirations by denoting her as "Misses DeNoel." And that led to the question; Why?

"Please get in, sir," the driver said from the other side of the car.

I ignored him, watching the entire sequence, from Nicoli guiding her by the elbow, to some conversation taking place as he helped her up the stairs and into the plane, where they both disappeared. Nicoli exited five seconds later, and returned to the limo, where I was waiting. He knew I knew, but what could he do? It was most certainly planned by his superiors, who from behind their mahogany desks forgot the realities of the field.

"Sorry about that," Nicoli said in French.

"I'm sure that was none of your doing," I replied in kind, and he nodded thanks before we both got into the back of the black state limo, no longer dubbed BGC with my personage weighing not too heavily upon its shocks.

"Vodka?" Nicoli offered, and took a bottle out of a small portable cooler, along with two glasses. "I love this brand."

Smirnoff. What Vodka lover didn't like the brand. "Sure, after you."

I didn't wait for him to drink first. An old expression from the poisoned drink days. A sign of good faith. Nicoli knew it well, and I appreciated his knowledge of ancient customs. Especially since the newfound revelation had him working for Vladimir, which cast a whole different light upon his charade. It was both good and bad, in that Nicoli was connected to the commandant, yet disturbing, for it gave new meaning to running into someone. Surely, Nicoli and Vladimir wanted more than to just check on my relationship with Sylvia.

"Does Vladimir know what's going on?" I continued in French.

"Oh yes." He pointed to the black upholstery behind the driver's seat, and motioned with a gesture that it was a monitoring device.

They were elsewhere nowadays. I nodded my head and continued my conversation on a mundane subject, hoping that his revelation with regard to his connection with Vladimir was a field command decision, and not one that has come down the line, tainted with administrative scheming and calculation.

The rumble of jet engines turned into a scream, and I allowed my gaze to drift past Nicoli's profile to the windows of the plane. Was she inside looking down at this car, or was she restrained by the military men who'd stayed aboard? Was she cursing my name, again? Were her eyes watery in my absence? Those hauntingly sexy green eyes, with their dual individuality, miniscule imperfections making them striking. I remembered checking for pupilary responses in the darkness of the cave, those greens and lesser blues and blacks beautiful under flashlight. Ah, those intricacies of nature that made us all unique beings, no matter the mold we all shared. Was my intent at the time to imprint myself upon her brain, and had her whisper—Why'd you let them get me?—implied that I was imprinted on her brain? Was she just being the tauntingly cute litte brat she'd seemed to be, after waking up, the lady just beneath the surface of the girl, a prize to be gotten by patience, and only in time?

"Good stuff," I said after I drank my fill, then brought out my toys. Inside the briefcase I carried a debugger, a scrambler, the wavelength fluctuation device that would scramble any sensors, which might lurk with their micro antennae through the specifics of my electronic noise emanations. Nicoli's eyes brightened as I revealed more techno tricks, which the Russians would have in about two years, no matter what I showed or did not show. Mankind, technologically speaking, evolved no matter what; i.e. any industrialized country with think tanks and secret government-sponsored research would sooner or later figure some technology out. It was a matter of time, just like the atom bomb. Had the U.S. not arrived at that point sooner, the Germans would have.

I kept speaking about the wiles of Russian vodka, as I typed a message to Nicoli on my MPC; "Scrambled communication; what's the deal with Vlad? Why Mrs. DeNoel?" I gave him my arm, so to speak, so he could read and type a message, as I spoke about the other uses for potatoes.

He hesitated, looked at me, then typed a message, as he changed the subject to Andalusians and their training and breeding.

"I want to defect!" I lost my conversational thought.

"Why tell me? I can't help you any more than a John Doe. Besides, I'm more world citizen than U.S."

"I would like to join your org!"

"Bullshit! I'm a private contractor! I don't have many contacts, only friends in high places. Quit bullshitting and tell me what gives. Why Sylvia?"

He chuckled at that and typed; "We want to know what your ties are to DeNoel. Her husband's a member of the President's cabinet."

"DeNoel? Yeah right. I know every cabinet member and there's no DeNoel there. What about the nukes? Does Vlad know?"

"You are too knowledgeable. DeNoel is an asset we have invested a lot of rubles in, and don't want to waste. As for the nukes, you and I will handle them according to our agreement. The deal holds with Peroskvi. The Russians must play a part in the capture of corrupted politicians and thieves.

Minski can be disposed of at any moment, but he will be allowed to assist, so long as he's cooperative."

"—Ah, but there's no substitute for good breeding," he said aloud.

"I agree, but there are tricks to that trade, as I'm sure you know."

"Ah, but there are secrets to every trade, are there not?"

I gave a holler to JD; "TRACK FLIGHT PATTERN OF MY SECOND, POR FAVOR!" My number two, if it was still good, was a bug I'd placed on Sylvia's clothes the moment I hugged her.

"CAUGHT SIGNAL THE MOMENT IT WAS ACTIVATED. BOUND FOR MOSCOW. CLEAR SIGNAL."

"PRIORITY THREE FOR MY SECOND. WHERE'S THE WEASEL?" Henri.

"INBOUND ON BULG/YUGO MAIN HIGHWAY. AMBUSH SITE 10 CLICKS INSIDE BORDER. YOUR ETA IS 5, HENRI'S 23. WATCH YOUR BACKSSS." Meaning DTA, or don't trust anyone. "INBOUND HELI'S."

"Tell your driver our ambush site is five minutes ahead. What's the deal with the helicopters?" I asked Nicoli after he'd tapped the window.

"Backup."

"Backup?"

"Yes. A Spetz team, trained in handling nuclear weapons and bomb disposal."

"Have any jamming equipment?" That was the most important thing now. If Henri alerted his friends, then the other missions would be jeopardized. The terrorists might even decide to just blow one up where it was.

"Yes," Nicoli said offhandedly.

I knew he was hiding some new invention. Probably a SATDEF system, which tracked any type of electronic signal and deflected it with exact frequency waves, like an ocean wave crashing over it, pushing it to the earth before it could reach its target. Too bad they didn't know that it was a fraud. Any simple modulation device could easily get past the SATDEF system. The concept of the system was great, but the application was seriously flawed, as was the case with many new inventions. The best way to jam signals was still to stuff the frequency, and those surrounding it, with so much electronic noise that the sender couldn't get the message through.

"I hope it's not the SAT-DEF system?" I said, poking fun. His reaction was a grimace, and he knew I knew, because he'd come to expect such letdowns; third-rate technology that his superiors claimed was top secret, as if the claim would make it so. But Nicoli was in a position to know better, and I knew he wasn't surprised. "I'll take care of it.'"

Nicoli looked away, embarrassed, before speaking. "There was a time when we were first.... VostokOne, Mir...." He said a few more, but I didn't listen. It was a pipe dream quoted by many democrats who still hungered for the pride propagated by the propaganda of communism.

I felt his eyes on me, as I was busy instructing JD, which I didn't have to do.

"You know, I still cling to the hope of the sickle and the bear, the May parades that meant more than bluffs and Machiavellian schemes. Ha, even you, one man, have better technology than our entire country."

Yeah, but I didn't have the mass. "JAM 41.9LAT/21L0."

I said aloud; "I have better technology than America."

"Yes, but that makes it no easier to take. And would you seriously part with something like this?" He touched my MPC.

"Not this one, but I see no problem hooking you up. You'll have to pay for shipping and handling, and your government will owe me one." I paused for effect. "Unless you're coming over?"

He shrugged, still unable to break free of the reins of hope, which kept him from leaving Mother Russia. I could not blame him either, for I knew his pain, I knew the depths to which his hope sank, like a barbed anchor into the flesh of his soul, from whence desertion would cause endless guilt. I'd seen it eat people away. I'd seen that betrayal of self, for that's what it was, eat away the soul, then the body, and finally, one's life.

"We're here." I tapped on the black glass that separated us from the driver.

"Tell me, is she in danger?"

Nicoli contemplated for a moment. "Yes and no. Her father is very powerful."

"And her husband?"

He shook his head; there was no husband.

It's as I'd thought. She was sent as a tool.

"Know where to hide us?" I said, using the driver's native tongue. He checked with Nicoli, in the mirror, before returning to me in the affirmative.

"So the game begins," Nicoli said in Russian, then pulled out a very large Makarov 49 semiautomatic pistol.

"How the hell do you keep that monster from toppling you over?"

"Years of compensation. My wife says that when I don't wear it I walk with a limp." He chuckled at this. "And you?"

"I usually don't bother with guns, but Henri left me a little souvenir."

The red phone buzzed within a stained oak box that formed the top of the minibar. Nicoli picked it up, listened, then hung up the phone. All humor was gone. He looked out of the window, at the sky, then shrugged. "There's been an accident."

I heard the softness of his voice. This couldn't have happened twice in one week, or even in one life time, I told myself, reinforcing the odds in my head, which surely weighed in my favor.

I typed, unconsciously; "JD, ANY REPORTS ON ACCIDENTS?"

"I LOST THE SIGNAL A FEW MINUTES AGO. MOSCOW REPORTS ACCIDENT AT KRUSHCHEV AIRPORT. STOP. SORRY."

I deleted my own message and typed; "KEEP WATCH. STOP. REPORT ON SURVIVORS."

"So it begins," I whispered just loud enough for Nicoli to hear, though it had been said only for my sake.

"She is dead, my friend. I am sorry."

Yes, but someone had to be held accountable, I thought, blocking sorrow and loss with anger, putting another patch over my holed soul.

Good-bye Franny, I said in my mind, then looked out at the tan scenery of wheat fields and field grass, where we would soon run into a nuclear bomb.

It was too easy. Too pat. Shadows lurked behind the walls my allies had put up. Within the dark corner of my mind, those places I created in Haifu Hell, I saw cospiracies in life, and in death.

Dean? I queried silently.

– CHAPTER 24 –

THE BLACK WRAITH APPEARED in the distance, a shimmering blight on the horizon, as if the radioactivity of the nuclear weapon inside it were giving off heat. It puzzled me, with all their money and planning, that they didn't use another means of transport. A plane, chartered bus, or something indigenous to the region.

"Maybe it's a decoy?" I said under my breath.

"Well, I still wouldn't want to be in that car." Nicoli smiled for the first time in a while.

I did not envy the persons in the approaching BGC, for though Mother Russia's sons and daughters weren't as technologically advanced as those of other countries, they were constantly inventing new means of employing old technology. A road spike had been placed on the side of the road; a steel dart attached to a thin strand of superconductive wire, which was mounted upon a power source and amplifier that would short-circuit the car, and anyone touching conductive parts of the vehicle. The downside was that if the gas tank wasn't well insulated the car would blow up and spread radioactive material all over the area, and us.

Was she hurt? Was she dead? Were there survivors? I kept coming back to the "what ifs," but I knew. Shadows danced a pattern.

Nicoli's touch brought me back to reality, behind a clump of tall field grass, ten meters from the road and behind a mound. "Maybe she's okay?" he fed me hope. "But there's nothing you can do now, and we've business to attend to."

"Where's your driver?"

"Over there. Irrigation ditch." He would do the wet work, if necessary.

"STEP UP JAMMING, JD!" I typed. "We might be too close?"

"Probably, but it's too late now." And Nicoli crouched down behind the bush, turning his face sideways to me. "You'd better hug the ground, it's been known to throw off a lightning bolt or two."

I joined him, flattened on the ground, as the sound of the powerful German-built engine approached, all the while hoping that our shallow foxhole would be sufficient.

The crackle was like positive wires crossing; a white flash of light that lasted three seconds, and overrode the bright day, accompanied by a loud boom, which we later saw were the four tires exploding as the air within them expanded instantly. There was no flash of orange, or explosion.

POP! POP! POP! A gun spoke.

"Don't kill him!" I barked in Russian, seeing the driver dragging a man out by the collar of his jacket. I recognized Henri instantly, even without his wire-rimmed glasses. I hope the popping sounds hadn't been for him.

Nicoli raced past me, gun at the ready, black gloves on, and went to the side door and yanked it open. A body fell out, accompanied by a stainless steel, lead-lined Samsonite standard-sized suitcase.

"He's alive."

"Who got the bullets?"

"The driver. His hands were on the steering wheel. The radio's in the back though?"

Our driver dragged Henri over to the side of the road, as the helicopter approached.

A mopup team, no doubt.

Nicoli put plasticuffs on the man that had fallen out of the car with the suitcase; most likely the one who would deliver and set the bomb. He gently brought the suitcase to the side of the road, and set it down on the grass.

I typed; "JD, MISSION COMPLETE! ANY SIGNALS?"

"HOLD. DOWNLOADING INFO."

"Shit," I muttered to myself, hating to be put on hold, but nervous because it meant that he was busy in his little room, receiving God knew what. He was monitoring Sylvia, looking for Boris, tracking about ten different subjects both for then and for the future. *Come on, God, you owe me a couple,* I thought, knowing that it didn't matter, for what had happened had happened already. No changing the past, unless you're a slick revisionist.

"It's our team," the driver said, then opened the suitcase using Henri's key. "And this is ours too," the driver turned nuclear engineer stated as a matter of fact.

I saw inside that it was a crude device, which according to my readings on the subject would produce only about five kilotons. Enough to take out a city block and infect a city with radiation for years to come. St. Petersburg; Gone. Enough to bribe a country.

"Good, Sergiov. Can you disarm it?" Nicoli asked the man, a tone of respect now in his voice.

"Yes, a crude device. Effective."

"Any chance of radiation?" I asked.

"Yes," driver turned nuclear engineer turned Sergiev informed us. "Its casing has been removed so less explosives will be necessary to reach critical mass."

I nodded in agreement, and went over to Henri. He was still out, his hair standing on end, looking like a blond porcupine.

"Wake up, Henri!" I slapped him across the cheek; left, then right. Bitch slaps. "Get yer ass up! I know you're awake, bitch!"

"Okay—okay!" Henri sputtered, looking for his glasses and, not finding them, reaching for his waist.

"Ah—ah—ahhhh. Looking for this?" I shoved the .380 barrel into his nose, and saw tears spring to his eyes. "Remember me?"

"I—I—" He looked over towards the suitcase, and then slumped, as if his own life was somehow determinable by the bomb. "Just kill me. I'm dead anyways."

"Not before we find out about the other bombs, Henri. I'm afraid we've only just begun, as the song goes, unless you're willing to testify. Confession's good for the soul, and you're a good Catholic, now, aren't you, Henri? Even still, my new KGB friends are certainly experts at retrieval."

"Yes—yes—" Henri began softly.

"Speak up!"

"Yes, do speak up, Comrade Stoiebski," Nicoli said with true menace in his voice. "You thought I wouldn't recognize you in your French disguise?" *Ptwhew!* Nicoli spat in the man's face. "Traitor!" he hissed.

This was something new, now, I thought to myself, stepping back mentally to reexamine the situation. Was this some sort of act? No. Nicoli was truly outraged at Henri, and Henri was sort of ashamed.

"I take it you two know each other?" I said, standing outside the sphere of their hatred for each other, or, Nicoli's hatred of Henri, aka Stoiebski, or whoever he was.

"It was Parovich that hired—"

Whack! Nicoli's hand struck the man in the mouth. "Don't lie! You think we are fools? You've never been a pawn in your life!"

"Well, who is he?"

"He's a traitor!"

"I understand all that, but what did he do that's got you in a tiff?" I saw his look of confusion. "Upset?"

"I gave the British and Americans our spy list, prior to the Soviet Union's fall." Henri smiled proudly. "And I was paid what I was worth, too!" *Wack!*

"We lost fifty-eight agents. A dozen more, including myself, were compromised. He—" Nicoli spat— "was the catalyst, some say, for the downfall of the Soviet Union."

"What's he doing working with Minister Parovich, if he's the bane of Russia?"

"Your agencies are fools to think—"

Whack! "You will see how foolish we are when you're on the table, Mikely Stiebsky."

The Russian Sikorsky 114 helicopter landed nearby, just beyond the mound, where our BGC was parked out of sight from the highway. Moments later men in silver radiation suits ran over the rise, four of them, in a double line, as if they were out for a morning jog on the moon.

Nicoli barked orders to Sergiev, and the man obeyed instantly, shutting the case.

"Where's it going?" I asked Nicoli.

"Ah, my friend, you need not worry about a thief robbing a thief," he said honestly, looking me directly in the eye.

"What about him?"

"If you want to kill him go ahead, but I know you know that we need information from him."

"I'm sure Dean would like the latter idea—"

Nicoli sprang at Henri, his thumbs shooting into the man's mouth, as the eyes of the traitor began to roll up. The smell of almonds was powerful in the air. Foam came out of Henri's mouth, and dribbled over Nicoli's hands.

I pulled Nicoli from the man, who still might have enough life to spit the toxic cyanide into Nicoli's eyes, or mouth. It only took a miniscule drop to kill.

"He's gone." I held Nicoli's heaving shoulders for a moment, then released him.

"I didn't think he had the stuff to do it," Nicoli said, wiping his hands on the material of Henri's jacket.

"Cowards usually take the easy way out."

Nicoli sighed in agreement, and I had the feeling that he may have truly enjoyed the uncivilized nature of interrogation and torture, stepping down from his otherwise civil bearing. Could his hate run deeper than my own, so deep that it would shirk off his humanity for the mere act of vengeance, albeit for a higher purpose; finding the bombs? I'd experienced the feeling, and had given in to it only once, but it was there. I imagine it's there in all of us, waiting for the trigger pull; a moment that strikes at our very soul, that violent ripping away of something precious, something necessary for happiness in life.

In the jungles of Asia I have allowed my rage to flow, naked, dripping with mud and feces, fleeing tiny men with beady black eyes and evil leers, and cruel intentions. I know not how many fell by my hand, nor care to recall. General Dung's torture techniques were much more crueler than kind, and I've the scars on either side of my fingernails to prove it. He took great care not to pull the fingernail out, but instead to break it about halfway up. In Dung's crudeness lay my saving grace, for I've a strong tolerance for pain and forbearance, and never did waver in my story; I was a tourist on vacation, but also looking for American investment opportunities in North Korea. I'd told them, and kept telling them, feigning weakness and timidity. The last session with General Dung, which to this day I cannot remember, and maybe don't want to, must have caused my synaptic relays to overload in my brain. Eight hours or so later I found myself in the jungle, naked, but free, stalking my stalkers. I recall the tiger in the greenery; white, orange, and black stripes gliding through the shadowy greens and browns, colored oil behind big fern fans, elusive, dreamlike, but real. And screams from North Korean soldiers, shots, automatic gunfire lighting up the night, like flashes of lightning that wouldn't be suppressed by the thick foilage. My feet took the brunt of the escape; jungles are a bitch on feet.

"Cort?" Nicoli said for the second time. "I'm sorry you could not do it yourself," he added, because my blank stare had been locked on Henri's pale blue face.

But I was glad I didn't have to kill him. I didn't want to kill him, or anybody.

The bomb was gone, and the helicopter's turbine engines were warming up to a high pitched whistle. This part of the mission was over.

My computer buzzed against my forearm. I unstrapped the cover and looked at the screen. "BORIS IS FOUND. STOP. NO SURVIVORS. STOP." JD always used proper e-com lingo when something was wrong, or serious.

Something struck me in the gut, then in the chin, but nobody touched me. It was like an invisible body blow, crunching into my solar plexus, impacting unseen soft points you don't realize you have until hope is cleaved from your mind. I exhaled a loud sigh, and had I had tears to give, I would have given them. But Dean's death had robbed me of that release. Instead, I allowed Nicoli to lead me into the back of the limo, whose driver had been replaced.

Nicoli looked at my uncleared screen, and put a glass of vodka in my hand, and watched me down it. Then another.

"Drink, my friend." He tossed back a gulp with me. "We still have other bombs to find."

"What about the other man?"

"If he knows anything, he will talk." There was a sheer and determined assurance to that statement. "The cyanide tooth will be extracted back at HQ. Until then, his mouth is locked open."

I nodded my head as the liquid warmed my chest and belly, a warm hand seizing the icicle that was my spine, melting the dirty debris that lined my nerves. I couldn't think straight. I'd lost assistants before, and even contacts, but never ever two in such a short span. What were the odds, I asked for the hundreth time. And my grief? For a woman—a girl—I barely knew? Had she ever even reciprocated my feelings? Or meant anything more than friendship, or thankfulness for my saving her ass? Had she meant what her eyes had said when she pleaded with me to rescue her from her handlers? From the man who I now shared drinks with?

"Where're we going, by the way?"

"Moscow." Nicoli took another drink. "I'm afraid you were right. Moscow is a target. A radiation device was tripped at Krushchev International X ray devices bound for Stalinov Hospital. They never arrived."

He looked at me, and I saw the shadow of death in his eyes; that fear of a great loss. It would be.

"If Moscow is nuked, won't those out of the loop think that NATO or the U.S. did it?" I wondered aloud.

"The military generals might. The communist party would shout it out. A bunch of fanatics who've lost the heart of the party...."

"And once the presidential office is destroyed, under your constitution, the military takes over supreme countrol?"

"Yes."

"They will launch."

"Yes. Probably."

– CHAPTER 25 –

THE *IL MARICELA* rounded the western tip of Crete, under full speed, in the black night without moon, relying solely upon radar and GPS navigation. A crew of twenty-eight men, all Columbian, save for a Finnish Captain, made up the detachment in charge of the ship's precious cargo.

"I'm going down below. Watch the blip on the screen, and call me when it reaches here." Captian Volf Daark pointed at the radar screen, making sure the South American could see what he meant. He hated this man, who didn't speak at all, and probably didn't even understand what he said, Volf thought to himself. They could've at least sent a man who spoke Portugese or French, even English. He doubted there was anyone in South America that spoke Finnish.

There were about 250 miles of open sea until Malta, and about 1,250 miles until the Strait. He could sleep for six hours, then come back when they were near Malta, then check for busy traffic, and return to the cot for much-needed catching up. The seas were calm, which was the norm in the Med.

After this trip, Volf dreamed, he'd have enough money to spend a year on Oulu, fishing, hunting, and 4x4'ing, maybe even find a good wife who would sprout kids for him— "What the hell!"

A haf a million tons of steel shuddered.

The Columbian unslung his CF9 submachine gun. A man, the leader of the Columbian forces, ran into the wheelhouse and snatched the radio off its cradle.

"What's happened?" Figuero Montero barked at his soldier, whose sole responsibility was to watch over the Captain. Any radio contact was monitored from another, secret room. Those radios had stopped working sixty seconds ago, and Montero had felt the dark night moving in on them. "Did he do anything with the radios?"

"Nothing, sir. He was just going to take his rest, and the ship shook."

"Prepare for attack," Montero told his soldier, then looked at the Captain. "We're under attack, Captain. We must get a message to the owners of this vessel," he said in perfect Finnish.

Captain Daark held out his hand for the radio phone, and put it to his ear.

"Nothing but static?" he replied in natural Finnish, still surprised at the leader's ability to speak. He looked at the GPS navigation, and the electronic radar tracking scope, and saw that they too were gone. The boat suddenly came under the brightest light any of them had ever seen, or ever would see.

The Captain opened his mouth to say something when the flash of thermonuclear heat blew over them, instantly dematerializing everything onboard in a white hot instant.

"Nice shot, Captain Ptrovic!" Commander Kirov told his chief fire officer some thirty miles away.

"Years of practice off the California Coast, commander."

The crew cheered.

"My first," a young officer said.

"And hopefully your last," Kirov hoped aloud, for although they were trained to fire nuclear missiles quickly, none relished the opportunity, and what its effect would be. The small tactical nuke had been delivered from the special weapons section of the KGB just yesterday, by order of the President, and had been easily mounted on a Kirolov 65 long-range torpedo. None, not even the men who'd delivered it, had expected it to be as bright as it had been. But it had done the job, Kirov noted, for when they arrived at the last known position of the *Il Maricela* there was nothing but ashes on the sea, and minuscule particles.

Radiation cleanup teams were ordered in, and later the area would be monitored by Russian trawlers that were more than they seemed. But essentially, the thousand-ton *Il Maricela*, and all its crew and cargo, had vanished into the blackest of nights.

"I can't raise her, *señor*," the Columbian radio operator told his boss, *El Jefe*. "It just cut out, sir. Maybe the antennae broke?"

"No!" He had not existed for twenty years, at the top, while all others were being busted or killed, without knowing when something was smelly. Instincts. They were speaking to him now. All he had to do now was give a sign, and Moscow would be exfoliated from the earth. But first they must be in place. He felt deep down that the freighter was gone; Montero was a good soldier, smart, and would have found a way to make contact if it hadn't been something final. Next time they'd use a stealth plane, or submarine. Easily attainable by a multibillionaire. But something was telling him, those instincts, that he needed to vacate this safehouse. It had been a good home for six months, but now it was time to go to the next one, which had been purchased three years ago, under some other name, as were all his estates, be they in Europe, Asia, Americas, or even Africa and Australia.

"We're moving."
"*Sí, señor.*"
"But first contact Miguel, find out if they're in place."
"*Sí, señor!*"

"Colonel Ramirez, big fish is making a move."
"Is echo team in place?"
"Yes, sir."
"Then let him go. Where's his security men?" Colonel Ramirez, thirty-nine, born in East Los Angeles, said into a throat mike.
"At alpha coordinates, sir." The coca processing plant, outside Cali Columbia.
Colonel Ramirez had had this DEA/U.S. Military adventure thrown in his lap, but he liked the adventure, chasing the "Big Fish," aka Edwardo Diaz, around the globe. They were a week away from the biggest bust to go down in international history. Many lives had been lost up to this point, he knew, and sometimes he wondered if human lives were worth prohibition, but they were here now, not back in the old neighborhood. The Big Fish had been tagged and tracked, under the highest priority. Major U.S. DOD satellites had been given to DEA and IDEA, actually the Department of Defense contracted out their personnel and honored all requests made by DEA or IDEA officials. Elusive suspects suddenly became easy to track, and in doing so they'd witnessed over two thousand executions worldwide, committed by the drug lords, either as a matter of business, or economy. Many times he himself had wanted to break cover and step out from beneath the straw hat and potato sack pants, and become the Special Forces Commando he'd been trained to be. His conscience ate at him, for not saving the lives of his own people, for though born in East L.A., he was Mexican, just like those poor farmers and traffickers, who were most often killed rather than paid. There were always more to take their place.
Now, outside a villa in Madrid, Spain, he leaned against the pole, looking like any old Spaniard waiting for one of the cabbies. Several men were posted around the area, waiting for the signal, which could be given at any moment. He'd better return to post, Colonel Ramirez thought to himself, and bounced off of the street lamp post, and began walking towards a small Spanish flat just down the block, but within sight of the larger estate. The DEA/IDEA Spanish HQ, which only two Spanish government officials new about. And they were sworn to secrecy, and paid handsomely by the DEA/IDEA, whose coffers were fat from seizures around the world.
"Sir? The radio man is calling long distance to Russia again. Should we

jam it, or let it go through?"

They had billions of dollars of sophisticated equipment, some even more sophisticated than the military had, since the DEA had been given priority from President George Bush Junior's administration. Budget limitations were on the order of billions. All just to fight the war on drugs.

Ramirez thought about the phone call as he took off his disguise.

"Sir? It's connecting."

"Have we heard anything from anyone?" Ramirez asked.

"None, Colonel. Not since the CIA message came down from DC to be on the lookout for any strange packages, aka bombs."

"Well, let it go through, but record it, and send it to the cyphers, and track trace the call."

The second the words left his mouth he felt a knot at the base of his skull, an intuitive resonance of doom, which he'd felt several times, and which had saved his life just as many. Ramirez rubbed his neck, and tried to shake the feeling all the way to the shower.

He couldn't.

– CHAPTER 26 –

RAJIID DISRAELI, NAMED AFTER the British statesman, stood near a post some ten meters from the rails, which now rumbled as a long passenger train pulled into the station. His eyes were upon Igor, waiting for the sign. He enjoyed this type of work, which was why he'd accepted Cort's offer of being the India Contact, though he did wish he knew more about what was going on that was so important as to drag him from his warm bed and wife in Bombay. But such was his line of employment. He and Igor would watch over Cort's back, while he was in Russia, and, as JD requested, be ready to save the day, or call God. He knew the pain that Cort was feeling over Dean's death, for he had experienced that loss when his son had been killed.

Rajiid wore a Bombay business suit, which would have made great camouflage on Wall Street, or in the London business district, but he stood out like a blinking McDonald's sign in the middle of Red Square, Igor thought to himself. He enjoyed the Indian's Hinduistic commentary when they'd time to congregate. He often visited Rajiid's family when he was within two hundred miles of Bombay, which was more often than not. Where was Fong at, Igor wondered, for as the Russian Contact, he was supposed to know where the other contacts were. Damn that independent-minded Fong! JD had told them all to be discreet, but not invisible. It was better that than being spotted by the Moscow Centre's intel Directorate, or the new KGB men.

Igor had positioned Rajiid so Cort would see him, and know that he had backup if needed.

Te Si Fong, five feet two, hid a stocky build under traditional Chinese clothes, and a serious demeanor behind a tourist's facade. He stood gray among the people, sipping a cup of tea at the furthest table just outside the train station. From his vantage point, across the street, he could monitor the enemy from behind blue-tinted glasses, with intelligent eyes of dark obsidian. His face held features that gave away his royal Cantonese ancestry. He lifted his cup, pressed his lips to the glass, but never touched the cold tea.

"Canton in position, enjoying the sights."

Igor heard Fong' s voice in his tiny ear bud speaker, and raised his hands, acting as if they were cold. "All go. ETA one minute. Igor out. Rajiid? Remember, don't make direct eye contact. My people will be looking for that. Just make sure you're seen, then leave."

Rajiid checked his watch, then nodded instead of risking speaking into the gadget in a crowd.

The new Minsk to Moscow bullet train skreed to a final halt, and Moscowvites prepared to debark, but this purpose did not detract from the loud conversations and smiles, in certain areas of the train where coworkers grouped. At the rear of the train a more solemn group stood.

I thought it odd that the new Russians were still afraid of old KGB, or even normal citizens wearing old KGB long coats. Even the youngsters, with their American and Western European ways, quieted instantly within the presence of the trenchcoats, and hard stares.

"Yes, and it's been years since we've taken dissidents into custody for questioning." Nicoli smiled in a manner that reminded me of a shark, though not too proud of his old teeth.

He'd read my mind. I smiled and said, "Yes, but you still pull citizens in for questioning.

"Like you Americans, we must fight the war on crime, drugs, and terrorism. Besides, we must keep up appearances, but none are executed or imprisoned without due process.

"Ah, qualifications." I saw him grin, for he knew I was correct in my assumption. The doors slid open and we moved within the flow, though surrounded by four KGB men; two in front, two behind.

Rajiid! What the hell was he doing here? I locked eyes briefly, and then he turned and boarded the train. I searched for other contacts, instantly knowing that JD and Igor must know something, or be up to something. Well, at least I had backup, and gave up looking lest I give my watchers away. I might just need them. Certainly I had enemies within Russia, and two foes in the higher echelons of the power structure. Though, as far as I knew, none were part of the KGB.

"We're at ground zero, Nicoli," I said as we stepped out into the cool polluted air of Moscow. A man, dressed in a business suit, stepped up to us, then looked off the bodyguards.

"Car for you." An American. Nicoli's facial expression changed momentarily. "Let's go."

It was common practice for Americans to secretly assist them under circumstances such as this one. Circumstances that would have a global impact.

I looked around without moving my head, using my tinted sunglasses to shield my eye movements. FONG! It was nice to see the smartest man I knew here in my stead, just in case shit went from bad to worse.

"Have you made the search?" I asked Nicoli in French.

"Mr. Falcon, your PC please," said the CIA agent, his left hand holding what looked to be an electronic suppression box, where my PC sensors could not pickup what was being done in the back of this black car.

"Why, and will it be harmed?"

"For our protection, and no, it won't be touched."

"Fine." But I knew it was quite possible that there was a second trapdoor from which my PC could be secretly taken, examined, and tampered with. But knowing this, I didn't mind it. In fact, I could use it to my advantage. "Allow me to sign off real quick." I typed; "JD. CIA TAKING MPC FOR MOMENT. STOP. SAW THE SIGHTS. THANKS. OUT."

"What're you typing?"

"Done. Here. I unclipped the MPC from the snug cloth rig, and handed it to the man, who gently placed it inside the box and shut the lid. It was placed inside with QAZ facing the rear of the car, and so it should return.

Me and Nicoli sat facing forward, while the CIA man sat facing the rear, with the front section of the limo behind the black glass.

"Why the secrecy? Well, we've located the nuke using our infrared detection satellite system. It's located in Minister Richtor's offices—"

Nicoli's face went white. "In Red Square."

"A short walk from the President's chambers, directly over the bomb shelter elevators. Anyone in there would die instantly from oxygen deprivation." I added my two cents, but was more interested in the InfraRad Sat System. I'd heard rumors of such a system for years ago. The only problem with it was that it was completely invasive, in that it would have to have eyes on the world at all times, which meant it was "Big Brother" in the sky. For example, if a burglar breaks into a house on Fifth Street in Phoenix, Arizona, at 14:00 hours, the system would detect and record it. On the other hand, say you didn't trust banks and wanted to bury your loot in the backyard. It would see that too. See all. It was the type of system this agent was telling us existed. Why was he telling us, was my unspoken question. But it didn't matter, because it truly was just a matter of time before such a system was over our heads.

"We've already spoken to your superiors," he said to Nicoli.

"We're going to Red Square?"

"Yes. Amnesty will be given to any spies that will be blown if their expertise is needed to fix the situation."

Why would he say that, I wondered. It was like an ace in the hole that had no purpose, unless a Russian decided to defect, or vice versa. Hmm? "And me?" I asked. If they had everything figured out, then why was I needed?

"I was told you were involved." He shrugged, opened the box, and handed me back my MPC. The secrets had been told. My personal recorder had it on a digital file.

It came out as it went in. Maybe it hadn't been tampered with? I doubted that.

– CHAPTER 27 –

WE DREW NEARER THE RED SQUARE, and it seemed that the air got colder within this protected area. Armed guards waved us through without even checking passes. The car stopped in front of the main administrative offices, where the President of Russia had had a new office built for him. Breaths came out in huffs of steam, but I felt hot within the newly donned parka.

I mentally scanned those around me, from behind my shades. I wouldn't see Igor or Fong, not within the protected confines of the Red Square, but at least I knew they were there. Nicoli led me up the stairs to the front entrance, a man stepped out of the double glass doors. Spetsnaz men, four on each side, came out of the woodwork, surrounding Commandant Vladimir Krinkov. I swore I recognized him, as he gave me a lopsided grin.

I'd only seen pictures of Vladimir, but now, standing before me, he was an impressive figure of manhood, if I be one to judge. He was sixty-three, born in Moscow, tutored by private teachers, and adopted into the old KGB by his uncle, a nonmemorable colonel who mostly shuffled papers. I put him at six feet tall, and I would bet money that he had a six pack of muscles beneath his blue pinstriped tailored suit. He wore the same type of sunglasses as I. From the CIA-generated biography, I knew he was an ambitious, and some say reckless, man in his youth, but he had made it to the top, and now there, he had become cautious. Like a bear roaming Wall Street. He had secrets on many in power, but he had also collected many political and economical defenses, so that if anyone tried to disturb his power base, or knock him off, it would cost the offender, and the country.

"Ah, wonderful. Mister Falcon," Vladimir greeted me with an easy smile. Quite a feat, considering there was a NUCLEAR BOMB TICKING OFF less than a hundred meters away! "Glad to finally meet you." He gave me his hand, and I shook it. "Nice trick with the phone."

Without admitting anything, I said. "The pleasure was all mine."

"Said the spider to the fly," he quipped.

I motioned with my hand. "But this web is yours."

"Nicoli." Vladimir nodded to the man, then led the way into the building.

PROCESS OF ILLUMINATION

Once past the door, and the eight Spetsnaz troops, he began to explain the situation; "We've a critical situation—you don't mind if I speak in Russian?—good. You see the American presence, and we've even a German scientist, as well as our own nuclear and bomb specialists. But we've had to keep this under the vest."

"And the *Il Maricela*?" I asked.

Vlad looked around before speaking. "It never existed."

Oooo, scary. I could think of a dozen explanations, and did not envy that ship of fools.

The foyer and the hallways were much the same as they were in the old Soviet Union days. Only the faces on the paintings had changed. The walls were still dark wood, the floor marble. Nothing to disturb the administrators from their task of serving the public.

I'd once—strike that—JD had once sent a floater into the the building. A small "MS" ("mini-spy" *à la* JD); a small electrically powered hovercraft with microcameras, passive radar sensors that could look behind walls. JD's plan was to map the entire building at night, over the weekend, while most of the administrators were gone. And it had worked, up until the point that the signal had been cut, either by a swat of the hand, or by an internal jamming system. I believed the former; JD believed the latter.

I'd find out soon enough what had really happened, because we were approaching the area where the MS had been lost. It was in the central offices that we stopped. A large ten-foot-wide, five-foot-deep chimney. Men had carefully taken apart the old bricks to reveal a long cigar-shaped torpedo. The nuke. Three men in white coats were looking at micromonitors, which were connected to wires that rested against the chrome of the beautifully evil device. None looked as if they were at any critical decision making point.

It had to have been dropped down into the chimney, and that said, it had to have been made to fit in it. And it was strategically located, right above the elevator system that went down into the fallout shelter.

"Is it deactivated?" Vladimir asked the Russian scientist, who turned and stood at near attention.

"It's a tamper proof system. The shell is ... seamless."

"How much time?"

"Thirty minutes, maybe less."

That's why they were fidgeting, looking at each other, and accomplishing nothing. I wondered how many people in Moscow actually knew what was about to happen. I could feel my own damp underarms. I took off my parka and threw it over a chair. Something about the bomb was familiar.

"Is this place jammed?" I asked Vlad, bringing out my MPC.

He gave me a 'you should know' look, then said, "Not now."

"JD! URGENT! PULL UP 2003 RECORDS ON MIN MO, AKA JAPANESE BOMBER."

"THOUGHT HE WAS DEAD?" my screen questioned. "OK. GOT THE FILE. ARE WE GONNA BE BOMBED?"

"LOOK AT BOMB SCHEMATICS FOR THE JB 21 FROM THE ONES OFF HIS DESTROYED HARD DRIVE."

"WE ARE CHARGING A FEE FOR THE TWO YEARS IT TOOK TO SCRAPE HIS BITS TOGETHER, RIGHT?"

"What're you doing?" Vlad's curiosity had been piqued.

"I'm going to save Moscow, if I can." *And in doing so, you'll owe me big time,* I didn't say.

"How?"

"First—hey! Don't go near that area!" I ordered the scientist, who was trying to pull out another brick. "There's a pressure pad near that area, I think."

My forearm vibrated. "Do you have a printer, with a fax modem hookup?"

"Over here."

I plugged my hook-up into the printer's standard jack, which most countries had thankfully switched to.

Did the Mo, aka The Japanese Bomber, still live? Did he know I deactivated his bomb by using a simple trick? The only way that was possible was if one of the four Japanese officers had talked about it. Then again, it could just be a shapely coincidence.

Twenty minutes and counting, my watch said.

Vladimir was on the phone. Nicoli approached. The printer printed.

I felt his presence, even as the schematics of JB 21 were being printed out. There were three views; top, left, right. The side view were wiring schematics.

"They say that the radiation levels are too high," Nicoli said to my back.

"That's why they're backing away?"

He nodded. I handed him the first copy of the schematics. He took it over to the scientists, then returned. "We needed a bomb disposal unit, with nuclear experience."

I laughed at the thought. The next copy came out, and I took it over to the table so I could lay it out and get a good look at it.

"The Japanese Bomber's dream bomb," I said to Nicoli, who followed me over to the table. "You know anything about bombs?"

"Not this kind." He shook his head. "I thought The Japanese Bomber was dead?"

That thing over there tells me he's alive."

The last known bomb made by Mo was four years ago, at a sushi joint in Kyoto. The bomber's accomplice had been given a prize, a blue jacket with a sewn-in tracking device, won from a radio contest. Even then, it was hard tracking the man in the crowded Japanese cities, where buildings and tight alleyways and people mixed and mingled, like spices in a complex soup. Kind of like trying to detect and track a scent in an outdoor food bazaar. And doing it from 300 miles up in the air. The accomplice had carried his oblong duffel bag, and when behind Fong Xu's Sushi bar, had placed the bomb inside the vent. You know, those back alley vents that steam in the mornings. We found out later that the bomb had been made to fit that specific vent.

That bomb could be described as a long silver shape, which once emplaced, was fixed. There were four touch points that sprang out against the inner walls of the vent. If anyone tried to pull it out, or move it, the bomb would detonate. I figure we'd gotten lucky with the magnetic detraction. I digress; within the bomb we'd found a series of dummy wires, filled with radon, which if bent or disturbed in any manner that disturbed the inner pressure, set off an electrical charge to the detonation core. There were several booby traps; motion detectors; those trip wires; placement sensors; and a backup power supply camouflaged by the batteries. What it didn't have was an internal motion detection system, because the bomb was sealed, and the bomber figured that if there was no way to get into the detonation core, there was no need to place a motion detector inside. We retrieved the bomb by placing my watch on the outer end of the shell, or the tip of the cigar. And that was where the detonation core had been found, magnetized. A hole was laser cut, and the detonation core was extracted as the bomb's timer struck 005. Minutes later Mim Mo's private residence was raided, but upon smashing down the door the entire house blew up, killing three officers and the next-door neighbors.

"Where's the X ray?" I asked the scientists, who were pointing sharpened pencils at the schematics.

Vladimir jerked his head to the Russian, who stood up and left the room.

"That should have been the first thing here," I cursed.

"Here," Nicoli said, pointing to the portable X ray.

I checked my watch. "You've got five minutes to locate and get a picture of the detonation core," I told the Russian, who I presumed would be in charge of the portable X ray. It was passive X ray, which shouldn't give off enough heat to cause any heat detectors to set of the detonators. It was the kind of X ray used to look through walls, to prepare a suite or room for the President's occupation in foreign countries.

I suspected that this bomb might not have the pin devices, which pushed outward from the shell once emplaced, because it needed all the space it could get inside for the required explosives. The core would have to be super compressed, super heated, before critical mass could be reached. The only way to do that was with enough explosives, perfect detonation sequences, and the micro circuitry to make it all happen. If I could move the Uranium core a millimeter off, it might throw the detonation sequence, or the explosive aim points. Or it might be possible to create a magnetic field which threw off the electrical sequencing, but I wasn't a genius, and it could actually set off the bomb. It all depended on whether or not The Japanese Bomber was alive, or only his dream bomb.

"What are we looking for?" Nicoli asked me, as six people stood around the small TV set, which showed an X ray picture of the bomb.

"Looking for a new sensor, which could detect interior motion, or magnetometer."

"It looks just like the schematics. How did you know?"

"Stop!" I pointed to a new sensor, one that wasn't in the schematics, near the detonation core. "That's it." Mim Mo was alive and well, I thought to myself.

"What're we looking for?" An American scientist from the DOE (Department of Energy) spoke for the first time.

"CIA?" I asked.

"DOE here on vacation with my wife. You?"

"Reporter slash dogooder." I saw his face pale. "We got a magnetometer?" I stood up from the television screen and looked at Vlad. "Time to show me what you got. Do you have a heavy internal jamming system?"

Vlad shook his head.

"Look, you either light this place up, or it's good-bye Doctor Shivago." I watched him think it over.

"Three minutes, sir? We were off," the Russian scientist squawked upon seeing the internal timer. "We were off, sir."

He took out what looked like a mobile phone, and dialed a number. "Done."

"We might have a chance."

"Hey, my phone?" the German said, staring at his own mobile phone, which he'd been using to say good-bye to his family.

"If you would like to say good-bye to your families, you'll have to leave the building now," Vladimir said solemnly.

Oh ye of little faith, I thought, taking off my shirt and my MPC. It would be a tight squeeze. "I need duct tape."

"Are you crazy?" the DOE specialist nearly cried.

Nicoli looked around in one of the three supply boxes, then brought me a roll of that silver lifesaving tape, known in every land, in every language. I imagined there were different names for it, but it was recognizable to most anyone on the planet earth.

"Tear me off two five-inch strips, will ya."

"Sir, you can't be serious?" the Russian scientist spoke. He addressed Vladimir, who was watching me and Nicoli.

"Have you any ideas?" Vladimir asked the man, looking him in the eye. When the man said nothing, he said, "Then shut up."

I placed the second strip over the other, so that there was an "X" that would hold my watch to the tip of the bomb's shell. The magnetic emission would face down into the bomb, and I hoped that it would pull the detonation core towards that end, throwing off the sequence, or short-circuiting the micro circuitry. Hopefully I'd be able to get out of there in time.

"Nicoli, hold my arm while I lean under. I don't want to knock the casing." The chimney wall was a foot thick, so I'd have to lean in, then reach up, and try to affix the watch top dead center. If the heavy jamming setup didn't interfere with the tiny patch sensor, then it would explode. *At least we won't feel anything.* "Here I come, Dean."

"Are you sure about this?" Nicoli asked quietly.

I nodded. "We'd never make it, Nicoli. It's this or nothing. Damn, it's hot in here?"

"Radiation?"

"You got doctors on standby?" I saw him look back at Vlad, then give me a nod of assurance.

I was thankful that my sweaty arm was providing a lubricating affect. Good thing the fireplace hadn't been used in a while, but there was still a fine black dust that tried to creep around my glasses, into my sweat-stung eyes. "Come on, Cort, we can do this." There! My bicep squeezed gently past the side of the bomb. Though the bomb had been made to wedge into the chimney, it wasn't the same shape as the flue. The bomb felt hot. I felt hot. Something buzzing in my head, a odd taste in my throat. Sweat beads popped up on every part of my body as I stretched. I felt the top of the bomb, and guessed the center, and pressed the button.

The world spun and then it went black. A hand tugged on my arm, then I heard ticking sounds. Did I press the magnetic pulse device? I felt a huff of heat, then nothing....

– CHAPTER 28 –

"WHAT? WHADAYA WANT?" I said, though they heard, "Wah—wahaya won?" Who was I speaking to? Dean?

I sensed my nakedness, and a cool breath of air blowing over my entire body, which felt raw, new, from my ankles to my face. A machine ticked off to the right. I smelled the antiseptic smell of a hospital.

"Mister Falcon?" a nurse repeated. "Are you awake?"

"Deah." Was my tongue stuck to the roof of my mouth or what? "Air ah I?" I noticed a certain fuzziness. "Dean? Dean, is that you?"

I tried to open my eyes again.

"I'm nurse Cyrus," the female voice said.

I didn't think I'd spoken aloud. Or did I actually make it past the pearly gates, or into that virgin-filled paradise? Though this latter sounded like more of a nightmare to me. My left eye unsealed, but the right would not. The whiteness of the room blinded me instantly, and I shut my one working eye. I worked my orbital muscles until I unseated the natural glue, and could open the right eye enough to squint. I could see a strange apparatus hanging over me, barely a foot, and it was the creator of the cool air.

"Doctor Gustafason? Patient one is awake," I heard the nurse speak, but I noticed now that she was speaking over an intercom.

Past my feet I could see a large glass window; an observation room.

"Mister Falcon? Mister Falcon?" A Swedish accent. Male.

"Yes." This was getting irritating. Where the fuck were they?

"I'll bet you were wondering who we are? Where you're at?"

Finally someone with brains. I tried to move, and some machines bleeped.

"No, don't move just yet. Your skin has been repaired, but you've been stationary for thirty-four days. This is the Moscow Burn Unit, a special section. By order of Mister Krinkov himself. Your personal things, at least those that weren't destroyed in the explosion—"

"Excuse me, is he awake?" Vladimir Krinkov interrupted. "Hello, Mister Falcon? Good to see your alive and well. We thought you might not pull through."

"Is the square there?" I asked.

"Minus a chimney." He chuckled. "Otherwise, except for you and Nicoli, there was not much damage thanks to you."

"Good. Water?"

The nurse came into the room, which was like a pressurized chamber, sort of like level four decontamination zones used by the Center for Disease Controls' (CDC) high-risk areas.

"The doctor will speak with you, and I'm going to check on Nicoli. He's been awake for a couple weeks. By the way, an Indian man, Rajiid, I believed his name was, inquired after you? I thought you'd have a Russian contact?"

"Too unreliable," I said, and heard him laugh as he left.

The nurse came in and gave me a drink of a sweet substance that had such a tartness it made my cheeks pucker.

"Sweet, eh?" She wiped my lips, and fed me the straw again. This time there was water. I grew tired almost instantly, and knew that I'd been had.

Sweet, my ass! It was medication. My eyes shut in mutual agreement.

I awoke violently. Strike that. Something awoke me. "What the hell's goin on?" I felt two sets of rough hands upon my new skin, then I was being carried like a baby by someone very strong. It was hot, then cold, and I smelled the outside. I opened my mouth, and puked off to the side.

"Thank you," a voice whispered.

I'M BEING KIDNAPPED!

– CHAPTER 29 –

"STOP STRUGGLING, CORT," Igor remonstrated.

I opened my eyes, and saw Fong's face. He was carrying me, then placing me into the chilled interior of a car. I blinked back the brightness of the day, saw the snow falling, and then the door slammed, wheels chirped, and the motor gunned. "Fong?" I couldn't believe it. "What's going on?"

"Yes, he's here too," Igor said from right next to me on the backseat. "Think you can put some clothes on?"

"I'm not sure how I feel. I just woke up from a long ass sleep." I moved, but even that required muscles that had not been used for a long time. "But yeah, I'd like to get dressed."

"Good. I've put some clothes together for you. We must hurry. Here, take these pills first."

He handed me two small yellow pills, and I swallowed them faithfully. I felt almost instantly better. "What were they?"

"Amphetamines. It'll help you get back to speed." He handed me the clothes. "We have to get you out of Russia."

"Why the urgency? Kidnapping me? They were taking good care of me."

Fong harrumphed from up front.

"Fong is correct. Something has happened. Word came down that you were to be taken to a secret facility. A place from where none have ever returned. Even the guards who go there rarely get out. I've never been there, and never want to go there. It is a place of torture, and execution.... Krinkov's, indeed, the country's attitude towards you, has changed. It seems you know something they don't want you to know."

A thousand questions raced through my mind, while I got dressed. The fabric of the clothes felt rough against my hypersensitive skin. I remembered what JD had told me about Sylvia, but what if she hadn't been killed? What if she were in a security-sensitive place, where I could possibly spot her, and know her true identity?

"Was there any mention of the nuclear fiasco in the media, or by the Russians?"

"None. Never happened," Igor said.

"What's their explanation to the other intel agencies in the know?"

"Only the CIA knows, and possibly the Brits. JD gave the files and operational details of the entire incident, from beginning to end, just in case. It's no secret that you saved a lot of asses, no pun intended. Why the Russians would want to kill you, since that woman is dead, is a mystery."

"Unless she isn't dead." I heard Fong concur with a grunt.

Igor hemmed in thought.

"If that's true, then the Russians go on persona non grata status." I was dead serious too. "Are my supplies here?" Suddenly the sky outside went dark, and the car stopped. "What the hell's going on?"

"We're in a warehouse. We'll take a secret tunnel to the train station. They'll try to shut the city down, or at least have it observed by satellite. This ought to throw them off."

"Secret tunnels?"

"Yes. And remember, Cort, it's not all the Russians. It's probably Krinkov, and a few of the upper level controllers."

Yes, I knew that, but I was thinking about 'unless she wasn't dead.' The thought found a happy home in my heart, while we moved towards the train station through an abandoned line. Fong lent me a shoulder as my legs rememorized their duties. In a matter of minutes I felt comfortable walking on my own, but my legs felt as if I'd just run a marathon.

Igor watched the Russian countryside pass by, lost in thought, the sound of the wheels thumping over irregularittes in the steel train rails. "There used to be some integrity in our game, eh, Comrade?"

"The old ways are fading, and I'm not sure I ever knew them, except as instinct." It was society that changed the morals and ethics of those around me.

"What gives with this woman?" Igor could hold back no longer. "It's not like you. And she's probably a deep cover Russian agent, raised Russian in another country."

I knew the type he was speaking of, because I'd met them before. They were children who'd grown up in one country while being taught the nationalistic lessons of another. Sometimes they rebelled outright, but the quiet ones were the most dangerous. They invidiously rolled through life with the secret inner makings of a bomb, to whoever's country they were a citizen of. When the time came for them to show the true flag, they could be an agent in the enemy intelligence service, or the President of the country. The latter would be the best case scenario. However, if you had someone as the President of your enemy, then your enemy wouldn't be your enemy anymore?

Need I answer him? Igor was a link in the Russians' chain, or had been. Was he completely loyal? I wondered, but stopped doing so when I thought of his actions over the years. They spoke louder than words, or my own disloyal thoughts. "Just a girl, my friend. I gave her my word."

"Bahhh. This is different. She's part of the machine. She's been bred, schooled, and trained at deceit her entire life, for the common good of Russia."

"Common good?"

"Yes. It's similar to the American way of thinking, or the greater good."

"I gave her my word." That was that. She'd asked me to help her, and I'd told her I would. Indeed, she'd cursed me for not helping her.

Igor persisted. "I still think it's dangerous. They've already tried to kill you, and when you made the promise she wasn't, ah, in her right mind."

I looked at Igor, but he stared out the window. He seemed to have aged. Or had I not looked at his weathered face in a while? "Our word is all we have left."

He sighed, then patted my knee. "Then I must give you my resignation at the conclusion of these matters." He avoided eye contact. "For Dean, or someone truly innocent, I would have no problem. But for romantic illusions I cannot risk my network, or my family."

"I shall miss you, my friend." Damn! I'd do more than miss him, I'd be in a bind without him, for I'd never find another as reliable as Igor.

He didn't respond, just continued to stare out at the countryside. We drifted within our silence, he to his thoughts, me to Dean, to Sylvia, and to Francesca. Was I wrong to keep my word? If what Dean had said was true, then Sylvia had already been a Russian agent, and had probably committed antithetical crimes against humanity. Or was she a passive agent? Information gatherer only? Although: the latter had been known throughout history to cause the deaths of more people than any other catalyst. I thought about Igor; was he in danger? Were the Russians on to him? Did they threaten his family and friends?

The station arrived, and the bullet train stopped. There were no trenchcoat-wearing Russian agents waiting for us. Only a few passengers got on, while several got off, including Mr. Fong, who I saw leave and return with a duffel bag.

Fong came into the car once the train began gaining speed. A duffel bag hung from his shoulder, and I hoped it contained some supplies. A new watch would be nice.

"Mister Fong, a pleasure to meet you again." I stood shakily, and bowed.

"Nice to see you are dressed." He handed me the bag, after taking a seat across the aisle in an empty section of seats. "JD san says you should check the side pocket first."

"Excellent!" I saw the watch had that new laser I'd requested.

"He say it works same as before, only with one new addition. He say you dial him moment you receive MPG. I'll be in contact." He tapped his ear to let me know he could hear me over the communications system.

"Thank you, Mister Fong."

He stood, bowed, and left the car.

"I don't know how he does it," Igor spoke finally.

"His chi is what makes him ... dangerously relaxed. Any more explanations will have to come from him. I do know that so long as he keeps his chi in check he controls life. When he loses that, then life controls him."

"Well put. Now where are we going? JD said something about a Francesca being held by the UAN?"

"Let's find out." I took my MPC, typed in my access code, and sent a message. "JD! BACK ON LINE. WHAT'S UP?"

My screen came alive instantly. "NICE TO HEAR YOU'RE ALIVE AND NOT TOASTED. BEEN WAITING. IMPORTANT. SYLVIA SURVIVED THE CRASH IN A SPECIAL SPHERE, SIMILAR TO THE AIR FORCE ONE BALL IN THE TAIL SECTION—"

Now that was something I hadn't thought of, and looking back, it made perfect sense. The Russians would take the debris and crash material into an enclosure on the basis of investigating the crash. But what about the pilots, and the two soldiers?

Had they been expendable for the "common good"?

"Anything interesting?"

"Yes." I looked at Igor. "You don't have any problems rescuing a woman from the UAN camps?"

He inclined his head.

"JD. WHERE'S FRANCESCA?"

"CHECK PRINTER."

"Where?"

"Right along the way." I saw the circled map. "Slovakia."

– CHAPTER 30 –

IGOR AND I CROSSED the border without trouble, which meant that the Russian intelligence people were still in Moscow. Good. I hoped they looked for a few days, and found nothing. Meanwhile Barry would print the story I'd written on the second leg of the journey.

The story detailed the theft of the nuclear weapons, the conspiracies, the murderer and his still unknown controllers, and the Russians' responses and actions towards me. All supported by transcripts and photographs. Those were the stingers, for they provided proof. I mailed the written story to Barry, and asked JD to help. Evidently there had been two U.S. stealth satellites above the *Il Maricela* when it had disappeared in a mushroom cloud.

"GOING TO RESCUE A WOMAN IN SLOVAKIA. TELL ME IF ANYONE WANTS THE STORY." It wouldn't be as tantalizing as the events surrounding the last few days, but it was a part of the story. Her tragedy was symbolic of many living in such hells created by man's need for more power. It was the result of that inherent evil called war.

Now, fully geared in comouflages, I led Igor through the sparse woodlands just outside the UAN guard perimeter. We'd already satviewed the camp, knew their routine, knew where the main barracks were and where the prisoners would be at during the time we'd be there. It was 14:00 hours. The detainees were all outside, under watch by only two tower guards. Now we had to locate the target.

"You have the picture?" I asked Igor, who seemed uncomfortable out in the field.

"Yes."

The two towers were about two hundred meters apart, at the corners of the perimeter fence. It was a rectangular field, approximately the size of two football fields. Two large Quonset huts, each capable of housing two 747s, were connected to the field by large sliding steel doors. Now those doors were locked.

"That her?" Igor pointed towards the right, the eastern part of the field.

I followed his sight line to that part of the enclosure, where only women sat. Some seemed almost dazed, and some merely accepted this as some sort of obstacle. I found Francesca among the former, seated alone upon a crude bench. She wore a gray dress, and brown shoes without socks. Her hair had lost its golden luster, and hung about her like seaweed. But it was her.

"Fong, come in," I said into the mike.

"Ready."

"In five—four—three—two—"

BOOM! BOOM! A distant thunder crackled, shaking the very ground.

"Damn!" Igor cursed in Russian, as a fireball erupted into the sky about a half mile away.

"Ready?" I asked him.

I looked down the 12x scope and aimed center mass, while Igor did the same. "Squeeze."

The air rifle kicked, the projectile flew towards the tower guard. I would hate to be hit by it, but it was the only long-range nonlethal weapon available on short notice. JD called it a "thud", which is what it did when it hit flesh. A halfinch-long titanium needle, which injected an instant acting sleeping agent. It took time to master the trajectory, but one could do so quietly with the air rifle, which didn't make a sound. The range finder scopes helped overcome anything else.

Both guards dropped in their tracks, but none of their warders knew the better. At least, not yet.

"Let's do it."

Automatic gunfire chattered in the background, as we approached the perimeter fence. I slashed the fence with the wire eater; a modulated high-energy laser that was bounced between two lasers in a one-inch section. It was that area that I dragged along the steel wire, which instantly melted the metal creating an instant doorway.

I rushed into the compound, running as fast as I could towards the woman. "Francesca! Francesca?" I called, but she didn't even look, not until I stopped right in front of her.

"Francesca?" I whispered, then lifted her tear-streaked face. Her brown eyes were wet, but also, they were vacant. "I'm here to get you." I picked her light body up, and felt her cling to me, her bones poignant against my flesh, and my soul. Her head lay against my shoulder as I ran to the hole. Her fingers dug gently into my shirtfront, grasping on to the hope of possibly finding her family, of finally being rescued from this nightmare, but still waiting to wake up from it. Keeping alive the hope of the dead raising, of things not being as they are, as I clung to the hope of Dean walking towards me down a road, of Sylvia being an innocent, of the world righting itself before it toppled off into the blackness of space, giving some other creation the last laugh in our universe. Her head burrowed into my chest, and as I passed through the opening I felt her sigh. The bones to which I held sagged in my arms, and I sensed her last joy even as she joined her loved ones in that great beyond. She was free. Each of us deserves as much.

Fong came around the fence, not running, but moving very quickly. He looked at me, noticed the woman. He nodded. It was about honor.

Igor fired a pistol, to urge the prisoners, then we three and a body left through the woods to the waiting vehicle.

"A matter of honor," Fong answered Igor's looks, their eyes locking momentarily, two bulls deciding a point.

Down the road a ways we found the small church, and I spoke to the chaplain, making a donation to the church. I gave him the date she died, the same day as her son and husband.

I saw the twinkle in the chaplain's eyes, his gray beard like an ancient stalactite, resting against his black frock.

"God has an interest in you," the old priest said, then took her body personally, and left.

Now, my son, Sylvia, and a man named Boris.
Dean?

*

K.L. Caldwell is 36 years old, and lives alone in the deserts of the world, searching to create a bluer sky above us all. He is an internationally published author, poet, and playwright.